Mary Selby is a doctor, married to another doctor, with five small children. She lives in a quiet Suffolk village and plays the organ in the local church. Her first novel, *A Wing and a Prayer*, is also published by Black Swan.

Also by Mary Selby

A WING AND A PRAYER

and published by Black Swan

THAT AWKWARD AGE

Mary Selby

BLACK SWAN

THAT AWKWARD AGE
A BLACK SWAN BOOK : 0 552 99671 8

First publication in Great Britain

PRINTING HISTORY
Black Swan edition published 1997

Set in 11pt Linotype Melior by
County Typesetters, Margate, Kent

Black Swan Books are published by Transworld Publishers Ltd,
61–63 Uxbridge Road, London W5 5SA,
in Australia by Transworld Publishers (Australia) Pty Ltd,
15–25 Helles Avenue, Moorebank, NSW 2170
and in New Zealand by Transworld Publishers (NZ) Ltd,
3 William Pickering Drive, Albany, Auckland.

Reproduced, printed and bound in Great Britain by
Cox & Wyman Ltd, Reading, Berks.

This book is dedicated
to Neville
who brought magic into my life
by filling the spare room with it

Chapter One

Deepest rural East Anglia, where the skies dominate the earth to the extent that artists sometimes go quite mad trying to get the clouds right, is a land of green wellies, mud and sugar beet, a land where combine harvesters block winding single-lane roads to the very best of their ability, and experimental agricultural policies get their first try-out. It is neither flat nor truly hilly, but gently rolling, its patchwork curves spread and rounded like the breasts of huge, reclining, naked women. Landscapes are best not likened to men, as occasional pylons can then cause embarrassment.

It is also a very green and pleasant land, its studding of farms and windmills and pretty villages resembling precious jewels in a scattering of gigantic navels. The farm workers have left, for modern farming practice replaced them long ago with large tractors, but an endless mix of would-be rural dwellers expressing their primeval need for green grass, fresh air and original Georgian paint colours on their walls have rushed to replace them. On their tail, in turn, has been born a vast industry in magazines, books and interior designers specializing in the Country Style, and the villages now look far more authentic than they ever were when they were first inhabited.

The village of Bumpstaple was one such jewel, and its new vicar was just in the process of moving into its new vicarage. In this he was being aided by Albert,

Eric, Joe and Wilf of Happy House Removals, Limited.

There is only one kind of person who drinks more tea than a vicar, and that is a removal man. Unlike vicars, removal men constantly demand excessive quantities of tea – they actually appear to need in excess of twenty cups a day merely to function. (Entire learned papers may well have been written on how it is that they manage never to need the bathroom.)

Those who are being removed invariably keep out their second-best mugs for removal day; the stained ones, the chipped ones, the ones which came free with a can of motor oil. They would not mind too much if the removal men broke them, in fact they rather hope they will, for it would save having to find them cupboard space in the new house.

Unfortunately, removal men never break anything which is dispensable, but only those things which have been particularly carefully and deeply packed. The end result is the aptly named Old Mug Syndrome, whereby neighbours dropping by for the first time to offer welcome to the newcomers, and to ascertain what sort of people they are – that is, their sort or not their sort – are unwittingly given a completely false impression of them.

This was what happened to Robert Peabody, the new vicar of Bumpstaple when Olive Osborne, village postmistress and moral guardian, called round when he was moving in and discovered a large and visually distressing mug on his kitchen unit. It was decorated with a large and vulgar cartoon penis, which had an extremely inappropriate facial expression. It is difficult to say what an appropriate facial expression would be, as penises are not generally blessed with them. The chances are, in any case, that Olive would have been just as offended by a faceless penis, and removing the face would have removed the whole point of the joke on the mug.

There were several reasons why Olive was so offended. First of all, this was not the kind of thing that she expected a vicar to have on his china. Secondly, it was not the sort of thing which should be on china anyway; china should have flowers on it, or little fluffy kittens. Thirdly, the infrequency with which her husband Ernest exercised his marital rights meant that Olive did not like to be reminded of what she was missing when drinking tea. Lastly, some women are offended by most things anyway, and Olive was one of them.

Olive was a small woman who looked, on first glance, like a guinea-pig who has recently been given a suppository. She had small, sharp features, rather staring eyes, and lips which seemed always to be pressed together in a condemnatory fashion. She ran the Post Office, and liked to feel that she also ran the village of Bumpstaple. She had never been contradicted in this assumption because no-one had ever dared. They might never have received any Christmas cards again.

Robert, wandering into his new kitchen to look for the box with the washing-up things in it – in order that he could wash up some mugs and make more tea for Albert, Eric, Joe and Wilf – came across Olive staring with a rather fixed expression at something on his kitchen unit.

Months afterwards, if she had known all the facts, Olive could have said that she had known from that mug that there was something rather rude about Robert Peabody, something decidedly unvicarish. Perhaps, then, it was fortunate that she never did know all the facts. Very few people ever did.

'Hello,' said Robert, wondering if Olive had been at the sherry. A lot of women of a certain age in his last parish had drunk sherry in the mornings, but when you considered what had happened to the place, it was perhaps hardly surprising.

9

Olive started. 'Oh. Hello, Vicar,' she blinked, recovering fast. 'I just popped in to welcome you. I saw the van.'

Robert smiled charmingly, mentally sending a prayer of thanks Heavenwards for his wonderful ability to remember faces and names. 'Mrs Osborne, of course. I remember you from my interview. Secretary of the PCC.'

Olive half melted. Only half of her ever melted, the inner core could not be touched. She was like a horse chestnut: once you have got through the prickly bit, there is an even tougher nut beneath. Now she remained very wary because of That Mug. 'How nice of you to remember, Reverend Peabody. Are you settling in?'

'Oh, please do call me Robert. Well, as you can see, we are rather at sixes and sevens,' he said, wondering if anyone had ever settled in whilst Albert, Eric, Joe and Wilf were drinking tea.

Olive's question had been purely rhetorical, as they usually are in such circumstances. It is rather like saying, 'How are you?' to someone strung up in traction. The chances are that they feel pretty lousy, but those who ask rarely want to hear this, they just want an excuse to sit and eat the grapes they have brought.

'You must let me know if you need anything,' she said, slightly more warmly. She could still see the offending mug out of the corner of her eye. After a lifetime of nosiness, her peripheral vision was particularly well developed.

'That's very kind,' said Robert. 'I was just making tea. Would you like some?'

Olive dithered. She rarely refused tea, but to drink it from a mug with a penis on it would probably have choked her. As she dithered, Wilf appeared. Albert, Eric and Joe, he pointed out, were rather thirsty.

10

Olive saw a way in which she could be impressively useful. '*I'll* make the tea,' she told Wilf forbiddingly. 'As you can see, the vicar is *very* busy. *If* you could manage a few more boxes, tea will be half an hour.'

Wilf was married to a woman like Olive. This was why he had become a removal man; the job entailed long hours away from home. He recognized defeat, and went off to explain to Albert, Eric and Joe that half-hourly teas were now off. They would be disappointed, as he was, for half-hourly teas were a useful tool in stretching out the day, particularly as tea breaks lasted at least twenty minutes – that was a Union Rule. The increase in unloading speed consequential to the increased inter-tea interval was, therefore, quite phenomenal.

Olive, meanwhile, organized Robert's kitchen with frightening efficiency while delivering a run-down on local services, and washing up all the mugs except That One.

Robert had realized what was upsetting her, and he regretted causing her embarrassment. The mug had been a gift from his son Josh, and represented Josh's sense of humour rather than his own. Although not a prudish man, he had never felt compelled to display penises on any of his kitchen utensils. He had always kept it out of sight in the box of unmatched china. Now he wondered how to remove it from Olive's presence without being obvious.

He was spared the need, for Josh, coming down the stairs, took in the situation at a glance, and saved him. 'Dad, where on earth did that dreadful mug come from? Was it here already, or does it belong to the removal men? Oh,' this to Olive, 'hello.'

Robert beamed. Although, as a long-time single parent, he often felt guilty that he did not have a difficult and rebellious teenage son, he was at times extremely glad of it. He introduced them gratefully.

'I'm delighted to meet you,' Josh told Olive.

Olive eyed him suspiciously. A teenage boy who spoke pleasantly was obviously up to no good. Still, one couldn't really blame the vicar for the age of his son. 'I really must be off,' she said, delivering a final wipe to the taps. Her voice was warmer now, more like a cold tap than a glacier. 'I expect Mavis Entwhistle will be in later –' a faint hint of distaste there '– she always did for the last incumbent.' She was still not quite sure about the mug, but was prepared to give the benefit of the doubt to Robert, as the sexual obsessions of teenage boys and removal men were far more likely to be suspect than those of vicars. 'Don't let those removal men slack, now.'

She busied herself out of the door, and subjected Albert, Eric, Wilf and Joe to a hard stare on her way down the drive. It unnerved them so much that they became quite thirsty.

'What did she want?' asked Josh.

'To check up on me,' said Robert with a smile. 'Actually she's on the PCC. I wonder if I had her vote.'

Josh picked up the willy mug. 'Libran willies like a good tickling,' he read. 'Do you think she'll go straight to the Bishop?'

Robert grinned. 'No, I think you saved the day. Sad to think that one's reputation can rest on such a small thing.'

'Speak for yourself,' said Josh.

'Now, Josh,' said Robert, 'that will do.'

'Sorry, Dad.'

'Er, ahem, is that kettle boiled yet?' asked Wilf, and they got on with the business of the day.

Bumpstaple lay prettily in one of Suffolk's more charming hollows, surrounded by woodland and fields of smug horses. It was in fact a smug village, its inhabitants fully aware that it was so attractive that passing

12

helicopter pilots became quite lyrical when flying overhead. One should never be deceived by villages, though. However picturesque, they are as much the nesting ground of envy, greed and sexual indiscretion as the best parts of Knightsbridge. Such things began in villages, after all, and all of life can still be found there, concentrated and distilled by isolation, like the best of single malt whiskies, into its purest form.

St Julian's church stood, patiently, conveniently and rather appropriately, opposite The Cricketers Arms in the centre of Bumpstaple. It was appropriate because St Julian was patron saint of publicans, and convenient because most funeral parties finished up in the pub. The previous vicar had encouraged this, believing a little light-hearted revelry to be good for the soul on such occasions. Of course, no-one really believed he had owned shares in the brewery, but he had retired early with a liver complaint, and Bumpstaple's services had been taken by Oliver Bush, the rector of neighbouring Great Barking, for the best part of a year. Some people thought the poor dear man often seemed quite inebriated himself, but no-one had liked to comment.

Bumpstaple lay only a mile away from Broomhill, a rather functional little market town. Having no immediate prospect of acquiring a Marks and Spencer, Broomhill's status was limited to functional, for in the world of market towns the essential next step up, after a book shop and a Woolworth's, is a Marks and Spencer. Without one a town can only be so grand. On such small things rests the whole demography of England.

On this particular September day, Bumpstaple's collection of chocolate-box houses were looking particularly prettily lit and inviting, for it was one of those grey kind of autumnal days which remind one uncomfortably that Keats was wrong – or high – and there is

13

nothing mellow about seasons of mists and fruitfulness. The sky was dull and overcast, and cars were lighting up even though they could be seen perfectly clearly by anyone fit to be out alone.

Claire Kettle alighted from the school bus at the crossroads, regretting the fact that she had refused to take her coat to school today. It had been her mother's suggestion that she should, which meant she had been obliged to ignore it. Tessa had not yet realized that she should be suggesting that Claire went to school naked apart from a pair of stilettos and a tattoo. That way they both would have been happy, Tessa because Claire would certainly defy her and dress sensibly, and Claire because she would be both successfully warm and successfully defiant.

She was the only girl from St Hilda's who got off in Bumpstaple, and the doors of the buss hissed shut almost before her cello was clear of them. She sighed loudly, but the bus driver had long since become oblivious to the loud sighs of teenagers, either on or off the bus, and he departed with a swoosh of air brakes.

Claire glared after the bus, then picked up the cello and headed down past St Julian's church and the New Rectory towards the Old Vicarage, which was her home. As she walked she dragged her feet, scuffing the toes as firmly as she could against the asphalt. It was a classical teenage drag, for it did not signify some terrible impending neurological disorder, but merely the desire for new shoes. If Claire had been honest with herself, she would have to admit that her mother was not to blame for her annoyance with her present shoes. St Hilda's specified that she must wear plain black lace-ups, so it was not really surprising that Tessa had not been interested in buying the lime green Doc Martens with the fluorescent toe caps. Claire, however, was fifteen years old and was therefore rarely honest with herself, even on a good day, and never if it involved giving ground to her mother, so she blamed Tessa entirely for her dissatisfaction.

She stopped beside the New Rectory to examine the scuff marks. Not much there yet, but give them a week and she would quite legitimately be able to plead for more. Even if Tessa didn't give in, Richard would. Richard was her stepfather, which meant that he started with a kind of guilt-handicap even before she had begun to plead for anything. Claire believed that step-parents were useful creatures; Cinderella must have messed things up somehow. As she picked up the cello again she glanced through the New Rectory gates. The house had been empty for many months, but now there was a removal van parked in the drive.

She wondered, although with little real interest, what the new vicar would be like.

Claire was not much interested in vicars. They came in the same category as mothers, umbrellas and tampons, in that you only required them when something unpleasant was happening. She noticed Mavis Entwhistle hovering in the doorway, and hurried away hastily.

Mavis had not seen her. She was looking out for her daughter, Sally, hoping to flag her down and introduce her to the new vicar, but Sally was late. Mavis gave up and went back in to fetch her coat, and so she just missed seeing Sally's little blue car trundle past the New Rectory, slow slightly as though considering calling in to offer a welcome, then change its mind and pick up speed again. In distant Valhalla, though, the fates who dice with the souls of men noticed, and giggled mysteriously.

Claire, who had unknowingly adopted the pained expression which all cellists wear when remembering the number of times a witty passer-by has said, 'That's a big violin!' – for Mavis said it every time she got the chance – did see Sally, and waved at her. She regarded

15

Sally as one of the very few bearable adults in her life.

Claire had trouble with most people over the age of fifteen. Her stepfather Richard wasn't too bad – her mother could have chosen worse – and Dad and his new wife, June, were fine, of course. Otherwise, well, her cello teacher was OK, and then of course Sally Entwhistle, despite being daughter to Awful Mavis. That was about it, really.

Walking up the drive, she was relieved to notice that the garden gate was closed. That beastly pig Lysander would be unable to get through and snot on her. The presence of a pig as a pet was, she felt, testament to her mother's enduring weirdness, and was one of Claire's many points of dissatisfaction with her.

She let herself in through the back door of the Old Vicarage. Tessa was in the kitchen, sitting at the table filling out forms, with the brainless giant hound lying across her feet. Some conversation was therefore unavoidable.

'Hello,' Tessa said, far too reasonably, 'had a good day?'

Claire realized belatedly that she had been too busy thinking about Lysander to decide what mood to adopt. She opted, on impulse, for surly and unresponsive. 'OK. What's for dinner?'

'Kedgeree,' said Tessa, sighing. She recognized the mood at once, of course. It bore a remarkable resemblance to most of Claire's other moods, but it was nice to live in hope.

'Oh,' said Claire, conveying in a single syllable her total disappointment with anything her mother said, did and, particularly, cooked. She stalked off towards her bedroom, forgetting to scuff her shoes, but dragging the cello spike spine-chillingly along the stone-flagged floor.

Tessa winced and wondered, not for the first time,

16

how the charming child in the photograph on her dresser had managed to metamorphose into someone who seemed to detest her so absolutely. True, everyone said that fifteen was a difficult age, but at present there seemed little prospect that sixteen, seventeen or eighteen would herald any sort of improvement.

She returned to the paperwork, opening the car insurance certificate which had arrived in the morning post, and then glaring at it. It was correct as far as it went. It was just that being listed as 'housewife' did so rankle. It was such an inadequate term for all she did in this house. This year she had finally made a stand and entered herself as 'family and zoo manager' on the form. A letter had come back from the insurance company enquiring as to whether or not she had any elephants or black rhino. (Interestingly, they had specified black rhino. Presumably white ones were OK by them.) Regrettably, if she did, they would have to double her premium, presumably on the basis that this made her car more likely to collide with passing big game than the cars of other, lesser mortals. She had been forced to telephone them to clarify matters, and they had been awfully miserable about it. Either they had no sense of humour at all, or the prospect of insuring a rhino-keeper (black) had so enlivened their lives that they had been quite devastated by the disappointment. Either way, now she was again listed as 'housewife'.

It was perhaps a good thing that she had not confessed to being an artist, particularly if they had realized that she was currently working on a picture of the pig, Lysander. He was not, of course, vicious but he was quite noxiously flatulent. You had to consider the health consequences of the fumes, which was why, much as she loved him, he lived in the garden.

She felt a little flutter inside, and patted her stomach reassuringly. It was strange, feeling a baby moving

17

again after all these years. She was only thirty-five, certainly not past it in childbirth terms, but having had Claire so long ago, it felt rather like doing it again for the first time. She remembered the evening when they had told Claire. She supposed that, with the benefit of hindsight, it had been a doomed evening from the beginning . . .

It had been a bad day. She had spent an awful hour trying to get sun block onto Lysander – as he was a pale-skinned pig, this was most necessary in the summer – and after finally succeeding, had realized that she had used Claire's secret supply of the self-tanning variety by mistake. Lysander had turned a very odd colour, and Claire had demanded reimbursement for lost melanin. She had reasoned that she would now have to spend her entire life slightly paler than she would otherwise have been and this, apparently, could make 'all the difference'.

The problem with hindsight, though, is that it is never there when you need it, and consequently gives pleasure only to TV critics and philosophers.

'Oh God,' Claire had said, when they told her about the baby, 'how embarrassing. I suppose you'll be wanting to breastfeed, too.'

'You were breastfed,' Tessa had pointed out, reasonably, she thought. Claire had feigned the urge to vomit and Richard, who rarely attempted to mediate, (for in battle he who attempts to interpose himself between the warring parties is inevitably the first casualty) had felt obliged to say, 'Now Claire, be reasonable.'

Claire had been determined not to be reasonable, not then, not ever, she had made that more than clear. She had simply opted out of the conversation in the way which she found the most satisfying and Tessa the most annoying, allowing her eyes to glaze over and her focus to wander into the middle distance as she said, 'OK,' in the kind of mildly exasperated tone of voice which she imagined one would use with small nagging children. Then she had sloped off to her room.

Tessa sighed. Claire seemed to dislike her so much that she would not have been surprised if she had decided to live with her father and his new wife, June. Sometimes, she thought guiltily, I wish she would. Richard thought that Claire actually liked living in Bumpstaple, and that her endless implying that Daddy led a far trendier life in London was just teenage point-scoring. Tessa was not so sure, but it was time to make the kedgeree, so she turned her thoughts to that.

A short distance away, Robert Peabody and his son were already sitting down to their first meal in the kitchen of the New Rectory. It was, since Mavis Entwhistle had prepared it, a pie. Mavis's addiction to making and eating pastry was so absolute that she turned almost everything she cooked into a pie. It was a shame, really, that with so much practice she made such indigestible pastry.

As it was their first Mavis meal, Robert and Josh were not yet aware of the grim future which loomed, a future in which their attempts to dispose of Mavis's pastry in an environmentally acceptable, and Mavis-invisible, manner could possibly come to dominate their every evening. The previous vicar had usually buried it in the garden, but unfortunately it was the kind of substance which, like disposable nappies, can take at least two hundred years to break down, and there were, therefore, not many sites left for interment.

The kitchen was not bad for a modern rectory. Many old village vicarages had been sold off by the church, being too large and expensive for the modern vicar's needs. New, squarely unexciting replacements such as this had been built in their grounds. Perhaps they were all designed by the same architect, for the outside of the house closely resembled others in which Robert and Josh had lived. The previous vicar of Bumpstaple, however, had made it quite comfortable. The kitchen had a red Aga, and there was a jacuzzi in the en suite bathroom. There seemed something a little risqué about having a jacuzzi attached to his bedroom, Robert thought. It would certainly be wasted on him.

Robert and Josh were instantly identifiable as father and son. They were both tall and rather rangy, with large noses, dark eyes beneath bushy eyebrows, and unruly black hair. To the romantic eye they were a pair of Heathcliffs. Unlike Heathcliff, Robert was a quiet and earnest man. His wife had divorced him many years earlier, in order to marry a country and western singer named Jed, from Arkansas. This had not surprised Robert, as it was a mystery to him why she ever married him in the first place. He was a modest and oddly innocent man, even for a vicar, and had never worked out what it was that had brought her to his bed, all those years ago. His great regret was the fact that she maintained no contact whatsoever with her son.

Robert had spent the last eight years as vicar of the parish of Rumpleton on the north-east coast of England. It had been a small parish, even to begin with, but, as the cliffs began to crumble into the North Sea, it had become even smaller, until it had reached the point at which there were no parishioners at all, and even the inhabitants of the graveyard had required reinterment elsewhere, lest they should be given a burial at sea that they had never requested. Very few vicars can actually claim to have seen their parishes shrink before their very eyes quite as literally as had Robert Peabody, not even these days.

Josh Peabody, Robert's son, was sixteen, and as supremely confident as his father was shy. He had welcomed the move to Suffolk, reasoning that as he would be leaving home in a few years they needed to go somewhere fresh, somewhere where there were some live parishioners, so that he stood a reasonable chance of finding a decent woman for his father. Josh did not want his father to be lonely when he left home, and he hoped that here in Suffolk he could find him the perfect bride.

Josh and Robert were very close. They had been united in adversity when their village sank into the North Sea, just as they were now united in adversity by the prospect of finishing Mavis's pie.

'I think,' said Josh, giving up on his, 'that I should see if anyone round here delivers pizza.'

'I don't know,' said his father. 'We must be careful not to offend our cook.'

'I take exception to both of your last two words,' said Josh, idly folding the pastry which he had removed from his portion of pie, and discovering that it kept its crease like damp cardboard. 'There must be an industrial use for this stuff.'

'Just put yours in the bin,' said Robert, feeling obliged to continue with his.

'She would see it,' said Josh, darkly, 'and I daren't feed it to the birds – they would drop like stones.'

Robert gave up, his cutlery was not up to the task, and the mental image of kamikaze great tits falling like hail all over the village was not helping his appetite. 'I believe she left our dessert in the fridge,' he said.

Josh went to look. It was apple pie, and he sighed deeply, wondering if his father had committed them to a lifetime of the same. Doubtless he had felt sorry for the woman – probably some mousy little spinster who lived to 'do for the vicar', and had not had the heart to turn her down, for fear of offending her.

Supper in the Old Vicarage was also not without problems. It began in the usual way, in that Claire glared malevolently at the food on her plate, then scowled at her mother. 'Isn't there anything else?'

'No,' said Tessa, thinking that anything else which she had also cooked would be likewise unacceptable in any case, 'I thought you liked kedgeree.' I must try to be reasonable.

Claire looked at her with disdain. 'I like June's kedgeree.'

God, thought Tessa, give me strength. Since June married Tom, Claire's father, she seemed to have been beatified and canonised. 'This is only tuna, egg and rice,' she said aloud.

'Exactly,' said Claire, in the tones of a restaurant critic. 'June uses smoked haddock. She's a cordon bleu, you know.'

Part of Tessa longed to say, isn't that a French tart, but she couldn't bring herself to do it. The fact that Claire had always declared unmitigated loathing for smoked haddock seemed far too petty to mention. 'Well, I'm sorry, but there's nothing else. Make yourself a cheese sandwich.'

Claire sighed, the type of sigh which said clearly that Tessa was most unlikely to have purchased the Right Sort of cheese, and then wandered off to the fridge, leaving her kedgeree arranged on her plate as a smiley face.

'I see that the new vicar has arrived,' said Tessa.

Richard, who until now had been deeply involved in the contemplation of his novel – his agent was pushing him to finish it – looked up briefly from his plate. 'Have you met him yet?'

'No, I just saw the van. Did you see anyone, Claire?'

Claire shrugged in order to suggest that if King Kong had moved into the village she probably would not have noticed him, particularly in her present state of malnourishment. She constructed a sandwich so bulky and unappetising an object that Tessa was quite certain that if she had presented it to Claire, her

22

daughter would have professed not to know what it was.

'I daresay we'll meet him in good time,' said Richard, returning to his innermost thoughts.

Tessa watched him head for his study as she cleared up the dinner things. He could be withdrawn like this for days as he neared the end of a book, but the reunion at the end was always worth waiting for. At least, she corrected herself mentally, it used to be, before I grew to the size of a house end.

She ran water into the sink. Claire had, as usual, made herself scarce at the first sound of a tap, and she tried not to feel that Richard ought to be more help. He seemed to feel that the pursuit of his muse exempted him from responsibility in other areas of life, and his muse had been playing extremely hard-to-get ever since she had become pregnant. Tessa found this particularly upsetting.

She tried to remember how Claire's father had been when she was pregnant, then baulked at her own thoughts. She did not want to find herself comparing Richard unfavourably with a relationship which had ended in disaster. She left the sink and went to find him. 'Why don't you take the evening off?' she asked him. 'We could put our feet up and argue about baby names.'

'Oh – hmm – sorry, I'm at a bit of a crucial point, don't want to lose my train of thought. You have a think.'

'It's supposed to be a shared thing,' said Tessa crossly, thinking that his train of thought never objected to his stopping work to eat – although clearing up afterwards clearly stretched its patience – 'You'll only object if I decide to call him something silly.'

Richard tried not to sigh, but sent a small wave of exasperation her way without meaning to. 'There's lots of time,' he said, 'you'll be pregnant for months yet.'

That, Tessa reflected, was perhaps part of the problem. Much as Richard wanted a child – they had, after all, been trying for several years – he seemed unprepared for the fact that the process involved her being pregnant for a full nine months. Pregnancy was, he seemed to feel, a 'woman's thing', and it should not impinge on him particularly. It was rather like his attitude to periods. He always seemed to know, instinctively, when she had a period. He never made sexual advances towards her when she had a period. If she had asked him why, he would have claimed that she was imagining it, yet so perfect was his timing that she had actually wondered if he checked the tampons in the bathroom cupboard every night to see if she had taken any out. Perhaps she should just keep a number tally on a blackboard next to the loo to make things even easier for him.

'Is there any ice cream?' Claire interrupted her reverie.

Amazingly, the house-end sandwich seemed to have been eaten. It had been the kind of sandwich which pubs with very blunt bread knives try to market with a pickled onion as a ploughman's lunch. 'In the freezer,' said Tessa.

She started to clear the table, half listening for Claire to declare the ice cream to be the Wrong Sort. It would be nice if the new vicar had a family, she thought, a nice teenage friend for Claire. With her luck, he'd probably be some doddery, prim old thing with no children and an over-starched wife. Tessa ran water into the kedgeree dish and opened the dishwasher, unaware for now of just how glad she would be to be wrong.

In his study, Richard battled with his final chapter, and wondered why he hadn't become a farmer like the rest of his brothers. Two answers presented themselves fairly swiftly: first of all, the urge to write had always been immense and secondly, well, he didn't like animals. Lately, though, writing had felt like hard work. He wrote murder mysteries, intricately crafted and with a hallmark, rather mournful tone which he had never had to reach hard for – until now. Recently he had begun to wonder if he and his hero, Inspector McTavish, ought to go their separate ways for a while. He no longer liked the man, and felt that his creation had developed bad habits and mannerisms which had not been intended. Richard had even, recently, found himself idly plotting McTavish's unpleasant demise. The plots were becoming increasingly peculiar.

Perhaps, he thought suddenly, looking at the scattered papers on his desk, it is I who have changed, and McTavish is still the same. Perhaps I should retire him, write about someone new. Dare I make such a change, though? This is my livelihood, my family's too, the only thing I do well, and if I leave McTavish now, I might lose him completely, for ever.

Richard dragged his mind back to his final chapter. But as he wrote, a little voice in his head kept suggesting to him that he burn his boats right now and remove McTavish from the picture. Just retire him, though. Nothing more. No need to burn the boats by having him eaten by a Triffid.

Chapter Two

Robert Peabody need not have worried about offending Mavis Entwhistle, for she was not an easy woman to offend. She was certainly never offended by anyone's opinion of her pastry. She understood its effect on the digestion only too well: she had eaten a lot of it herself over the years, and her physique reflected the fact. She also regarded Robert as the answer to her prayers. Mavis had been praying to St Uncumber. This admirable woman, famous for having grown a beard and moustache to fend off unwanted suitors – in this, she did actually bear some resemblance to Mavis – is traditionally invoked by women who want to get rid of their husbands. Mavis had called upon her more than thirty years ago, and shortly afterwards her husband Albert fled to Thailand in order to become a Trappist monk. Mavis had seen this as sure evidence that St Uncumber was on her side, for it had not occured to her that there might be something in her own personality or physical form which could have driven a man to seek a life of seclusion and celibacy. Mavis's more recent prayers to her saint had not concerned her own romantic life, for she required none, but that of her daughter Sally. Now she saw that Robert Peabody was the ideal answer to them. He had most of his own hair, all of his own teeth and presumably, as he was a vicar, no excessive sexual appetites. As soon as she set eyes on him, she had experienced The Sight, a gift which she took very seriously indeed. Her Sight told her that this was the man for Sally.

Robert, perhaps fortunately, given his vocation, did not possess The Sight, so he had experienced nothing earth-shattering upon being confronted with Mavis. She was not, alas, a prepossessing woman. Olive Osborne often said that when they were handing out good looks in Heaven, Mavis had omitted to join the queue, having queued in the wrong place and got two bottoms instead. She had an impressively hairy mole on her nose, and the kind of figure which is more often compared to a building than to an hour glass. Her corsetry was a miracle of engineering, and she sported a bosom so fearsome that if she turned too quickly it was liable to catch passers-by a serious blow as it followed her. However, she possessed another important quality which modified her surprising ugliness, a quality often found in those who are bereft of any desirable physical attributes, and unduly endowed with the other sort. Mavis was endearing. She inspired the same kind of tolerant affection as do the red river hog, the fossil fish and the rainbow-bottomed baboon – all creatures so peculiarly ugly as to be strangely appealing. She was also interferingly helpful, rudely curious, clumsily friendly and offensively blunt, but she meant well, and this made up for a great deal, in most people's eyes at least.

Given Mavis's physique, it was perhaps fortunate for the male sex that she was only ever lascivious on her daughter's behalf. She herself had had all she ever required from the Opposite Sex when Albert Entwhistle had had the nerve to Impregnate her in her sleep. She had decided after this that sex was not for her. Albert had reached a similar conclusion, and the rest, as they say, was history.

Perhaps every village has its Mavis Entwhistle, a person who, by the very immensity of their difference from the rest, makes the rest look so much tamer. Rarely, though, do these Mavises appear in quite as florid a form as was the case in Bumpstaple.

Mavis lived in a small cottage at the top end of the village with her daughter, Sally. She had a small, secretly earned income, and she also looked after the church and the rectory to keep her hand – and her nose – in. Even Sally did not know the true source of her mother's money. She knew that Mavis sent manuscripts to London, and had long since accepted her explanation that she was a freelance proof-reader. In fact, Mavis was Arcane Rose, the *English Covens' Herald*'s expert on herbal magic, and she was also Leila Stargazer, astrologer to the *Broomhill Gazette.* What's more, she now intended to bring all of her powers to bear to make very sure that Robert Peabody recognized swiftly that his destiny lay with her daughter.

There is nothing wiser than hedging your bets, though, so to make doubly sure that all possible forces of fate were on her side, including the Almighty, she meant to become a regular and devout member of Robert's new congregation. She would begin this Sunday.

Unaware of the plans which Mavis had for him, Robert Peabody was making his own plans for Bumpstaple's church. Nothing radical, of course, for he was not a radical kind of man, but he believed that it is entirely possible for any church to make itself into the hub of the community of which it is a part. This task is particularly easy in villages, where the limits of the community are fairly easy to define, and where most of the population are within walking distance. Robert had decided to centre his subtle campaign on Christmas. He planned to stage a proper Festival of Nine Lessons and Carols on Christmas Eve. He would put together a small choir for the occasion, and the whole village would be invited to attend.

Oliver Bush, the Rector of Great Barking, who had been covering as vicar of Bumpstaple for the last twelve months, tried to dissuade him. 'My dear Robert,' he said gently, over coffee in the New Rectory kitchen, 'you do not realize what a nest of vipers may be stirred by this well-intentioned plan.'

'What do you mean?' Robert could see nothing wrong with the idea. He had done something similar in Rumpleton, and although admittedly his congregation had been fairly small at that stage, it had been quite a success. He said as much to Oliver.

Oliver, whose sweet nature generally permitted him to speak ill of no-one, wrestled with his conscience, for he did not want Robert to make problems for himself. 'I'm afraid, Robert, that there is a tangled social web in Bumpstaple, rather more tangled than you may be accustomed to. It lays many traps for the unwary. It might be better to leave the organization of such an ambitious event until you have had a chance to settle in, get to know everyone.' It was the closest he could come to warning Robert that Olive Osborne would invariably upset everyone else if given a prominent role in anything – and she would certainly expect a prominent role in anything.

Robert, though, saw only good in others, and he shook his head, smiling. 'I'm sure that this is just the thing to unravel those webs and improve everyone's sense of community,' he said earnestly.

Oliver did not want to say any more. He admired Robert's wish to breathe life into his church, and if, in breathing life into things, not all of what subsequently flourishes is what we intended, that does not mean that the intention is any less worthy. This was Robert's parish now, after all, and Oliver was sure that he would be guided.

He therefore turned the conversation instead to the recent lightning damage to the weathercock on his own church. The insurers had refused to pay, he told Robert, they had said that Acts of God were excluded from the accidental damage cover, apparently on the basis that God does nothing by accident. There had in the circumstances, he explained, been no arguing with that. Meanwhile, Bumpstaple began its downward trundle towards Christmas, like Thomas the Tank Engine with brake failure, gathering momentum as it ran.

As Oliver was taking his leave of Robert, Josh Peabody was riding home on the school bus after his first day at St Joseph's. He was pleased that his father had allowed him to opt for the local Catholic boys' school rather than the mixed school in Broomhill. Robert had felt a little awkward, as an Anglican vicar, but Josh had wanted a single sex school, and this was the only one. He had recently come to realize that boys need a sanctuary from which to do their leering. St Joseph's also offered something at which to leer, as it was admirably situated next to the playing fields of St Hilda's school. Already he had had an enviable opportunity to assess the local female population's thighs, when a hockey lesson had coincided with his study period in the library, which overlooked their hockey field. Such observation could save wasting an awful lot of time on chatting up a girl who might later turn out to have thighs like tree trunks.

St Joseph's had the added advantage that the boys did not tease him for having a vicar for a father. The Catholic boys, unable to have priests as fathers, were curious rather than scornful. Today they had wanted to know where his father got the Communion wine from, and Josh had enjoyed telling them that it was made in a special Anglican monastery, where monks trod the

30

grapes barefoot after the Bishop of Bath and Wells had personally inspected them for veruccas. Tomorrow he looked forward to enlightening them as to how supplies were moved at dead of night in great secrecy to avoid hijack by gangs of marauding Catholic priests jealous of its very high quality.

The bus had disgorged more than half of its occupants at Broomhill bus station, where a queue of mothers with first cars which they hoped others would assume were second cars chatted about the high expectations of teachers and the high cost of school uniform. Now it was trundling around the various villages.

Claire sat a few rows behind Josh, trying desperately hard not to look at him, but taking in every detail. The desire for a boyfriend was so all-consuming that her subconscious could take over at such times.

She noticed that he wore the St Joseph's uniform with a fashionably scruffy air – tie crooked, top button undone, huge overcoat – and he looked a little older than she. He had no obvious spots, although he might be on something for them, as she was. Still, suppressed spots were marginally better than none, even if she always felt that they were still there, lurking beneath the surface, waiting to pop out at the first hint of a chocolate biscuit. His hair was not greasy, and was floppy in a trendy, uncontrived kind of way. He was OK.

She eyed the other girls on the bus surreptitiously. It was clear that they were all eyeing Josh too. She sighed. There was Jackie Johnson from the fifth form – she wore lipstick as soon as she got outside the school gates and had breasts that wobbled when she ran – and Zoe Ormondroyd, who had perfect skin and knew how to French kiss. She, Claire, could not hope that he would notice her.

She was terrified when Josh stood to leave the bus at

Bumpstaple. From praying that he would notice her, she now veered violently towards praying that he would not. She even toyed with the idea of staying on the bus as far as Great Barking, but rejected it on the grounds that everyone else on the bus would notice and wonder what she was doing. Like most girls of her age, she yearned for attention, but hated to be the focus of it, so, reluctantly, she and the cello struggled down the aisle after Josh, and the bus regurgitated them all at Bumpstaple crossroads.

In the end it was very easy to start talking. One of the problems facing girls at single sex schools is that they begin to see boys as alien beings, but when Josh offered to carry her cello, Claire's tongue became unknotted and she found herself walking along beside him, chatting. Other girls at school generally implied that the minute you smiled at a boy he was liable to snog you, unless, of course, you were a complete dog, but now she discovered that the sexually-obsessed-but-desperately-pimply louts of their stories obviously shared their classrooms with a few normal people such as Josh Peabody.

By the time they parted company, after a long chat outside the Old Vicarage, they were on their way to being friends. Tessa, watching surreptitiously from the hall window while chatting to her sister on the tele-phone, was glad to see her daughter talking to someone with such natural enthusiasm. She resolved to be excessively careful not to ask who it was. Hell hath no fury, she had learned, like an irritated teenager.

When she came in, Claire, who had heard about Mavis's pastry from Josh, felt an unfamiliar desire to tell her mother about it, even though she generally tried to avoid having unnecessary conversation with Tessa, lest it be interpreted as weakness on her part. In any case, describing the awfulness of the pastry might be taken as implying that Tessa's was rather better, so she resisted the temptation. Tessa's cooking left a lot to be desired – it had given her spots.

Claire would have died rather than admit to her mother that she was worried about her spots, and she had affected great reluctance when Tessa took her along to Dr Potter on one of her own antenatal appointments and casually mentioned the problem. However, she now took the tablets he had prescribed with religious commitment, and monitored her skin every day with the magnifying side of the shaving mirror.

Such mirrors make even the most perfect of complexions look like the surface of the moon, so, unsurprisingly, Claire was not satisfied with hers. When she looked at the cruel reflection, she hated being a teenager. Childhood had been so much easier; no spots then, and the ability to live in the same house as one's mother without such an EFFORT. The transition into adulthood was an uncomfortable one, and one which she would have preferred at times to abandon.

Claire had a problem particular to teenage girls: although they need their mothers, they also begin to see in them what they themselves will become. This is hard to accept when, like Claire, you had planned to be either a princess or an astronaut. Therefore she had developed a protective paranoia, and this enabled her to blame Tessa for, amongst other things, her spots. Why couldn't Tessa be more . . . befriendable, Claire thought. In teenage TV soaps, the heroines had wonderful friendships with their mothers. I mean, pregnant, I ask you! No-one else had a pregnant mother. Their mothers had all presumably realized that sex was for teenagers to worry about, and had slipped decently into the menopause and separate beds as soon as their daughters hit thirteen. It was just typical, wasn't it, that she should be the one with the ridiculous mother.

Despite all this, she surprised herself by being pleasant. 'I've just met the new vicar's son. He's named Josh Peabody, and he's very nice.'

Tessa wondered whether this was a test, whether Claire had seen her watching from the window. 'I wondered who it was,' she said casually, 'I saw you from the hall. I was on the phone to Sarah.'

'Oh yes. What did she want?' Claire quite liked Aunt Sarah, who provided trendy hand-me-downs, and did not dress like a reject hippie like her mother did.

'She's off to America with Miles,' said Tessa, 'for three months. Something to do with his research.'

'Oh?' said Claire, wondering yet again what it was that Uncle Miles found so interesting about lobsters' nerves. Perhaps it was all a scam, for it certainly meant that his family got to eat an awful lot of lab-reject lobster. She wondered if all Cambridge scientists ate those things which they experimented upon. Not much fun for the ones working on bugs. 'Why is Aunt Sarah going? She doesn't usually.'

'Well,' said Tessa, hesitating briefly but then deciding to tell this friendly Claire. It was important to consolidate these small advances, particularly when the news which she would shortly have to impart would be so unwelcome. Three months . . . 'She's been saving for cosmetic surgery. She's having her breasts enlarged in a private clinic over there.'

'Oh, gross,' said Claire, wondering how old she would have to be to have the same. She feared that Aunt Sarah's lack of bosom might be genetic, and that her own had stopped growing already. 'Is horrible Hugh going too? Perhaps he could have his brain enlarged.'

Tessa swallowed. This was it, the worst news anyone had to give since Chamberlain had to tell the

34

King that Adolf Hitler fancied a holiday in Poland. 'Er-no,' she said awkwardly, trying not to laugh, for, after all, Hugh already possessed the frightening intellectual precocity of Dr Who on LSD. Perhaps it was because he had been raised as an only child in a house which was regularly filled with Cambridge research scientists. Claire, of course, saw her ten-year-old cousin in the same category as vermin – indeed he kept a lot of vermin about his person. During his recent attack of hand, foot and mouth disease she had tried hard to convince Sarah that he needed to be shot and buried in quicklime. 'No, I'm afraid the bad news is that Hugh is coming to us.'

'You're kidding!' Claire's friendly mood exploded like a bubble, lost without trace, as she visualized her fledgling friendship with Josh being ruined by the interference of a ten-year-old red-headed gremlin. 'Why? When?'

'Saturday,' said Tessa apologetically. 'Sarah and Miles didn't want to take him out of St Joseph's for three months and disrupt his schoolwork, and in any case there would have been nothing for him to do over there. Miles will be busy, and Sarah will need to recuperate.' She did not add that her sister feared that if Hugh got himself invited into the cockpit of the Jumbo on the way across the Atlantic, as he surely would, the pilot might have a nervous breakdown and take them to Murmansk. It did not need saying.

'So instead he'll disrupt my whole life,' said Claire tragically. 'Can't we say "no"?'

'I'm sorry.'

'He peed in my wellingtons.'

'He was only four.'

'He still is, mentally,' said Claire darkly. 'He collects bugs.'

Tessa felt some sympathy. Hugh had a fondness for the kind of practical jokes which amuse no-one but the perpetrator, and he was constantly equipped with stink bombs and matchboxes containing things with more than their fair share of legs. He was living proof of the fact that in every generation there is at least one Gerald Durrell. 'I'm sorry, Claire,' she said, 'I couldn't have said "no", you must see that.'

Claire was even sulkier because she did, but would have preferred not to. There is nothing worse than having to agree with the enemy. 'Just when I've made a friend,' she muttered.

Tessa heard. 'I'm sure Josh won't go off you just because of Hugh.'

Claire glowered. 'Go *off* me? Mother, I've just *met* him, for God's sake. I don't fancy him. I don't think about sex *all* the time, you know.' She longed to add, 'as you obviously do', but did not quite dare. The words hung unsaid, together with the condemning 'Mother'.

Tessa sighed. She was 'Mum' on a good day. She struggled to undo the damage, like a fish in a net. 'I didn't mean in that sense. I meant as a friend, not a boyfriend.'

'Boyfriend? No-one calls them that these days,' said Claire scornfully. She had slipped back into character. 'Hugh is a pain. Don't expect me to look after him. What's for dinner?'

'Spaghetti bolognese,' said Tessa sadly, knowing that this was unlikely to improve matters.

Claire sighed loudly. Because it was not salad, and if it had been she would have complained that it was boring as she had had it for lunch, it represented yet another battle in the Spot War. 'I'm going to do my homework.'

Tessa watched her go, and wondered if she had really just seen a glimmer of light in the mother and daughter relationship. Years ago, when Claire was young and nice to her, she had wondered how it happened that parents fell out with their teenage children, why it was that communication failed. Now she wondered how anyone ever got it right. She returned to the bolognese, hunting for the garlic crusher. It was, like much of her food these days, a low fat recipe, as she hoped it would help Claire's spots. Those tablets were helping a little, but best to attack on all fronts. She never dared mention her efforts to her daughter, as she might then refuse to eat at all, on the principle that mothers 'had no business' interfering. It was one of her favourite arguments as it could, with a little thought, be applied to almost anything Tessa did.

Richard, tempted in a few minutes later by the smell of the garlic, offered to help with the salad, then sat at the table eating olives. 'When do we get the little monster?' he asked.

'Saturday,' said Tessa.

'Not much notice,' he mumbled, and Tessa knew he was foreseeing disruption to his novel. 'How did Claire take it?'

Tessa was silent for so long that he thought she hadn't heard him. Finally she said, 'I suppose not as badly as I expected, on the whole.' I must be positive, she thought, it could have been worse. She didn't threaten to go and live with her father.

Sally Entwhistle, Mavis's daughter, was also arriving home, as yet entirely oblivious to the plans for her future being hatched out by her mother. Sally was a rarity, one of those few villagers who was genuinely welcome in neighbouring villages too. This honour was hers because she manned the mobile library, and also because she was an extraordinarily nice person. People who live in villages can be far more isolationist even than certain anti-European politicians. There was an unbreachable gulf between Bumpstaple and Great Barking, a village notorious for the monstrous privet penis it had once displayed in its churchyard. Unaware that they might actually be suffering from a particularly literal form of penis-envy, the people of Bumpstaple practised 'villageyness' to a high degree. In fact, if you lived in one village then you were more likely to move to a yurt outside Ulan Bator and start trading in camel dung than attempt to live in the other. The last person to try it had been a postmaster, who had gone from Great Barking to Bumpstaple in 1964. He had been doomed. The Bumpstaple outlet had been larger, but he had not made any profit, owing to the dreadful smell which followed him into his new premises, and which lingered there until he finally moved out. It had been rumoured that someone had put a curse on him, and only Mavis Entwhistle, who started the rumour, had known that the smell owed as much to the pound of haddock which she had sewn into the hems of his curtains as to the secret spell which she had incanted as she did so.

Sally did not resemble her mother; indeed, the fact that she was such an attractive and well-adjusted girl was a source of constant amazement to most people. Unfortunately though, Sally had had a series of failed romances, and she tended to view the opposite sex with a somewhat jaundiced eye.

Her failures were largely due to the machinations of her mother, who had not only arranged the dates but actually contrived to be present for some of them. Sally had come to dread her mother's favourite phrase: 'Sally, I have met the most charming man today . . .' The men had ranged from the washing machine repair man (bad breath, false teeth) to the milkman (hopelessly gay) and the baker's assistant (personal space problem, no deodorant). The words had always heralded another excruciating evening. Sometimes sheer acting ability had kept her going, particularly in the case of the washing machine man. After her plastic

38

buck teeth had failed to put him off – he had, in fact, been quite jealous – she had been forced to stage a very effective reproduction of an epileptic fit in order to prevent him from kissing her. Only the timely intervention of the barmaid at the Cricketers Arms, where she was well known, had prevented him from attempting mouth-to-mouth resuscitation – he had even taken his teeth out in readiness. Sally had put her foot down since then, refusing all her mother's dates.

She was therefore not impressed, on entering the cottage, to be greeted by Mavis enthusing coyly and obviously about the new vicar. 'I will not come and meet him,' she said again.

'But you'll like him,' pleaded Mavis in dismay. Even St Uncumber could not be expected to do much if Sally would not meet the man. Surely The Sight had not let her down?

'No,' said Sally firmly, tossing her blond hair as she put the kettle on.

'You'll have to meet him in church, anyway,' said Mavis.

'I won't,' said Sally, 'because I shan't go.' She knew as she said it that it was not true. Unlike her mother, she was a regular member of the congregation, for she ran the Sunday School in the vestry. Still, it would not do to let Mother think that she could win on this one.

Mavis tried a different tack. 'I shall be attending church again,' she said rather smugly.

'Again?' queried Sally, pouring tea. '"Again" implies that you have been before.'

'I have,' said Mavis indignantly.

'Not since Aunt Agatha's funeral in 1983,' said Sally.

'I go in every week to clean,' said Mavis. 'That gives me plenty of time for praying.'

'Huh,' said Sally, thinking her mother was more likely to go into spontaneous orbit than pray. 'What's for tea?'

Mavis looked her smartly in the eye. 'Chicken pie,' she said balefully, and Sally knew that the lines were being drawn for a battle of wills. She firmed her mental backbone. She could take the pastry.

'Good,' she said, 'I'll go and change.'

Later that evening, Claire casually offered to take Charlie for a walk; despite possessing some incredibly un-doglike pedigree Irish wolfhound name, he had always been called Charlie, because he had always been one. Normally Claire was mercilessly unwilling to walk the dog. She insisted to Tessa that none of her friends ever had to walk dogs – Claire's accounts of her friends were a constant source of amazement to Tessa, for the largesse of their parents, their lack of involvement in any domestic tasks, their unusual freedom and their vast wardrobes. A swift observation of the quantity of concealer stick which Claire had applied to her face (she had concealed almost all of it) suggested that Charlie was a means to an end, so Tessa wisely said nothing.

Claire called casually at the New Rectory. Robert Peabody answered the door and said yes, of course Josh would come for a walk. Claire could not help gloating a little, just to herself, as they headed through the village. If only Jackie Johnson could see me now.

They walked towards the woods which bordered the village, chatting as they went. Charlie, vaguely understanding that the chances of a good stick-throwing session were not high, pulled hopefully. As he was a large dog, this meant that Claire's arm was almost dragged from its socket, so she let him off.

Pheasant abounded. Charlie lived in hope of catching one, although he never had thus far. Hope is the driving emotion in most dogs. Much as they adore their masters, rage after intruders and lust after every passing bit of canine skirt, they are powered for the most part by hope. Hope of a walk, hope of dinner, hope of catching a rabbit – you can see it in their eyes.

Despite being a wolfhound and therefore one of the fastest things on four legs, Charlie had never caught so much as a rabbit. This was because what his genes had gained in speed they had lost in finesse. He had a huge, lolloping gallop, but a congenital shortage of fine tuning, so that he stood no chance at all of catching anything which changed direction. In truth, he had no fine tuning at all, but when it came to lolloping, Charlie was your dog.

Now he was desperate to pursue things. He forgot his pheasant plans as soon as he was free, for he was not unduly burdened by memory, and rushed to investigate a very interesting tree. It was interesting because it smelled of dog, which was unsurprising as he had relieved himself upon it that very morning.

Claire and Josh strolled slowly after him, watching him nose his way from tree to tree, clearly thinking 'WOW!' all the time.

Now that she was actually with Josh, talking as new friends do, Claire wondered if she should have used so much of the concealer stick. He was nice, she did not want him to think she was a tart. For once she felt glad that her breasts did not jiggle when she ran. 'Don't you ever see your mum, then?' she asked him curiously.

'Never,' said Josh. 'I don't have a mum in any real way. You're lucky.'

'I don't know,' said Claire, 'my dad's in London.' She was fond of saying that she was from a broken home, but it seemed a little inappropriate to say it to Josh.

'At least he didn't run off with the lead singer of a group called the Hillbilly Mangoes,' said Josh.

'No,' Claire had to agree, 'but I sometimes wish I could go and live with him. Mum is such a pain, she's always nagging me. I have fun with Dad.'

'Don't you think he'd nag too, if you lived with him?'

41

'That's what Mum says, but I can't imagine Dad nagging, and at least he isn't having another baby.'

'Well, I think you're really lucky, you've got two families: two parents, two step-parents.'

'I suppose I am,' said Claire thoughtfully. The absolute truth was that she didn't really want to go and live with Dad, for that would mean leaving her friends, her bedroom, her secret hiding place in the oak tree. She did not allow herself to feel that leaving her mother would in itself give her any second thoughts, and certainly she would be glad to see the back of that pig. A thought occurred to her. 'Do you think your dad would marry again?'

'I plan to make sure of it,' said Josh, who had thought of little else for years. 'He just needs a push in the right direction – vicars are no good at that sort of thing. I need an ally, actually. Will you be it?'

'Yes, of course,' said Claire, delighted. 'What can I do?'

They stopped and sat on an upturned log. There was a strong smell of wet dog, thanks to Charlie having found the same wow-provoking pond which he found every day, but it was her favourite spot for sitting and thinking. She wondered whether to tell Josh that this was her special place, but decided that, on top of the concealer, she might seem too keen.

'Well, I have to find someone first,' said Josh. 'Who do you know that's eligible? Someone local, preferably in the parish.'

Claire suggested Sally Entwhistle immediately. Josh thought that she sounded hopeful, although he was afraid that she might be too young as his father was forty-two.

'But she's thirty-three,' said Claire in surprise. 'That's ancient.'

'There's still a nine-year gap,' said Josh, eyeing her. 'I think two years is ideal, don't you? Like us, I mean.'

42

Claire gasped and flushed. 'Er – what for?' she asked. Josh grinned and she found herself smiling back, delighted that he liked her. 'We can easily get them together,' she said. 'Introduce them after church.'

'There's always a crowd chatting after church,' said Josh. 'We need to introduce them more personally. Perhaps . . .' he took a deep breath, 'perhaps you could introduce me as your boyfriend now, on our way back, and I could invite her to meet Dad.'

'As my *boyfriend*?' It just slipped out. So much for trying to be cool. Claire watched him nervously. Was this when the snogging started? Would it be horrible and slurpy, like Antonia said?

Josh slipped an arm around her cautiously. This was when they sometimes slapped you. Girls these days seemed to have a bit of a thing about slapping faces, as if you hadn't lived till you'd socked some poor guy. 'If that's OK,' he said, a little nervously.

Claire heard the hesitancy and it reassured her. He was just as nervous as she, just as Mum had always said it would be. 'It's really OK,' she told him. 'I'd love to.'

By the time they had sealed the bargain, she decided that Antonia had clearly never kissed anyone. There was nothing slurpy about it at all.

On the way back they remembered Sally and Robert and The Plan. 'Come on,' said Claire, 'you'll have to brave Mavis, though.'

'Oh,' Josh could still feel the bit of pastry he had eaten earlier, and was afraid it would lodge in his appendix and perforate it. What if he should run into Mavis and she should ask how he had enjoyed the pie? 'OK,' he said bravely, so they fastened Charlie on his lead and headed for Mavis's cottage. As luck would have it, Sally was in the front garden, putting out the bin, and Mavis tended her giant hogweed in the back, so there was no need to discuss pastry at all. Claire introduced them, and it all went rather well until Josh asked her if she would like to come down to the New Rectory and meet his dad. She didn't refuse, exactly, just glanced swiftly over to where Mavis was clearly eavesdropping, then said that some other time might be better, she was having an early night. They might have tried harder, but Charlie was clearly desperate to get on and check an interesting scent which he had found – it was his own, and it led home – so things were left in a some-other-timish kind of state.

'Never mind,' consoled Claire, 'there's plenty of time. At least you've met. We can always keep her talking in church on Sunday, make her hang on till everyone else has gone, then she can meet your dad.'

'Good idea,' said Josh, cheered both by the thought and by Sally. She looked a definite possibility. 'Here, let me.' He took Charlie and her hand, and this time Tessa ducked down below the hall window when she saw them at the gate. Some things mothers are not meant to watch, however accidentally they happen upon them.

Chapter Three

The following day, just after Claire had left for school, Tessa turned to the back page of *The Times*. She always read newspapers backwards, feeling that this gave a much more balanced sense of the relative importance of things than starting at the front. Today the word 'ducks' jumped out of the page at her in the way that certain words do, bypassing the usual word-filtering processes and taking the green channel directly to the centre of the brain marked 'important'. She had been following the ducks for ages, ever since they had been washed overboard from a container ship in the northern Pacific Ocean, and had begun their exhausting voyage.

It had been *en route* from Taiwan to California, crossing one of the last great wildernesses, home only to albatrosses and film crews doing Alistair MacLean remakes. One container, caught by a freak wave, was lost overboard and had split, releasing twenty-nine thousand yellow plastic ducks to an uncertain fate. The crew had been unable to save them, concerned as they were with strapping down the blue whales and red hippopotami which remained on board, so the ducks had bobbed cheerfully away and the eye of the world's press had turned upon them.

There are some days when editors are short of news, and the duck flotilla had filled a gap. There were those who had reflected that if the blue whales had been the

45

ones to be lost, they could have had a great deal more fun with the story. Yet the story had endured as, indeed, had the ducks who were, after all, designed to withstand children.

Readers had demanded duck stories, and the fearless gentlemen of the press were despatched in pursuit. As a result, Tessa and the world knew when the ducks crossed the date line, and when the great transpolar currents drew them inexorably into the Arctic Sea. Intrepid reporters had found them when they froze in the ice, wedged together, duck upon duck, their little yellow heads protruding hopefully above the pack ice, patiently awaiting the spring thaw.

Tessa had followed the ducks throughout, for they seemed to her to demonstrate what can be achieved by stoicism alone. Today, at last, and after a long wait, there was some real news. Two thousand yellow plastic ducks had been sighted off Iceland by a cod trawler. There was a real possibility that they might reach the Hebrides before Christmas.

'Richard, do look,' she said, 'the ducks are in the paper.'

'Oh,' said Richard, not looking up. When you are tangled in your epilogue, a bunch of globetrotting plastic ducks can seem unimportant, even when they are the first to sail the transpolar current since Fridtjof Nansen in 1893 – the Press had proved to be a positive treasure trove of little-known facts.

'Just think,' mused Tessa, as a man on the TV breakfast news grew terribly irate about juvenile crime. It was all, he said, due to lust.

Richard sighed and came down from the astral plane of his epilogue. 'Just think what?'

'Well, what a triumph, that plastic ducks should make it so far.'

'But they didn't do anything,' said Richard, 'they just were.'

'That's the point,' said Tessa. 'All they had to do was endure, and everything worked out. It's like faith.'

'Sounds more like having no brain to me,' said Richard, 'after all, they didn't have any choice. What did you expect them to do? Fake a mass suicide and move to Argentina?'

Tessa sighed, feeling that she and Richard were on slightly different wavelengths. 'Well, I think it's a lovely story,' she said stubbornly. 'If I had one of them I'd treasure it.'

'I bet you'd keep it on the mantelpiece,' said Richard dryly.

'I would too,' said Tessa. 'It would remind me that you can beat the odds.' She was silent for a moment, then added, 'Sometimes I feel that no-one in this house is transmitting on the same frequency as me.'

Richard imagined she was thinking of Claire and the trials of adolescence. Since he felt himself far too intelligent to utter the usual platitudes about teenagers going through awkward phases, he said nothing, and Tessa felt suddenly weary of having no soulmate. I'm sure he understood me better before I was pregnant, she reflected. We were much closer. Especially after sex. Even after a row, one quickie in the bath always made us lovers again. Sadly it seemed, at the moment, that a quickie in the bath was about as likely as a massage from the Swedish prime minister.

If only he understood about the ducks. His not understanding about the ducks seemed to define the essence of the problem. Tessa shoved her thoughts away. 'Coffee?'

'Mmm,' said Richard, distantly.

Thoughts we don't like are not easily shoved away, thought Tessa, falling over Charlie in the kitchen. They are like the vegetables you put in the bottom of the fridge and forget about. They fester. They wait, silently, for their chance to jump out and get you.

Then, when you are looking for something else entirely, they fall out and make a squishy mess all over your feet.

Richard was also struggling to suppress unwelcome thoughts which leapt from metaphorical fridges. Here he was trying to retire McTavish, a man never notable for his retiring qualities, and all the time these odd, surreal jokes about ducks and Argentina kept popping into his head. How could he sustain a mournful literary tone when he could barely resist having McTavish accidentally fall off the edge of the world?

A short distance away, once he had seen Josh off at the door – Josh had headed straight for the Old Vicarage and Claire – Robert sat down to plan his day. He hoped that fate would be smiling upon him as he met his new parishioners.

If he had realized then that, far from merely smiling on him, fate had been at the gin and was laughing hysterically, he would still not have turned back, but he would have been very surprised. Since the defection of his wife to a life of music and passion with the Hillbilly Mangoes so many years ago, he had led a calm and ordered life, and he thought that he knew himself well. If someone had told him that deep within his soul there was hidden a streak of abandoned passion, he would not have believed them.

Robert planned to begin by calling from house to house, introducing himself to those in the village who spent their days at home. He was aware that this would involve him in the consumption of a superhuman quantity of tea, (the Happy House removal men would have been terribly jealous, had they known) and that most people feel rather awkward if the vicar asks to use their bathroom. It still surprised him that people seemed to think that a vicar was too spiritual to have functioning kidneys.

He had never seriously expected to marry again. It is difficult for vicars, for even these days some bishops believe that those who contemplate such a step should be buried for eternity beneath enormous smouldering heaps of fire and brimstone. True, he had at times felt lonely in Rumpleton, particularly when his flock had all departed (even the dead ones) and since he knew that fire and brimstone can be difficult to obtain in any quantity nowadays, even for bishops, he was aware that romance was not totally out of the question.

Although he never admitted to the loneliness, especially not to himself, somewhere far in the recesses of his mind hid the thought that, some day, he would look into the eyes of another lonely soul, and they would find a gentle happiness and companionship as the years went by. He never consciously looked for anyone, for he knew that when you look too hard for something, you often find something quite different and mistake it for what you sought. He was no fool, though, and as he went from cottage to cottage, sipping sherry, drinking tea and popping back home every so often to use the bathroom, he began to notice the number of times that sweet little old ladies asked if he had yet met Mavis Entwhistle, then added, 'You must meet her daughter Sally.'

The syndrome of villagers trying to match-make their least marriageable resident to an incoming clergyman is frequently discussed in theological college as one of the job's potential hazards. Adding this to the fact that every time anyone said Mavis's name his stomach rumbled sadly, Robert could not be blamed for imagining that a woman who produced pastry of such terrible indigestibility must have produced a daughter of unenviable awfulness.

This, of course, left him totally unprepared for Sally. Perhaps nothing could have prepared him, but certainly his defences were down.

*   *   *

By mid-morning they had heard all around the village that Robert Peabody was planning some sort of Festival of Lessons and Carols for Bumpstaple. There is no substitute for village gossip when it comes to the dissemination of information. Scientists who spend years studying particle theory and the speed of light perhaps ought to turn their attention to gossip, for at times it appears to contravene all known laws of physics. Indeed it is quite possible that when we finally set out to explore space, the furthest giant space ship travelling at many times the speed of light to a wretchedly distant planet will arrive to find that gossip has beaten them there.

In Bumpstaple there was a more prosaic explanation, which was that Mavis Entwhistle had gleaned the information from eavesdropping on Robert and Oliver Bush the previous day, and she had a mouth the size of Felixstowe Harbour. When Tessa went into the Post Office, they were already discussing it. Marjorie Smythe from the manor was in there, and Olive Osborne particularly enjoyed gossiping to her. It made her feel socially elevated, especially as Marjorie was such a mouse and always agreed with everything she said.

'I do hope our new vicar will fit in,' Olive was saying conspiratorially. 'Although he seems a nice enough man, he is divorced, after all.'

Marjorie refrained from saying that if he was occasionally sober he would be an improvement on the last incumbent. 'Did you hear that he is planning a proper concert for Christmas, with a village choir?' she asked Tessa.

'It is such a marvellous idea. I have always been musical, and I have often said to Ernest that we should do something of the sort,' said Olive, wanting to make it clear that she knew all about it. 'Don't you agree, Mrs Kettle?'

Tessa knew that Olive was well aware that her name was no longer Kettle. But then Olive disapproved of second marriages, and she particularly disapproved of Tessa's because it had taken place in St Julian's, despite her own presence on the PCC. Today, though, she felt strong, for the baby's sake. 'It's Mrs Bennett, Olive,' she said stonily, 'as it has been for eight years. I would have thought that you would remember – you were at the wedding.' Indeed, Olive had invited herself to the wedding by the simple expedient of turning up at the church, wearing a very obvious hat.

'Of course, dear, how silly of me,' said Olive, hating to be shown up in front of Marjorie.

Marjorie Smythe liked Tessa, and she smiled. It was a pretty smile, and actually it was on rather a pretty face. Unfortunately this was more than adequately disguised as she was wearing one of her awful head scarves, a mud-coloured tweed skirt, and brogues. They did not suit her at all, but were the uniform which she had felt obliged to adopt throughout her married life. 'It will certainly provoke a sense of rivalry in Great Barking,' she said.

Tessa thought it sounded like a well-intentioned recipe for disaster in which she, as organist, would be obliged to figure prominently. 'It's quite ambitious,' she said mildly, 'when we don't even have a choir. I hope everyone takes an interest.'

'I'm sure they will,' said Olive, in tones which suggested they would be denied a postal service if they did not. It occurred to Tessa that Olive could have intimidated Rasputin himself into turning up for the service, had he not already met a rather more unpleasant end.

'How are you, anyway?' asked Marjorie. 'Are you looking after yourself?'

'Fine, very well, thank you,' said Tessa, remembering that the entire village had known of her pregnancy

51

almost before she did, owing to the fact that the postman, who delivered her hospital appointment card, dared conceal nothing from Olive.

'Must have been a bit of a shock,' said Olive, fishing.

'Not at all,' said Tessa, feeling annoyed on her baby's behalf, 'we had wanted children for a long time.'

'Oh, dear, I didn't know you had suffered from infertility,' said Olive, making it sound like a contagious disease. She had the lateral thinking powers of a tabloid journalist. 'Did you have the test tube treatment?'

Tessa lost her composure, something which she rather enjoyed doing from time to time. 'Not at all,' she said, too sweetly. 'We were just having a lot of fun practising. It really does make your hair curl.' She stalked out, tossing her curly hair pointedly. Marjorie gazed after her admiringly, wishing she had the nerve to be rude to Olive – heaven only knew, she deserved it often enough.

'Well,' said Olive in affronted tones. Temporarily lost for words, she glared after Tessa. Her own hair was as straight as a yardstick, and she wondered if perhaps it was related to Ernest's inability to perform. In her youth she had possessed curls. Tessa had struck a nerve, even if she had omitted to buy any stamps.

They were still discussing the festival when Sally dropped in on her way to the car park of the Cricketers Arms with the mobile library, and asked Olive for a box of tissues.

Olive glared disapprovingly. 'Aren't you at work?'

Sally dimpled; she had almost undentable good humour, providing that no-one was trying to kiss her without their teeth in. 'Of course,' she said disarmingly, 'I'm due on the car park in five minutes. No, the tissues are for the library. You'd be surprised how many of my customers have a little weep over *Dr Zhivago* in the mobile.'

Olive was not disarmed. Sally might have had more chance with an Afghan resistance fighter, even one with a surface-to-air missile launcher in his rucksack. She raised her eyebrows to indicate her disapproval of such a waste of public funds. After all, she was not the sort of woman to weep in a library, not even over *Dr Zhivago*. 'I suppose our taxes pay for people to blow their noses into these,' she said darkly, handing over the tissues.

'Certainly not. My wages pay,' said Sally indignantly, and there was nothing Olive could say to that. 'I'll see you later, will I?' she added as she departed.

Olive and Marjorie said that she would.

Smiling to herself, Sally returned to her van, pulling out from the Post Office and heading for the pub. Was there, she wondered, a grumpier woman than Olive anywhere? The new vicar would have his work cut out there.

A short distance away, Robert had reached the house of Ivy Postlethwaite, one of the village's more ancient residents. As Sally parked the library ready for business, he was fighting off what appeared to be half a pint of sweet sherry. Ivy had a great deal to say about vicars and why they should not be single, however many divorces they required before they got it right, and Robert felt honour bound to listen to all of it. As her memory was not good, and she repeated herself constantly, it was quite a long visit, and by the time he got away – and that was only by dint of giving three quarters of the sherry to a rather happy-looking cheese plant – Sally and the mobile library were *en route* for Great Barking. He did check the car park, but since he had as yet no real idea of what he had missed, felt only slight regret that the library was gone, as he shrugged and headed for the Smythes' house.

Marjorie Smythe arrived at her door rather flustered,

as usual, having had to fight several dogs for the privilege of getting there first. She quite surprised him by congratulating him on his idea for the Festival of Nine Lessons before he had even mentioned it, indeed, before he was even in through the door. She offered him tea, his seventh cup so far, and he accepted and followed her through to the spacious kitchen with its huge cream Aga and white butler's sink. She was not, he thought, a truly contented woman, and he was curious to discover why.

His intuition was correct. Marjorie had, on the surface of things, everything she had ever wanted. She had aspired to become a certain sort of woman, the kind who lives in a manor, arranges flowers and is gracious to her gardener, and she had done so. She lived in a very elegant house – indisputably the best house in Bumpstaple – and her husband, Keith, was a JP and pillar of the community. The house was filled with green Hunter wellingtons, green waxed jackets and copies of *Country Life.* The Aga had four ovens, the dairy had marble shelves, the gun room was full of guns and tweeds, and they had no less than six golden Labradors. However, Marjorie had not been born to such greatness. She had grown up as a very ordinary girl in Stoke-on-Trent. Her mother, who had had plans for her daughter from an early age, had sent her to elocution, riding and ballet, and had bought her a Barbour jacket at sixteen so that it should be suitably worn by the time she was properly launched via local point-to-points and the Hunt, into County society. There, Marjorie had quickly met Keith, and had been introduced to an East Anglian County set who knew nothing of her more humble background. The transition had been made, but it was not a comfortable one. Deep in Marjorie's subconscious, so deep that she had almost, but not quite, succeeded in hiding it from herself, the truth lay grumbling. This truth was the root of her discontent, for it was that she hated the Aga and its foibles, detested the Barbours which waxed her hands and her hair, hated cold muddy point-to-points full of jolly hearty people with snooty horsey children, despised green wellies for their association with mud, hated the Range Rover which she could not park, and whose tail gate she could not open, and, oh, most of all she hated being a dog person.

Some people are born doggy, some achieve dogginess and some have dogginess thrust upon them. Marjorie was one of the latter, so it was particularly unfortunate that Keith's dogs had always believed themselves to be unreservedly hers. All six Labradors adored Marjorie with every wet, salivating, doggy breath in their bodies, and they are not a breed remarkable for the dryness of their mouths. They followed her remorselessly around the house, and howled miserably when they were parted from her. They licked her face, laddered her stockings and emitted unpleasant smells from their bottoms wherever she happened to be, and she was aware that, whatever beautiful and exclusive scent she layered upon her body, they always overwhelmed it with indisputable essence of dog.

Neither had Marjorie ever got on with the essential uniform of her new status. She knew that brogues did not suit her slim ankles, heavy tweeds made her short figure appear frumpy and head scarves made her look like an escaped character from a documentary about rationing. She wished she could appear publicly in the white stilettos which she had bought secretly and kept hidden in her wardrobe, but she did not wish to embarrass Keith.

So now she sat, in her gracious kitchen, pouring tea for Robert while the dogs competed to lie across her feet and moult on her skirt. 'I think it's a marvellous idea,' she said again, 'so good for the village.'

'I'm so glad you think so,' said Robert, wondering if he would be able to taste his drink through the smell of dog. 'I thought we might get a small choir together.'

'Oh, wonderful,' said Marjorie, surreptitiously easing a couple of dogs off her left foot, which was going numb. She had never adapted to the smell – it put her off her dinner. 'I would love to join. I'm an alto. You should speak to Tessa Bennett – she plays the organ for us.'

'Indeed I will,' said Robert, 'although I wouldn't want to put upon her too much; I hear she is expecting.' He fished for a notebook and pencil, made a note, then looked at Marjorie. She had the kind of clear hazel eyes that return a gaze directly and honestly. He felt she had great unused capabilities and a lack of self-esteem. He would enlist her as his chief ally. 'I thought perhaps *you* could give me a little advice,' he said.

'Ask away,' Marjorie was flattered. Keith never asked her advice, and her grown-up children were far more prone to giving it than listening to it.

'Well, you know the village,' said Robert. 'Who should we enlist into the choir? We need people who will actually turn up, but some of them, at least, need to be able to sing.' He knew very well that there were many factors contributing to the make-up of successful village church choirs, and the ability to sing was only one of them.

Marjorie understood perfectly. She included Olive in the list of names she suggested, for she did not like to think what might happen to Robert if she did not. She was well aware that Olive's voice had the kind of penetrating warble which a rutting turkey might envy, but at least she could certainly be counted on to turn up. Heavens, she would probably run the whole thing, Olive always took over everything. She sighed.

Robert heard the sigh, wondered at its cause. He

shook her hand as he left. 'You really have been a tremendous help,' he said to her.

Marjorie blushed, overwhelmed. No-one ever called her a tremendous help these days. 'If you need anything, don't hesitate to ask,' she said. 'Keith will be very sorry to have missed you.'

'That's very kind of you,' said Robert, who had the feeling that he would have got far less out of Marjorie if anyone else had been present. What a shame that such a nice, friendly, attractive lady should have such an inferiority complex. He had seen it shining right out of her, like a beacon. Such a shame, too, that she didn't dress a little differently – that country gentry outfit must do nothing for her self-esteem.

After he left the Manor, Marjorie sat at the table thinking for a while. She had been a real help. She felt rather proud of herself. It was an unusual feeling for her, and she celebrated it by shutting the dogs in the kitchen and heading upstairs with a good book. The dogs howled a little, as that was what they felt was expected of them, then settled down happily for a nice snooze.

By the end of the afternoon, Robert was becoming quite worn out, and very full of cake. He had now found Olive. It was half-day closing in the Post Office, so she had invited him into her parlour to take tea in her nice floral china cups. She had not mentioned Robert's Awful Mug to anyone, except Ernest, and he had seemed quite disturbingly interested. Now she was doing her best to make clear to Robert how much he needed her.

Olive had run the Post Office and Village Stores ever since the departure of the previous postmaster and his Awful Smell. Once she had faced a robber across her counter. True, he had been armed only with a can of furniture polish, but she liked to say that it could have been nasty had he not been thwarted by Mavis Entwhistle, who had entered the store behind him, tripped, and fallen upon him from the rear propelling him forcefully into the liquorice bootlaces. He had been grateful when the police arrived to take him away, for he was quite terrified by Mavis's insistence that he meet her daughter. He had begged the magistrate to jail him, and when offered Community Service, had punched the court clerk on the nose in order to get his sentence increased. The magistrate had been most impressed, and was still trying to think of a way in which the deterrent powers of Mavis Entwhistle could be used for the common good.

Olive never gave credit where it was due, though, and she disliked Mavis for being so obviously happy all the time, despite having no husband. Those who are chronically frustrated cannot bear happiness in others. 'I know the ins and outs of Bumpstaple,' she told Robert now, as he chewed on a fruit slice. 'There are subtle rules in villages like this. For example, Oliver Bush used granary bread for the Eucharist last month, and poor Miss Postlethwaite got a seed caught behind her dentures. One does not wish to be seen trying to spit out the Communion bread – it is, after all, the Body of Christ.' It was important, she felt, that Robert should understand what sort of a vicar he was meant to be. He might have seemed the right sort at the interview, but she had heard terrible tales of vicars who appeared conservatively cerebral at interview, only to turn out to be closet evangelists who leapt upon the altar during services waving their tambourines and singing 'Lord of the Dance' in the wrong key.

'Indeed, no,' said Robert gravely, 'although I am sure that it was not Oliver's intention to inflict an uncomfortable denture on Miss Postlethwaite.' He had learned not to smile when amused, but Olive looked at him suspiciously. 'These are very nice fruit slices,

Olive,' he added hastily, 'did you make them yourself?'

'Oh, yes,' said Olive, who had brought them in off a shelf in the shop. It did not occur to her that, as a vicar, Robert was almost certainly familiar with every known variety of commercially produced cake. She made a mental note not to sell that particular brand for a while, lest he should see it. 'Now,' she said firmly, 'the congregation were most upset when the Rural Dean used the mordern version of the Lord's prayer . . .' she hushed her voice a little, making it sound as though the congregation had been forced to recite a black mass, 'AND we had that awful hand-shaking. One never knows, these days, what one might pick up . . .' Her voice trailed away, as she suddenly worried that he might be offended.

Robert, being a vicar, was never offended, at least not visibly. He was genuinely interested in the un-written rules and foibles of Bumpstaple's devout, even though he did not particularly intend to observe them. He felt that unwritten rules have a habit of piling up in parishes until there is a very real danger of being buried by them. The only way to prevent this is to stride forward, making your own way through, scatter-ing the rules and then carrying on while the dust settles. Dust always settles eventually, unless someone keeps stirring it. He distracted Olive by telling her about his plans for a choir and a carol service.

'I am a soprano,' she told him at once, 'and I pride myself that my voice carries well. If there are any solos . . .'

Robert added hastily that such details would be arranged later as he himself had no ear for music, and Olive showed him the sympathy the musically gifted like to accord to the tone deaf. 'Oh dear, what a loss for you. We must ask Sally Entwhistle to join, she is so modest, but she has a sweet voice.' This was uncharac-teristically generous of Olive, but she did qualify it by adding, 'I don't know where she gets it from. Mavis has a voice like an old frog, poor dear.' Already, in her mind, she was organizing the whole affair.

Robert kept his voice even. He could feel his stomach rumbling again, and felt that he must depart lest Olive think her fruit slices were responsible. He did not want to cross her. It was not that he feared her disapproval – vicars have to put up with far worse – but he felt that she was a rather unhappy woman, and he did not want to add to her problems.

Olive watched him go, fiddling with her straight grey hair. He seemed all right, and he had allayed her earlier suspicions that he had more lust in him than was proper for a vicar, surely a vicar should have none. Yes, he would do nicely. She had never actually told him that she would run the choir, though. Still, plenty of time. It wasn't as though there was anyone else to do it. As he disappeared from sight she began to practise her trills.

On his way to see Tessa, Robert found Ernest, Olive's husband, waiting for him outside the New Rectory. His surprise was tinged with pleasure, for he enjoyed a bit of personal counselling, and Ernest looked like a man with problems. Although he was a tall man with an upright, rather military gait, something worn in his expression suggested it. Perhaps it was the way his eyebrows had the same rather mournful droop as his moustache.

Robert suspected that Ernest's problems would have Olive at the root of them, and he was not far wrong.

'Hello, Vicar,' said Ernest. 'I wondered if I might have a word with you, in confidence.' He had the rather unrufflable manner common to those men who have been so thoroughly hen-pecked that they are finally emerging from it onto a higher plane of complete immunity.

'Of course,' said Robert, shaking his hand, 'if I can help, then I will.' He led Ernest into the kitchen and put the kettle on. Fate seemed to be conspiring against him, for Mavis had clearly found That Mug somewhere, had washed it and left it out on the draining board, and now he managed to give Ernest his tea in it. The more he put it away, the more it popped up. Rather like the real thing, in some people at least. He suppressed a smile. Blue humour was not appropriate when wearing the dog collar. Sometimes he wondered where these thoughts came from.

Ernest, drinking, felt that the Hand of Fate had touched him. From the moment he was given his tea he knew that this was a man he could talk to frankly, a man whose advice he could take. He began to talk.

It had often struck Robert that people frequently brought problems which really belonged to their doctors, and laid them at his door. Doubtless doctors were bedevilled with issues of faith and collapsing marriages. He quite understood, though, that a man does not lightly broach the subject of his willy with a stranger, even one in a dog collar, so he did his best to advise. It was, he thought, particularly ironic that someone should come to him about sex, when the popular perception was that single vicars did not indulge. He had long since accepted that sexual relationships are not easy for rural vicars, when even holding hands might prompt a call to the Bishop by some concerned parishioner fearing for their immortal soul. Still, if not the blind leading the blind, then you could certainly call it the neglected leading the limp. Ernest said that he was most grateful that Robert had been frank. Robert managed not to make Josh's joke about not being Frank but hoping to be Ernest. Oscar Wilde might have turned in his grave. He was glad to have helped, even though all he had really done was to reassure Ernest that it would do no harm to keep his

61

clinic appointment. It was amazing, he reflected, what medicine could do these days, especially when you were in BUPA.

Sally sat at Tessa's kitchen table as Robert bade goodbye to Ernest. Hers had felt like a very long day, and during the course of it she had had Robert's virtues extolled to her by several of the old ladies who were her regulars, and several more who were not. Now she sat in Tessa's kitchen, sipping tea and giving vent to her exasperation. 'Do you know,' she said, 'if one more person remarks on how handsome a man can look in a dog collar, I think I shall scream. It's bad enough hearing it from Mother every meal time. She's been giving me pie again because I haven't rushed into the rectory in my wedding dress and hung around until he proposed.'

'Oh dear,' Tessa sympathized. She was feeling particularly anti men today, as Richard had been shut in the study ever since breakfast and had glowered at her when she took in his lunch. 'Who else has been hinting?'

'All the old ladies, for a start,' said Sally. 'Miss Postlethwaite got quite carried away on the subject. She reads all that Esme Smuts lust. It's all sex, book after book. In fact I'm sure all she ever thinks about is sex.'

'Sally! She's eighty-three.'

'Yes, and still a Miss,' said Sally, unrepentant. 'I expect I'd be the same in her position. She's been without sex even longer than she's been without teeth, I should imagine. She enjoys it vicariously, you know. She likes to read about it and imagine that we're all having a wild time.'

Tessa giggled. 'That's rather Freudian.'

'What is?'

'You saying "vicariously". It ought to mean pertaining

to vicars. Perhaps it does, really. I can see you have vicars on the brain.'

'I have not,' said Sally, 'nor, before you ask, sex. Speaking of sex, though, how are you and Richard?'

'Shush,' said Tessa, 'Claire might be listening.'

'I haven't seen her come in.'

'No,' said Tessa, 'but she may be lurking. I find that the teenage years bring with them a remarkable ability to lurk.'

'Olive lurks,' said Sally. 'She lurked in the library today. She comes to inspect the returns shelf, you know, to see what Ivy Postlethwaite has been reading.'

'What does Olive read?'

'Very acceptable novels,' said Sally, 'Jane Austen, the Brontës, Dickens. At least, that's what she borrows from me. I suspect she has a secret stash of airport novels. She's another vicarious one. I somehow don't think poor Ernest sows many oats.'

'I'm beginning to think I'm another,' said Tessa, sobering as Charlie wandered in in search of his dinner, and dropped his big doggy head onto her lap in a mute pleading. 'I get more physical affection from this dog than the rest of my family put together.'

'Has Richard struck a bad patch with his muse?'

'His muse,' said Tessa, 'would have to be in darkest Uzbekhistan without benefit of a telephone, to justify the time he's spending looking for it. No, that's just an excuse. His book is fine. He's avoiding me, I know it.'

'I'm sure you're wrong,' said Sally. 'Richard loves you.'

'I know he does,' said Tessa, 'and I know he's just a bit put off by my bulk. I think he thought he'd find pregnancy wildly sexy. Especially the boobs, you know. The trouble is, they've got so big that I think he's afraid of suffocating. It's odd, when my family are all so flat-chested; my sister has resorted to buying some new ones, you know.'

Sally grinned sympathetically. 'So he doesn't find pregnancy wildly sexy?'

'Not even a little bit sexy,' said Tessa sadly. 'I know it's only temporary, logically, but I still feel rejected. I suppose I'm afraid that by the time I'm back to normal he will have forgotten why he ever fancied me.'

'That's rot,' said Sally, 'and you know it. Talk to him. Perhaps he really is having trouble with Inspector McTavish. After fourteen books, I should think he feels like a change.'

'I doubt it,' said Tessa, 'his work has never upset him before. McTavish comes easily to him – he never even gets writer's block.'

'Well, you know best. Look, I must go. I need to make myself a sandwich before Mother gets home and threatens me with pie. She's gone over to Saffron Walden to see her friend Joyce. She says they talk about bridge, but I'm sure they just discuss my love life.'

As Sally left, Tessa reflected how unlikely a pursuit bridge was for Mavis. She did not strike her as the bridge type, except in the sense that she was almost big enough to be one.

Not terribly far away, Robert let himself back into his kitchen in a state of embarrassment. After Ernest's departure he had heard music coming from the village hall behind his house, and decided to investigate. Expecting to find an after school tea club or a lace-making society, he had been unprepared for the sight of the Broomhill and District Aerobics Club. The club members were drawn from all around the area, which was at least some consolation, as it meant that Robert would not be seeing most of them in church. After all, he would never be able to look at any of them again without being mentally transported to a bouncing mass of offensively luminous leotards, most of which were worn a size too small in the erroneous belief that what is squeezed away in one place will not pop out somewhere else.

He had apologized profusely for interrupting them and had left very quickly, prompting a great deal of giggling and general comment on the unmanliness of vicars.

This was rather unfair. It is one thing to address a fully clothed group of people, but quite another to have to introduce yourself to all of their thighs at the same time. There is something particularly daunting about thighs *en masse*, and they can have even the boldest of men fleeing for home. Robert therefore returned home without calling in on Tessa as he had previously intended, so he missed Sally too. Perhaps, in view of subsequent events, this was for the best.

Chapter Four

Mavis, meanwhile, was chatting to her friend Joyce, who was the proprietor of Astral Suggestions, a small shop in Saffron Walden specializing in the magic arts and crystal healing. Mavis was her chief adviser on herbs and astrology. Joyce had the distinction of being almost as peculiar to behold as was Mavis herself: she had fewer warts, but considerably more facial hair. Together they looked like a pair of witches. Indeed, Ned Perkin, roving reporter from the *Broomhill Gazette* had once been sent to investigate the two of them in the hope of getting a good coven story. This, Ned knew, had meant one with plenty of sex and virgins in it. He had visited the shop, but upon meeting Joyce he had decided that if she was a virgin she was welcome to stay that way, and left in a hurry after receiving a lecture on her gynaecological problems, which had quite unnerved him. This is of course the way that most people feel when confronted by the gynaecological problems of ladies of a certain age. Only doctors are forced to sit and listen, which may account for the high level of stress in that profession.

Joyce was interested to hear that Mavis had plans for a new love potion. 'Do you really think you can do something this time?' she asked.

'I've been growing hogweed,' said Mavis. 'It's very powerful in the love stakes.'

'It stings,' said Joyce, 'and it's banned. And it's

poisonous if you don't do it right. In any case, if you grow it again then the Council will want to come and dig it up again.'

'It's that stick insect Olive, from the Post Office, who reports me, you know,' said Mavis. 'She's got nothing better to do than spoil other people's enjoyment.'

'Have you made up a hogweed love tonic?' asked Joyce, who had her sights set on her bank manager and so had more than a professional interest in Mavis's recipe.

'I've nearly finished it,' said Mavis. 'I've been working on hogweed for years, you know. I shall write it up when I've finished. In the meantime, though, I'm giving him nettle and sage to get him primed.'

'Well, if you do write it up, let me sell your book here,' said the manageress. 'Mind you, I'm not sure that you're right to try it out on a vicar. He might be terribly virtuous.'

'He's still a man,' said Mavis. 'It will work. Now, I must get home and put some hogweed in Sally's pie.'

It was as she let herself in through the front door that she found the letter on the mat. It was in a brown envelope, which made it undesirable from the very beginning, but to make things worse, it appeared to be from the Council. Sally was in the kitchen, eating a sandwich.

'When did this arrive?' Mavis waved the letter at her.

'Second post,' said Sally. 'I came in the back way, didn't see it.'

'Will you open it?' asked Mavis, deciding not to take issue with the sandwich for now.

The Council, who wrote to Mavis every year about her hogweed, were nothing if not predictable. 'Dear Madam,' the letters always began, and Mavis would then refuse to read them on the basis that she was not and never had been a madam – a ploy she used with all official documents. 'Dear Madam, we understand that your garden contains a Dangerous Weed, the giant hogweed, *Heracleum Sphondylium.* This Weed can only be grown Under Licence. Please take steps to remove this Weed from your garden. If you fail to comply with this order then an official may be forced to arrange destruction.' Every year, Mavis cut the hogweed down in early October, when it had seeded – she had cut it back last week, in fact, as it had finished for the year. Every year the Council came and found it gone. They could not see the seeds in the ground, so they ticked a box on the Dangerous Weeds form and went home. They were paid by the job, not by the hour.

Sally read out the usual letter. 'It's signed Cyril J. Bender this time,' she said. 'He must be new, but otherwise it's the usual letter. Do you really have to grow this stuff, Mum? I'm sure that one day the Council are going to turn up with men in space suits and incinerate our garden.'

'It's just a lot of silly fuss over a harmless plant,' said Mavis, defensively.

'It's not harmless,' said Sally, 'it stings, and it's probably poisonous. What do you do with it, anyway?'

'It doesn't sting,' said Mavis sadly, 'when it's cooked.'

Sally, who normally regarded Mavis's herbalism as an inoffensive form of alternative medicine which rarely worried anyone but the Council, was alarmed. 'You've been cooking with a Notifiable Plant? Oh Mother, really. What's this Cyril person going to say when he finds out?'

'It's perfectly safe to cook with,' said Mavis indignantly. 'I've used it for ages.'

Sally was tempted to say maybe that explained a few things, but refrained. 'Well, you'll have to stop,' she said. 'One day you'll get into trouble.'

Mavis sniffed and muttered something.

'What was that?'

'Oh . . . nothing. I'll get dinner,' said Mavis, thinking that she had an excellent store of the leaves drying in the garden shed. There would be plenty of hogweed brew for Sally and Robert. She smiled to herself. Perhaps she should give Olive some too – it would serve her right for telling tales to the Council. It was bound to have been her.

Mavis was not the only person in the village hoping to stir up a little romance. Richard had run Tessa's bath that night, and she hoped this was a step in the marital harmony direction. The hope died when she got into it.

'Oh, *Richard*.'

'What?'

'The bath's cold.'

'Oh come on, it's quite warm.'

'This bath isn't warm. This isn't the kind of bath you get into to soothe your aching muscles, it's the kind you use to reduce bruising.'

'You mean it's cold?'

'To anyone who is not a penguin,' said Tessa, drying herself and shivering. She displaced so much water these days, she reflected, that it would soon not be worth putting anything in the bath at all. 'Perhaps I should just sit in an empty bath,' she said glumly, thinking, I just want to be cosseted a little, to be fussed and tucked into bed, brought cocoa, have my bath stirred. The trouble with men is that they've no idea how to cosset.

'How about a cocoa?' asked Richard as she came into the bedroom.

Tessa softened at once. 'Yes, please.'

'Perhaps,' said Richard, not hearing, 'you could bring me mine whilst I'm in the bath.'

He shut her out of the bathroom and turned on the hot tap.

Tessa dropped her towel and stared at her body in the bedroom mirror. I'm not going to feel hurt, she told her bulge fiercely, it's his loss if he's not interested in me. I am still the same person underneath. But you're *our* baby, not just mine. I didn't change shape by myself. He's just a selfish old fart. She frowned fiercely. I hope he can't find the soap, I hope it's dissolved.

Later, in bed, the fierceness had gone. Silly to get so steamed up about a cold bath. She could always have put the hot water in herself. Richard lay on his back, hands linked behind his head, feigning extreme tiredness – she could always tell – and she snuggled up to him, wondering what he was thinking.

He couldn't help not liking it, the snuggle. Tessa's body made him feel rather odd at the moment, but Modern Man is meant to adore all aspects of his wife's pregnancy, so he could not say so. He didn't even really know why. He didn't feel excluded, it wasn't that. He had worried at first that he might feel that her body had changed from a sensuous sexual object into a kind of obstetric conduit, a demystified model with cervixes and uteri which had not previously been at the forefront of his mind when things got physical – but that wasn't the problem either. So why had he lost his appetite for sex? Tessa was beautiful, she glowed with pregnancy, she was Madonna-like in her inner calm and beauty, but he still felt uncomfortable, even when she just wanted to cuddle. He knew that she felt rejected, but what was he to do, pretend? He wondered how quickly he could feign sleep, and began to work on his breathing rhythm.

'Richard?' she said.

'Hmm?'

'What are you thinking?'

'Sheep,' he lied.

Tessa sighed. However much she told herself that he just found her pregnancy unappealing, not herself, it still hurt, especially when what she really wanted was for him to stride around the garden singing 'My boy Bill'. It wasn't really the sex – although that would be nice – it was the closeness. They didn't even talk properly any more. She turned onto her side.

Richard, like most people who have pretended too hard to be sleepy, was wide awake. His thoughts had turned again to Inspector McTavish, and his own recent and peculiar urge to have him sucked unexpectedly into a black hole. His mind never used to work like this. He wondered what Tessa would think, but she was asleep, and in any case he didn't want to worry her. It would hardly be fair, when things were so awkward between them at the moment. Eventually he got up and went to his study, where his fourteen previous McTavish novels were lined up on a shelf in chronological order. Switching on the desk lamp, he settled down to look at them. Upstairs Tessa stirred, wriggled up against him, discovered him to be a pair of pillows, kicked them out of bed, then fell properly asleep.

When Robert met Tessa the following day, she lost no time in assuring him that the word on the street, as she gathered it was now put, was that he was already quite a hit. Even Olive seemed to have softened her attitude towards divorced vicars, and Olive was normally about as soft as a freeze-dried fruit bat.

'I'm delighted to hear it,' said Robert, thinking it was amazing what a vicar can achieve just by drinking vast volumes of tea. Odd, really, that the same wasn't true of removal men. 'I just hope my preaching style is as popular. So far, all I've done is eat cake.'

'And pastry,' said Tessa, smiling sympathetically.

Robert nodded. 'And pastry.' Some things did not need to be said.

'You know, as long as there's no total immersion during Communion, and the congregation don't have to sway when they sing, I think you'll find us pretty easy.'

It would have taken a particularly mean-spirited kind of person to have said, afterwards, that Robert was to find some of his new congregation rather easier than others.

Hugh arrived that Saturday morning. Claire had not planned to be around when he made his appearance, but was caught out when he was dropped off early, while she was still trying to extract extra pocket money from Richard. Aunt Sarah, it seemed to Claire, deposited Hugh with almost indecent haste before speeding off towards Audley End railway station to catch the London train. It was amazing, she always thought, that you could begin a trip at Audley End station that could end in America. It gave Audley End a kind of worldliness which was at odds with its appearance.

Claire had always been fascinated by Audley End station, a tiny white country station which had been hijacked by commuters. It sat out in the midst of green fields and tiny cottages, decorated with hanging baskets and posters of local attractions, looking like the kind of house Sooty would go to on holiday, but surrounded by an absolutely vast car park. It had a pleasingly surreal quality.

Hugh was ten years old. He had ginger hair and freckles, and he seemed to be formed into a perpetual question mark. If a question mark could be personified, then Hugh was it. Unfortunately for Claire, fifteen-year-old girls were just about his favourite subject for baiting, and he was master of the art. He had an unerring ability to embarrass, and an insatiable appetite for collecting creatures with more than their fair share of legs in matchboxes and jam jars. Gerald Durrell and Hugh could have been soul mates.

Tessa felt rather sorry for Claire, as she waved her sister off. She had been plagued by a Hugh of her own when she was Claire's age, in the shape of her little brother – they obviously ran in the family – and she could clearly recall the frustration of being endlessly angered in a multitude of small ways, none of which sounds like anything to get steamed up about when recounted to an adult. No-one but another sufferer could possibly understand how utterly mortifying it is to have your first bra used to store marbles. Nevertheless, Hugh was family, she told Claire as he negotiated the stairs with a large plastic tank which no-one else was allowed – much less wanted – to touch. It contained a large and rather stupid-looking lizard.

'He's the black sheep,' said Claire, pocketing the extra five pounds keep-the-peace money she had extracted from Richard.

'Every family has its black sheep,' said Tessa.

'Some,' said Claire darkly, 'are blacker than most.' The lizard, she felt, confirmed her greatest fears. The last pet Hugh had threatened her with had merely been a white rat, but then, ownership of peculiar creatures seemed to run in her family. Down the maternal line.

Relieved to have found a way to blame her mother for both Hugh and his lizard, she headed upstairs. She must get to her room before the little creep put anything black and hairy in her underwear drawer.

When she got upstairs, Hugh was there already. 'What are you doing in my bedroom?' she demanded.

Hugh grinned, his snub nose wrinkling in the way that elderly aunts have been known to find appealing. 'I came to say "hello",' he said, 'and to borrow your skin cream.'

'What do you mean, borrow my skin cream?' Claire

stood protectively in front of her dressing table, wondering whether ten-year-old boys got acne.

'It's not for me, it's for Larry,' explained Hugh, patiently. 'He doesn't like to ask.' He revealed the two tubes he was holding behind his back.

'Give me those!' Claire made a grab for them and he hopped away. Retrieving her dignity, she attempted a shrug, determined not to sink to the level of brawling with him. A girl with a boyfriend was far too adult to be goaded. She tried a different tack. 'Please yourself,' she said, shrugging in what she hoped was an uninterested manner, 'but don't be surprised if your friend is allergic to it. It's special cream, not designed for boys.'

'Larry isn't a boy,' said Hugh, surprised, 'he's a lizard.'

'Oh God!' Claire forgot her resolve. 'You can't put skin cream on a lizard!'

'Aunt Tessa puts sun cream on Lysander, and he's a pig. What's wrong with putting it on a lizard?'

'It might poison it,' said Claire, 'or make it grow breasts.'

Hugh peered at the cream, his genuine fondness for his lizard vying with the thought of the fame which could be his if he possessed a lizard with breasts. 'It doesn't say anything about breasts on here,' he said doubtfully, 'and it certainly hasn't done much for yours.'

Claire gritted her teeth, searching for a cutting response.

'It says on here that it's for spots,' said Hugh. 'Have you got spots? How revolting!'

'No, I have not got spots!' said Claire, praying that the other tube he held was not her concealer. 'Nor freckles, you little speckled pain. Anyway, you just wait. Boys get much worse acne than girls. You'll probably look like a toad in a few years' time.'

Hugh grinned. He was impossible to annoy – experts had tried. 'It says "deep cleanses and putrefies" on this label,' he said. 'Ha ha, that explains a lot. You women are all weird. Did you know that my mother's gone to America to get some new breasts? You can buy them over there. Imagine if she bought a pair that didn't match, by accident. D'you suppose they'd let her take one back?'

'You are stupid,' said Claire witheringly. 'Give me my creams. They'll upset your toad.'

'Lizard,' said Hugh, relinquishing one. 'What's green and hard?'

'Get lost.'

'Frog with a flick knife,' said Hugh, peering at the second tube of cream. 'What's this? De . . . depil . . .'

'Depilatory cream,' said Claire, 'for hairy armpits. I wouldn't put that on your creature if I were you.'

'Hairy armpits? Have you got those? It must be gross, just like a baboon.'

Claire, who privately felt that it was, threw a can of styling mousse at him. It missed and hit the wall, the top broke and white foam began to erupt from it, making strange Mr Whippy shapes on the carpet.

Hugh grinned annoyingly. 'Now look what you've done.'

'Pig!' shouted Claire, enraged.

Hugh left the room casually, airily. When he got to the door he added, 'Teenage girls are *so* messy,' then fled before any more projectiles came his way.

Claire sat at her dressing table, exhausted by the conflict. Why did she get so riled? What peculiar quality did Hugh possess? He was like a little gremlin. It was only a shame he didn't explode on contact with daylight, like the real thing. She peered into her mirror. Oh God! Was that the beginning of another spot? It was the beginning of another spot. Josh would go right off her when he saw this. Should she put the spot-zapping cream on it? That would get rid of it, but not without making it red and obvious first. Should she conceal it? No good for viewing at close quarters, though, and it would make it more spottish underneath. She tried talcum powder. A pale patch was better than a red one. Why do spots always come out when you least want them? she asked herself despairingly. Why can't we get spots when we're seventy, and no-one cares what we look like? Why does it have to be NOW?

She rooted in her top drawer, muttering. Hugh had clearly caused the spot. It was stress. If her mother had never agreed that Hugh could stay, she would never have got the spot. It was obviously her mother who was primarily responsible. In her heart of hearts Claire knew this was not at all fair. She was not accustomed to listening to her heart of hearts, but on this occasion it popped out and reminded her that it was her hormones, not her mother, that controlled her skin, and she was conscious of a faint but surprising feeling of guilt for thinking otherwise. Finding the anti-spot antibiotics distracted her from this unusual train of thought, and she decided to double the dose. She would ask Zoe Ormondroyd, who travelled on her bus and whose skin was perfect, what her secret was.

Tessa had reached the stage of pregnancy when indecision predominates, and she spent endless fruitless minutes in front of the supermarket cold shelves trying to decide which of several effectively identical brands of margarine to purchase. This was, she thought, an activity of such singular pointlessness that it was actually depressing.

She ran into Sally when trying to decide on some trout at the fish counter. One had a rather nice smile, and she felt it would be rather mean to eat him. The fish assistant did not seem sympathetic to this view.

'He *is* dead already,' Sally said over her shoulder, as

the fish assistant sulked uncompromisingly. 'If you eat him, his sacrifice won't have been in vain.'

Tessa cheered up slightly at the sight of a friendly face – other than that of the fish. 'I could give him to Hugh, I suppose,' she said, 'he'd appreciate him. OK. I'll have all four trout.'

The sullen assistant seized the last remaining trout, which she had hoped would be unsold and thus available at staff discount at the end of the day, and loaded them onto the scales. 'Heads on?'

'Yes, please,' said Tessa, 'and tails. You can't often have both, can you?'

The assistant looked at her, undertakerishly.

OK, as she told Sally later, it wasn't her best joke ever, but it wasn't that bad. Shortly afterwards, trying to select bread from an inexplicably vast and confusing array, particularly when you realized it was all brown and sliced, she saw Robert Peabody. He was, she noticed, a man who chose his bread decisively, flinging it into his trolley, a man who knows that food shops are for buying food and not for agonizing in.

She was not quite correct, for Robert had spent some time agonizing over what he could buy in order to ensure that he and Josh would have everything in the house that they required for a nutritionally sound diet, but nothing for making pie. He greeted Tessa, insisting on helping her with her trolley, which wanted to go in a different direction altogether.

'Did you see Sally?' she asked him, forgetting that he hadn't met her, would not know her if he saw her. 'I was talking to her by the fish a few minutes ago.'

But Robert said he had not. He felt sure that the notorious Sally, if she resembled her mother at all, would have been more than obvious, even from several aisles away, and he did not wish to arouse any more speculation than there was already by asking for details of her appearance.

Odd, really, that they had missed by just yards, thought Tessa. In Valhalla, though, the fates did not think it odd at all. They thought that, thus far, it was the best game they had had in ages.

By the time Tessa got back with the weekly shopping an hour or so later, Hugh and Claire had made themselves scarce. This, she felt, was all part of the great skill of lurking, which involves melting invisibly into the wallpaper when there are chores to be done, and appearing swiftly, silently and irrevocably when there are chocolate biscuits to be eaten. Hugh, although not even a teenager yet, had always been an effective lurker.

She unpacked groceries wearily, thinking about those cheerful midwives who insisted that pregnant ladies must never lift anything heavier than an egg. She wondered on which planet such ladies of leisure lived. 'It seems,' she said to Charlie, who seemed to be the only one who would listen to her, 'that we must have a matter transporter in this house, for there were three people in here when I got home, and now there seem to be none. Someone has clearly beamed them up.'

Charlie said nothing. If he had been thinking constructively he would have found it most odd that anyone should wish to make themselves scarce when a bag of dog biscuits had just entered the house. Thinking constructively was not, however, one of Charlie's strong points, so he raised his eyebrows hopefully and nudged Tessa instead.

Richard wandered into the kitchen, then tried to sidle out, as he was awfully caught up in his study.

'Stop right there. You can help me unpack,' said Tessa, not wanting to nag.

'OK.' Richard leaned down and picked up a carrier bag. There was a packet of chocolate biscuits in the top. He decided to unpack that first.

Tessa found the bread. It was, as usual, beneath the bag of tins. 'Blast,' she said.

'What's up?'

'Whatever I do, I always squash the bread.'

'You should put it through the till last,' said Richard, 'then it would be on top.'

'I did, but then it gets put into the boot first.'

'I see. Does it really matter?'

'Well, I suppose not, except that it means we get funny shaped toast. It looks like smaller toast, but I suppose it isn't really, it's just got less air in it.'

'Ah,' said Richard, 'but then you can fit less butter and marmalade on it, so you need to eat more toast to fill up.'

Tessa tried to plump up the bread, but only succeeded in squashing it further. 'Do you remember those adverts for slimmers' bread, where the girl became so light that she floated away in a hot air balloon?' she asked wistfully. 'I wish I felt light enough to float. It would take a crane to get me airborne.'

Richard singularly failed to contradict her. 'Put the kettle on, love,' he said.

Where would we be, thought Tessa, fishing out her herb tea from the cupboard, without hot drinks? It is not the drinking of them that is so vital, nor even the ceremony of pouring them out. It is the act of putting on the kettle. It is such a wonderful displacement activity. It acts as the watershed between two conversations, dividing that which we do not want to discuss from that which we do. Without it we would have to say, 'I'm bored, shut up,' whenever we wanted to change the subject, whereas 'Put the kettle on' is far less offensive, even though it means the same thing.

She had, astonishingly, just unpacked the very last bag of shopping when Hugh and Claire rematerialized. Feeling weary and puffed out, she watched them raiding the biscuit tin, to which a few biscuits had made the hazardous journey, in spite of Richard, and it struck her that she had never really stopped breast-feeding, at least in the metaphorical sense. When they stopped draining you in one direction they started in another. However many biscuits she bought, they never saw the sun set over the kitchen window. For a moment, her family seemed like inconsiderate strangers.

'I suppose you want your lunch,' she said, hoping that they would jointly cry, 'No, you put your feet up while we make you a smoked salmon sandwich.'

'Can I have hot dogs?' demanded Hugh.

'Ugh,' said Claire, 'junk food. I'll have cheese salad.'

Richard had gone.

Tessa went to look for hot dogs in the larder, and underwent the slightly surreal experience of finding three rolls of Sellotape where the baked beans ought to have been. This was doubly peculiar, because she had spent some hours the previous day looking for even one roll of Sellotape. There had been none anywhere then, she could have sworn, not even on the beans shelf, yet now, here they nestled, three rolls like London buses, smug in their togetherness. She sighed. 'Would you like,' she asked Hugh, 'Sellotape with your sausages?'

Hugh looked at her with the kind of disdain of which only ten-year-old boys are capable. 'Mad,' he said, 'quite peculiar.'

Tessa wondered briefly whether to look for beans in her desk drawer, but dismissed the idea as too ridiculous. 'Then you can have them on their own,' she said. The absent-mindedness of pregnancy was taking her over, she knew. As she fed the ungrateful horde she reflected that she was beginning to feel as though her brain was becoming bovine. It was slow, ponderous, cud-chewingly forgetful these days. 'I wouldn't be surprised,' she said aloud, 'if I woke up tomorrow and discovered that I had turned into a cow. Actually it might be a relief. Nothing to do all day except chew the cud.'

'Not quite,' said Hugh, 'you'd have to have your udders squeezed twice a day. You wouldn't like that.'

Tessa just refrained from saying that she wasn't so sure about that.

Sunday dawned, and as little old ladies everywhere became excited at the thought of their weekly dose of *Songs of Praise*, and supermarket check-out girls everywhere whiled away their shifts working out how much they were earning per minute on double time, Mavis Entwhistle was putting on her best coat in preparation for her attendance at Robert's first Sunday service at St Julian's. It was a dreadfully purple coat, but somehow it was right for Mavis. She checked her appearance in the hall mirror. She had become accustomed to her face. She had had a good many years in which to do so, so meeting it in the mirror did not accord her the kind of startled surprise which others felt when confronted by her particular style of make-up. She had always worn purple lipstick, after all.

Mavis thought that she looked her best today. She had shaved the hairs off her moles, as she felt that they were rather un-churchlike, and had even powdered her nose. She nodded at herself in approval. She was going to become a fine upstanding member of the congregation, a veritable pillar. She would give her full support to the man she already saw as her future son-in-law.

'Sally,' she called up the stairs, 'come on down, you'll be late for church – I can hear the bells.' She knew that Sally would not really miss the service just to avoid meeting the new vicar.

Sally trudged down the stairs wrapped in her

dressing-gown and looking awful. 'Sorry,' she whispered, 'you'll have to go without me. I've got a migraine.'

It did not even cross Mavis's mind to disbelieve her; she had never known Sally to lie. 'Oh dear,' she said, 'let me make you a poultice.'

Sally suppressed a shudder. Some of her mother's herbal remedies could be so revolting that they actually provoked migraines themselves. 'No, thanks,' she said weakly, 'you go to church. I've had my tablets.' She retreated to her bedroom, and Mavis had to go alone.

Mavis walked to church cautiously. Although the roads were quiet, it is wise to swivel your head frequently as you walk in East Anglia on a Sunday morning, for its leafy lanes are often rendered hazardous by the reckless, bicycled meanderings of multiple-parished vicars who have finished off far too much Communion wine. They must then balance upon ancient and brakeless bicycles to travel from church to church. The problem reaches its peak just before evensong, when the worst affected may be on their fifth or sixth service, and may be winding merrily down a road many miles from where they are meant to be.

Richard was not a churchgoer. It was not that he did not believe, more that his mind was so full of other things that he had never felt the need to think about it. Now, as Tessa left for church and he realized that he still had Hugh, he resolved to make an effort. 'Do you like detective stories?' he asked.

Hugh, guzzling breakfast at an ecologically alarming rate, muttered something derogatory about the Famous Five.

'I mean my Inspector McTavish,' prompted Richard. 'You've seen him on TV, haven't you?'

'Boring,' said Hugh, who was not known for his delicate tact. 'I mean, when you've seen one murder story you've seen them all.' He had heard his father say that. He refilled his bowl.

Richard was interested. This was precisely the conclusion he had come to himself on his late night reading stint. When it came to it, there was only so much to be said about Inspector McTavish, and he had said it all. Perhaps this explained his strange urge to have him meet some terrible end. 'What sort of things do you like to read?' he asked curiously.

Hugh glanced at him suspiciously, wondering if there was a trap. Teachers did this, then when you said you liked adventure they gave you a pile of dreadful sissy stuff about wet children with stupid dogs. 'Science fiction,' he said cautiously, 'with kids and monsters – and plenty of violence.' He watched Richard carefully for signs of condemnation. He was expert at spotting it, as there had always been plenty for him to spot. There was none. Richard was busy remembering just how much those sort of books appealed to him, too.

The church was quite gratifyingly full – Robert's village rounds had paid off. He knew that not all were likely to come regularly, some would have come out of curiosity, but he took the view that once was better than never. Tessa was pleased, too, as it was not often that she could pull out all the stops on the organ without drowning out the congregation entirely. Robert's sermon was rather fun, she thought. He began with a bit of a joke – his tutor at theological college had emphasized the importance of capturing his audience's attention in the first few minutes. This is every bit as important for a vicar as for a stand-up comic. (In fact Robert had often reflected that the similarities did not end there.)

He told them all about Rumpleton, and its unexpected move south when it was deposited as silt in the Humber estuary. It provided a good example, he explained, of how one man's misery – the loss of his retirement bungalow overlooking the North Sea – can become another man's misery too, if he does nothing to help the first man. Such a man was the Rumpleton and Bunbridge MP. He had not supported the Rumpleton residents' request that their coastline be shored up and protected at great expense, as unlike Bunbridge they had been predominantly Labour voters, and he had a small majority. As chance would have it, he had also been a passenger on a millionaire's yacht when it was grounded on the very silt which had once formed a part of his constituency, as had his very attractive researcher. His wife had then told the Press exactly what her opinion was of his politics and this, Robert told them, just went to prove that ignoring the misery of others can be more foolish than you think.

While the congregation were nodding and smiling, delighted at the fall from grace of a lying, cheating son-of-a-peer, he got in a quick plug for God as the eternal dispenser of justice, then moved swiftly on to the creed.

His inclusion of the hand-shaking at the exchange of the peace took them aback a little, particularly as he insisted on walking through the congregation, greeting them each in turn. Olive was particularly put out because she was forced to shake hands with Mavis, something which she could not recall having done in thirty years.

Mavis was very impressed. Church was much more fun than she had imagined. It was really quite jolly, and she was enjoying herself. She had discovered, to her surprise, that her ability to outsing Olive Osborne was quite striking.

The rest of the congregation were quite struck by it,

too. It was like having a pair of mating dodos carousing in the back pews. Even with all the stops out and the swell pedal fully open, there was a risk of the trilling duo entirely drowning out the organ. At least they could be thankful that, as Mavis sang rather sharp and Olive rather flat, to a certain degree this cancelled out, so that in chorus they almost seemed to be in tune.

On the whole, though, even Olive was impressed with Robert. Despite being divorced, he had cast no lascivious looks at the ladies in the congregation. He had used the old version of the Lord's Prayer, she had known the tunes to all the hymns, and if the hand-shaking had been a bit unwelcome, well, he had clearly forgotten her advice just on that one matter. One could forgive him a little, and at least he had shown no tendency to shout 'Hallelujah!' or play the bongo drums at any point during the service. The vicar of Broomhill had done something along those lines, shortly before taking early retirement, and some parishioners in the town were still reeling from the shock. No, Robert would do very well, she thought. She hung back at the end, enjoying the feel and smell of the church, so that Robert would have more time to speak to her.

Mavis watched everyone leave with her cleaner's eye. They had trodden dirt into her nicely hoovered carpet, and she hoped that the congregation would not always be quite so large, but it had been very enjoyable; she had shaken hands with as many people as she could in the time allowed, and she loved Robert's stand-up speech. She had laughed and clapped far more loudly than anyone else. Poor chap, the others had all been so po-faced. He had got a bit serious every now and again, of course, but you could forgive him the odd slip – after all, he was a vicar.

Marjorie Smythe followed her husband, Keith, out

of the front pew which they habitually occupied. She enjoyed coming to church as it was one of her few chances to leave the dogs behind, although this unfortunately meant that she had their welcome to face when she got home.

Keith waited for her at the head of the aisle, took her arm and smiled at her. Marjorie adored Keith. Her adoration of Keith had made her what she was, and it continued unabated. It was for him that she wore the clothes, tolerated the dogs, drove the Range Rover and refrained from setting about the Aga with a sledge-hammer. He was her hero. She just wished – oh, she never knew exactly what it was she wished for. A spark of admiration or surprise when he looked at her, perhaps? She knew he loved her dearly, she just hankered after a bit more desperation. She read historical romances in secret, and the heroes she admired most in those books were the ones with a good line in desperate adoration, like Mr Rochester when he wept over Jane Eyre.

'Morning, Vicar, I enjoyed your sermon. Welcome to Bumpstaple,' Keith was shaking Robert's hand. He had a grip like a carpenter's vice, Marjorie knew, but Robert did not flinch. 'Keith Smythe. Pleased to meet you. I gather you've met my wife, Marjorie.'

Robert heard the glimmer of pride in his voice, could see he was a reserved man. Marjorie did not notice it, for she did not expect it to be there. Robert wondered what a bit of self-confidence would do for her.

'Yes, indeed, she has been a great help to me,' he said, and Marjorie flushed with pleasure.

'Oh, really, it was just minor advice. Anybody would have said the same.'

Robert shook his head. 'Actually,' he said, 'I have another favour to ask. I wondered if you would be able to organize the choir for me?'

'Oh . . . I . . . Well, surely Tessa . . .'

'Tessa has rather a lot on, I think,' said Robert, 'and you sprang to mind at once.'

'Oh. Gosh. Yes, well, I'd love to.' Marjorie was overcome.

Keith observed this in some surprise. As someone who had never lacked confidence himself, he had never before conceived of the idea that his wife might not be as secure in her role as he was in his.

Olive Osborne, who was hovering, waiting to speak to Robert, was furious. That was her job. Of course, he would have asked her if Marjorie had not been in front of her in the queue filing out. Why, if the dreadful Mavis hadn't drowned everyone out, he would have heard her remarkable singing voice. (He had, and he had indeed thought it remarkable.) Then he would definitely have asked her. Well, this could be sorted out right now, in just the same way as the flower rota had been removed from Marjorie's control before she had ever had it. She hurried forward into the group.

'Oh, Reverend Peabody – Robert – good morning Keith, Marjorie – I was just about to offer to organize the choir myself. Dear Marjorie has so much else to do, and I am quite chorally experienced.'

This was not absolutely true, but she had sung the role of third angel in the Great Barking nativity of 1952, so it was only a slight distortion of the truth.

Robert was a little taken aback by the swiftness of her attack, although it was not entirely unexpected. Rather a bully, he thought.

Marjorie had become visibly embarrassed. 'Oh, of course, if Olive . . .'

'Nonsense,' said Keith, who was cursing himself for not having realized before now that Marjorie might have allowed herself to be pushed out. 'Marjorie will do a grand job. She was a most accomplished singer when we met, weren't you, my dear? I'm sure you too have a great deal to do, Mrs Osborne. We all admire how much you take on, we cannot ask you to do more.'

'Oh. I . . .' Olive was torn between anger at being crossed and pleasure at being flattered by Keith, who was, after all, a magistrate.

Marjorie, who had watched Keith in some amazement, now came to her own defence, surprising herself as much as Olive. 'It's kind of you to offer, Olive,' she said firmly, 'but I shall enjoy it. I have time on my hands. I do hope you'll come and audition, though.'

Robert grinned.

Olive's jaw dropped. 'Audition?'

'What fun that will be,' boomed Keith before she could say more, 'auditions. A grand idea, don't you agree, Olive? I shall audition too. Thank you, Vicar, I have enjoyed myself.'

He swept a rather glowing Marjorie out of church, leaving Olive somewhat nonplussed. He had, in fact, enjoyed himself immensely.

'Good to see you here, Olive,' said Robert.

'Oh, I never miss a service,' said Olive primly. She disliked being treated as if she was just any member of the congregation, who might or might not turn up. She felt that the regularity of her worship gave her added rights, and she had never been terribly keen on the idea that people who repented at the last minute got into Heaven just as easily as those who had been churchgoers for years.

'I'm sure you don't,' said Robert, smoothing her feathers. 'I know you are very busy, but I had hoped to ask you to take charge of decorating the church for our Festival of Nine Lessons. It needs to be something rather special, as I'm hoping for an extra-large congregation on Christmas Eve. Can I leave it in your capable hands?'

Olive mellowed at once. He had asked so nicely that she quite forgot that this was a job which she considered hers anyway. 'Of course I will. You can depend on me, Robert. Come along now, Ernest.' Ernest Osborne, who was chatting to Tessa, was whisked past Robert with barely a chance to wave. Robert nodded at him gravely, wondering if their little chat would pay dividends.

Robert and Tessa were left alone. She locked the organ console and finished stacking her books. The mice had been nesting in the large print edition of *Hymns Ancient and Modern*, and she tipped the droppings onto the collection plate. 'I see you have Olive organized,' she said, smiling. 'I've never seen her so won over.'

'I hope so, she seems a very unhappy lady,' said Robert. 'Now, how are you?'

When Tessa reflected afterwards, it struck her that he was probably right about Olive. She resolved to try to be nicer to her in future.

Chapter Five

Claire and Josh had been in church too, hoping to engineer a meeting or even some kind of a date between Robert and Sally. Sally's unfortunate non-attendance had foiled their cunning plan, but at least church had rescued them from Hugh, who had previously been following them around with his camera, claiming to be doing biology research. Turning the organist's pages in church, he had told Tessa, was uncool, and coolness was very important in class four. Claire and Josh were therefore able to hurry out of church at the end of the service without being followed, in hope of an unobserved snog behind the war memorial.

It was not to be, as Olive saw them when she walked home with Ernest. Snogging teenagers annoyed her, and she sniffed self-righteously. 'Disgraceful display,' she said to Ernest, 'and in public, too.'

'It's hardly public, dear,' said Ernest mildly, reflecting that it was only public if you were a giraffe or had eyes on long stalks. Then again, Olive did have eyes on long stalks. He sighed. A snog behind the war memorial would be quite nice. It was no good, though, when not all of his plumbing worked as well as it should. Something was wrong with his crank shaft, as he had told the doctor at the clinic, and it meant that things were a bit quiet on the piston front these days. It was true that this did not prevent him from indulging

in a good snog, and it would probably do Olive the
world of good, but he took the view that there was no
point in starting the engine when you couldn't get into
gear. He sighed again, reflecting on times past when
Olive would not have had time to decorate the church
and would certainly not have sung flat. Still, she might
yet be in for a surprise . . .

'Don't dawdle, Ernest!' snapped Olive. 'People will
think we're nosing.'

We bloody well were, thought Ernest, but said
nothing, as usual, out of guilt.

Back at home, Sally Entwhistle lay with her eyes
closed in a darkened room, listening to the distant
church bell. She was genuinely sorry to have missed
the new vicar's first service. His son seemed very nice
– he would be good for Claire, she was sure. Poor boy,
he had even tried to be polite about Mother's cooking,
but she could imagine his true feelings on the matter.
Some opinions were universal. It was a shame that
Mother would insist on trying to match-make; she was
always so painfully obvious, and it wasn't as if Sally
was likely to fancy a vicar anyway. She and her mother
had different requirements of Sally's future soul mate.
Souls aside, Sally required that he should be extremely
sexy. Mavis plainly did not think this important at all.

Somewhere in far away Valhalla, the fates listened to
her thoughts and winked smugly at one another.

Claire and Josh were not aware that Olive had seen
them. They were indulging very thoroughly in what
has variously been called necking, snogging, kissing
and lip-awareness practice. It was going quite well, in
that they hardly ever got their noses locked now.
Unfortunately, just then the tenderness of the moment
was cruelly shattered by a voice behind them.

'Imagine what would happen,' said Hugh, 'if you

were sick. It would pass straight from one stomach to the other.'

They broke apart, flustered and furious.

'Go away, you nasty little creature,' said Claire.

'What's it worth?' asked Hugh, grinning demonically.

'It's worth me not leaving you tied to the war memorial,' said Josh, seizing him.

Hugh considered this. 'I don't think that your dad would approve of you tying small boys to memorials,' he said.

'You're not a small boy,' said Josh, 'you're a devil. Devils can be tied to any sort of monument – it's church law.'

Hugh was not sure about this. 'If you threaten me, I'll tell the whole school you were snogging,' he told them.

Josh didn't care and said so. Claire rather hoped that he would spread it about – she'd been trying to think of a way to do so herself.

Hugh looked mutinous. He was rarely beaten. 'You've got to come home,' he said to Claire, 'Lysander's got out.'

'Oh God,' said Claire. The last time Lysander had fled from his expected fate of hideous pampering until death, it had taken them hours to catch him. He had eventually been found in Ernest Osborne's vegetable patch, where he had eaten two cauliflowers, and he had consequently smelt truly disgusting for ages. Tessa had found him too noxious even for painting, and so no-one had gone within ten feet of him for days. 'Where did he go?' she asked.

'He was in the churchyard,' said Hugh, 'eating flowers.'

But when they got there, Lysander was no longer in the churchyard, nor were there any flowers to be seen. They went to find Richard, who they could hear behind the rectory, whistling loudly in a manner clearly meant to be tempting to pigs.

'Where's Mum?' asked Claire.

'Round the back of the pub, calling it by name,' said Richard in disgust. He felt that if you must name a pig you should at least have the decency to call it Percy. Whoever heard of a pig named Lysander? Richard was not fond of pigs. He had not thought that they would ever figure prominently in his life, apart from at breakfast time.

'How did he get out?' asked Josh.

'Ask him,' said Richard, pointing at Hugh and glaring. To think that this was a child whose literary opinions he had earlier thought of value. So, he liked violence, did he?

Hugh glared back defiantly. 'I just wanted to take him for a walk. He always comes when I call him in the garden, so I thought he'd do the same if I let him out.'

'You silly prat,' said Claire, 'he's permanently trying to escape. He only comes to you in the garden because he wants to get into the house; he's the kind of animal who always wants to be somewhere else.'

'He was on a lead,' said Hugh, mutinously.

'You put a pig on a lead?'

'Well, why not? I put Charlie's collar on him, but as soon as we got out he pulled too hard and I lost my grip.'

'You,' said Claire with relish, 'lost your grip years ago. You were born without grip.'

They set off in different directions, calling Lysander. Lysander, though, was the wiliest of pigs. He was well aware that the sound of his name being called in a variety of tones, both sugared and furious, indicated that there were those who wished to restrict his liberty. Freedom was particularly important to Lysander, for there were many interesting things growing in Bump-staple, and he planned to eat most of them. This

93

burning desire had now led him to Mavis Entwhistle's garden, where he set about the sage. In this he demonstrated the limits of his intelligence, for a pig would surely be thought foolish in selecting a herb which effectively pre-flavours him for roasting. (It was a shame, really, that she had cut the hogweed, which would perhaps have been even more appropriate.) He was a trusting pig, though, and had no idea that most of his siblings had already met a fate in which sage played a prominent rôle.

It was Claire and Josh who found him. This was not difficult, in the end, for a ranting Mavis confronted them and demanded that he be removed at once. You could not blame her, for her sage patch looked as though someone had gone particularly wild in it with a can of Agent Orange. She toned herself down from enraged to slightly cross when she saw that her possible future step-grandson was present, as she wanted to keep up the good impression she was sure she was making with the vicar.

'Please could you remove this pig?' she asked, with commendable restraint.

Hugh appeared from nowhere. 'I'll help,' he said.

'You caused the problem,' said Claire, ungratefully.

Mavis eyed Hugh balefully. 'Your pig has eaten my sage.'

Hugh stared at her, mesmerized. How could someone who looked like Mavis ever have had a husband? Perhaps she hadn't, perhaps she had had Sally by artificial insemination, like a cow. He wondered if he should ask, but decided that it might perhaps be unwise just now. He turned his attention to Lysander. 'Hey, pig!'

Lysander ambled cheerfully off towards the corner of the house.

'I'm sure Mum will replace anything he's damaged,' said Claire, edging after Hugh. The last thing she wanted was to be trapped in conversation with Mavis.

'Aaargh!' shouted Hugh from around the corner of the cottage. They rushed to see what was wrong. He lay on his front amongst the remains of Mavis's dandelions. Lysander stood beside him, chewing as innocently as a pig can in such circumstances. 'That smells like poo on you,' said Claire, sniffing.

'That,' said Hugh, getting to his feet and eyeing Lysander threateningly, 'is probably because it *is* poo on me.'

They walked home some distance behind Hugh, as there was a following wind. For once, even Mavis had not been inclined to prolong the conversation. Marjorie Smythe passed them, walking her dogs. Fortunately they adored her so much that they were not tempted to get involved with pigs or small reeking boys, however fascinating their scent. Claire and Josh exchanged polite greetings and explained what had happened.

'Dear me,' said Marjorie, glad, for once, that she only had dogs to worry about. 'Tell your father I did enjoy the service.' She was looking brighter and happier than usual, and she was not wearing a head scarf.

Josh said that he would, and Marjorie headed off towards the woods. She felt good. She had felt empowered since meeting Robert Peabody, and she had thrown away her head scarf. In fact, she had thrown away all of her head scarves. They had gone into the bin, and tomorrow she planned to buy herself a new hairband. A domed velvet one.

'Stop watching those dreadful children and come and lay the table!' snapped Olive. She could see that Ernest was daydreaming as usual, gazing out of the front window at that ridiculous pig Lysander being dragged home. 'Whoever heard of a pig named Lysander?' she demanded crossly of no-one particularly. 'I suppose it's named after some pop star or other.' They had not taught classics at Olive's school.

'Now, my dear, I think they are rather splendid young people,' said Ernest, 'and I remember that there was a time when you and I held hands behind the war memorial.' He had indeed been daydreaming, but not about pigs. His mind had been on the days when he and Olive were first married. She had been a different woman in those days. Actually, the less he had oiled her hinges the more prudish she had become and that, Ernest believed, was entirely his fault.

'Ernest, really,' said Olive, who chose not to remember that she was ever young, lest she be tempted into sympathy with today's teenagers. She began to scrape a carrot, rather furiously. 'Held hands, we may have done, but we did not indulge in that liposuction which was going on earlier.'

'French kissing, dear,' said Ernest mildly, smoothing his moustache. 'Liposuction is cosmetic surgery.'

'Oh, and how would you know that?'

'I read it,' said Ernest blandly, 'in a leaflet at the private hospital.'

Olive dropped the peeler. 'What do you mean? When were you at the hospital?' Anxiety sharpened her voice, which was quite an achievement in itself.

'I have been to see a urologist,' said Ernest, with calm banality, 'privately.'

'A urologist? You mean about your . . .' Olive could not immediately think of an acceptable word.

'Erection, dear,' said Ernest matter-of-factly, 'or lack of.'

'Ernest!' Olive gripped the carrot fiercely and blushed bright pink.

'Now, Olive, dear,' said Ernest, 'a couple of our mature years should be able to discuss these things.'

Olive looked down at the carrot, then put it down in

some distaste. 'Why?' she asked. 'I didn't expect you to discuss my menopause.'

'No,' said Ernest, 'but then you were not impotent. This problem affects us both . . . and so does the treatment.'

'Treatment?' Olive was horrified, as images of the possible treatments which a private clinic might offer an impotent middle-aged man swam into her mind. Lascivious women with huge thighs, at the very least. They would almost certainly be Swedish. 'You can't possibly . . .'

'It is to be an implant,' said Ernest implacably, 'I am going to have an implant.'

'I really don't want to hear about this,' said Olive, horrified at the turn of conversation and hating herself for imagining where the implant was to be put, and what it would consist of. Was Ernest planning to acquire an extra organ? Would it be motorized and whir into action? She retreated into the kitchen.

Ernest smiled to himself. It would clearly do Olive the world of good. He was a kind man who loved his wife dearly and who humoured her constantly. It was a reflection of his skill in people-management that she had never known she was being humoured, and had always believed herself to be in charge. 'It will not be visible, dear,' he called after her, 'it goes on the inside. It can be bent. A delicate hand motion will render it up, or down, as required.' Olive had her fingers in her ears.

Ernest was very happy that his problem could be solved. Despite his phlegmatic approach to life, he had not wanted to face a future in which erections failed to feature at all, and he believed that the same was true of Olive. With a cheery smile, certain that, underneath her layers of embarrassment, he had improved Olive's day, he started to lay the table.

*   *   *

Lunch at the rectory seemed at first to represent a sign of variety in Mavis's cooking, as it was casserole. Unfortunately, though, it merely signified that she had run out of lard, for it was really pie without the pastry. It was the only variety they could expect, but as this in itself represented a huge improvement, Robert and Josh did not complain.

It was not a bad stew, comprising chicken, mushrooms and green bits. The green bits tasted a little like spinach, which Robert did not like.

'You and Claire seem friendly,' he said to Josh.

'Mmmm,' said Josh.

'Very friendly.'

'D'you think these are nettles?' asked Josh.

'Perhaps there shouldn't be quite so much public canoodling.'

'I think they're nettles,' said Josh decisively.

Robert thought that he had made his point. Josh was like that. 'The congregation was a good size today,' he said brightly, buttering his baked potato.

'Mmmm,' said Josh, then saw a window of opportunity.

'I saw Mavis there, but apparently Sally, her daughter, is ill.'

'Oh dear,' said Robert non-committally, having heard all this from Mavis earlier.

'Don't you visit the sick, to take them Communion?'

'Only if they ask me to,' said Robert.

'Oh,' said Josh, wondering whether he was being too obvious.

'And I have not been asked,' added Robert, who could spot an ulterior motive when it was disguised as a camel trader in Outer Mongolia, let alone when it was actually in his kitchen with him.

They finished their main course in silence. Pudding was apple pie, as Mavis had had a little bit of lard. Their pastry holiday was over.

'I've met Sally,' Josh tried again, 'she's awfully nice. She runs the Sunday school, you know.'

Robert put down his spoon. 'Josh,' he said mildly, 'just because your love life has erupted with Vesuvian vigour, don't assume that I need help with mine.'

'You don't have one,' pointed out Josh, perfectly reasonably, he thought.

'Well, after your last attempt, that's a relief,' said Robert wryly. He was referring to the occasion when Josh attempted to set him up with Helga, the mother of his best friend in Rumpleton. He had eventually been invited to dinner by Helga, an invitation which had later turned out to have been blackmailed out of her by her son. On arrival, he had been introduced to her other half, a statuesque blonde named Rowena. They had been as unprepared for his dog collar as he had for their sexual orientation, so the evening had not been an unqualified success.

Josh remembered it only too well. He decided to drop the subject, and offered to wash up whilst Robert worked on his sermon for evensong.

It was after supper, well after Lysander and Hugh had been respectively restored to garden and cleanliness, that it struck Claire that, despite having to retrieve a pig and peel potatoes, she had rather enjoyed her morning. Indeed, Tessa had been quite taken aback by her sheer willingness to lay the table – she had not previously thought that the adjective 'willing' was one which could be applied to her daughter in any circumstances. It partially compensated for Richard's odd mood. At least he was sitting with them, not drinking his coffee in his study as so often recently. Perhaps, thought Tessa uncharitably, he's come in to moan at me about my pig. She knew that Richard had never liked Lysander, whose presence in her life had been firmly established long before she met him, a case of 'love me,

99

love my pig.' Recently she had begun to feel as though she owed Richard a series of apologies for disturbing his previously ordered life with pigs and dogs and teenagers. *He didn't have to marry me. I have nothing to apologize for.* She decided to start her own conversation before he could.

'Mavis really was very good about Lysander,' she said brightly.

Richard nodded agreement. He had actually come in hoping to be sociable, to relax his mind sufficiently to finish his chapter. But how could he finish a serious novel when his life was so filled with farce? Perhaps if he just wrote novels about pigs he would find things easier.

'It was only because Josh was there,' said Claire. 'She didn't want to rage in front of the vicar's son. She was really peeved underneath. You could tell – her moles were throbbing.'

'Gross,' said Hugh, looking up from his computer game.

'Poor Mavis,' said Tessa, 'she can't help having her moles, and if Lysander devastated her garden, then she had every right to throb them.'

'I think she's a witch,' said Hugh. 'She looks like a witch.'

'She's certainly very keen on her herb garden, for someone whose cooking is legendary for all the wrong reasons,' said Tessa, joking.

'Perhaps she's not growing herbs at all,' said Claire, who had attended a talk from the drug squad at school. 'Perhaps she's growing cannabis. You'd better watch Lysander. Make sure he isn't high.'

'I don't know how you'd tell,' said Richard, draining the last of his coffee. 'I think he's weird all the time.'

'You're all being silly,' said Tessa crossly. 'Lysander is not weird, he's a pig, and if Mavis is a drug dealer

100

then I'm Santa Claus. Nor a witch, Hugh, before you say anything else.'

Hugh grinned. 'Jingle bells, jingle bells, jingle all the way,' he sang cheerfully.

'Witches don't grow herbs,' said Richard. 'Black magic is all about sex, not herb gardens.'

'I bet you're wrong,' muttered Hugh, retreating to his hand-held computer game. It made highly irritating bleeping noises at intervals, and Claire was awaiting an opportunity to grind it underfoot and blame it on Charlie. She could even hear it through the walls at night. She knew Hugh knew she could, too, and that was the worst thing.

'You don't know anything about sex,' she told him scornfully, 'so how would you know?'

Tessa and Richard exchanged glances and retreated into the kitchen to make more coffee.

'Everything,' claimed Hugh. 'I bet *you* didn't know the female spider eats the male after they've mated.'

'Ugh,' said Claire, who didn't like anything that was black and wriggly.

'And dogs lock together,' went on Hugh, relentlessly, having watched David Attenborough on TV, 'and pigs produce two litres of semen. I've seen a man whose job it is to . . .'

Claire had had enough. She fled.

Hugh grinned. He had won possession of the whole room. He was not, however, as knowledgeable as he liked to make out. His interest in all creatures great and small had led him to observe the mating habits of fish and spiders rather more than of anything mammalian, and he had some doubts about this vagina theory. It was all very well teaching about sperm and willies, but who would honestly want to do such a thing with theirs? In any case, where did a spider keep his? Hugh had inspected some of his spiders very carefully, and could not find anything remotely willy-like. No, he reckoned that the sperm and willy thing was a front, just some weird entertainment adults had devised for themselves. God would never have come up with anything that peculiar. The test tube idea was far more likely – he had read something about it in the newspaper. Maybe they didn't have test tubes in prehistoric times, but they could have improvised with coconut shells, couldn't they? He had tried to ask the teacher in the last Social Biology class, but the teacher had already learned that at certain points in the curriculum Hugh's raised arm was Best Ignored. Hugh was therefore convinced that they were concealing the truth from him until he was older. This is the kind of thing you come to expect when you are ten.

Chapter Six

Some weeks have auspiciousness thrust upon them.

Not everyone has the knack of doing this, but Mavis Entwhistle was able to thrust auspiciousness anywhere, as she had a direct line to the most superstitious and suggestible members of the community through her rôle as Leila Stargazer, astrologer to the *Broomhill Gazette.*

Those who read the column discovered on that Monday morning that it was to be an unusually auspicious week on the romantic front for those born under the sign of Libra.

Mavis had discovered that Robert was a Libran, which was why this week's Libran horoscope was so interesting. You never knew, she reasoned, vicars might be superstitious, so Leila hinted that any unattached Librans should keep their eyes very closely peeled this week, for their perfect other half would be appearing in their lives. She went further, even, than that, stating categorically that a church would be a likely setting for this meeting, and Sunday a likely day. All Librans had to do was turn up in church, she implied, and they could expect their eyes to meet those of their soul mate across a crowded congregation. As a result, almost a twelfth of Broomhill's population turned up at church the following Sunday, mystifying the vicar both by their presence and their persistent gazing at one another.

Robert, unfortunately for Mavis, did not read horoscopes, so he was not remotely prepared for what lay in store for him when he looked out of his study window and saw that the mobile library was parked outside the Cricketers Arms on the Tuesday morning. He was unaware of just how passionate a heart beat beneath his clerical shirt; perhaps, indeed, like a good Stilton, it had taken some time to come into its full maturity. Had he known, he would still probably have gone out and faced any risks this might present, for that is what vicars do. Thus they have more in common with Batman than most of their congregation ever realize.

'Ah, good,' he said to himself, realizing that this would be a chance to meet the dreaded Sally Entwhistle without Mavis or Josh presiding over the conversation like the Jewish matchmaker in *Fiddler on the Roof*. As he set out, the wheels of fate creaked into action.

Inside the mobile library, Sally was helping one of her regular old ladies, Ivy Postlethwaite, to select a large print romantic novel. Miss Postlethwaite was a good example of how the meekest and most spinsterish of old ladies were the most focussed on the physical side of written lust, for she was one of the meekest and most spinsterish of all.

Miss Postlethwaite liked to read Esme Smuts, a romantic novelist whose terribly sexual stories invariably detailed the path to Nirvana of an assortment of argumentative, but admirably agile, young people. Esme Smuts was to literature what Mavis Entwhistle was to the world of fashion swimwear, in that her standards were so different from everyone else's as to be unrecognizable. She was rumoured to be a reclusive spinster with no real window on the world, who plagiarized the rude bits of other novels then strung them together as a book. Whatever the truth, she certainly had a following.

'I like Esme Smuts, dear,' Ivy Postlethwaite was saying, 'I like the sex, you know. You don't get much at my age.' She peered at the large print shelf. At that moment the doorway darkened as Robert ducked through it to introduce himself. Somewhere in Valhalla the fates thundered into action, doing the fatalistic equivalent of nought to sixty miles an hour in half a second, whilst Destiny grinned wickedly and stirred the air with his fickle finger.

As the van rocked slightly under his weight, so too rocked the worlds of Sally Entwhistle and Robert Peabody. The peal of heavenly bells as their eyes met was drowned only by Miss Postlethwaite's sudden fit of coughing. An instant, for it could surely only have been an instant, seemed to take an eternity to pass, and they were frozen in acknowledgement of one another. Miss Postlethwaite, not the most observant of women, rarely allowed reality to intrude upon her enjoyment of the outpourings of Esme Smuts, as she felt that reality was rarely as exciting. Now she took the book Sally was holding from her nerveless fingers and allowed it to fall open at the most thumbed page. ' "His hot, throbbing manhood pressed against the centre of her very being. She gasped, flooded by sensations she had never before . . ." Ooh, I've read this one, dear.'

Sally barely heard. She was covered in confusion, aghast at herself for gazing and blushing, alarmed by the obvious racing of her heart. This was ridiculous. She shook herself mentally. This was madness. There was no such thing as . . . she could not even bear to frame the words in her head.

Sally was no romantic. She was, after all, the daughter of a woman who many felt was the very antithesis to romance, and her mother's matchmaking attempts had set her determinedly on a course of sensible distance-keeping where men were concerned.

She would not, could not believe in love at first sight, even though she had just fallen victim to it. She forced herself, by tremendous act of will-power, to concentrate on Ivy Postlethwaite.

'Sorry, have you? I've got you down as having read *The Trail of Desire*, but this one has only just come out in large print. It's by the same author, of course.'

'Oh. Well, what's this one called then?'

Sally dragged her eyes from Robert's and wondered where her stomach had gone. '*The Heat of Desire*,' she said weakly, reflecting that variety was not Esme Smuts' strong point.

Ivy Postlethwaite nodded sagely. 'I'll take this one then. The trouble is, my dear, once you've come across a few throbbing manhoods, they all seem the same.'

'I suppose,' said Sally, trying not to look at Robert, who still stood as though frozen in the doorway, 'that there aren't too many ways to put it.'

'Oh, you couldn't be more wrong,' enthused Ivy Postlethwaite, who was rather deaf, and quite unaware of the presence of the new vicar of Bumpstaple behind her. She was also glad to have the chance to talk about something on which she was so knowledgeable. She had applied to *Mastermind* earlier in the year, offering the novels of Esme Smuts as her specialist subject, but so far they had not replied. 'I've heard it called his hard maleness, the heat of his desire, the centre of his being, the focus of his pleasure, his tumescent muscle, his heated manhood . . . I could go on, dear, as I'm sure you can imagine . . .'

'Yes,' said Sally, rather desperately. She could smell his scent. It smelt . . . wonderful. Tantalizing. Warm and spicy . . .

'Personally, I prefer hard manhood – it has a nice ring to it, but then Esme Smuts has always had a way with words. In the last one I read . . .'

Sally risked a look at Robert. There was no doubt in

her mind that everything she was feeling was reflected back at her in his dark eyes. She swallowed nervously and sensed his attention following the movement of her throat.

Miss Postlethwaite had clearly been visited by a sixth sense which told her she was not alone. When she turned and saw Robert's clerical collar, the colour came and went in her face with alarming speed. Gathering up *The Heat of Desire* with undignified haste, she rushed away, muttering something about the pills she was on making her ramble.

Sally and Robert were left staring at one another. Sally was definitely aware of the swelling chords of a heavenly choir working their way towards the end of Part Two of the *Messiah*, and reaching the Hallelujah chorus.

They must have said something. She vaguely recalled saying, 'Do you feel it too?' And Robert saying something quite perfect in response. Afterwards, it always seemed to her that he had come towards her in slow motion. He took her in his arms with amazing gentleness whilst time was put on hold. She felt herself turning into an Esme Smuts heroine as her eyes shone, her lips parted, her head tilted back . . . she never had any recollection of which of them had shut the door.

There are some kisses which are just kisses, but there are others which come from the heart, and when two fully grown-up people, who thought that such things were not for them, come together in one of those, sometimes there is nothing to hold them back. A pair of deeply passionate souls, buried for years under layers of clerical collars, good sense and shyness, took over the situation completely. As they were engulfed by something which some people don't believe can happen outside a fairy tale, their inhibitions fell away like leaves from a boiled artichoke, and they behaved in a way that neither of them had ever behaved before, but of which Esme Smuts would have been proud. If the Hallelujah chorus had been playing actually on the outside of their heads, it would quickly have become very loud indeed.

Esme Smuts' heroines, despite falling prey to tumescent appendages in all kinds of exotic locations, have probably never made love in a mobile library, particularly not one bought with money raised by the Broomhill Ladies Circle. Indeed it is doubtful that, despite Esme's extensive descriptions of conflict and lust, they have ever made love quite so unexpectedly and delightfully anywhere. Sally forgot her old ladies, who had all called in already, luckily for her, forgot that she was due in Great Barking at twenty past, forgot her mother, and even forgot the washing machine repair man with the false teeth. Her world was entirely filled by this man, this wonderful man who had barely said a word beyond 'I'm Robert Peabody', something which was quite unnecessary as she had already guessed it.

Robert, too, had forgotten everything. Although he had not been entirely celibate in the years since his ex-wife decided she preferred country music to organ, the feelings which now overtook him were quite new and unfamiliar, and they were overwhelming in their grandeur. Impossible as it might seem, he knew he was in love.

Afterwards. they held one another closely on the nylon carpet between the plastic chairs.

'I'm not this kind of girl,' whispered Sally, touching his face in amazement. She felt absolutely stunned, struck by a metophorical thunderbolt. She knew she couldn't possibly be dreaming, because she never had dreams like this.

Robert kissed her, marvelling at her beauty. To think he had been avoiding his son's attempts at match-making with this perfect creature. What time they had wasted! 'I know. I'm not this kind of man, either,' he said, stroking her cheek, 'but something impossible has happened to me today.' They kissed again, seriously, deeply, lovingly, then as Sally tried to speak he added, 'I know you feel it too, this incredible thing.' He held her hands tightly and Sally nodded, speechless, 'I have fallen in love with you, I have fallen at your feet. I want to hear you tell me the same.' The passion in his voice was almost hypnotic.

Sally gulped. 'I . . . this is impossible, isn't it?' Her eyes searched his.

'Say it.' Had Cupid been there, he would not have bothered to load another arrow.

'It's the same for me,' said Sally, and giggled weakly, self-conscious at her own words. 'I am at your feet. This is what they mean by love at first sight.'

Robert laughed his happiness, pulling her to her feet as he stood. 'I love you, I love you, it sounds more possible the more you say it. I love you and I want you to be mine for always. I want you to marry me!'

'Oh I do want to!' cried Sally, astonished to find that all her plans had just been upended, and what she had thought about marriage first thing this morning was not what she thought about it now. 'I will! I do! Oh, but don't you think it's going to seem a little hasty? Perhaps we should give things a decent interval. Your new parish will think us indecent. We *are* indecent.'

Robert hugged her tightly, then sighed. 'You're right of course, my darling,' he said, kissing her hands. 'We should keep things secret for a while; I don't want to ruin your reputation.'

'I think yours is the one we should watch,' said Sally. 'Everyone in this village has been waiting for me to do something strange since the day I was born. They would just say, "It's Mavis Entwhistle's genes." You, though, are the vicar, and you've only been here five minutes.'

'Five minutes is all it takes to fall in love,' said Robert romantically. 'In any case, vicars are no less passionate beings than the rest of mankind, although I must admit I had not realized quite how unlike the popular perception of my calling I could be.'

'I'm so, so glad,' said Sally, kissing him, 'but I must go. We're frightfully lucky no-one has tried the door, and I'm very late for my next call.'

'Heavens,' said Robert, realizing that events had so carried him away that the potential presence of most of his future flock, watching the mobile library rocking tellingly on the pub car park, had not concerned him at all. 'It was impossible to be circumspect when I saw you.' He straightened his clothes a little, unlocking the door. 'When can I see you again?'

'Tonight. I'll come round,' said Sally, looking for her shoe. 'Mother will be at home, so I'll come to you. It's rather ironic actually, she's busy trying to get us together.'

'So is my son,' said Robert, 'interferingly so. I shall enjoy stringing him along.'

'He can't have anything on Mum,' said Sally. 'I could tell you a few stories.'

'I can hardly wait,' whispered Robert, helping her round to the front of the van, and glancing around surreptitiously for observers. 'Until tonight, my dearest.'

'You'll need to go and find another dog collar,' said Sally, still rather shy, as she put the van into gear, 'before someone sees you.' (Later, finding it behind *Wuthering Heights*, she blushed, making Rose Bush in Great Barking a little suspicious. In her experience, young women who blushed were always up to something.)

As Robert hurried off, she drove towards Great Barking, floating on cloud nine. Even the restive crowd of ladies on the car park of The Baying Hound could not disturb her mood, and she was so sweet and accommodating to them that even the impatient Rose Bush was mollified. They were, in any case, so caught up with their own village scandals that they really had not noticed the time passing. Sir George Ormondroyd and his wife Angela had been seen cavorting in their stable by the postman. There really was no other word for it – well, actually there was, but Rose Bush did not wish to repeat it. At their age!

It was a beautiful day, anyway, thought Sally as she drove on, why should they have minded a little wait? She felt delightfully used. Even the knowledge of the sheer foolishness of what they had just done could not mar her mood. True, Bumpstaple would be scandalized if she had Robert's baby nine months from today, but if that happened then it was welcome to be scandalized. In any case, it was unlikely – this was not an Esme Smuts novel, much as it had begun to feel like one.

She grinned to herself and changed gear, thinking that the mobile library would never seem the same again. She was full of joy.

Back in Bumpstaple, Robert, wearing a fresh collar, drank a sherry. He felt truly overwhelmed, both emotionally and physically. This was an unfamiliar sensation, and he wanted to enjoy it a little. He would have liked to rush into St Julian's and thank God for giving him Sally. He saw no conflict at all between the celebration of his sexuality – which, after all, God had chosen to bestow upon him – and his vocation, but he did realize that others might not see things in quite the same way. There was also a very real risk of encountering Mavis in the church, and he felt that it was best to delay meeting anyone, particularly her, until he felt a little more vicarish. He would have a long hot soak in the bath.

It was only when he was wallowing in the water, and even that was unusual, for most vicars rarely wallow, it being a rather extravagant kind of activity, that it struck him that he was probably the only vicar ever to have made love on the floor of a mobile library. Vicars just don't behave that way, nor do gentlemen, and he had always felt himself to be a very typical vicar and gentleman. This meant that virtually everything he had ever believed about himself was wrong. He hoped that Sally was not reflecting on events and thinking him a loose and immoral kind of person – but there had been nothing he could do. The surge of feeling which he had experienced on meeting Sally had been far too powerful to suppress, even in a mobile library. He had no regrets.

Robert had gone back out when Josh got home and raided the biscuit tin, partly out of hunger and partly out of a wish not to be hungry later on. This was because Mavis was in the kitchen, preparing supper.

'So you enjoy my cooking?' Mavis asked, as she pottered around looking for a rolling pin with which to beat her shortcrust pastry to death. The question seemed innocent enough, but the sudden gimlet gaze which accompanied it gave it real force.

'Er – yes,' said Josh, too polite to say that Mavis's pies were his idea of torture. 'So does Dad, apart from the green bits. He left them – he thought they were spinach.'

'Oh,' said Mavis, disappointed, 'right.' She beat at the pastry then, deciding that it was the wrong shape for the pie, balled it up and rolled it out again. She usually did this several times, which was part of the secret of her pastry. So, she thought, Robert had been leaving the nettles and sage. That was no good. She must definitely move into phase two of her operation.

'Oh Mavis,' Robert came in through the door. 'Another of your excellent pies, I see.'

Josh winced. Mavis beamed as she put the pie in the oven. 'Indeed it is. No spinach this time.'

'Oh, thank you,' said Robert, wishing that there was no pastry either. Perhaps he should be saving it and taking it by the truckload to the workers on the Broomhill bypass – it would make excellent ballast. 'I wonder if perhaps we could have a little less pie,' he said cautiously. 'I am watching my weight, you see.'

Mavis beamed. How admirable, she thought. Perfect for Sally. What's more, the whole village was saying what a nice vicar they'd got, so how could Sally fail to fall for him? 'Of course,' she said. 'You must try my herb tea, too. Most invigorating for those who value their health. My daughter Sally swears by it; I will send her down with some later.'

'I'll look forward to that,' said Robert, trying not to sound too enthusiastic, lest she should become suspicious.

Josh, admiring his ability to sound pleased when he must surely be filled with dread, reflected that his father would probably drink the brew, however revolting. Vicars acquire an immunity to disgusting tea: he had always thought that perhaps God struck their taste buds very early on in their calling as a perk, a little favour to help compensate for night calls and dog collars. Still, it would get Sally Entwhistle into the house. They would meet at last.

Mavis hurried home, feeling triumphant. There was nothing like a good herbal tonic, far more effective than nettle stew. Mind you, Josh had eaten the stew and was already involved with Claire Kettle. The old recipes were always the best. She did not hold with the New Age magic which appeared in the *Covens' Herald* these days – all this chanting and dancing naked around electric pylons and mobile phone transmitters. The only effective magic was herbal magic, and when

113

she had succeeded with Robert and Sally, she would write it up for the *Covens' Herald.* That should improve both her standing and her salary.

'Hi, Mum,' said Sally, emerging from an early bath when Mavis got in.

'Hello, dear,' said Mavis, not noticing Sally's shifty look in her rush to finish packaging the hogweed tisane she had been working on for a few days. 'I've to pop back down to the vicarage – I promised them some of my herb tea.'

Sally followed her into the kitchen. 'It's not the same one that you gave to the Broomhill Cystitis Support Group, is it? The one that gave them hives.'

'No, this is a tonic. For all-round health,' said Mavis, adding coyly, 'Would you take it down for me? My arthritis is troubling me today.'

Sally reflected that for once her mother's unsubtle attempts to kick start her love life suited her very well. 'Of course,' she said, 'it will give me a chance to meet the new vicar without this entire matchmaking village egging us on like a pair of wrestlers.' She turned away quickly to hide her blush. The idea of wrestling with Robert was a little too close to the truth.

'Here,' said Mavis craftily, handing her the bottle, 'stay there and have some. Find out if he likes it.'

As Sally left, Mavis reflected that with any luck Robert would look up, across his kitchen table, and when his eyes met Sally's over a mug of steaming hogweed, nature would take its course.

Mavis had more in common with Esme Smuts than she knew.

Sally knocked at Robert's back door, her cheeks pink, her heart racing. The day still seemed unreal. She was in love, even though yesterday they had not even met!

Josh answered the door and, desperately keen that

the meeting should go well, introduced them. He was so keen not to appear as though he was matchmaking that he failed to spot their appalling acting. It is extraordinarily difficult for two people who have just consummated their passion on the floor of a mobile library to pretend that they have never met.

'Hello,' said Sally awkwardly, 'I'm Sally, Mavis's daughter. I've brought some of her herb tonic.'

'Hello,' said Robert, about as relaxed as a Punch and Judy puppet. 'Lovely to have you – meet you, at last.'

Sally spluttered and turned it into a cough.

'Would you like me to boil the kettle?' asked Josh, adding fiercely, 'We were about to have a drink, weren't we Dad?'

Honestly, he thought, how could his father expect to get anywhere with chat-up lines like these? He wondered whether to stay and make sure they got talking, or to just go and hope that they hit it off. Caution got the better of him – they were clearly a little awkward, so he would stay and offer conversational help.

'Sally's a librarian,' he told his father as he made up the herb tea.

Sally's eyes shone at Robert. Robert's shone back. Oh dear, thought Josh, silence. This isn't going well. 'You ought to go and see the mobile library,' he said encouragingly, 'I bet it's a really good place to get to know people from the village.'

'Er – yes,' said Robert, in a strangled voice.

Sally cast around desperately for something neutral to say. 'Where was your last parish?'

'Rumpleton,' said Robert. 'On the North-east coast.'

'Oh dear, isn't that the one that . . . ?'

'Yes,' said Josh, 'sank without trace.'

'Oh. How awful.'

Josh rooted for mugs. He still hadn't worked out where everything was kept, and so, despite trying very hard to avoid the mug with the penis on it, he actually gave it to Sally, who was making perfectly painful conversation about coastal erosion. He sighed.

'Haven't you got homework to do?' asked Robert.

Perhaps, thought Josh, they'd do better without me. Let's face it, they couldn't do worse. He left them to it, and to his credit did not listen at the door. After he had gone, the lovers gazed at one another over their drinks.

'I can't believe this morning really happened,' said Robert.

'Neither can I,' said Sally. 'I don't usually behave like that in the library, you know.'

Robert grinned. 'I expect it's against fire regulations. There's no-one else is there?'

'No of course not,' said Sally, 'not even recently. Not even in living history, really. I wouldn't want you to think that I had sex on the rebound.'

'Now, there's an interesting idea,' said Robert.

She blushed. 'Don't you think we ought to tell your son, at least?'

Robert looked uncomfortable. 'I've spent the last few years preaching caution to him. In any case, I think today's events are just too precious to tell anyone about.'

They held hands for a while, whispering things which Esme Smuts might have found rather soppy.

'I think,' said Robert after a while, 'that we should just keep things quiet for a while, then after a decent interval we just spring it on everyone and tell them that we've been growing closer for months.'

'Months?'

'Well, you know, vicars are allowed to love, but when it comes to the desires of the flesh we are expected to maintain very high standards.'

'I thought,' whispered Sally, 'that your standards were extremely high earlier.'

He kissed her. 'So were yours. I am burning up for you.'

Sally trembled inside. 'Will you marry me?'

'On one condition,' he took her hand between his own.

'Name it.'

'That you talk your mother out of feeding us pastry ever again. This herb tea isn't bad though, she's welcome to keep feeding us that.'

'You're on,' said Sally.

She stayed for quite some time. Josh, wandering downstairs a few times to ask his father what he had thought of her, was pleased to hear the murmur of conversation, and left them alone. At least they seemed to have hit it off. It was quite late when Sally left so Robert walked her home. (They would have liked to hold hands, but you never knew who might be about.)

'I'm not a very good actress, you know, I might give the game away,' said Sally, at her gate. 'My last part was as an angel in the Sunday School Nativity.'

'I bet you were a beautiful angel,' said Robert.

'I was awful,' said Sally. 'I dropped my candle into the crib and it caught fire. Mary ran off screaming with baby Jesus and the lamb. There hasn't been a Nativity here since.'

'There could be one this year,' said Robert, 'as part of the Festival I've planned.'

Sally thought this a marvellous idea. Mavis, listening hard on the other side of her front door, heard them discussing the concert and was pleased. They sounded friendly. She pottered off to the kitchen so as not to be caught eavesdropping when the door opened.

When Sally came in, after a deep look and a very surreptitious squeezing of hands, her mother appeared, wanting to know, basically, everything. Sally was very casual. Yes, he was very nice. Yes, they could be friends. Yes, she would be helping with the carol concert. Mavis was quite satisfied. It was the best she could reasonably have expected, and far better than the washing machine salesman had managed. If she had secretly hoped that they might fall in love at first sight, she did not admit it to herself. Such things don't happen in real life. Even hogweed takes time.

Josh also wanted to know how it had gone. 'Did you think she's pretty? Did you fancy her?'

'I'm a vicar, Josh,' said Robert, grinning.

'Doesn't mean you can't fancy her. You fancy Michele Pfeiffer.'

'OK, OK. If you really want to know, yes, I thought she was lovely, and yes, I do fancy her.' He had always found it best, when concealing the truth, to stick as closely to it as possible.

Josh was delighted. He shook his father's hand.

'What was that for?'

'Stage one,' said Josh. 'Next week you'll be smooching.'

How right you are, thought Robert, but wisely said nothing.

Tessa had been dreading the first choir rehearsal, which was scheduled for the following evening. It had not been a very good day. The discovery by the electrician of five dead mice under the fridge, when inspecting the socket behind it, had not helped. Richard's unsolicited opinion was that those who looked under fridges deserved all they got, which he apparently thought was a pearl of wisdom. The electrician did not agree – he thought there should be danger money for dead mice – who knew what he might catch? He then demonstrated to Tessa, by means of a meter which he knew told her nothing, the general appalling quality of her wiring, and uttered the immortal words so beloved of tradesmen everywhere: 'I don't know which cowboy did this job. It'll all have to come out.'

The only redeeming feature of the whole occasion

was that he had tried to flirt with her, a sensation so odd to anyone who has been pregnant for nearly seven months as to be almost worth celebrating. She was quite unaware that the electrician would have flirted with her dog if he thought he might get an extra cup of tea that way, and so she had a slight spring to her step when she interred the mice with a brief ceremony next to her dandelions.

Unfortunately, she now had backache, probably due to the murine funeral; and the prospect of taking the massed vocal cords of Bumpstaple through their paces filled her with dread.

Marjorie also dreaded it, albeit with the kind of butterfly dread with which we await things which we also would not miss for the world. Despite having thrown away her head scarves in a flash of self-confidence, the layers of self-doubt were still firmly adherent to her shell.

Nevertheless, she felt that she had reached an important junction in her life, and the path of the choir led to changes which she wanted to make. Robert had sown a seed of confidence in her – some might say that sowing seeds seemed to be his strong point – and it was just beginning to germinate. Even Keith had noticed. She was not oblivious to the admiring looks he gave her on the way to the rehearsal.

The choir arrived at the church in dribs and drabs. Claire and Josh were there, together in a very ostentatious way. Hugh was there too, together with a variety of villagers, some of whom clearly hoped they would appear on the Sainsbury's Choir of the Year.

In fact, not since the Heage Big Nose Society was disbanded in 1885 for singing the Hallelujah Chorus while drunk in charge of a horse and wagon had such a surprising band of people gathered to make music.

Olive was being officious, as always. She still felt she

should have been organizing this. The threatened prospect of an audition also loomed large, so she wanted to establish herself as an essential member of the choir before she actually had to sing. It was not that she felt she should have anything to fear from an audition, in normal circumstances, but what if Marjorie simply wished to exclude her out of revenge for all the years of having the flower rota taken away from her? She therefore designated herself choir secretary, and was brandishing an attendance book, feeling that this was her best route to a prominent musical rôle.

'First,' she said, 'are there any apologies?' She looked around.

'That depends on your point of view,' whispered Hugh to Claire, in one of those schoolboy whispers which reaches all four corners of any room with great clarity. Claire dug him in the ribs to shut him up, but it didn't work, for he added, 'There are quite a few apologies here.'

'What should anyone want to apologize for?' asked Mavis, 'we haven't done anything yet.' She wondered if Olive thought that someone had farted.

'Hush, Mother,' said Sally, but Mavis would not hush.

She was just warming up and she wanted to help, she wanted to get involved. 'Would it help if Sally apologized for being late?' she asked Olive kindly.

Olive glared at her. 'You don't apologize for being late, you apologize if you don't come at all.'

Mavis looked at her steadily. Olive was definitely becoming a little strange. That hogweed tonic might actually do her a great deal of good, and she could give her dandelion biscuits, too. They were excellent for those awkward years some women go through.

'How can you apologize for not coming?' asked Hugh. 'If you did then you'd have to come to say you couldn't come, but then you would have come even though you didn't mean to come, so you might as well stay and there wouldn't be any point in apologizing.'

There was a general sense of not getting anywhere.

'Look,' said Keith, 'I don't think we need apologies. I'm sure we are all here.'

Olive pursed her lips, making a trout face, but said nothing. Let them be disorganized if they wanted to be. She would have done it properly, but she was not going to argue with Keith.

Marjorie, quiet until now, took a mental and physical deep breath. If she didn't take charge of the proceedings now, then she never would. 'Right,' she said, quite startling Olive with the booming quality of the word, 'let's get started. I see no need for auditions, but I would like a rough idea of how we all sound, so let's begin with some scales. Tessa, could I have a middle C please? Now, on a count of three . . .'

The Associated Board of the Royal Colleges of Music might not immediately have recognized what followed, but it would probably have given marks for effort. Marjorie, betraying admirable skills on the field of wince-suppression, led them through their scales with great forbearance until she knew just what their strengths and weaknesses were. Having concluded that volume was their main strength and also their main weakness, she divided them into two parts and set to work.

It was not easy. Apart from Hugh's surprisingly pure soprano (but then, the grubbiest, naughtiest little boys are always the best sopranos) Sally's sweet contralto and Keith's strong baritone, the choir were not musically gifted, although most seemed to suffer from the bizarre delusion that they could have been in the Covent Garden chorus but for an accident of birth. Mavis and Olive were particularly noticeable for the violence of their trilling, and there was the knotty problem of

121

their constant slight deviation from the required note –
in opposite directions – which was harder on Marjorie's
musical ear than if they had been completely tone
deaf.

'Do you think,' she asked a little desperately at one
point, 'that it might be possible for you to warble a
little less?'

Unfortunately Olive and Mavis each thought that
this was a dig at the other, and both continued to trill
like psychotic nightingales.

Even so, they made progress, so much so that an
hour later, Marjorie felt there was a reasonable chance
that by Christmas no-one would run out of church
screaming when they sang. Olive, however, was now
about as cheerful as the ghost of Christmas yet to come,
as she had gathered that there definitely would not be
any solos for her.

Keith sang strongly, deeply, and Marjorie heard his
voice through the rest and felt the familiar little tremor
at it that she always did. She hoped he would not think
her too bossy, but she had found her feet now and she
knew she could be good at this. 'One more scale,
before we close,' she said. 'Slowly, and *listen* to
yourselves.'

She was quite exhilarated by the end, when Olive
took her aside. 'Might I have a word, Marjorie?'

'Of course,' said Marjorie, reflecting that if Olive was
going to offer to take over then she would tell her to
jump in the river.

Olive, though, was no fool. She could spot assertive-
ness when it stood at the front and told her what to do.
'It's Mavis,' she whispered, 'she's trying to drown me
out.'

'I'm sure she isn't,' said Marjorie, 'it's just that you
both have quite, er, powerful voices.'

'Penetrating,' said Olive with some pride, and
Marjorie felt that this was apt.

'We'll all blend in by Christmas, I'm sure.' She wished she was. 'We'll be working a little more on intonation next time.' That's right, blind her with science.

'Oh,' said Olive, a little uncertainly, 'that's good.'

'It will be,' said Marjorie grimly, and Olive buttoned up her coat and left in a hurry in order to find a dictionary before she had forgotten the word.

As soon as she had gone, Mavis hurried over. 'Oh, Mrs Smythe, I have enjoyed myself. You are such a good conductor.'

'Well, thank you,' Marjorie was pleased. 'Music is meant to be enjoyed.'

'Oh, I truly did,' said Mavis, checking that Sally was out of earshot, 'but where was the vicar?'

'Oh, he would have come but he was sick visiting,' said Marjorie, looking around for Keith.

'Oh, good,' said Mavis fervently, '– that he would have come, that is. Do you think we'll make a good choir, then?'

'Oh, I'm sure we will,' said Marjorie, thinking that removing Mavis's vocal cords would help.

'I'm sure I can do something about Olive,' said Mavis, lowering her voice to a whisper. 'I couldn't help noticing that she sings rather flat.'

Compared to you she does, thought Marjorie, raising her eyebrows encouragingly.

'I have a recipe,' said Mavis theatrically, 'for biscuits.' She paused for effect. 'Dandelion biscuits. They're the herbalist's HRT you know, tighten things up a treat. Even voices.'

'Perhaps we should all have some,' said Marjorie, before she could stop herself.

Mavis took her seriously. 'Do you think so? I'll bring some along. There's nothing like a dandelion, you know.'

'Oh. Right,' said Marjorie, startled, 'that will be nice.'

Mavis did not strike her as a person with experience of HRT. Her appearance was an illustration of many of the things women use it to control: weight, warts and weirdness.

Mavis beamed.

'It's no good, you know,' said Tessa to Marjorie after they had all gone. 'You'll never tune Mavis *or* Olive. They just represent the in-built variety of village choirs. At least they make up in enthusiasm for what they lack in skill.'

Marjorie straightened her spine a little. 'I'm not admitting defeat,' she said firmly. 'You'll see: by Christmas we'll sound like King's College Choir.'

Tessa admired her determination. So did Keith. He had enjoyed himself, watching her take charge. She was like a diamond, he reflected, sparkling . . . Yet she had been long overdue for a polish. Had he been guilty of neglect?

Keith Smythe had always thought himself married to a good, but not particularly unusual woman, the sort who manages the household accounts, walks the dogs, knows exactly how much money to give the dustbin men at Christmas, and never forgets her mother-in-law's birthday. He loved her, of course, but he took her for granted, assuming that she was as secure in her domain as he was in his. If the head scarves she usually favoured were not particularly becoming, that was up to her. Head scarves, like puffa jackets and powder compacts, were part of the mystery of women.

But this evening, he suddenly felt that he had lived for years without really seeing his wife, he felt like someone who suddenly discovers that champagne is meant to have bubbles after years of drinking it flat. He felt very proud of her. 'I did admire the way you organized us all,' he told her as they got home. He had deliberated all the way over whether such a statement would sound patronizing. Even this was unusual, for he was accustomed to saying exactly what he thought, without needing to deliberate at all. He was, after all, a magistrate, and in his professional capacity he had never been a man to say nothing when something would do.

'You did?' Marjorie wrenched her sensible slippers off a helpful dog, wishing for a pair of fluffy white ones devoid of dog slobber. The dog sighed blissfully, out of sheer pleasure at having been of service. Despite spending the evening without his mistress, he had had a pleasant two hours sucking her slipper, which he regarded as an acceptable substitute and therefore equally worthy of adoration. This type of anthropomorphism is common to all Labradors, who are, therefore, a particularly slipper-friendly breed.

'Of course,' said Keith, 'it was marvellous to see you holding your own against such a motley crew.' His own slippers sat untouched by the door, and he put them on.

Marjorie sighed. Keith used 'marvellous' very freely. He thought Sainsbury's decision to sell underwear was marvellous, chicken Kiev was marvellous, new flavours of dog food were marvellous. She was not sure that she wanted to be marvellous too. 'Thank you, dear,' she said, and Keith sensed that his attempt at a compliment had somehow fallen flat. 'But there is rather a problem with the choir. Didn't you notice that almost the entire village – at least those who go to church – are in it? Who is going to be left to form our audience?'

'Ah,' said Keith thoughtfully. 'Hm. I'm sure we can think of something.'

Marjorie was doubtful. 'I don't know,' she said. 'You know how villagey they all are around here. Rose Bush from Great Barking would rather be burned at the stake than show her face in St Julian's, even when her husband was our acting vicar. People like her won't support our concert.'

Keith said nothing. He was conceiving a masterly plan. Marjorie deserved an audience, and she should have one.

Chapter Seven

Half term leapt threateningly into the picture, as it so often does. It can be a difficult time for parents. Just as they have finally got used to the school run and begun to appreciate a little daytime peace and quiet, with the accompanying reduction in throughput of chocolate biscuits, the beloved progeny are back at home for a week. It is hard enough for parents who work, to manage half term, but their trial is nothing compared to that of those incarcerated in their homes with their bored, peer-deprived offspring.

Tessa always forgot about half term. Claire had been at school for ten years, yet half term still took her completely by surprise every time. This time, not only was Claire looming gloomily over the cornflakes at nine o'clock on a Monday morning, but Hugh was also skulking about somewhere. It posed something of a dilemma, as she had an antenatal appointment that morning in Cambridge, and had hoped that Richard might accompany her in the rôle of Supportive Husband. She had also hoped that the presence of all the other Large Ladies with their adoring husbands might trigger in him a different response to her body than the one he currently enjoyed, one which she enjoyed not at all.

Predictably, the idea of a family outing to Cambridge did not appeal to Richard. Tessa could not honestly blame him. It would mean taking Hugh, and the prospect of an hour's wait in an antenatal clinic with Hugh making his usual loud and witty observations on life and pregnancy did not appeal to her either. She would have to go alone.

Claire was not impressed. 'I thought you could give me a lift to town. You said you would at half term.'

'I will. There are four more days of half term,' said Tessa.

Claire glowered. Josh was unavailable today, having gone on a school field trip, and today was therefore boring. She sighed heavily, another deprived teenager.

'Why don't you come with me?' asked Tessa. 'We could shop in Cambridge afterwards.'

She did not really want Claire to come, not in her grumpy mood. She wanted to hold Richard's hand and smile at an ultrasound screen, to talk quietly and intimately with him about her birth plan and the idea she had about playing South American pipe music against her abdomen. She had a picture in her mind which she had seen in a pregnancy magazine, of a smiling husband proudly hugging his pregnant wife, both gazing adoringly at her growing bulge. She wanted that picture to be herself and Richard. The thought of that adoring man being replaced by her sulking, grumbling teenage daughter was, by contrast, distinctly unappealing. While she wanted to put more effort into the mother-daughter relationship, she didn't want to do it right now. There are some days, she felt, when you just don't have enough energy to spend the entire morning with someone who is guaranteed to be unpleasant to you.

Claire considered the invitation. She was mildly curious to see the antenatal clinic, although she would have died rather than admit it, and as the alternative appeared to involve remaining in Hugh's vicinity, she decided to accept. 'OK. I'll come,' she said, in tones grudging enough to make it clear to Tessa that she was being done an immense favour.

Tessa put a brave face on it.

She tried to talk to Claire as they drove to Cambridge. 'I saw three magpies today,' she said brightly, 'and four yesterday.'

'So?' said Claire, clinging ferociously to her sullenness, which she had wrapped around herself like a security blanket. She had no real idea of how to escape gracefully from such a mood once she had decided to assume it, but had in any case no real wish to try.

'Well, you know. Three for a girl, four for a boy.'

'Perhaps you're having a hermaphrodite,' said Claire.

Tessa tried not to say, 'Do you have to be so miserable?' but failed.

Claire snorted. She had been practising a really good haughty sniff recently, but it kept coming out as a snort.

There was a low mist hanging over the road, and strange shadows loomed threateningly out of the murk at the side before revealing themselves as trees and road signs.

Tessa, concentrating hard, tried again. 'It's not a very nice day for shopping,' she ventured.

'I suppose that means we're not going,' said Claire, in martyred tones.

'I didn't say that. If you want to go, we'll go.'

'I've got no money anyway,' said Claire, sullenly.

'Well, if you see something you like I'll pay.'

'That's no good. It takes all the independence out of it.'

'Oh.' Tessa negotiated a roundabout and drove guiltily past a large, lone hitch-hiker with a psychopathic expression and a sign saying 'Leeds'. She had never stopped for hitch-hikers since seeing a horror film about one who turned out to be a werewolf.

'You ought to have given him a lift,' said Claire.

'He might have been an axe murderer,' said Tessa.

'He didn't have an axe,' pointed out Claire, determined to argue, 'and he was going to Leeds.'

Tessa thought this was quite an interesting statement. 'Don't axe murderers go to Leeds?' She tried to introduce a teasing note into the conversation.

'Don't be stupid,' said Claire, 'anyway, I've still got no money.'

'Suppose I give you twenty pounds?'

'It won't buy shoes.'

'Did you want shoes?'

'I didn't say that. I just said it wouldn't buy shoes. You need leather shoes if you don't want crippled feet. Leather shoes cost at least thirty pounds.'

Tessa sighed, half wishing she had swapped Claire for the Leeds-bound psychopath. 'At least we didn't bind your feet,' she muttered to herself.

'What? What did you say?'

'Nothing. Nothing at all.'

Claire glowered that shimmering teenage glower which is so like the heat haze above a volcano which feels like having a little fun.

One of the signs jumping out of the mist announced the imminent presence of the maternity hospital, and they lurched awkwardly into the car park.

'Will you get me a ticket from the pay and display?'

'I've got no—'

'Here's the money.'

Claire went. Tessa locked the car, unlocked it, found her handbag, her maternity notes, her gloves, locked it again. She wasted a moment envying Claire. The older you got, the more you seemed to have to carry.

Claire returned, carrying the ticket. She was, of course, also still carrying the chip on her shoulder. 'Awful having to pay at a hospital,' she said.

'Yes,' said Tessa mildly, thinking the same.

'If you were really ill, you might forget and get a wheel clamp,' said Claire.

'Hopefully you wouldn't have driven yourself then.'

'You might. If there was no-one at home and your phone was out of order, you might have to drive yourself.'

'Perhaps,' said Tessa, 'you should write and tell them.'

'I might,' said Claire, surprised not to have been disagreed with. It is something you come to expect when you are a teenager. Perhaps, she thought, she ought to try and be cheerful. On the other hand, that would only draw attention to her now.

'Mrs Bennett?' A midwife, efficient in blue, called her name, and Tessa jumped to her feet, anxious not to miss her turn.

'Are you coming?' she asked Claire.

'No. I'll wait,' mumbled Claire. She hoped, once Tessa had gone, to get a better look at a magazine on the table.

Tessa followed the midwife into a small blank room where she was weighed. Her weight was astonishing. No wonder I'm tired, she thought, carrying all that about.

'Right, dear,' said the midwife, 'is this your first?'

'Second,' said Tessa shortly, thinking, surely in that huge dossier they keep on me there's something to tell them that.

'When are you due?'

'Just into the New Year.'

'Baby moving?'

'Yes.'

'And how are you feeling?'

Tessa wondered whether to tell her she felt like a football with a bladder the size of a pea. 'Fine, really,' she said, cowardly.

'Let me check your blood pressure, then. Have you brought a sample?'

Tessa suppressed a smile. She wondered whether these rather coy references to samples were ever misunderstood, whether anyone had ever handed the midwife an Avon trial pack instead of a pot of wee. She handed her the bottle, and the midwife went out, leaving her to wait for the doctor. You did a lot of waiting for people when you were pregnant. She settled down to read the kilograms to pounds conversion on the wall.

Outside, Claire successfully located the article on how to have a happy sex life and scanned it avidly and with mounting disappointment for any direct and specific reference to the mechanics of sex. It was all about Relationships During Pregnancy. Presumably they assumed you knew all about the mechanics if you had reached that stage.

Claire was desperate to find out about sex from those who were actually Doing It – but not her mother. That would be too gross. She knew what you did, she knew what went where, the nuns had covered that, but what did it *feel* like? Why did people do it in the first place? Where exactly was the fun? All around her sat huge ladies, the end result of something that sounded so strange and mechanical on paper, yet which clearly had something, since people appeared to want to do it more than once. Claire thought they all looked rather like spiders, with their huge bulging stomachs and spindly arms and legs. They all seemed to be wearing rugby shirts and leggings, unlike Tessa, who wore Indian tent dresses. She felt a momentary grudging sense of pride that Tessa, whose dress sense was so sixties, was at least different from the crowd.

She felt terribly conspicuous. There was a girl of about her own age who clearly had not benefited from the dire warnings of Social Biology class, and Claire began to fear that the other ladies might think that she, too, was pregnant. She wondered how to make it clear that her mother was the one who was gestating.

A woman with a clipboard sat down next to her.

'Excuse me, dear, I'm doing a survey for the management. Could I ask you some questions?'

'Er . . .' said Claire.

'Good,' said the woman, whose last job had involved asking passers-by in a Chelmsford shopping centre about their views on sanitary towel advertising. She had therefore become accustomed to interpreting 'er' as she pleased. 'Did you find it easy to park?'

'No,' said Claire loudly, thinking here was a chance to have her views heard. 'It was rubbish.'

'Right,' said the woman, ticking laboriously. She wore a credit card-type badge with a ghastly photograph of herself, looking like a TV weather girl on speed. It said 'Aurora Peach. Management Survey Clerk'. 'Would you say that the —' she lowered her voice conspiratorially, '— *lavatory facilities* were attractive, unattractive or mediocre?'

'I haven't been,' said Claire, 'so I don't know. Is that really your name?'

Aurora Peach ignored her. It was a question she was asked so often that she sometimes regretted paying for the deed poll. At least Aurora Shufflebotham had been her own. No-one had ever thought she might have chosen it. 'Is this your first visit here?'

'Yes — I mean, no. I'm not on a visit.'

Aurora Peach looked concerned. Claire's responses had to fit in a box. 'Have you been here before?' she asked patiently, her pen poised above her chart.

'No,' said Claire.

'Have you required infertility treatment in the past?'

'Of course not. I'm fifteen.' Claire was getting riled.

'Oh. Are you having twins, triplets or more?' Aurora was immune to exasperation. In Chelmsford she had asked her questions until people had rushed, shrieking, to the escalator to escape. The woman she had been trapped with in the scenic lift for two hours had been the only one to complete a whole questionnaire, but she had been taken away on a stretcher when the firemen got them out.

'I'm not PREGNANT!' shouted Claire. All around her heads swivelled. A dozen pairs of eyes pinned her to the new-look-NHS seating.

'All right, keep your knickers on,' said Aurora Peach, revealing her true colours and nailing them to the mast in a big way.

'They were never off,' said Claire haughtily.

'Well,' said Aurora Peach, moving off in a strop. 'Well.'

Claire tried to shrink a little. The heads had turned away, and she did not want them to turn back.

Tessa reappeared. 'Hi. I'm all done.'

'Oh. No scan?' Claire had hoped to see.

'No. Sorry.'

'Why are you sorry? I'm not bothered.'

Oh dear, thought Tessa, things have not gone well out here. She glanced surreptitiously at the magazine Claire had been reading. '101 ways to please your lover', it claimed. Tessa thought, If I know men, a hundred of them will be food and the other one watching female mud wrestlers. 'I'll tell you what,' she said, 'wait here a minute.'

'Where are you . . . ?' Claire sighed. Surely her mother couldn't have gone to the loo again? She noticed Aurora Peach having a difficult time with a huge lady who appeared to be getting on to all fours.

Tessa reappeared again. 'Right. Come on. Let's go shopping. I've made a hairdressing appointment for us later.'

'But I don't want my hair cut.'

'Then have it styled. It's up to you.'

'I . . .' Claire could have argued, but the chance to go to the hairdresser's was too good to pass over. Her hair was usually cut by Aunt Sarah in the kitchen. She hadn't been into a proper salon since she was four and had poured purple hair rinse into someone's coffee so that they had got purple lips.

They left the clinic. Behind them, Aurora Peach was desperately begging her victim not to push yet, whilst two midwives tried to heave her into a wheelchair.

You could tell that it was late October as soon as you got into Cambridge, for the shops were bedecked with Christmas garlands and the sales assistants wore the habitually anxious expressions of those who are required by their contracts to maintain a permanent, helpful smile.

Tessa and Claire trekked glumly from shop to shop, each reflecting that she could have had a far better time by herself. Claire, gazing into a shoe shop window, on Tessa's prompting, at another pair of hand-decorated Doc Martens, wished that they could give up and have something to eat. She did so hate shopping with Tessa, and it escaped her understanding that she would never, never be satisfied with any plain black shoes which the shoe industry could produce whilst there were shoes with daisies on them in the shops.

The various Cambridge clocks within audible range chimed twelve, and Tessa stared. 'Heavens,' she said. 'Hair.'

She had actually first had the idea of taking Claire to the hairdresser's for a little female bonding some time ago, when watching one of those sit coms when everyone sits chatting at the salon beneath those driers which looked like alien brainwashing machines. (Perhaps, she had sometimes thought, that's what they were). She had dismissed it at the time as a crazy idea, but her daughter's miserable face in the clinic had called for desperate measures.

The salon was bustling. Someone was just being finished off in front of a mirror, but although their stylists were not yet free, it was made very clear to Claire and Tessa that they were late. They were offered, and accepted, coffee, then, just as they tried to drink it, a shampoo. Tessa, with her head completely ricked backwards over a sink with a half moon cut out of it to accommodate an alien's head, reflected that the coffee was no great loss. Hairdressers make the worst coffee in the world. Even when they have a filter machine and real milk it tastes like the product of a drinks machine in a tyre and exhaust centre, only colder.

'Ouch,' said Claire, neck extended over the next sink.

'Sorry,' said the girl insincerely, attacking Claire's scalp as though she was training to be a Turkish masseuse. 'Is that better?'

It wasn't, but Claire said nothing, perceiving that Tessa was suffering the same. Clearly this was part of the hairdressing experience.

Some time later, she obediently nodded and smiled on being shown the back of her own head in a mirror. It had been worth the pain. She had always wanted a decent French plait, but Tessa was useless at it. You'd think an artist would be good with their hands.

'You've got nice thick hair,' said the stylist, 'just like your mother. You're lucky.'

Claire mused on this. If she had nice hair and it was like Tessa's, then Tessa had bequeathed it to her. If someone else had been her mother she might have had horrible hair. June's hair was horrible. It was all frizzy. She realized that, in hair at least, she was glad that Tessa was her mother. In any case, June put bacon in her spaghetti bolognese. It was disgusting.

*   *   *

As it was half term, there was no food left in the house by Tuesday. Tessa was far too exhausted by the trip into Cambridge to face the war zone that was the supermarket, a place which purported to sell food, but which actually sold Serving Suggestions and whispered promises of perfectly browned trays of nibbles prepared by serene and unflusterable women. In any case, it was a dangerous place on pension day; it always seemed to her that beneath many a sweet old lady was a frustrated tank driver trying to get out, and, once given a supermarket trolley, they reverted to character and turned into mean fighting machines, cruising the aisles looking for someone to ram like half-crazed tyrannosauruses with blue rinses and pension books.

However, if you let your husband do the shopping, and let the Hughs and Claires of the house go with him, then it is best not to look too carefully at what they bring back. Claire and Hugh staggered through the kitchen door ahead of Richard, carrying a huge pumpkin, the kind you have to harvest with a crane. They planned, they said, to make a lantern for Hallowe'en.

'Oh yes?' said Tessa, remembering last year's pumpkin, which had slowly turned into a green mush in the corner of the pantry because no-one had got around to carving it.

'We thought,' said Richard generously, 'that you'd like to help.'

Tessa put down her paintbrush. 'A Hallowe'en lantern,' she said expressionlessly.

'I'll make it,' offered Hugh. 'Have you got a big sharp knife?'

'I won't answer that,' said Tessa, 'on the grounds that I might incriminate myself. You can help unpack the shopping.'

It was actually better not to watch them unpack, she

told herself, attacking the pumpkin with her best carving knife whilst endless biscuits, crisps, sweets and the kind of breakfast cereals which normal people throw away in disgust after locating the plastic gremlin and the holographic sticker of a prepubertal pop star, emerged from carrier bags and skulked off to the cupboards.

'I suppose,' said Tessa, hacking away at the pumpkin's left eye, 'you actually plan to eat that stuff.' It often struck her as odd that these days the manufacturers of the gremlins and stickers put them inside the plastic inner with the cereal, rather than between the cereal and the box, as they used to. You'd think they would realize that as the plastic inner now had to be breached, there was a serious chance that some of their product might get into someone's digestive system.

Hugh, it transpired, had already eaten half a packet of chocolate biscuits on the way home.

'You'll grow up to be a fat spotty pig,' said Claire, who tended to regress when Hugh was around.

'Takes one to know one,' said Hugh, aggravatingly. 'Anyway, I'm going to grow up and be a spy like James Bond.'

'Oh yeah?'

'Yeah. I'll have a portable phone and a car full of gadgets, and I'll talk in code so no-one understands.'

'That sounds like our plumber,' said Richard dryly, 'except he makes more money. What's for dinner, Tess?'

'That depends,' said Tessa, 'on what you've bought. So far, it rather looks to me as if we're having gremlin flakes with marshmallow bits in followed by chocolate biscuit wrappers.'

'Great,' said Hugh.

'Oh God,' said Claire, 'why can't we have bolognese?' She thought her spots had regressed a little over the last two weeks, and they had eaten bolognese twice.

'OK,' said Tessa, grateful that there was something that she cooked which Claire appeared to want. She carved feverishly at the pumpkin's nose.

'Mum?'

'Yes?'

'Would you not put any extra oil in the sauce?'

Tessa was surprised. Claire's tone was almost friendly – mind you, she did want something, so it did not yet meet the criteria for spontaneous niceness. 'Sure,' she said mildly, starting the mouth.

'Won't stop you being fat and spotty,' said Hugh. Claire stuck her tongue out at him. 'And ugly,' he grinned, hopping from foot to foot like something annoying invented by Tolkien.

'For Heaven's sake, Hugh, cut it out,' said Richard, emerging from the larder, and Hugh did, contenting himself with pulling faces at Claire behind Richard's back. Claire retreated to her room and Hugh, losing his victim behind her bedroom door – what a blessing for teenagers is the bedroom door – strabbaged out into the garden to look for bugs for his latest matchbox.

Richard boiled the kettle for Tessa and himself. 'What's this?'

'Herb tea,' said Tessa, 'it's one of Mavis's. Sally brought it – she says it's quite nice.'

'OK. Here.' Richard had resolved to make an effort today. He had just finished his first draft, and McTavish had retired safely, neatly avoiding being caught in any of Richard's strangely feverish alternative plots. He could relax a little, mend some fences. 'How's it going?'

She sipped. 'What?'

'Well, I didn't mean the bloody pumpkin,' said Richard, embarrassed at his own awkwardness. 'That.' He pointed at her stomach.

'Much the same as yesterday,' said Tessa darkly, reflecting that perhaps she should just have gone to Sainsbury's herself.

139

'Is it moving?'

'It's not an it, it's either a he,' said Tessa, 'or a she. Not an it. And yes, he's moving. Do you want to feel?'

Richard touched the bulge gingerly. It moved and he snatched his hand back, startled, even though he had felt it once before.

'For Heaven's sake,' she was rattled, 'this isn't *Alien* you know. He isn't going to burst out and eat you.'

'Well, it felt funny. Sorry.'

'You'd feel a lot bloody funnier if you were the pregnant one,' said Tessa crossly. It was all very well trying to make excuses for Richard – it was, after all, his first pregnancy, and a lot of men go off their wives then – but there's a difference between going off and being repelled. She put down her knife. 'I need a cuddle,' she said, not liking her train of thought. Richard looked nervous. 'Look,' she said, 'I'm not going to jump on you and crush you. I'm just feeling lonely. Insecure.'

Richard hugged as much of her as he could, feeling guilty that he seemed not to be able to give her all she needed, but not knowing how to make up for it. 'I do love you, you know.'

'I know,' she leaned against him, 'and I know you don't fancy me when I'm pregnant . . .'

'I do. I—'

'You don't, it's obvious.'

'I'm just tired, that's all,' said Richard. Somehow he felt that admitting to having gone off sex would make things worse. Anyhow, he had had a lot on his mind recently. It was just stress.

It's the fact that he won't admit it, thought Tessa, that hurts the most. I bet he blames everything on his work, it's an easy way out. 'Will you help me with dinner?' she said aloud. She could see that he was grateful for the change of subject. At least chopping the onions would give her an excuse for a bit of a weep. She rooted about in the fridge.

There were several pre-breadcrumbed chicken portions in there, and a large over-ripe avocado with a reduced price sticker on it, but there were no onions.

Fortunately for Claire, Josh got back from his field trip the next day, so her half term improved considerably. They were walking Charlie, or at least Charlie was wandering around in the woods while they snogged, when they got around to discussing parents.

'I think your mum's really nice,' said Josh.

'She's OK when she's asleep,' said Claire, suddenly remembering that her stepmother June slept in the nude, which was far worse than Tessa's nighties.

'No, I really think she's smashing,' said Josh, 'so does Dad.'

'Why?' asked Claire, startled to imagine that a proper adult might think Tessa smashing. Richard didn't really give that impression lately, after all. The thought surprised her, annoyed her oddly.

'She's different,' said Josh, 'and so pretty. Just like you.'

'Oh.' Claire pinked. 'Do you mean it?'

Josh proved it conclusively. Claire was not accustomed to thinking anyone over twenty-nine pretty. Thirty-five was positively menopausal, except that it obviously wasn't. Look at Mum. Pregnant.

'She is odd, though,' said Claire after a while, as they strolled back down through the village. Olive watched them disapprovingly from the Post Office window, hoping to catch them canoodling again so that she could tell her next customer how disgusting it was. 'How many mothers do you know of her age who are long-haired and pregnant? She dresses like a hippie, and she actually loves that pig. I heard Richard say that if she dies he thought it would inherit first.'

141

'She's one of a kind,' said Josh. 'You wouldn't want a clone mother with highlights and a manicure who spent every Friday night at Weight Watchers, would you?'

'No,' said Claire thoughtfully, 'I suppose I wouldn't.'

'You do look like her, you know,' said Josh, clearly admiring.

Claire couldn't help feeling pleased, because it was clearly meant as a compliment. Until recently, she had hated any suggestion that any of Tessa's genetic material might somehow have sneaked into her own, for what nineties child wants to be programmed to become a hippie? Now, though, so soon after the hairdresser's comments, she had a glimpse of Tessa through Josh's eyes. You could say she was trendy, really. The sixties were in again, and hair like that took years to grow. She fingered her own red curls.

'You know,' said Josh, 'they say that if you want to see what a girl will be like in thirty years, just look at her mother.'

'Oh God,' said Claire, 'what a thought.'

'Don't you want to be like your mum?' asked Josh curiously, watching her.

'Well . . .' Claire considered, forced into honesty by his serious expression, but reluctant to solidify her thoughts by speaking them aloud. 'I wouldn't mind so much, I suppose, if it wasn't for the pig. And the smocks.'

'Well, you don't have to have a pig,' said Josh. 'I'm sure pig ownership can't be coded for in your genes.'

'I suppose not,' said Claire, 'definitely no pig. Just a nice little budgerigar.'

Josh laughed. 'Why a budgerigar?'

Claire shrugged. 'I suppose because a budgerigar is everything that a pig is not.'

Josh liked that. 'You ought to be a philosopher,' he said.

Claire wasn't quite sure what a philosopher did, or if they got paid well, but didn't like to say. She made a mental note to ask Richard whether they got a company car. Dad had a company car. The radio worked, not like in Mum's old Landrover. That had what Mum called built-in air conditioning and live music, which meant that it was horribly draughty and they all had to sing when they went on holiday. Josh wanted to be a doctor. Claire didn't fancy that. All that poking around. She still remembered being taken to casualty with Hugh when he lost a jelly tot in his ear. She had often suspected it was still there.

'I thought I might be an English teacher,' she said, 'at a girls' school, with no Hughs.'

'You needn't worry,' said Josh, 'there are no other Hughs.'

Ten yards ahead of them was the war memorial, with Hugh dawdling around it in a suspect manner. He was hoping that they would smooch so that he could laugh and point. Now, sensing that he was under discussion, he hurried over. 'Can you lend me any money?' he asked.

'Dream on,' said Claire.

'Get a life,' said Hugh, nastily.

'I'll lend you some,' said Josh, 'here. Go and annoy Mrs Osborne in the Post Office.'

Hugh said nothing. He had been trying to collect two pounds for one of his more nefarious schemes and now he had succeeded. He would phone Freddy Cartwright tonight, and tomorrow they would strike.

Hugh had set his sights upon a petrol station in Broomhill, which many believed to be unique in the whole world, for it boasted a maggot dispenser. What's more, it offered a choice, upon insertion of two pounds, of white maggots, red maggots, mixed maggots and worms.

Joe Hanratty, who ran the station, was a keen fisherman, the kind of man who is only happy when encased in oilskins and braced waist deep against a current, the kind of man who actually watched angling videos. Such was his enthusiasm for the sport that he had persuaded his bank manager – aided by the gift of a twelve-pound trout – to allow him to purchase a maggot machine. The machine did not manufacture maggots. Only God, Joe Hanratty liked to say, manufactures maggots, but it kept them chilled and pre-pubescent for up to a week, dispensing them in cardboard boxes with plastic lids to those as keen to fish as he.

The machine was famous as much for the unlucky Japanese tourist who thought it was sushi and ate a whole lot of red ones, as it was famous for its complete out-of-bounds-ness to local schoolboys like Hugh. This was due to an incident in St Joseph's school kitchens which had resulted in rice pudding being taken off the menu indefinitely. The perpetrators who had put the maggots into the rice pudding were never unmasked. As a dish, it had never been popular, so the rest of the school felt that they owed them a debt, but since the headmaster had eaten a large portion, they had wisely laid low. As a result, the machine was doubly out of bounds to boys from St Joseph's. It was trebly out in Hugh's case, as he had freckles. Joe Hanratty mistrusted freckles. Freckles, he always felt, belonged on fish.

The machine was, essentially, an adapted chilled food machine. Refrigeration was essential, of course, for everyone knows what maggots want to be when they grow up. Joe Hanratty changed them every few days, to prevent them from succeeding.

It stood on the forecourt, where Joe Hanratty's cashiers were under instruction to keep a careful eye on it for all the twenty-four hours a day that the station was open, for you never knew when a small freckled boy might strike. (Joe was rarely there himself, for at every moment in a river somewhere the trout are rising, and his mission was to be there to greet them.)

Hugh felt that his collection of small and wriggly creatures was incomplete without a tub of maggots and, in any case, he wanted to watch one transform itself into an insect. The attraction of this, to someone of Hugh's Durrellesque tendencies, was indescribable, so he had planned his assault on the station very carefully, and he needed Freddy to make it work.

It was simple, really: all they had to do was distract the cashier. Freddy Cartwright was dispatched into the garage shop to have a funny turn.

The cashier was accustomed to a multitude of ploys used by other small boys with vendettas to pursue against teachers, parents and girls, but despite this inbuilt suspicion he was unable to ignore a ten-year-old writhing on the floor and foaming at the mouth.

He leaned over Freddy suspiciously. 'Are you OK?'

Freddy blew bubbles and choked convincingly. The soap tasted horrible.

The cashier peered at him uncertainly. He did not like children who foamed. Dogs who foamed had rabies and bit you. 'I'm calling an ambulance,' he said decisively, picking up his phone. 'Yes – operator – I need an ambulance . . .'

Freddy stopped foaming. This was getting serious. 'Er – I'm feeling better now,' he said.

'Shush,' said the cashier, 'I'm talking to the amb . . . Hey! Is this another maggot job?'

'I'm sorry, caller, what was that?' asked the operator.

'Oh. Oh God, sorry. Nothing. I don't need an ambulance. I've been duped!' He slammed the phone down and ran for the door, but was not in time to prevent Freddy and Hugh from legging it over the field at the back with a box of chilled maggots as their prize.

When they were safely away, they divided their spoils equally, as agreed. This took quite some time, as the meticulous fairness which small boys apply to their dealings with one another obliged them to count all the maggots out. Hugh had opted for red ones, and there were two hundred and fifty-one. Interestingly the one was white, so they called him General Custer on the basis that he, too, was outnumbered by Reds, and rather than exercise the judgement of Solomon, Hugh gave him to Freddy. If school history teachers only knew of the sheer wealth of information contained in the heads of small boys, they would perhaps despair rather less than they do.

They were quite nice, surprisingly dry to the touch, as if they had been rolled in sawdust. Hugh planned to show his off at home – he was sure everyone would be impressed.

Tessa, oblivious to what lay in store for her on the maggot front, was at home thinking about the carol concert. She had been trying to sort out nine readers for the lessons, and it was rather a headache. Robert suggested that Hugh should read, as a choirboy traditionally goes first. A senior clergyman traditionally goes last, and they planned to invite the Bishop. In between, you had to work up in steps from Hugh to the Bishop. This was, in itself, an intriguing idea, linking as it did Hugh and the Bishop in one continuum. It also meant, though, that even if she managed to give readings to everyone who would be offended if they were not asked to read, they could still be offended by the order in which they read. Then there was the choice of readings. They wanted to include 'Journey of the Magi', but someone – Olive – was bound to take offence at the camel men who featured in it, for cursing and wanting women.

'Look, Aunt Tessa, I want to show you something,'

said Hugh, for once a welcome diversion. His voice was innocent enough, but there was something shifty about his eyes.

'You're up to something, Hugh, I know that face.'

'It's my usual face,' said Hugh indignantly. 'I can't help it if I've got the sort of face that looks as if I'm up to something.'

'You generally are, though,' said Tessa. 'Go on, show me what's in your hand . . . Ugh! Hugh! Where are they from?'

Hugh held only three maggots on his palm, having hidden the rest for safe keeping in case Tom, Dick and Harry got a frosty reception. 'I got them off Freddy,' he said truthfully, omitting any reference to the other one hundred and twenty-two outside. 'I thought they were interesting.'

'They're maggots,' said Tessa unnecessarily. 'If you drop them anywhere near me I'll kill you.'

'Oh. You don't like them,' said Hugh sorrowfully. 'They don't have much of a life, you know. It's a bit much when no-one gives them a chance.'

'That's anthropomorphism,' said Tessa.

'What's that?'

'That means that you're assuming that maggots feel as you would feel if you lived their life. Maggots have a different view of things.'

'How do you know?'

'Well, if they didn't they'd commit suicide when they saw what they were getting for dinner,' said Tessa logically.

Hugh liked that. A different view of life. It explained so many things which worried him: why spiders didn't get bored and Lysander liked left-overs, for example. 'Do you think sloths have a different view of life?'

'I'm sure they do,' said Tessa. 'It's upside down, for starters.'

'Oh,' said Hugh, 'but Mr Rushton said in French that

we all acted as though we were raised by sloths, yet none of us were upside down.'

'I don't think that was quite what he meant,' said Tessa. 'Now please take those out and promise me that you won't bring them in again.'

'OK, I promise,' said Hugh sadly. It seemed to him that he had severely limited his options. It would not be keeping to the spirit of his promise, though it would be to the letter, if he were to bring in a different three – or even thirty-three – maggots to put in Claire's underwear drawer.

Chapter Eight

As Bumpstaple Post Office closed for a half day on Fridays, Tessa stood in the queue in the Broomhill one, trying to put most of her weight on the leg without the sciatica. It was Hallowe'en.

The queue was a carefully controlled 'S', hemmed in by cord barriers intended to act as reminders of the correct queuing etiquette. The queue stood, calm but bored, watching brain-numbing loop videos on Post Office services, and picking up leaflets about savings plans and health insurance.

Tessa found queuing a tense pastime. There was this desperate boredom until you reached the front of the queue, then all of your senses had to go on alert, eyes all over your head were required, for it became imperative to watch all six counters simultaneously so as to be instantly aware when one became vacant. A delay of even a second risked incurring the tutting wrath of the remainder of the queue, who saw their waiting time being extended by your inadequacy. Worse, the clerk at the desk was usually so irate that you had not materialized instantly in front of her that she would call 'next' in clear and disapproving tones, whilst the rest of the queue shuffled and muttered in chorus with that particular brand of mass nastiness of which S-shaped queues are so very capable.

Hugh was superficially with Tessa, but he was busy

watching people having passport photos taken in the booth. She decided not to tell him off for peering under the curtain and annoying them, partly because she preferred the rest of the queue not to think he was her responsibility, and partly because she felt that anyone sitting in the booth waiting for it to flash would probably benefit from being distracted from the dreadful contemplation of their own image in a darkened mirror.

The queue was moving very slowly. There seemed to be a lot of partially deaf people with very complex requirements regarding TV licences and car tax refunds. Tessa, charged with posting Richard's first draft off to his agent for an opinion, could not give up. She moved forward a step, wondering idly if he ever got bored with McTavish. Mind you, in his current uncommunicative mode, he probably wouldn't tell her.

'Excuse me,' said the woman behind her, 'I can't see the video.'

Tessa moved back, amazed that people actually watched it. Perhaps, she thought, it's full of subliminal images which transform normal people into obedient zombies who form queues and watch loop videos. Perhaps I should get Hugh to watch it.

'You're being ages,' said Hugh, appearing at her elbow. Several people behind her shuffled their disapproval at his having ducked under the railing and so breaching the unbreachable barricade.

'People have a lot to do,' said Tessa mildly.

'You're pregnant,' said Hugh more loudly, 'you shouldn't have to stand in line.'

'Sssh,' Tessa was embarrassed. In front of her the queue tried not to notice her pregnancy.

'You've got a bad back,' said Hugh with piercing clarity, 'and yet there's nowhere to sit.'

The queue in front wavered a little. The man in front of Tessa asked if she would like to take his place. She thanked him, embarrassed, and tried to nudge Hugh to shut him up.

'Oh thanks,' said Hugh with appalling clarity, 'she could give birth at any minute, you know.'

The other three people in front of Tessa melted out of her way, and she found herself propelled to the front of the queue. She wondered what they were so afraid of. Perhaps they thought her waters might break and wash them out into the street.

The counter clerk was unnervingly polite. There was probably a special clause in the new Customers' Charter about pregnant women.

The manuscript cost an absurd amount to register, but it all seemed straightforward enough until she asked for something special.

'I know it's delivered the next day,' she said to the clerk, 'but tomorrow's Saturday and there'll be no-one there. Can it be delivered on Monday instead?'

The clerk's studied helpfulness faltered slightly. 'If you want it delivered on Monday you have to post it on Saturday,' she said.

'That's not the next day,' said Hugh.

The clerk ignored him. 'If you post it now it will be delivered Saturday.' She looked at Hugh. 'That's tomorrow,' she added, thus fulfilling the 'helpful' clause in the charter to her personal satisfaction.

'There's no-one there tomorrow,' said Tessa again. 'I just thought it would save the postman a wasted journey.'

'What do you mean?'

'Well, he'll only have to go back on Monday.'

'No he won't,' said the clerk, 'he'll just leave a card telling them to go and get it from the sorting office.'

Tessa sighed. 'If I sent it second class would it be delivered on Monday?'

'Probably not,' said the clerk, 'and you can't register it if it's second class.'

'So would it be delivered on Monday if I post it in Bumpstaple tomorrow?'

The clerk consulted a list. 'No. The collection goes at eight from there. You'd miss it.'

Tessa gave up, defeated by red tape. Richard would have to come into town tomorrow. He would not be pleased. Mind you, she thought, I am not pleased today, and I don't suppose that worries him.

'God,' said Hugh loudly, 'it's no wonder the country is going to the dogs.' He heard his father say that all the time.

Tessa fled, embarrassed, clutching the parcel. Those left in the queue tried to look as though they did not agree with Hugh, which was difficult, because they did. The clerk sighed. 'He's right,' she said to no-one in particular, and went off in search of the particular form required by those who want to read the new Customers' Charter in Braille.

Outside the Post Office they ran into Olive Osborne, who had just come out of the chemist next door, wearing a furtive expression and a strange floppy hat. She clutched the paper bag which she had obtained inside very protectively against her chest.

'Oh. Hello Olive,' said Tessa, steadying herself, 'I didn't recognize you for a moment. What an interesting hat.'

Olive subjected her to a hard stare, then decided that no insult had been intended. 'The weather forecast said rain,' she said, untruthfully, for the purpose of the hat had been disguise. 'How are you?'

'Oh fine. Out of breath.'

'She's got a bad back,' said Hugh.

Olive ignored him. She preferred large rats to small boys, and that was saying something. 'When is the baby due?' she asked, hoping that no-one could see her prescription through her bag.

152

'New Year's Day,' said Tessa, 'but Claire was late, so I'm not holding my breath.'

'You couldn't,' said Hugh. 'Why *are* you so puffed out?'

'Because I'm carrying a lot of extra weight.'

'Seems a bit silly.'

'Why?' asked Tessa.

'Well,' said Hugh, 'God should have planned for it. If I'd have been God I'd have given women bigger lungs. Mind you, you'd need bigger chests then, and if Mrs Entwhistle had a bigger chest she'd—'

'Now, Hugh,' said Tessa sharply, 'don't be rude.'

'But it's true. Women were only created for having babies, so you'd think they'd be designed for it.' Tessa, who had thought much the same at times during her pregnancy, frowned at him. 'Mind you,' Hugh continued, his terrifying train of thought rolling on like Thomas the Tank Engine fleeing the Fat Controller, 'at least He got lips right. Imagine if they were on the back.'

'Really,' said Olive, wishing God had given Hugh an 'off' switch.

'You'd never be able to see what you were eating,' said Hugh. 'It could be quite useful for kissing goodbye though, and for kissing people you don't like. My mum says it's particularly important to kiss people you don't like. Don't you think so, Mrs Osborne?' He turned appealing eyes on Olive. They were wasted. A Chieftain Tank might have stood a chance of softening Olive – but only might.

'What a silly idea,' she said quellingly. 'Now, I must be off—'

As she turned to go, the pharmacist appeared at his door. 'Oh, Mrs Osborne! You forgot your leaflet!' Olive stopped and turned. 'Here you are.' He held out a coloured leaflet which Olive seized and crammed into her handbag, but not before Tessa and Hugh had time to see its cover: 'HRT AND YOU – THE FACTS'. There was a smiling woman in tennis kit on the front.

Hugh opened his mouth. 'What's . . . ow!'

'Oh, Hugh, sorry, was that your toe?' asked Tessa smugly. 'I'm afraid pregnancy makes me very clumsy.' She just managed to stop herself adding, 'It's my hormones.' How is it, she wondered, that the things we most want not to say are the hardest to avoid?

'You've crushed it,' said Hugh melodramatically. 'I shall need a note for PE.'

'No chance,' said Tessa, 'come on. Home.' Checking that Olive was out of earshot she added, 'And before you ask, HRT is Hormone Replacement Therapy, Hugh. It gives middle-aged ladies a new lease of life.'

'Does it make them like her?' asked Hugh.

'Well,' said Tessa, 'I think the point is that it makes them unlike her. Now, you're to promise not to mention it to anyone. People like their medication to be very private.' Hugh said nothing. 'Hugh? I mean it. You spread gossip about Olive and I'll circulate that photo your mum took when you were three.'

'OK, OK. My lips are stitched up,' said Hugh hastily. He knew the photo. He could be bought.

Olive drove home with her heart still beating a little fast. The lady GP had been horribly smirky and chummy, and went on at length about hot flushes and libido, despite the fact that she looked about sixteen and probably wouldn't have noticed a dry vagina if it had sat in the waiting room shouting 'I'm dry! I'm dry!' Nevertheless, Olive felt a secret twinge of excitement at the thought that, like the woman in the picture on the brochure, she was about to revert from old prune to young grape via the twice-weekly application of an oestrogen-impregnated patch to her bottom.

The thought of the word 'impregnated' made her feel quite odd. She had been reluctant at first to try the treatment, but the flushes had been such a nuisance, and the GP so convincing, that she was now looking forward to it. She could not admit, even to herself, that Ernest's imminent reinforcement at the private clinic had anything to do with her change of heart.

She was so eager to begin her transformation that she let herself into the Post Office shop, closed for business, and applied a patch at once while hiding behind the birthday card counter. Then she hid the packet up on the medical shelf behind the aspirins, where Ernest would not spot them. She had always believed that the mystery of a marriage must be retained. This was why she always wore long flannelette nightdresses. Indeed, Ernest had always found them a mystery – at least, he had found the way in a mystery. It involved finding her ankles as starting point then going on from there. In the past, before deflation set in, she always knew what it meant when he felt for her ankles.

Olive smiled to herself, then jumped as the doorbell went. Everyone knew the Post Office was closed on Friday afternoons.

She pulled back the blind. Mavis Entwhistle stood at the door looking, Olive thought uncharitably, like a sack of something squidgy. 'We're closed,' she said unhelpfully. Mavis did not hear her through the glass, so she opened the door and said it again.

Mavis nodded. 'I know. I've brought you some of my herb tea, and some biscuits.'

'Why?' asked Olive, who was not the type of person who gave spontaneous gifts, and who therefore rarely received them.

Mavis had an answer prepared. 'I thought you might try them with a view to selling them in the shop,' she said.

This Olive could understand. 'Oh, well thank you,'

she said. 'Of course, I can't promise anything.'

'That's all right,' said Mavis cheerfully, 'but do try them. I would value your opinion.' She was confident that Olive would try them, for she was not the sort of woman to miss out on a freebie. Well, the biscuits would improve her voice. As to what the tea would improve, well, that remained to be seen.

Olive shut the door. Poor woman, she thought, with an odd gush of charity. Living alone for all those years, and so ugly. No wonder there's never been another man.

Poor woman, thought Mavis, hurrying home, hiding in the shop like that. She must just be desperate for some privacy after all these years of marriage. She chuckled to herself as she walked.

When Tessa and Hugh got home, Richard was nowhere to be seen, and the rat man from the Council was waiting to be let in.

'Oh, I'm sorry,' said Tessa, 'we were expecting you, it's just that my husband was meant to be here.' The trouble with authors was that you never knew when an idea would strike them and cause them to rush off somewhere to think.

'That's all right, love,' said the rat man, 'I was just reading my paper.' He nodded sideways at the printed matter on the seat of his van. It seemed to be light on news but heavy on breasts. 'I believe you think you saw something in your house.'

Tessa let him in. 'I saw a rat,' she said, 'in the glory hole.'

The rat man looked dubious. 'We get a lot of calls about rats,' he said, reaching, on a scale of one to ten, patronization level ten. 'Mostly mice and escaped guinea pigs, they turn out to be.'

'It was a rat,' said Hugh firmly, behind Tessa, 'she knows rats. Are you really called the Ratman?'

'I'm a Pest Controller,' said the man, haughtily. 'I control pests.' Like you, added his tone.

'So you don't exterminate them?' asked Hugh. 'Can I have the rat, then?'

'If it *is* a rat,' said the man, who privately thought that no woman would know a rat if it jumped out of a hole marked 'RAT', waved a rat protection banner then ran off shouting 'I'm a rat, I'm a rat,' 'then I will get rid of it.'

'The stuff won't hurt my pig, will it?' asked Tessa.

'Your pig,' said the man carefully. He wondered what she was on, and if he could have some, 'and would this be a wild pig?'

'Don't be stupid,' said Hugh, 'he's called Lysander.'

'Look, why don't I just show you where it was?' asked Tessa.

The rat man looked pointedly at the kettle.

'Would you like a cup of herb tea?' asked Tessa wearily. The rat man said that he would, and she put the kettle on to boil. 'You don't believe me, do you?' she asked him.

He looked nervous. You never knew what pregnant women might do if you upset them. Still, this boy was here to act as a witness. 'No,' he said.

'Come with me,' said Tessa, 'I'm going to show you something.'

The rat man followed her cautiously. All through his working life he had fantasized that some day a huge woman would leap upon him during a house call, and teach him all she knew. He hadn't expected one quite this big, though.

Tessa found him the droppings she had swept up earlier, then tried not to sound smug. 'I don't mean to be smug,' she said, smugly, 'but doesn't this prove that I know a rat when I see one?'

The rat man agreed grudgingly, and went to get his humane traps.

I'm tired of this, thought Tessa. I'm tired of being treated as if I've got a strange mental and physical disease. What is it with men? What is it with Richard?

The rat man, who thought himself a sensitive man, returned with the traps and got a sense that he had better not ask for more tea.

'Do you know,' said Tessa to Sally, later, 'men treat you as though you're not a woman when you're pregnant.'

'Oh dear,' said Sally sympathetically, 'Richard stuck in his epilogue, still, is he?'

'No, actually I've been to post the novel,' said Tessa, 'not that I succeeded. No, I should imagine he's plotting the next one. He never stops – he might have to have a decent conversation with me.' Or even sex. 'It's not just him, though, it's all of them. Pregnancy makes them strange.'

I hope Robert won't be like that, thought Sally.

'Except Robert,' said Tessa aloud, and Sally jumped and blushed. Tessa did not notice. 'Robert treats me like a normal person,' she said. 'Still, I suppose it's because he's a vicar. He doesn't have to worry that I might get the wrong idea and jump on him.'

'Why shouldn't he?' Sally was unable to stop herself. 'He is a man as well as a vicar.'

Tessa looked at her in surprise. 'Well, yes. I just meant that . . . is there something you're not telling me, Sally?'

'Of course not,' said Sally hastily, 'I just meant that vicars probably get parishioners chasing after them all the time.'

'What a thought,' said Tessa, wondering. No. No, Sally couldn't have the hots for Robert, not yet – they'd barely met.

*   *   *

The fact that Hallowe'en fell at the end of half term week was just plain unfortunate, for it gave the modern day equivalent of Things That Go Bump In The Night – children – ample time to plot how best to deprive the residents of their village of money, sweets and sanity in one fell swoop.

Claire and Hugh were going trick-or-treating. Claire had not wanted to go with Hugh, as his presence was not conducive to canoodling with Josh. She was given no choice, though, for Tessa insisted that it was not safe for Hugh to wander around the village alone after dark. It was not Hugh's safety she feared for, she said, but everyone else's.

She had to admit, as she lit the pumpkin lantern for the hall window, that they had made quite an effort. Hugh looked even more of a gremlin than usual, with a pale green face and a pair of plastic fangs. Tessa thought Claire's trick with the black lipstick was particularly striking. They were also taking Charlie with them as the Hound of the Baskervilles, although since he was the soppiest creature ever to claim descent from wolves, they had to make his identity clear by attaching a label to his collar. Tessa drew the line at Hugh's plan to sprinkle him with something from his chemistry set to lend him a phosphorescent glow.

Hugh complained loudly, 'That's what they did in *Sherlock Holmes.*'

'I don't care,' said Tessa, 'you're not phosphorescing Charlie. It might not come off.' She wondered what the RSPCA would have to say about a dog who was also forced to act as a light bulb. Hugh glowered briefly, but he had other things on his mind. 'I do like the black lips,' said Tessa to Claire, hoping that the truce which she had sensed occasionally this half term might still be lingering around.

'Black lips. BLACK lips?' Claire rushed to the hall

mirror. 'Oh my God! Hugh, you little slimeball, did you put black lipstick in my make-up drawer?'

Hugh looked shifty. 'I might have by accident.'

'By accident? How can you put black lipstick in someone's drawer by accident? Mum?' she appealed to Tessa.

Tessa tried to look stern, realizing that if she laughed now she might as well write off the mother-daughter relationship for the next decade. 'Now, Hugh,' she said, as angrily as she could manage.

'She put it on,' pointed out Hugh defensively, 'I only put it in there as a present.'

'He's got a point,' said Tessa to Claire, 'how did you manage to put it on without noticing?'

'It was bloody red when I put it on,' growled Claire, 'wasn't it. Hugh? You know what I'm talking about, don't you? This is one of your joke shop tricks.'

Hugh looked sheepish. 'I thought it would look good on you.'

'Perhaps you'd better just wash it off,' said Tessa reasonably. There was a knock at the door. 'Oh no, it's Josh! Mum, stall him, please!' Claire fled upstairs.

'Borrow my lipstick!' Tessa called after her, glad of a chance to be a friend in this particular altercation.

'Yours are all horrible!' shouted back Claire, and Tessa was forced to agree that lip gloss and Chap Stick, even if it was mango flavoured, weren't particularly Hallowe'enish. If only I wore bright red lipstick, she thought, I could have saved the day.

Hugh was letting Josh in. He was dressed as Count Dracula. 'Hi, Mrs Bennett,' he said, 'where's Claire?'

'She's got black lips,' said Hugh in some satisfaction, and sure enough Claire's lips were still black when she came downstairs. Although it was not immediately obvious, the hand pressed across her mouth suggested it to be so.

'Let me see,' said Josh, and Tessa froze, fearing

laughter and then the end of a beautiful friendship. Claire removed her hand carefully. 'Wow,' said Josh, clearly impressed, 'sexy.'

Claire glowed. Hugh glowered. Not only had his first joke of the evening backfired, but the green stuff on his face had begun to feel tight and crumbly – not being a teenage girl, he had until now been unaware of the joys of the face pack.

Tessa, who was not convinced that she wanted her fifteen-year-old daughter to look sexy, eyed Hugh doubtfully. 'You'd better not smile, or your face will crack.'

'Ha ha,' said Claire.

After she saw them off, Tessa spent a bored evening. Richard was too busy with The Great Revision to devote any time to her, and she was at that stage in pregnancy when TV adverts made her weep, even when they were for engine oil, so she switched the TV off. After a while she heard a rival gang of trick-or-treaters creep past the window muttering, 'We got Quality Street here last time.' They probably kept a dossier on the best houses. Playing the game, she opened the door to an assortment of ghouls and gremlins, and dispensed Mars bars with obvious alarm.

'Ta very much,' said the leader, a tall and heavily warted fiend. Behind him she could see a small spectre taking notes.

'How did you do at the vicarage?' she asked, hoping for conversation.

'Rubbish,' said the fiend, 'no answer. Upstairs, I reckon. Up to you know what.'

'I don't think so,' said Tessa, disapproving of such casual rudeness about Robert. 'He *is* the vicar.'

'That doesn't matter,' said a member of the Adams family, 'vicars do do it, you know.'

Yes, thought Tessa, I suppose they do, given the

opportunity, and that's the second time that's been pointed out to me recently.

She frowned to herself, thinking. Had Robert and Sally hit it off particularly? They seemed reasonably friendly at choir rehearsals. Was there room for romance? No, Sally had some furtive relationship on the go already, she had sensed it a couple of times now, something very sexy. Well, that was hardly likely to be Robert, he hadn't been here more than two minutes, and Sally wasn't the sort to leap for the condoms on the first night, even if he hadn't been a vicar.

Next door, Sally was dressing while Robert watched her from the jacuzzi.

'I hope that wasn't Josh who knocked. He might wonder why you didn't answer the door.'

'He wouldn't come here,' said Robert, 'and in any case, I'd just say I was in the bath.'

'It's a bit of a risk,' said Sally, sitting on the edge of the bidet to pull on her woolly tights. 'I'm only supposed to have come to deliver more herb tea.'

'Well, you haven't been here long,' said Robert, 'I could have used you for much longer.'

Sally giggled. 'I bet you could. I did bring you some more herb tea, by the way. I didn't just come for a quickie.'

'You got two,' said Robert smugly.

Sally blushed. 'So I did.'

'You're blushing.'

'I'm not.'

'You are. You are quite adorable, do you know that?'

'Soppy thing,' said Sally, 'you'd better hope that no-one tells Mother that you didn't answer the door while I was here.'

Robert sighed. 'I don't like deceiving everyone,' he said. 'We must start dating officially.'

'I know,' Sally pulled on her boots, 'but I dread the

wagging tongues. They'll watch us like hawks, too. I
don't think I could fake a first date after this.'

'Just as long as nothing else is fake,' said Robert, and
she giggled again.

'I should say not.'

'Well, we aim to please.'

'Conceited man; but I can't even officially come for
dinner without Josh breathing down our necks. He's as
bad as Mum.'

'Sometimes,' said Robert, 'it's like living with Oprah
Winfrey. He'd want to know everything.'

'You're lucky, though,' said Sally, 'he's such a nice
boy.'

Across the village, Josh's niceness was being tested to
its very limits. He, Claire and Hugh were haunting the
war memorial while they shared out their spoils. 'What
did you say you'd done?' he asked Hugh in horror.

'Well, you have to do something to the ones who
won't give you a treat,' said Hugh mulishly.

'Well I think you're just meant to scare them,' said
Josh.

'This will scare them,' said Hugh, picking at his face
mask.

Claire, keeping her distance from Hugh, said in
strangled tones, 'Have you got any more?'

'I had a hundred and twenty-five,' said Hugh, 'but a
lot came out in my pocket. Here, feel.'

'No, thank you,' said Claire. 'What did you do with
them, then?'

Hugh muttered something.

'Speak up,' said Josh.

'Mrs Osborne's letter box,' said Hugh, adding with a
hint of defiance. 'She shouldn't have called me a
horrible little pest.'

Claire felt a surprising twinge of agreement. 'No
you're right, she shouldn't,' she said.

163

Hugh stared at her in surprise. Was this the same girl whose knicker drawer had been the planned final destination for the rest of his maggots?

'Well, we're going to have to own up,' said Josh soberly. 'She'll only guess anyway, and then it will be worse. We'll all go round tomorrow.'

They trekked home soberly, each imagining how it would be when Hugh told Olive he had put twenty-four maggots through her letterbox. So preoccupied were they, that they said only a brief hello to Sally, hurrying home the other way. If they had given any thought to it, they would have assumed she had been with Tessa, but they did not. They had agreed not to tell Tessa or Robert, in the hope that if they owned up to Olive, she might be reasonable. No-one could remember her ever having been reasonable before, but they could hope, and if they got there as soon as she opened up and grabbed the maggots quickly, she might not even notice. They had also arranged to meet on the dot of eight-thirty, outside the Post Office.

Tessa was puzzled to see Claire and Hugh up so early on a Saturday. It was not surprising that they might be up to something, but it was surprising that they might be up to it together.

Claire's lips were still slightly black. Tessa avoided mentioning it, asking Hugh instead whether his pores felt refreshed and stimulated.

He peered at her absently. 'I haven't got paws,' he said.

'On your face,' said Tessa. 'How does your face feel?'

'As if it's been painted with Copydex,' said Hugh. 'C'mon, Claire.'

To Tessa's astonishment, they went off together, and there were still Cornflakes left in the packet, too.

They met as planned, a sober group. Olive was just shooting the bolts.

'She hasn't screamed yet,' said Hugh.

'Give her time,' said Josh. There was an ominous silence, then the door opened.

'What do you three want?' asked Olive, surprisingly cheerfully.

'Er, can we come in?' asked Hugh, hurrying past her and looking around quickly.

'What are you up to?' Olive was suspicious now. In her experience, boys like Hugh always wanted something, and it was usually free liquorice bootlaces. Claire and Josh were inspecting the floor from the bottom of the steps. Where were the maggots? Surely they couldn't have crawled far?

'D'you think they legged it?' whispered Claire.

Josh shook his head. 'Can't have. That would be a real marathon for a maggot,' he whispered.

'Er, about last night. We've come to apologize,' he began, advancing up the steps. He felt that as he had been in charge, it was up to him to take the blame.

'What for?' asked Olive, raising the blinds and keeping a wary eye on Hugh who was pacing the floor frantically.

'Last night,' said Josh, looking around.

'I should think so too,' said Olive, 'knocking on doors like that.'

'It was very foolish, we know,' went on Josh, working up to the confession.

'Yes, you did look silly,' beamed Olive, picking up her duster and swatting at a rather dopey-looking fly which was sitting on the till. She liked apologies.

Hugh stared.

'No, we don't mean that,' said Josh, 'we mean—'

'Aaaargh!' shouted Hugh, throwing himself to the floor. 'Aaargh. I fell. I've hurt my knee.' It had been all he could think of to shut Josh up. He clutched his knee, which he actually had injured as he fell, and wafted

165

another drunken baby fly away, sending a pleading look at Josh.

It was Claire who came through first. She rushed to his side. 'He's cut his knee, Mrs Osborne. Look, it's bleeding. Could we have a plaster?'

Perhaps it was because she was flustered, perhaps it was because one had come out of the packet and lay on the shelf. Either way, it was not an Elastoplast that Olive handed to Claire, not even realizing her mistake when it was on Hugh's knee, since it looked from a distance quite ordinary. Hugh and the others were in such a hurry to get out that they, too, noticed nothing.

'You are so stupid,' said Hugh outside, 'you nearly told her.'

'You've got a short memory,' said Claire angrily. 'Josh was going to take the blame for your revolting trick. Not half an hour ago you'd have been grateful to get away with being strung from the steeple by your ankles while Olive threw wet socks at you.'

'Well I didn't know they'd turned into flies,' said Hugh. 'It must have been the warmth in my anorak pocket.'

'What about your pocket?' said Josh in horror.

'Oh God!' said Hugh, realizing he was wearing it.

It was fortunate really that no-one ever found Hugh's anorak. The flies got out in the wheelie bin, of course, but no-one is surprised to find flies in a wheelie bin, least of all bin men, who find much worse things from time to time. In any case, Fred Perks, who looked after the Bumpstaple and Barking refuse round, had long since worked out which wheelie bins were worth exploring and which should be put straight onto the winching gear. Since it was Olive's bin into which they put Hugh's anorak, there was no chance of Fred having a look inside. Olive was even mean with her rubbish.

Hugh was quite pleased. He had always hated that anorak, and his day was further improved by finding the rat man's humane trap in the glory hole was occupied. 'I've always wanted a rat,' he said to Tessa.

'Takes one to want one,' said Claire. They were back on a war footing. It was only the fact that he felt rather queasy over the next twenty-four hours that prevented him from fighting harder to keep the rat, but as it was, he went to bed with a tummy bug and Tessa released it somewhere in the woods, where it spent a few hours getting its bearings before heading straight back to Bumpstaple.

The following day, however, Hugh was quite sick, and he had not got out of bed by the time Tessa went to church. It was very unlike him, especially during such good beetling weather, and he was no better by lunchtime, sloping about the house like an odd sock, crumpled and out of sorts.

Tessa called their GP. 'I'm sorry,' she told John Potter when he arrived, 'I know it's probably nothing, but it's so unlike him.'

'I've been called out for less,' said John cheerfully. 'Come on, Hugh, let's have a look at you.'

Hugh sat miserably on his bed while John moved his head about, felt his neck and listened to his chest with a stethoscope.

'Well, you seem fine,' he said eventually, 'it's probably just a tummy bug. There's no rash anywhere, is there, or any odd bruising?'

'I don't think so,' said Tessa. 'Hugh?'

'I've got some good bruises,' said Hugh proudly, rolling up his pyjama legs.

John Potter looked. 'Hugh! Where on earth did you get that?'

Hugh covered his oestro-patch protectively. 'It's a plaster,' he said.

'I can see that,' said John, wondering how he would

167

cope when his own twin boys reached Hugh's age. 'Where is it from?'

'The Post Office,' said Hugh reluctantly.

Tessa peered. 'Oestro-patch. That sounds a bit hormonal.'

'That's because it *is* a bit hormonal,' said John. 'It's HRT.'

Hugh looked sheepish. 'Hugh?' Tessa prodded him. 'Did you know what it was?'

Hugh muttered something inaudible. 'Hugh?'

'OK, I knew,' said Hugh, 'but only after I got home. I thought it would make me better at PE.'

'Whatever gave you that idea?' asked John. 'The only bits of you it makes better, Hugh, are bits you haven't got. This is the culprit, Tessa, causing the sickness.'

'It's not fair,' said Hugh, rousing mild indignation out of his nausea. 'Girls have all the fun. I saw it in your magazine, Aunt Tessa. The women taking it said they got a new lease of life, but all I got is an itchy knee and to feel pukey.'

'That's life,' said John, reflecting that it was, really. 'Perhaps that'll teach you. It's probably lucky you haven't grown breasts. Have you got any more patches?' He wondered if they were being illicitly swapped for cigarettes now in school playgrounds.

'No. Mrs Osborne stuck it on me by accident,' said Hugh. 'It was a mistake after I'd been looking for maggots. Could I really have grown breasts?' It seemed to him extremely odd that his mother should have gone to America to buy breasts if they could be grown this easily: first Claire's cream and now Olive's plasters.

'Probably,' said John, winking at Tessa.

'Will he be all right?' asked Tessa, wondering what her sister's reaction would be if she returned from America to find her son was a bigger cup size than she was.

'I'm sure he will,' said John, 'give it a day or so. At the moment he's got morning sickness, that's all.'

Hugh looked mournful. 'You won't tell Claire, will you?'

Tessa took pity on him. 'Just as long as you'll sing solo in the carol concert.'

Hugh felt so grotty that he agreed.

Chapter Nine

Tessa was glad that half term was over. The amount of food that Hugh could put away in a day had proved quite unnerving, and the increased throughput of washing had resulted in an odd-sock pile of ghastly proportions. Some of them could not possibly have fitted anyone in the house. Others could not possibly have fitted anyone on the planet. She was just scaling its North face when Sally knocked at the door.

'Come in. I was just torturing myself with socks,' said Tessa.

Sally seemed hesitant, peered past her, did not laugh.

'No-one home,' said Tessa. 'Richard's gone to the library to look something up, the others aren't back from school yet. Herb tea or coffee?'

'Coffee, please,' said Sally, seeming uneasy.

I wonder what's on her mind, thought Tessa.

Sally wandered around aimlessly while Tessa filled the cafetière. She always made coffee properly, the little ritual reminding her of bachelor afternoons in coffee shops which she had never actually experienced, but which everyone puts into their memories once they have seen the right advert.

'Find some biscuits, Sally.'

'No biscuits,' reported Sally, looking in the cupboard.

'No, I have a secret stash,' said Tessa, 'hidden from Hugh. He hoovers them up.'

'Where are they then?'

'I don't know for sure,' said Tessa, 'it was some-where safe.'

'OK, let's play hunt the biscuit,' said Sally, then, after a while, 'Did you know there were three tins of beans in your desk drawer?'

'It doesn't surprise me,' said Tessa wearily, 'although I might have been mildly impressed if you had found them in the larder.'

'Oh dear, that bad, is it?' Sally spotted a packet of digestives behind the dog biscuits. 'It's better than Mum's kitchen. It's so full of herbs at the moment that there's no room for anything else. She's mass-producing herb tea.'

'Perhaps she's a witch,' said Tessa, whimsically.

'Ha ha,' said Sally. 'She'd love you to think that. Don't ever tell her, it might make her worse.'

She sat down and began to dunk digestive biscuit in her coffee with the kind of blatant disregard for calories which only those in mental turmoil and those in love display. An awkward silence landed obviously on the table and flapped metaphorical wings to attract their attention.

'Look,' said Tessa eventually, 'I know you want to say something. What is it?'

'Well,' said Sally uncomfortably, 'I was in two minds, you know, whether to say . . . it was a confidence, but you are my best friend and . . . well.'

Tessa felt quite alarmed. What kind of things does your best friend worry about telling you? She examined her mental list. It contained, alarmingly, only unfaithful husbands and halitosis. She swallowed.

'It's Claire,' said Sally, 'she asked me about the Pill. About whether or not a doctor would tell her parents if she was on it.'

'Oh.' Tessa didn't know whether to be relieved or horrified. She sat down. 'I had no idea things had got

171

that far with Josh. I should have realized. God, I must be such a useless mother.' She looked at Sally miserably.

'Don't be silly,' said Sally briskly. 'Look, the rules are different these days. Some of them get into sex almost before they kiss.'

Tessa winced. 'You're a great help.'

'Oh I'm sorry. I just meant there aren't any signs to spot. Anyway, they probably aren't. She probably was just after information. He is a vicar's son.' What a stupid thing I just said, she thought, and I should know.

Tessa was not consoled. Charlie put his head on her lap and she petted him absently. 'I just wish she'd talked to me. Do you remember your mother talking to you about sex?'

'Golly, yes,' said Sally cheerfully, 'she more or less told me the world was a seething mass of penises in search of someone to impregnate, with men as something rather helpless attached to the other end.'

Tessa giggled. 'Mine said that it happened when you slept together. I thought you actually had to be asleep, and it just kind of popped in by itself.'

'How did we grow up sane?' asked Sally, wishing suddenly that she could talk about Robert. She blushed thinking of him, of his touch.

Tessa saw the blush and was intrigued. 'Are you having a secret romance?' she asked, but Sally would not say anything for fear she said too much.

Richard was in Broomhill library, looking around the children's section. Why shouldn't he write children's books, anyway? Looking around here, there were plenty of authors whose names he recognized from a more adult genre. He was sure he had it in him to do the same.

Should he talk to Tessa about it? Not yet – she had

172

a lot to deal with, and they weren't communicating terribly well. He'd talk to her when he'd thought it through, when they were through this rather awkward patch they seemed to be in. He did not allow himself to think that this might mean he planned on having no important conversation with her until after she had given birth. In any case, his idea might not work out, in which event he could always bring McTavish back. It was a good job he hadn't followed Hugh's suggestion of having him crushed by a giant radish.

Later, after spending a considerable amount of time trying to work out how to discuss the Pill with Claire without letting on that Sally had told her, Tessa got it, as usual, Completely Wrong. 'I wondered,' she said carefully, when Claire came in, 'if they had talked about contraception at school.'

'Course they have,' said Claire, looking for a health food bar.

'So you know about everything you want to know about?'

This was hardly for mothers to discuss, thought Claire. Far too embarrassing. 'Yeah,' she said aloud, pulling up a chair to look on the top shelf.

'So if you wanted a condom, or, say, the Pill, you'd know where to get them?'

Claire wheeled around on her chair and wobbled precariously. 'You've been talking to Sally!' she accused.

Tessa nodded. 'Well, she did think I ought to know. She is my best friend.'

'Bloody traitor,' said Claire. 'She promised.'

'Look, get down from there, I'm not angry,' said Tessa, 'I'm just sorry you didn't feel you could talk to me. If you and Josh are—'

'Having sex? Of course we're not bloody having sex,

Mother. It's all parents ever think of. I just *knew* you'd react like this!'

'Like what? How am I reacting?'

'All . . . understanding and, I don't know, over-reasonable.'

Tessa, who could never remember having thought her own parents over-reasonable, but who had often wished she had cause, was mystified. 'Would you rather I raged and swore?'

'Of course not. I just meant I knew you'd go on about sex. Everyone's parents push them into sex these days. They go on and on about it as if they're desperate to get you started.'

'Don't be silly. We just want you to be careful if you—'

'I know, I know.' Claire was exasperated, 'But you ought to know I'm not having sex. You're my mother.'

'I'm not psychic,' pointed out Tessa – quite reasonably, she thought.

'Oh, mothers always know,' said Claire impatiently, and it struck Tessa that this was one teenage myth best left undisturbed.

'Well, OK, I'm sorry. You don't want the Pill, you were just asking for information.' Tessa had a brainwave. 'Is it for one of your friends?'

'Oh, for God's sake!' Claire was goaded beyond belief. 'Sex, sex, sex, that's all anyone ever talks to teenagers for! Well, it's nothing to do with sex. If I wanted sex I'd buy condoms. Millions of big thick coloured knobbly ones, but I don't want sex. I want to get rid of my SPOTS!' She stormed out of the kitchen. Tessa could hear her going up the stairs muttering, 'Sex on the brain.'

She felt rather silly. Of course, some girls had the Pill for spots, and Claire's current tablets, although they had helped, had not completely cured the problem. It was a shame that Claire had to be so touchy about them – still, it was nice to know that she had not been completely wrong about her relationship with Josh.

Hugh appeared at the door. He was wearing his tie as though someone had tried to strangle him with it. His shirt hung out of his trousers at the back. (How is it that such a small thing has such a profound effect? she thought – but then, you could say the same of willies.) The tongues of his trainers were on the outside. He muttered something at Tessa before submitting to the magnetic force which apparently dragged him, protesting, to the biscuit tin every evening.

'You should be called William,' said Tessa, feeling a surge of fondness for him. He was so wonderfully uncomplicated.

'William What?' asked Hugh.

'Just William,' said Tessa, and got the giggles.

'Mad,' said Hugh, shaking his head and treading mud through the kitchen. 'Must be her hormones.'

Claire had not told her mother the complete truth. It was true that she wanted to try the Pill for her spots, but everyone at school said that it was a great way to get put on the Pill in advance of needing it for sex, and without all the attendant family grillings or the worry of your parents finding the pink blister pack in with your dirty sports kit. She felt that she must plan for when Josh asked her for sex – as some of her teachers were nuns, she had been left in no doubt that he would ask.

Claire's sex education was in some ways complete, but in others woefully inadequate. She was both fascinated and repelled by the idea of a male organ getting anywhere near her, and she could not honestly say that it was something she would ever have thought of doing if the nuns had not told her that this was what you did. She had only ever seen three penises – one on Hugh when he was four and weeing in her wellingtons, one on an alabaster Greek god in a Cambridge museum, and one on the revolting peeing cherub in the Smythes' garden. As the cherub was very old and his extremities were somewhat weathered, he didn't really count. There had also been the Great Barking penis, of course, but since that had actually been about seven feet tall, it had to be considered too abstract to give her a true idea of what she was facing.

She had understood from the Greek statue that they must grow as boys did, unless Greeks were particularly different from other men. Of course they think they are, but Claire had no idea as yet about the relationship between willies and egos in the male. From Social Biology, she did realize that they looked a little different during sex, rather like dogs' ones. She was not, however, very clear on how this was achieved. She assumed that, as in the dog, the thing was normally partially concealed. Perhaps, like an iceberg, only a tenth of it was usually visible, the rest lurking beneath the surface ready to jump out at the slightest provocation.

Her Social Biology text books had been unhelpful – the diagrams in them looked like plumbers' blueprints, and gave no real clue as to where the wretched thing was stored. Her friends, as far as she could tell, were equally mystified. They rarely discussed sex, as it was no longer particularly fashionable amongst teenagers. It was rather passé compared to crystal healing and reflexology, so it was unacceptable to interrupt an argument about pyramid power to ask whether or not some boy had tried to put his tongue in. They all thought about the tongue thing all the time, of course – and the rest – sex constantly worms its way into the minds of all teenagers, along with the conviction that the girl next to them in the shower is becoming a lesbian. They liked to feel, though, that they were far more rational and mature than their parents had been at their age, so they could not admit to their obsession.

As a result, Claire faced her dilemma with the feeling that it should not be a dilemma at all, arguing with herself repeatedly about whether to say yes to Josh if he asked her if he could, and whether she would be able to manage not to laugh if they did it.

Josh could not help being obsessed by the thought of his first, yet-to-come sexual encounter. From the virginal point of view, this is equivalent to entering the gates of Disneyworld on a free three-year pass: once through the turnstile, undreamed-of vistas open up. However, the knowledge that he would have to instigate things himself, coupled with the fear of rejection – and the fear of being punched in the mouth by Richard, Tessa or both, if it all went badly wrong – meant that he feared it as much as he longed for it. He also had a sneaking suspicion that the first occasion might not be all that other boys claimed.

It was a matter of great relief when French kissing with Claire had evolved naturally without real planning, and they hardly got their tongues locked at all, but it seemed unlikely that anything else would happen so easily. The more he and Claire kissed and groped, the more two emotions battled within him, fear and desperation, until he feared that he might actually explode.

He decided to ask his father how you got started. Robert had always been that sort of father, the sort of whom you could ask anything. Not that his father was likely to remember his own sex life, of course.

'Dad?' he said as they worked their way through Mavis's fish pie. It was not bad, as it had no pastry, only potato. She liked cooking with fish, and today she had particularly liked the facial expression on a pair of big trout in the fishmonger's.

'Hmm?' Robert was thinking of Sally, seeing her in his mind, sailing towards him down the aisle in a cloud of the palest ivory tulle – white would not, after all, be quite right.

'If you fancy someone a lot, how do you let them know that you want to have sex?'

Robert gulped hard and swallowed far too much pie. His own train of thought had been so exactly along those lines that for a moment he thought he had been rumbled. 'What do you mean?' he asked.

'Well, me and Claire,' said Josh. 'I'm not sure if I should – you know – discuss it.'

'Good Heavens, Josh, she's not sixteen yet,' said Robert in some alarm.

Josh, who, like most of his peers, had not given a great deal of thought to the age of consent, realized that he must tread carefully. 'I don't mean that we're – I mean, I want to know if she expects me to discuss it.'

Robert felt horribly inadequate. He could hardly talk about his own experience and lead by example after leaping upon Sally in a mobile library with a lack of reserve normally seen only in midwives. 'You must respect her age,' he said firmly, very conscious that a Higher Authority would hear any hint of hypocrisy. 'And don't forget that her family are our neighbours, and I am their vicar. You must behave impeccably. Anything you do or don't do could affect all of us for a very long time. In any case, if in doubt, it is always worth waiting, you know.' Well, he thought, I wasn't in doubt.

Josh thought that that was a no, basically. He was half relieved, but half frustrated. It was all very well for Dad, he *knew* what he was missing by being celibate. But how could you make an informed judgement on whether something was worth waiting for if you had never had any of it in the first place?

Tessa's week did not improve. Not only did Richard seem to think that, if he got too close to her, she might lower her activation energy barrier and spontaneously combust, but she had also run out of oranges.

She sat at the kitchen table, nursing a cup of herb tea and trying to control her deep and abiding craving for oranges.

Richard wandered in from his study in search of a drink. She could see that he was in his focussed mood, and these were normally best undisturbed, as there was a risk of being accused of interrupting crucial thought processes, but she was too out of sorts to worry.

'I'm out of oranges,' she said pitifully.

'Mm,' said Richard.

'I need to get some more. I hate the supermarket at the moment – the delicatessen makes me feel really queasy.'

'Mmm,' said Richard.

'Do you know,' said Tessa crossly, 'you are about as sympathetic as a custard tart. Here I am, looking and feeling like a giant pumpkin—'

'Mm,' said Richard, 'do we have any proper tea?'

'We never drink it,' said Tessa. 'I've some herb stuff from the Post Office. It's very nice. Do you want to try some?' Best not to tell him Mavis had made it. He was always saying she must be a witch. 'Shall I make you some?'

'Mm,' he disappeared back into the study.

Tessa brewed up the herb tea, reflecting that the day was not going to get any better. There was to be a choir rehearsal this evening, yet already she felt in need of a good hot bath and an early night. The choir could be hard work. Olive persisted in singing loudly and flat, and at times the rest sang with the verve of a bevy of tranquillized funeral directors celebrating the Festival of Dirge-Like Voices. Only Mavis was on top of the notes, and she was so painfully on top that no advantage was conferred. Hugh called her the Great

179

Warbler. Some of her sudden crescendos reminded Tessa of the background noises on the Labour Ward when she was taken round for a quick frightening.

In all, life seemed to be grinding her down, like a stick of solid deodorant, and she wasn't sure how much there was left of her to keep pushing up from the bottom.

At the other end of the village, Mavis was unaware that she was affecting the quality of Tessa's day. She was looking forward to choir practice. She was baking a large batch of dandelion biscuits to give out at the end. She was quite sure that they would cure Olive of her flat voice, but as everyone else was slightly flat, too, compared to her, she had baked enough for everyone. Upstairs, Sally was drying her hair. She was beginning to feel a wicked delight in these evenings spent with, and yet not with, Robert. There was, for a girl who had spent most of her life being entirely good, a delicious naughtiness about rehearsing 'Silent Night' while exchanging secret looks with the man she adored, looks which said, 'Just wait until later.' He always came along to support the choir, and to look at her. It was like being a teenager again, she thought, although it was actually much better because now you knew what you were waiting until later for. Once you let someone's sexuality out, she thought, it's like polystyrene packing material: it never goes back in again.

Robert was feeling the strain. His innate honesty made hiding his feelings very difficult, and the particularly physical manifestations of desire in the male meant that there was a risk of his feelings revealing themselves without his permission. Rather than wear a cassock all the time, or stand with his hands in his pockets in a rather awkward way, he generally chose to sit in the second pew, lest lascivious thoughts should seize him during 'We Three Kings'. He had settled in to Bumpstaple so well, winning even the most reticent of his congregation – Olive – round to the hand-shaking he liked to include in his services, that it would be a shame to upset them all now. Fortunately for Robert and Sally, the choir was so lacking as a group in any natural musical ability that it took all of their concentration simply to sing. There was none left for observing Robert.

It struck Marjorie, not for the first time, how strange it was that a group of people all, or almost all, capable of turning out a perfectly acceptable carol had become musically incoherent when put together. Perhaps, she thought, this is the phenomenon which led to the emergence of pop music. Still, she was sure it could be overcome.

So, with Previnesque skill, she coached her hopeful charges into two-part harmony. She tried not to think of what the Phantom of the Opera might have felt about them, for then the temptation to hide in the panelling and drop chandeliers on them might have become overwhelming. That would not do at all, not with Keith being a magistrate.

Mavis handed round her biscuits at the end. Since they looked fairly innocuous, and there was nowhere to put them without being rude, most people ate theirs, except Tessa, who gave hers to Marjorie. She wasn't sure if dandelions were safe in pregnancy, and she didn't think Mothercare would know. Hugh had pockets, and collected several. He was ten, after all, and everyone knows that ten-year-olds never refuse a biscuit. When he got them home he found that they were the exception that proves the rule, and saved them for Lysander.

Now that they were back at school, Christmas seemed to be rushing at them. Carol of the Year Competitions were on all the local radio stations, and large china manufacturers everywhere were advertising their Christmas plates, in limited editions of however many they thought they could sell. The hour had gone back, adding to the general wintry feel of things, and the air smelled of frost.

The tendency of teenage boys to put on flimsy shorts in such circumstances, and then to run around muddy fields grappling with one another continued unabated, and Josh was in the school First Fifteen.

As a result, Claire walked alone from the bus stop on the Thursday after half term. She would have stayed to watch Josh, for she much admired his thigh muscles, but she could not bear the thought of being labelled the bimbo on the side line. She had planned to call in and see Sally, as the library closed at lunchtime on Thursdays, and Sally was usually home. Today, though, she was not.

'Where is she?' Claire asked Mavis, who was snipping herbs in the front garden.

Mavis looked very smug. 'Gone to see the vicar,' she said. 'She's taken him some more of my herb tea. Very popular, it is.'

'Oh that's good,' said Claire. Sally was with Robert. Something was surely bound to happen if they were spending time alone together. They were so suitable – both single, neither with spots.

'Thank you dear,' said Mavis, misunderstanding. 'I do make a good herb tea. Want to try it?'

Claire was tempted to say, 'I'd rather be flogged with a wet loofah,' which Tessa had said last night in reference to eating Mavis's pastry, and which Claire thought rather witty, but she did not. By the time she had decided not to, Mavis had fetched her a packet.

'Here. It's excellent for love.'

Claire took the packet and stared at Mavis. 'Do you mean it's a *love* potion?'

Mavis took a decision. She did not reveal her secrets

182

lightly, but as Walt Disney knew so well, every sorcerer needs an apprentice, and she hoped Claire might be interested. She nodded sagely. 'I prefer to call it herbal magic, dear. I don't go in for chanting and sacrifice, you see.'

'Wow,' said Claire. 'Does it work?'

'You tell me,' said Mavis. 'Robert Peabody drinks it, so if he falls for Sally . . . well.'

'And Josh drinks it?'

'Yes.'

A terrible fear struck Claire. What if it really worked, and it was the only reason Josh had fallen for her? 'When did you first give it to them?'

Mavis smiled benignly, although the effect was not benign, for her face did not easily align into benignness. 'About a week after they moved in.'

Claire breathed a sigh of relief. That was OK then. 'I must go,' she said, 'I'll be late home.'

'Well,' said Mavis, 'don't say a thing to your mum or anyone, but if you ever want to know more, just ask.'

'I won't tell a soul,' said Claire, who loved a good secret. This was one of the best: Mavis, whose witch-like appearance had been remarked upon for years, actually was one, and she, Claire, knew it. She wondered how many other people in the village were taking Mavis's potions. Perhaps she should get some for Mum and Richard. Poor Mum didn't seem very happy lately.

It was an oddly sympathetic thought for a girl who had recently thought that her mother was only marginally preferable to the last of the dinosaurs to have very sharp teeth.

Robert and Sally were in fact drinking a post-coital mug of the very herb tea under discussion. They had not wanted to waste her half day, and much as Robert argued with his conscience about the morals of

183

premarital knowledge of the biblical variety, the passionate side of their relationship was too powerful to deny. Like a slimmer given a sudden, succulent rum baba for breakfast, they were unable to stop at one. If it had been rum babas they were indulging in, they would by now have gained a great deal of weight.

'You know, your mother makes quite a good brew,' said Robert.

Sally smiled. 'I quite like it, but I never tell her that. Some people think she's a witch, you know, and I sometimes think she believes it herself.'

'Well, you never know,' said Robert. 'Just imagine, if she was, this could be a love potion that we're drinking.'

'I hope not – it could cause bedlam,' said Sally. 'Half the village are drinking it.'

Robert sobered. 'I don't know what everyone in the village would say if they knew about this. I really am taking advantage of you in a most unchivalrous way.'

'It works both ways,' said Sally, 'and in any case, we did try celibacy, didn't we?'

'For about five minutes, if I recall. What do you suppose would be the response if we just came out with it now, told them that we were engaged?'

Sally thought. 'It would probably be a nine-day wonder, although you never know what Olive Osborne might have to say. She'd probably write to the Bishop.'

Robert sighed. 'She's a very unhappy woman. I certainly don't want to upset her – nor the Bishop, of course.'

'Perhaps we should give her some of Mum's potion,' said Sally. 'It might give her something to smile about, although I don't know how Ernest would feel about it.'

'Oh, I think he probably has hidden depths,' said Robert, 'but I wouldn't go giving anyone love potions, real or imaginary. You never know what might happen. Look at us.'

Sally poked him playfully in the ribs. 'You're not supposed to believe in that kind of mumbo-jumbo.'

'I merely believe,' said Robert, 'that the mind is a powerful tool, so that if someone believes that they have drunk a love potion, then it might very well work.'

'Then that means the person drinking it has to believe?'

'Perhaps,' said Robert, 'but perhaps there are more things in Heaven and Earth than we can explain.'

'Well,' said Sally, 'I was in love with you before you touched a drop.'

'That's all right, then,' said Robert, 'now leave me, wench, before Josh springs us. Rugby practice doesn't last all night, you know.'

Sally, hurrying home, passed Claire lingering by the war memorial. Sally's eyes had that particular shine which is only brought on by true love. Claire waved hello. She was not lacking in observation. Sally and Robert, she thought. I bet it has happened already, right under everyone's noses. If so, Mavis's magic had worked!

She hugged the knowledge to herself. It was her secret. Not a soul would she tell, not even Josh, for the power of magic must surely be diminished by spreading it around.

Marjorie Smythe was now a woman with a mission, and any misgivings she felt about throwing away her tweed skirts seemed trivial by comparison. They might be from Harrods, they might have been expensive, but they were the colour of dishwater and they smelled of dog. She wouldn't even insult Oxfam with them. She put them in the bin. Trousers would do until she knew what she wanted to replace them with.

185

Fred Perks, emptying her bin later that week, saw them there and decided that they would make nice warmers for his rabbit hutches, and in this way Broomhill's unique recycling scheme sprang once again into action, and matter was conserved. No doubt Einstein would have been delighted, had he known.

Marjorie's mission was simple: the Bumpstaple Festival of Nine Lessons and Carols was just the beginning for her choir, for they could go on from it to great things. She was beginning to feel quite a glow of satisfaction at rehearsals. 'Evensong at the cathedral,' she told the dogs as she put their food in the backyard and shut them out there with it. 'Then the Albert Hall,' she told them through the door, 'Carnegie Hall.'

Keith, arriving home a little early, was surprised to hear her singing. He paused at the door to listen, and all the dogs rushed to fall over his feet in delight. What a striking voice she had! What a striking woman she was! And thank goodness she had shut the dogs out for once – there were times when he felt she thought more about the dogs than she did about him. It rather put him off his stride, so to speak, when they spent the night on the bed, particularly their inopportune growls. Perhaps it was time he suggested to Marjorie that they should stay in the kitchen at night.

He slipped in through the door, deftly keeping the dogs firmly outside.

Marjorie, startled, broke off in the middle of her song. 'Oh, Keith, you're home early.' She seemed different, he thought, and not just tonight. Her cheeks seemed pinker, her eyes more sparkling – but no, it was more than that. What was different about her?

'It's a new hairstyle,' said Marjorie anxiously, seeing his puzzled face. 'I went to a different hairdresser.'

'It's lovely,' said Keith, 'very becoming. Where did you go?'

'Cambridge,' she said. 'Robert Peabody walked the

186

dogs at lunchtime so that I'd have time to get there. He is such a nice man. I'm so glad he asked me to take on the choir.'

'You mollycoddle those dogs,' said Keith, trying not to be exasperated. After all, how often must he have told her to get someone else to help with them? Yet clearly they were ruling her life.

He had never said anything, of course; like most long-married men, he had come to believe that what he thought and what he said aloud were one and the same as far as his wife was concerned. Now he sighed. 'I do wish you would take someone on to walk them, at least some of the time.'

'You wouldn't mind?' Marjorie was delighted at the reprieve. Oh, bliss. An hour at lunchtime in which no-one farted or moulted in the kitchen could be hers. Still, she mustn't appear too pleased. I mean, she thought, I suppose I do love the dogs, but Keith adores them.

'Of course I wouldn't,' said Keith. Small steps, he thought, can eventually take us long distances. Get someone to walk the dogs for her, and perhaps by the end of the year we'll be able to make love without anyone farting and moulting in the bedroom. Still, mustn't say that to Marjorie. I love the dogs, of course, but she adores them.

Marjorie's new sparkle was not dulled by the rehearsal that evening. It actually went quite well. She had definitely got the choir to hold a two-part harmony; admittedly, neither part was pitched quite where it should have been, but the fact that the members of each vocal part managed to sing roughly the same thing as one another was, she felt, something to be quite proud of. Now she looked forward to a dog-free night with her husband.

Hugh was not keen that she should leave so fast.

After Claire and Josh laughed at him for pronouncing the 'b' in 'womb' during 'Hark the Herald Angels Sing', he decided that he needed a gullible adult to clear up a few points for him. Marjorie looked gullible, he thought, popping up beside her like a suddenly ripening mushroom.

'What's a virgin's womb?' he asked.

Marjorie was nonplussed. She eyed Hugh suspiciously, suspecting a trap. 'Do you know what a womb is?'

'Course I do,' said Hugh, 'Aunt Tessa's got one.'

'That's right,' said Marjorie, gathering up music.

'So what's a virgin's one for?'

Marjorie glanced around for help, but none was forthcoming. 'Well, do you know what a virgin is?'

'A sort of olive oil,' said Hugh, whose sex education had so far not covered the more subtle semantics.

Marjorie decided that the time, the place and the person were all wrong for a detailed discussion of the virgin birth. Well, on reflection, this was probably the right place, but that was all. 'I think you'd better ask your Aunt Tessa,' she said, sending a mental apology to Tessa, and Hugh skulked off, disappointed but determined. In his experience, those questions which adults put off replying to generally had the most interesting answers. He would make it impossible for the next person he asked to put him off – he would ask Mr Jenkins, the RS teacher, in front of the whole class.

Chapter Ten

The following day, Hugh put up his hand in Religious Studies and asked Mr Jenkins about virgins and their wombs. Unfortunately he had reckoned without Mr Jenkins's extensive experience of small boys. Whilst individual small boys may vary in malevolence, it is entirely predictable that in every class of thirty ten-year-olds there will be one who asks the RS master what a virgin is. Mr Jenkins had worked out how to deal with them many years ago. Hugh was mortified to find himself under instruction to research the question and return to the class next lesson with a short explanation which he would be expected to deliver while standing at the front.

What to do? He briefly contemplated truancy, but was realistic enough to know that this would merely postpone the day of reckoning. A serious illness might have helped, but he had tried that last week on the day of the French test. It had proved a bad idea to claim period pains, but he had heard Claire being given a day off with the very same thing. How was he to know that only girls got it? Sexual discrimination, that's what it was.

No, the only solution was to brazen it out. He would find out what a virgin was, and he would explain it to the class. There was bound to be a dictionary with it in at home.

There's always a risk with dictionaries that the truth

which they reveal is a little too literal, lacking the finer nuances that a personal explanation might provide. In Hugh's case, the discovery of a thesaurus on the shelf next to the dictionary added to the problem, as extensive cross referencing provided him with a whole variety of useful words to use in his talk. He could hardly wait.

Sally met Robert furtively that day, a secret day off, in a tea room in Cambridge, a sensible sort of meeting place for a couple who did not think of themselves as sensible any more. The tea shop was intended to be quintessentially English. The waitress, unfortunately, seemed not to speak any, and was even surlier than her Parisian counterparts in the cafés overlooking the cathedral of Notre Dame. This did not matter a great deal, as most of the customers were American, and if the waitress had smiled at them or made any sort of suggestion about the quality of day she hoped that they would have, they would have thought the place inauthentic, and left.

Sally was quite amazed at the way she had changed. Before, she had been the sort of girl who wore white underwear, read PG Wodehouse at bedtime and only rented videos if they were made by Walt Disney. Now, though, she was more of a Charlotte Brontë reader, a viewer of *Gone With The Wind*, a True Romantic, and it was awfully difficult having to keep it hidden.

She longed to tell Tessa just a little of the story, but how can you open a floodgate and then expect to be able to let through only a drop? It would be impossible, and her first loyalty was now to Robert. He still felt that they must not go public yet, because the parish might be upset. Bugger the parish, she thought crossly, just because he is a vicar, why should he not be a passionate man?

She said as much to Robert as they buttered the

scones on their 'Special Tutorial Tea', the kind which tourists imagine most students retire to after exercising their brains, but which most students can only afford to dream of.

'People have a narrow view of life,' said Robert, holding her hand across the cucumber sandwiches and feeling himself drowning in her blue eyes. 'They see a vicar as a kind of moral guardian, and he has to be beyond criticism for them to have faith.'

'*Quis custodiet ipsos custodes?*' quoted Sally. 'But what about my morals? It's making a dishonest woman of me.' She kissed the backs of his fingers one at a time.

'Oh, excuse me, your reverence,' said an American lady at the next table, leaning across.

'Yes?' Robert turned.

'Aren't you the Bishop of Huntingdon and Ely?'

'Er – no, sorry,' said Robert, mystified. It was the first time, he reflected, that he had ever had to apologize for not being a bishop.

'Oh, I'm so sorry,' said his questioner, looking flustered, 'it was just her kissing your rings like that, and you do look rather like . . . but you are a priest, aren't you?'

'I'm a vicar, not a priest,' said Robert patiently. 'That's a Church of England clergyman.'

'And I was kissing his fingers, not his ring,' said Sally.

The woman looked suspiciously at Sally. She was not sure if vicars were allowed to do this kind of thing.

'Don't worry,' said Sally, 'I'm his fiancée.' She had never said it before, apart from quietly to Lancelot, her stuffed lion, at night. It sounded wonderful.

Their American friend melted at once. 'Oh, how perfectly charming,' she said, now looking at them as if they were a pair of terribly quaint English Doulton figures to be purchased tax-free and sent straight to Heathrow. 'I'm delighted for you. I'm Gloria O'Flynn

191

from Wisconsin.' She lowered her voice conspiratorially. 'I'm afraid for a moment there I suspected you might be – you know – a priest going through that awkward time of life.'

Robert thought the encounter just about summed up their problem. 'You see,' he said to Sally, as they walked back to their separate cars on separate levels in the multi-storey car park, 'people always leap to the worst conclusions, and then they become terribly undermined. They have to depend on their vicar to be a gentleman.'

'So what can we do?' asked Sally, visions of conducting an entire long-term relationship in multi-storey car parks and coffee shops. She was going to get awfully fat that way.

'We'll go public,' said Robert, 'at Christmas. That way they'll feel we've had time to get to know one another properly, and we can get married in the New Year. It will seem quick, but not indecent.'

'Well, all right,' said Sally, 'just as long as we're married by Easter.'

Robert took her in his arms, riskily, behind a concrete pillar – you never knew for sure that dozens of Bumpstaple residents weren't lurking in the lift.

'It's a deal,' he said. 'I do love a dominant woman.'

Back in Bumpstaple Post Office, Olive was feeling like a new woman. She was sure that her breasts had grown, and she was beginning to look at Ernest with a hungry interest which quite unnerved him. True, she had been much keener on that sort of thing years ago, but was he ready for this at his age? Although the subject of his impending implant had not been discussed between them again, Olive was tremblingly aware of the entry on the calendar which made it clear that Ernest was spending two days next week at the private clinic.

She had been back to her coy GP to report that she had never felt better, and to ask for more of the magic patches, since the first pack had worked terribly well and she did not wish to run out. She also wanted to ask whether, in view of the athletic-looking woman displayed on the HRT leaflet, to take up running, swimming, riding and tennis now, or whether just to wait for the sex. The mere thought of just waiting for the sex ought to have given her a hot flush as soon as she mentioned it, but thanks to the patches, hot flushes were a thing of the past. Now she practised pelvic floor exercises while dispensing pensions, and thought thoughts which she had rarely even had in her youth, when her hormones were entirely her own.

It never occurred to Olive that there could be any other explanation for the extraordinary change in her attitude to life and, particularly, Ernest. Even if it had, the fact that she had been drinking a large quantity of Mavis Entwhistle's herb tea was not something she would have connected with it.

Mavis, though, had a different view of things, and if she had had any doubts about the effectiveness of the hogweed brew, they were laid to rest when she went into the Post Office for a pound of lard and found Olive with a very strange facial expression, and a fairly racy sparkle in her eye. For the first time, she even felt slightly surprised at the potency of her own weapon. Olive was actually drinking herb tea right there, and what's more, she was not drinking it from a china mug with flowers on it. True, the mug was china, but it was not floral. It did not have pictures of little fluffy kittens on it, either. Instead it bore the legend, 'Postmistresses Do It Behind The Counter'.

Mavis stared. Had she overdone it? Olive might have needed perking up a bit, but she had never planned to make her dangerous. 'I see you are drinking my herb brew,' she said cautiously.

'Indeed I am,' said Olive brightly, 'I find it quite invigorating. I believe the vicar enjoys it too.' As she spoke, Ernest came into the shop behind her. There was no mistaking the lascivious look on Olive's face when she looked at him.

'Hello,' he said to Mavis, 'how are you?'

Mavis hardly heard – in fact, her pound of lard went right out of her head and as a result she made no pastry for Sally that night, so some good came of it. She, Mavis, had done this to Olive!

Delighted by her success, she hurried from the shop, making some excuse about forgetting her purse. Just wait till she told Joyce in *Astral Suggestions*. The hogweed was working! She must write that paper on hogweed. Ernest and Olive were surely *en route* for the throes of passion, and up until recently she had had him down as another one bound for Bangkok. He had worn that look which she had seen so often in Albert before he decided that he preferred to dress in orange and do a lot of chanting: the look of a man who cannot cope with his wife.

Mr Jenkins was surprised that Hugh was so cheerful at the beginning of his next RS lesson. Surprised and, if he was honest with himself, slightly alarmed, especially when Hugh got a crib sheet out and prepared to deliver his talk. All of Mr Jenkins's previous victims had been blushing and awkward at this stage. He adjusted his spectacles with a nervous gesture, and gave a little mental space to his usual de-stressing fantasy, which involved Hugh, a stage trapdoor, a large, boy-eating dragon beneath and, most importantly, his own hand on the lever.

'We are all virgins,' said Hugh in Churchillian tones, beginning as inauspiciously as he intended to continue, 'except for Mr Jenkins, 'cos he's got Mrs Jenkins.'

Mr Jenkins pushed his spectacles further up the bridge of his nose, reflecting that he might just as well have remained a virgin for all the fun that Mrs Jenkins provided in that department. 'Go on,' he said, realizing that he had to see it through.

'Girls can be virgins too,' said Hugh, 'but not often once they've been behind the bike sheds. When they go there they lose their hymens.' Mr Jenkins winced. 'Once they lose those then they're not virgins any more. If you look behind the bike sheds you can sometimes find the hymens the next morning. Usually they're pink, but I found a red knobbly one last week.'

Mr Jenkins cleared his throat noisily. The class were giggling and shuffling. 'Yes, well, thank you Hugh. That's not entirely correct, but—'

'I haven't finished yet,' said Hugh, 'I know where my mum lost hers. It was on the beach in Cromer. I expect it got washed out to sea, otherwise she could have got it back later.'

Mr Jenkins sighed, rather horrified by the vision of Hugh's deflowered mother hunting Cromer seashore for her lost hymen. Sometimes he wished it was not his job to educate. 'You can sit down now, Hugh.'

'Don't I get a house point, Sir?' asked Hugh, who was blessed with the ability to know when he had defeated someone, and therefore when best to push his luck.

'Sit down, Hugh,' repeated Mr Jenkins.

'Would I get a house point if I finished the speech?' asked Hugh. 'I've got a whole separate bit about hermaphrodites.'

'No. No, that's quite enough,' said Mr Jenkins firmly.

'House point?' prompted Hugh.

'About as likely as a knighthood, I should imagine,' said Mr Jenkins grimly, and Hugh got the message at last.

*   *   *

That evening, Tom rang, intruding into Tessa's kitchen like an echo from another life. Sometimes she really didn't like the phone. 'Come on, Claire!' she shouted outside Claire's door. 'Your father's on the telephone!' She knocked but did not go in, for it is a brave parent who enters the Teenage Bedroom. When occupied, it assumes the status of citadel, its doorway staunchly defended from trespass by its belligerent occupant. When empty, it lurks behind its closed door, a menacing presence whose very silent forbiddenness hints at the exponential multiplication of cockroaches, biro lids, and that peculiar grey-green mould which thrives only in coffee cups. Claire's room had become, in Tessa's mind, one of the last great unexplorable spots on earth, ranking alongside Low's gully and the high Himalayas.

'Coming!' shouted Claire at last, so Tessa was at least not forced to make any decisions about opening the door. When Claire was plugged in to her hi-fi, it could be impossible to contact her.

'It's your father on the phone,' said Tessa again, holding the receiver out, away from her body, as though it might criticize her. Tom had always criticized her, and the fact that they had been apart for nearly twelve years did not reduce his ability to make her feel small. She knew he thought her a bad parent – she knew it so well that he no longer needed to imply it – but that didn't stop him from implying it anyway. 'Claire! Do hurry up!'

'I heard you the first time!'

Tessa bit back the, 'Well, why didn't you come, then?' because he would hear. She returned to the kitchen table then, not wishing to be accused of eavesdropping, wandered into the sitting-room and began to play the piano. She had hoped that playing music during pregnancy would give the baby a musical ear. It hadn't worked for Claire, who doted on the latest banal products of single-earringed heart-throbs who looked like models from men's underwear catalogues. Her cello was merely a means of avoiding hockey practice, but that didn't mean it wasn't worth trying again. Tessa banged out the first chords of Beethoven's Apassionata Sonata, in the hope that this way the baby would also get used to loud music and wouldn't mind the shouting later. Actually, she reflected, if babies really did grow up loving womb sounds then we'd all spend our spare time listening to the plumbing.

Claire was on the phone for a while. Tessa always felt this boded rather ill for her. Tom was inclined to make suggestions which were destined to cost Tessa, not himself, time and money, but for which he then got all the credit. The last one had involved taking Claire ice skating, a drive of some miles followed by the weary experience of Claire becoming angrier and angrier when she failed to complete a triple Lutz in the first half an hour. It had been Tessa's fault for failing to buy new skates of championship quality. It was obvious, she said, that the hired ones were deficient. Tellingly, no return trip had been requested, but it remained Dad who had given her the chance to go skating, and Mum who had made sure that she did not do well.

Tessa had finished the sonata and begun another by the time Claire reappeared and stood, ghost-like, in the doorway. Eventually Tessa stopped, for a teenager waiting pointedly is not the most appreciative of audiences.

'That was Dad,' said Claire unnecessarily.

'Oh?' said Tessa.

'He wants a word with you.'

'When?'

'Now – he's waiting.'

'Oh Claire! Why didn't you tell me?' Galvanized,

197

Tessa rushed for the phone, annoyed to feel at even more of a disadvantage than usual. 'Sorry,' she said to Tom, 'I didn't realize you were waiting.'

'Never mind, it doesn't matter,' he said, his tone making it clear that actually it did. 'I gather Claire wants to spend Christmas with you this year.'

'Oh. I didn't know,' said Tessa, surprised at first.

'You haven't discussed it then?' Don't you communicate?

'You mean have we pressured her?'

'No, of course not,' mild exasperation tinged with reasonableness. 'I just wanted to say that's fine, but could June and I pop over on Christmas day, just for half an hour?'

'Oh. Yes. Yes, of course,' said Tessa, horribly afraid that she was about to feel forced to invite her ex-husband and his wife for Christmas dinner. 'Any particular time?'

'We'll arrange it nearer the event,' said Tom. 'June's mother lives in Bury St Edmunds and we'll be having lunch there, so it's no trouble.'

Oh, I'm so glad, thought Tessa, annoyed, we wouldn't want to put you to any trouble. How can he manage to sound so reasonable when he isn't? Is that what Claire thinks of me, she wondered, just too bloody reasonable? Aloud she said, 'Claire has a new boyfriend in the village. That will be why she wants to stay here.'

'Oh good,' said Tom, displaying what Tessa thought was Trendy North London Man's attitude to fatherly protectiveness.

'Doesn't it bother you?' she asked, feeling that for once she had the edge on proper parenting.

'No, of course not, if you didn't live so far from civilization I'm sure she'd have several,' said Tom, a trifle smugly.

Oh, another fault, thought Tessa, I live in the wrong

place. 'There are plenty of kids around here,' she said defensively.

'Oh, I'm sure there ·are,' said Tom, irritatingly placating, 'and she can always visit me.'

Tessa thought, I'm not sure I'd want her joining London's social scene. There's a lot to be said for rural backwaters. In London she'd have been on the Pill since twelve, and not for spots either. Aloud, she said goodbye. Talking to Tom always left her feeling as though she'd been put through several settings of a pasta machine, even though he was careful never to say anything too obviously derogatory. It was more a mixture of reasonable and patronizing, and it got to her every time. That *is* how Claire sees me, she thought, with a flash of insight, that's exactly how she feels. It suits her to cast me as the Great Female Dictator, it gives her something obvious to battle against. When I'm too reasonable it takes the wind out of her sails and she's left to struggle through the mire of being teenaged without anyone to blame.

Insight is not always a great help. Outside the kitchen door, Claire was seething. She had not yet realized that those who eavesdrop invariably end up cross. As Tessa put the phone down, she erupted back into the room. 'Boyfriend? *Boyfriend?* This isn't infant school. He's my friend.'

'And he's a boy,' said Hugh, coming in with his unnerving ability to spot an argument and join it.

'Sorry,' said Tessa, 'it was just a turn of phrase.'

'Well, you didn't have to tell Dad. He'll be just as bad as you. All . . . all . . . understanding.' Claire could not contain her infuriation.

'What's so awful about that?' said Tessa mildly, wondering if Claire knew the answer too. At least, she thought, I'm merely as bad as Tom. Usually I'm Jezebel to his St Michael.

'It's a front!' shouted Claire. 'It's a front to get what

you want. I know he's upset I'm not spending Christmas with him. I know you don't want me to have a boy-friend. Yet even though I know you know I know, you act as though it's OK.'

'You're nuts,' said Hugh, unable to enjoy an argument he couldn't follow.

Tessa was inclined to agree, but sensed that the situation would not improve if she said so. 'I like Josh,' she said mildly. 'You wouldn't stop seeing him if I asked you not to, would you?'

'No,' said Claire, agreeing cautiously in case this led somewhere she disagreed with. Parents were very good at sounding reasonable then leading on to something totally unacceptable.

'Well then, what would be the point? But in any case, as it happens, I don't want you to stop seeing him, so we're all happy.'

Claire was slightly mollified. 'Well, is Dad coming over on Christmas day?' she asked grudgingly.

Tessa sighed. 'Yes, of course.'

'Don't you mind seeing him?'

'No.'

'Why did you get divorced, then?'

'Oh, for God's sake. OK, I mind. Your father annoys me so I mind, but I'll have to put up with it, OK?'

'Good,' said Claire, pleased to have made some sort of a point. It struck her suddenly that her mother felt as irritated with her father as she did herself, giving them some common ground other than periods. It was an unusual feeling – she quite liked it. She just wasn't ready for a full truce yet. The transition from child to friend is a difficult one for both parties, especially as the teenage years are so terribly awkward on their own account anyway, and finding enough common ground to become friends with your mother is not easy when you have always regarded her as the Mad Pig-Painting Hippie From Hell.

*   *   *

The days were shortening and the nights drawing in as November drew to a close. Tessa remembered being told at infant school once, long ago, that the days were getting shorter, and crying because she thought that meant for ever, so that the best there ever would be had already been. She always got back a little bit of that feeling at this time of year: it triggered the memory, with its crisp mornings and dark, damp evenings on which people stamped their feet a little when they got indoors. A prehistoric reflex perhaps, she thought, to avoid frost-bite in our cave-dwelling days.

Claire was in the garden, cleaning Lysander's water trough. This was normally Tessa's mucky task, but Richard had bribed Claire to offer to take over for the remainder of her pregnancy. Tessa, unaware of the secret chink of cash, had been amazed at the offer.

The air smelled of Christmas, or black ice, depending on whether or not you were an optimist or a pessimist. Lysander, being a pig, took a rather narrow view of the future, which neither optimism nor pessimism could completely define. If he thought of anything, it was of food, and this did not vary with the season or his mood. Not so Claire. Although she had cultivated pessimism in herself for quite some time – it is, after all, the only fashionable attitude a fifteen-year-old girl can adopt – since Josh's arrival her pessimism had been quite diluted, and now she found herself thinking with pleasant anticipation of the festive season. She had given up her chance to have her usual moan about not spending Christmas with Dad and June, and had voluntarily forgone their turn. Christmas was better in Bumpstaple, anyway. Dad and June's rather trendy Islington Christmases lacked the essential appeal of home. Claire was, after all, still partly a child, and that part of her knew that Christmas is not Christmas when all the decorations are colour

201

co-ordinated, and there are no dangly chocolate Santas on the tree. Even so, she had until now felt the need to moan when she had to spend Christmas day with Tessa and Richard, as this stopped them from taking her for granted. This year, however, the added attraction of Josh's presence gave her an acceptable reason to admit she preferred to be in Bumpstaple. Actually, Josh had also begun to make her see Tessa's more acceptable characteristics. Mind you, this pig was definitely not one of them.

Tessa, washing dishes at the kitchen window, watched her thoughtfully. She was changing at last. The changes might not seem much from the outside, but when you are accustomed to being stamped on relentlessly by your daughter, even a blunting of her hob-nailed boots brings instantly noticeable relief. It was odd, really, she reflected, you would think that the advent of romance would make a teenager more, not less impossible to live with – but then, perhaps it was just that Josh was a good influence. If that was so, then Tessa hoped the relationship would not founder yet. Let's face it, she thought, the way things are going, my daughter will be the only one with any prospect of a sex life around here soon.

'Why don't you use the dishwasher?' asked Richard.

'It's full,' said Tessa shortly, blaming him for not having emptied it.

'Why don't you empty it, then?' he said, putting the kettle on the Aga annoyingly.

'Because my back hurts. Why don't you?'

'I should think that standing there doing that is just as bad for your back,' said Richard, feeling suddenly guilty. He wasn't the only one who worked hard, and he was enjoying drafting this new novel. He could put it down, too. He opened the dishwasher and began to unload it, with what Tessa felt to be an inappropriately saintly air.

In the garden, Claire finished Lysander's trough and gave him an apple. He was, as pigs tend to be in such circumstances, overwhelmed with joy. He suffered from a complete absence of any sense of proportion, as many pigs do. It is too philosophical an attribute for them, and so all of life's pleasures, be they apple cores or receptive female pigs, are greeted with equal ecstasy. He rolled on the floor and grinned piggily.

Claire found herself grinning back at him. 'You're not that bad, are you, you stupid creature?' she said fondly, then looked round in alarm to make sure no-one had seen her crack. *Oh God, I'm starting to like the pig.*

Lysander farted horribly, and Claire fled, holding her nose pointedly. How could anyone love a creature that passed wind when it got happy? But she did not completely forget her sudden rush of affection for him. *Perhaps,* she thought, with unusual resignation, *Josh is wrong, and I've inherited the gene for pig-worship.*

'Noble of her,' said Tessa.

'Hmmm?' Richard stacked plates in the bowl cupboard.

'Claire. Noble of her to clean out Lysander's trough.'

Richard decided to spare her the mercenary truth. 'We all ought to help you more,' he said.

Tessa thought that was rich, coming from a man who could not operate the washing machine they had owned for six years. Indeed, he had once called out the repair man when it would not wash, only to discover that it was not plugged in. She decided, in the interest of peace, not to mention this. 'Where's Hugh?'

'Post Office,' said Richard. 'He can't keep away from the sweet counter.'

'I asked him to get tissues,' said Claire, coming in from the garden. 'That pig has a runny nose.'

'Oh, poor Lysander,' said Tessa, 'he does hate having colds.'

'Anthropomorphism again,' said Richard. 'I some-times feel as though I'm married to Dr Doolittle.'

'He's only one pig,' said Tessa.

'And a dog who looks like a mutant giraffe,' said Richard. 'I live in the constant fear of what you'll decide to mother next. A monkey, perhaps, or a blue-bottomed baboon.'

Claire giggled. 'Did she tell you about our stick insects?'

'No,' said Richard, 'she didn't.'

'They had babies,' said Claire, 'twenty-three babies. Charlie knocked their tank over, and they got out. It was like having loads of bits of twig in the hearth rug.'

'I hope you caught them,' said Richard.

'We caught seventeen,' said Tessa, grinning.

'Oh God,' said Richard, 'you mean . . .'

'Yep. Somewhere in this house they're probably breeding like rabbits.'

'I've married into a very peculiar family,' said Richard, 'I know now where Hugh gets it from.'

Tessa put her arms around him, enjoying the teasing camaraderie. He hugged her briefly, then moved away, feeling uncomfortable.

'I'm going around to see Josh,' said Claire, not wanting to be embarrassed by them canoodling, failing to notice that they were not.

As she left, Richard went too, to his study, and Tessa was left feeling suddenly alone and dejected. Her family were like trout, she thought: if you grasped too desperately at them, they slipped through your fingers. She sat down, and Charlie put his head on her lap and sighed a long and mournful sigh. He found it brought more in the way of sympathetic petting than any amount of eyebrow wiggling.

'Elephants are pregnant for twenty-two months,' Tessa told him. 'I suppose I should just be glad I'm human.'

Charlie wagged his tail hopefully. He was not much interested in pregnant female elephants, said his expression, but a walk would be nice.

In his study, Richard settled back down to his book, thinking that perhaps God had sound reasons for giving him a low sperm count.

The sweet counter in Bumpstaple Post Office was one of those wonderful old-fashioned ones, loaded with liquorice whirls and cherry lips, and a variety of unidentifiable jelly objects of which several could be purchased for a penny – they even sold sherbert fountains with liquorice straws. Hugh spent a great deal of his pocket money in there, particularly since the maggot affair, as he had been expressly forbidden to spend any of it on the acquisition of anything capable of spontaneous movement.

Today, Hugh was sorry to find Olive behind the counter. Usually there was a young assistant in the shop on Saturday afternoons, a girl from a Youth Opportunity Scheme, although many people felt that working for Olive was less an opportunity than a sentence. She always allowed him to deliberate for as long as he liked over the sweets, whereas Olive would not allow him to rummage through the pot of cherry lips after the odd pair that were deformed and bigger than the rest. She insisted instead that he make his choice from a distance, whilst she loaded it into a paper bag with a pair of large plastic tweezers. He never got any extra ones free from Olive, and yet however much you have to spend it is always the extra one, the something-for-nothing, which is the best.

Olive did not like Hugh. When she was growing up, small boys had existed only to taunt small girls, and Hugh seemed to her like the crystallized concentrate of all the pigtail-pulling, stink-bomb cracking, paper-flicking, face-pulling small boys who had so dogged her childhood. 'Yes?' she said now, in Jack Frost tones. 'What would you like?'

'Tissues,' said Hugh, hoping to get her away from the sweets.

Olive eyed him suspiciously. 'Two-ply or three-ply?'

'Quadruple snot ply,' said Hugh, 'they're for our pig.'

Olive glared, sure that she was being had. 'Who sent you?'

'Uncle Richard,' said Hugh defiantly. 'He said he was fed up with that blasted porcine monster wiping its nose on his trouser legs.'

It had the ring of a direct quote about it, and Olive dropped her guard slightly, climbing to the man-size – there were none in pig-size – tissues up on her HRT shelf. The steps were a little unsteady, and her attention was taken completely by her climb. Behind her, Hugh's hand darted into the cherry lips and liquorice bootlaces, and he had the satisfaction of making his selection before she got back down again.

Olive snatched them back from him as soon as she reached the counter, and began to count them meticulously. Hugh noticed that a pair of mutant cherry lips of double thickness got counted as one, so he was moderately pleased. There was no point in asking her for his usual quarter of wine gums and expecting her to give him black ones.

Behind Olive, Ernest appeared with a big cardboard box. 'I shall have to put this on the top shelf, dear,' he said. 'I've no idea why we got sent such a large box, but we may as well keep it, they always get used. It will have to go up on top of the shelf unit.'

'Why? What is it?' asked Olive.

'Regular Tampax,' said Ernest cheerfully, setting up the step ladder just behind her.

'Oh Ernest, really,' said Olive, aware of Hugh's interested, grinning face.

Hugh saw that Olive had turned pink – even HRT cannot prevent those sort of blushes – and saw an opportunity to express his personality. 'What are Tampax for?'

'Nothing!' snapped Olive, faster than a mouse trap.

'They must be for something,' said Hugh reasonably.

'Nothing that need concern you,' said Olive primly.

Ernest, trying to manoeuvre what was actually an extremely large box of Tampax up the step ladder, began to chuckle to himself.

Accounts later varied a little over what happened next, but all were quite sure that the man who entered the Post Office in such a hurry had a stocking over his head. Olive thought that he had a gun, Ernest thought it was a truncheon, but Hugh, being lower down, saw at once that it was a piece of copper piping. Either way, the robber certainly pointed this weapon at Olive, and shouted 'Open the safe!'

Hugh, with the pluckiness usually shown only by springer spaniels and particularly stupid chihuahuas, flung himself at the raider's legs crying, 'All for one, and one for all!' He hung bravely on to one denim-clad leg, whilst the man tried to shake him off.

Olive, torn between fear that Hugh might actually be shot, and fury that someone should try to rob her again, said in shaky tones, 'Very well, but I shall need to get the key from behind the counter.'

'Hurry up then, lady,' said the robber, in what he clearly intended to be tones of growling menace. Through the stocking they were rather muffled, and he sounded more agonized than alarming.

Hugh, encouraged by this, tightened his grip on the leg as Olive rushed past Ernest's steps to get the keys. After that, everything happened very quickly. Olive knocked the steps in her flustered state, and Ernest went flying through the air. The box of twelve hundred regular protection tampons sailed from his grip as only tampons can sail, and Hugh sank his teeth as hard as he could into the would-be burglar's leg.

The robber opened his mouth to howl, and sucked in a mouthful of medium-support stocking, stolen the previous evening from the washing line of the rector of Great Barking. As he did so, he was struck just above the eyebrow by the flying box, knocked off-balance, and fell to the floor, banging his head on the ice cream freezer on his way down. It was later said of him that this made him the only man ever rendered unconscious by twelve hundred items of internal feminine protection and two dozen cornettos.

Hugh had always thought that being a hero could have its rewards. To be honest, he thought that his selfless action was worth considerably more than a pound of free wine gums, but to be fair to Olive, she had not yet recovered her composure. By the time the police had been and taken the teenage miscreant away in a satisfyingly ostentatious black maria, bearing the stocking of Oliver Bush's wife Rose in a plastic bag marked 'Exhibit A', quite a crowd had gathered. They applauded the police as they drove away, applauded Ernest for putting up a sign saying 'Business as usual despite attempted robbery', and even applauded Olive for nothing. They did not, to his great disappointment, applaud Hugh when he emerged with his wine gums and Lysander's tissues, for they had not yet heard the whole story. But he was confident that, when they did hear it, it would be on *News East*. He even planned to tip them off himself.

The first article on *News East* that night was all about the attempted robbery at Bumpstaple Post Office. There was Olive, looking, as Tessa remarked suddenly, more perky than usual. Ernest was interviewed about his daring lunge with the cardboard box, and then it was Hugh's turn.

He thought he had played it rather well. Long-time observation of the Esther Rantzen show about noble people had taught him that modesty pays when you are a hero, so he had been as modest as he was able, which was, in his case, horribly modest. Tessa and Claire, to his chagrin, fell about laughing as he answered the reporter's questions nobly and self-effacingly.

'And what did you do then?' came the interviewer's voice.

'Well,' said the modest Hugh, 'I just went for his leg. Instinct took over, you see, so without a thought for my own safety, I bit him.'

'Oh dear,' said the interviewer, 'what happened next?'

Claire and Tessa were helpless with mirth. Hugh glared at them and turned up the volume.

'Oh, it all happened very fast. Of course I had nothing to do with it. I hung on for dear life to his leg while Mr Osborne threw the Tampax at him.'

'That sounds very brave,' said the interviewer. 'Did you draw blood?'

'No,' said the modest Hugh, 'just sock. My mouth was full of cherry lips, you see.'

'And – er – what happened then?'

'He fell unconscious to the ground,' said TV Hugh, 'and Mr Osborne said that it was amazing what you could do with tampons these days.'

'Well, thank you very much,' said the interviewer in a choked voice, 'thank you Hugh Appleton. This is Moira Maddox, for *News East*, in Bumpstaple.'

Hugh felt it was truly unfair of them to be laughing so much. Just wait till Esther Rantzen rang, that would show them. He was, after all, a hero.

Chapter Eleven

'Don't you think it's remarkable,' said Tessa to Sally the following day, 'that Hugh should save Olive from being robbed?'

They were sitting in the kitchen, eating biscuits and drinking herb tea. Hugh was listening on the other side of the kitchen door, on the basis that if they were talking about him then he had a right to know, and if they weren't it didn't matter.

'I don't know,' said Sally, 'Hugh's not a bad boy, really.' Behind the door Hugh glowed a little.

'You didn't see the maggots,' said Tessa, 'but in any case I didn't mean that I was surprised Hugh tried to bite the burglar – he gets more like the creatures he collects every day.'

'Aaah,' said Sally, 'you don't really mean that.'

'Well, he eats constantly, he pops up all over the place, he makes a mess, he stores bugs . . . do you know, it sounds like the job description for a praying mantis.'

Sally started to giggle. Behind the door Hugh wondered where he could get one from.

'In any case,' said Tessa, 'I really meant that it was amazing that Olive actually needed saving. I'd have expected her to fell any would-be robber at a single glance.'

'She did think he was armed,' said Sally. 'She's not stupid.'

'No, but I've always thought she had a lot of Vlad the Impaler in her. D'you think they could be related?' She lowered her voice dramatically, 'Perhaps she *is* Vlad the Impaler, you know, reincarnated.'

Hugh was intrigued, wondering who this Vlad had been, and why Tessa was unable to pronounce impala properly. He must remember to tell her how to say it. He put his ear to the door, but they were on about babies now, so he wandered away, thinking about Vlad. Perhaps he was a legendary impala, a kind of impalan Pegasus.

In fact, he had a good few days, for Olive told all sorts of people what a brave boy he had been, how plucky, how positively Biggles-like! Hugh basked in the benefit of being in her good books, not realizing that a certain amount of this kind of praise was essential for Olive to save her own face in the situation. It had been bad enough the last time she was robbed, being rescued by Mavis's bosom, but now she had to admit to being a less effective guardian of the cash than a ten-year-old boy. She therefore vastly exaggerated the danger they had faced, until she had even convinced herself. So, for the moment, Hugh was enjoying a shower of free gobstoppers and sherbet fountains. It wasn't quite what he had hoped for, of course, Olive was certainly not generous enough to give away the water pistols from the toy stand, or the fluorescent felt tip pens which he so coveted, but he still planned to exploit it while it lasted, and he visited the Post Office at every available opportunity.

'I wish you were interested in herbalism,' said Mavis to Sally, wistfully pounding something in a pestle a few days later.

'I know you do,' said Sally, who was watching a dating programme in which two normal young men

211

and one with the charm of a dried dung beetle competed for a date with a girl who had impossible breasts and hair a Chinese restaurant could have made soup out of.

'It's a very useful hobby,' persisted Mavis.

'It wasn't much good for Aunt Flo's grey hair,' said Sally, 'it all fell out.'

'It got rid of the grey, though,' said Mavis, 'and the dandruff. Herbalism is like life: be careful what you ask for, they say, because you might get it. In any case, your late father took it very seriously.'

'I wish you wouldn't call him late,' said Sally.

'Well, he always was,' said Mavis, unperturbed. 'I don't suppose he's changed. I expect he turns up late for chanting every day, with excuses about fixing his prayer wheel.'

Sally dropped the subject of her Trappist father, which was never very productive except of insults. 'I hope there's nothing funny in that tea that you've been handing around.'

Mavis looked hurt. 'It's wonderful stuff.'

'That's what I'm afraid of,' said Sally. 'Didn't you just say you never knew what you might get?'

The girl with the impossible breasts and the dried beetle were pretending to be impressed by one another's physical attributes, whilst clearly wishing that someone an awful lot fatter/thinner/hairier/less hairy had been revealed when the screen went back.

'What do you think they'll get? It's only hogweed tonic,' said Mavis, quite sure that Sally knew nothing about the magical properties of plants.

'Blue-eared pig disease, probably,' said Sally. 'Come to think of it, things have been very strange in this village recently.' A couple from the previous week's programme were loudly demolishing one another verbally to the hysterical cheers of the studio audience. 'Marjorie Smythe is being assertive, there was the

212

tampon robber in the Post Office, and even Olive has a rather odd expression sometimes. They all drink that brew of yours.'

'So do you, dear,' said Mavis unperturbed, 'and you're not odd.' She watched Sally carefully. 'In any case, I thought you didn't believe in the powers of herbs.'

'I don't,' said Sally uncomfortably, 'I was being facetious.'

'Well,' said Mavis slyly, 'if I could work magic with my brews then I'd have you and Robert Peabody together by now.'

Sally's cheeks turned the colour of Ribena so swiftly that she could not hope to disguise it. She must be careful, she thought, pretending an interest in a loose thread on her chair arm, or someone would guess.

Someone had. Mavis was a mother. True, she was not a standard, scone-baking, rose-growing, PG Tips-brewing kind of mother, but with a Mother's Instinct and her Sight, she was well-enough equipped to interpret Sally's guilty expression correctly. I knew it, she thought exultantly, Sally is already seeing Robert. Something is going on!

She must send in her paper to the *English Covens' Herald*. Every month they ran a page of success stories, most of which were along the lines of 'I turned my boyfriend's mother into a hamster.' Mavis was sure that most of them were a mixture of wishful thinking and schizophrenia, but they did get paid twenty pounds for every published report. It did not worry Mavis in the least that her magical powers, if they really were responsible for all the changes in Bump-staple, were unleashing chaos on an unsuspecting world. She knew that magic, like the scent of chrysan-themums, drifts in all directions and gets up the strangest of noses, but this did not worry her. For her, magic was an end in itself. True, her only dramatic success before now, apart from the dandruff, had been the hex she put on the Great Barking postman, and even she had to admit that the smell of the haddock she had sewn into his curtains might well have worked even without the herbal spell she had cast. He had deserved it for trying to grope her once at the bus stop, and she had been glad to see the back of him, even though Bumpstaple did get Olive in his place. Still, even Olive was getting better since starting on the hogweed. Mavis was sure it would revolutionize her life.

Olive was on her way to visit Ernest at the private hospital. Her life was indeed facing something of a revolution, as he had had his operation and was convalescing in a single ward.

He lay rather uncomfortably. Since it was a private clinic, justifying at last his many years of private health subscriptions, he had the room to himself. This did make it far less awkward, having his dressings changed, than if he had been in a Nightingale ward full of old ladies with waterworks trouble and nubile young grand-daughters bearing bunches of pinks.

The nurses always got the giggles when they came in to see him. It was his own fault, he knew, for telling them he felt a bit stiff earlier in the day. It had been a reflex comment, one of his usual stock replies to questions about his health, when to answer fully would have been embarrassing, as it would have entailed saying, 'I feel as though my willy has just been scrubbed by a gang of Breton washer women with biceps like water buffalo.' It had, however, caused great mirth on the ward, and had given him an instant reputation for wit which he was rather enjoying.

Olive sidled in, looking extremely embarrassed. It was those nurses again. They knew. Worse, they knew she knew. It was not only what they were thinking, it

214

was what she was sure they thought she was thinking, that bothered her the most. She was glad to shut the ward door behind her.

'Hello, dear,' said Ernest cheerfully.

Olive tried not to run her gaze down his body. There was a tray over his bed, raised six inches above the covers. She dared not wonder how it was balanced there. 'Hello,' she said in a strangled voice, dragging her thoughts away from his groin. 'How is it – I mean, how are you?'

'Fine, thank you dear,' said Ernest, deciding to try his joke again, 'just a bit stiff.' Thanks to BUPA, he had had his eyebrows and his moustache trimmed, which had altered his expression quite remarkably. He waggled the eyebrows experimentally, the way he used to.

Olive blushed. 'Ernest!'

'Come, now, dear, I was only joking.'

Olive's face fell a little. 'Joking?'

Ernest, knowing exactly what she was thinking, patted the side of his bed. 'Sit down, dear. Yes, although I shall be home tomorrow, I shall be a little sore for a week or two. I hope we might have an interesting Christmas, though,' he grinned.

The colour came and went in Olive's cheeks, and he patted her hand. 'Don't be embarrassed, dear,' he said, 'they tell me that lots of men of my age have these problems. You'd be surprised how many are walking about with extra bendy bits inserted.'

'Oh dear,' said Olive, 'it's so . . . vulgar, Ernest. It's surely not what God intended.' The mental picture of Broomhill High Street crowded with men with flexible prostheses quite unnerved her.

'Nonsense,' said Ernest firmly. 'If God meant me to remain impotent he would not have given me the urge to seek treatment.' This was what Robert Peabody had said to him, and he felt it made sense.

215

Olive swallowed and ate one of his grapes, studiously avoiding the bananas. She also avoided Ernest's eye.

'Is there anything you want to ask me?' he asked patiently.

Olive gulped. She would have to ask. Even the truth could not be worse than her imaginings. 'How big is it?' she blurted out, almost inhaling her grape. There. It was out. If her husband was now the proud possessor of a two-foot willy which would need to be carried around in a special pouch worn at the hip, she would at least know.

'Just normal size,' said Ernest, 'no different.'

'Oh,' said Olive, emboldened, 'how does it work?'

'Well, you just bend it up to use it, and you bend it down when you're through. Apparently it's strong stuff, good for half a million goes.'

'What happens then?' whispered Olive.

'Well, it would probably snap,' said Ernest, adding at Olive's expression, 'now now, I'm only joking. We won't live long enough to use it that often. As soon as the dressing is off you can have a look.' He grinned wickedly. 'I'll let you have first go with it if you like.'

Olive felt that she had entered a kind of surreal pornographic world in which people talked about erections and organs as though they were fish and chips. Most of her was appalled by the conversation they were having, but one tiny, unexpected part of her was quite excited. 'I brought you some herb tea,' she said, 'I thought it would perk you up – oh, I mean—'

'Don't worry,' said Ernest, 'it is rather like being trapped in a blue comedian's show, isn't it?'

'When have you seen one?' demanded Olive.

'My sleepless nights,' said Ernest. 'Let's have some of that tea.' He winked as he pressed his call button for a nurse with hot water. 'Perhaps it's a love potion.'

'Don't be ridiculous,' said Olive, 'the vicar drinks it all the time.'

Tessa pushed her shopping trolley rather absently towards a checkout. Actually, pushed is perhaps not the right word, for the shopping trolley had its own ideas as to where it wanted to go. It did not want to go to the checkout. Neither, it appeared, did it wish to traverse any of the aisles selling essential household goods. Tessa suspected it of being deliberately doctored to drag her, protesting weakly, towards the smoked salmon and the speciality ice cream. In front of her was an irritated woman with a baby in her trolley. The cashier was having trouble with the till. The customer looked as though she still got time to use her hair drier, and the little girl wore booties which matched her hat, and a dress which had clearly been ironed. That had to be an only child. Tessa felt crumpled and hot in the presence of such efficiency.

The cashier looked flustered. 'I'm sorry,' Tessa heard her say, 'I've only just been till trained. Let me try one last time. Third time lucky.'

Tessa wondered with suspended horror if the till would swallow her if she pressed the wrong keys for a third time. Perhaps, like a hole-in-the-wall money dispenser, the till would only accept so much error before deciding that the perpetrator was a possible felon and worthy of digestion. She held her breath. The drawer opened, and to her relief there were no captive cashiers from earlier shifts already in there, awaiting the wrath of the Till Trainer.

The baby gurgled happily and passed wind loudly and delightfully; it is only ever delightful when done by a baby. The woman did not look pleased, and gathered up her purchases swiftly. She had bought patterned kitchen roll, Tessa noticed, so she must be rich.

She remembered with acute clarity supermarket trips during Claire's babyhood. Claire's acquisition of the consonants 'b' and 'g' before any others had endowed her with the ability to say 'buggerbuggerbugger' repeatedly to people in checkout queues. 'Shush' never had any effect. Even then she must have felt that adults were making unreasonable demands on her to fit their own agendas. Perhaps, Tessa thought suddenly, it is the ability to understand someone else's point of view which finally signals the transition into adulthood. Mind you, what would that say about politicians?

She was surprised to discover, upon unloading her own shopping, that she had bought a packet of Christmas crackers, although she had only come in for bread and toilet rolls. Really, she was becoming terribly absent-minded. Was it pregnancy, or was she really being controlled by her trolley?

'Buying early for Christmas?' asked the checkout lady chummily, and Tessa realized that she was pregnant too. Strange, she thought, how it puts you into a kind of temporary fellowship, bonds of shared adversity breaking the ice in advance to allow smiles and familiarity. It's rather like driving a Morris Minor. People in other Morris Minors wave at you. Mind you, it doesn't work so well the day you forget that you're actually in your Landrover, and you wave at all the Morris Minor people, and they glare and mutter.

Now she smiled at the checkout woman. 'I didn't intend to,' she said, 'they got in there when I wasn't thinking.'

'I know what you mean,' said the woman, 'last week I bought cat food, and we've no cat.'

Paying for her shopping, Tessa wondered if perhaps she should have joined the National Childbirth lot for a bit more shared adversity – it felt quite nice to be understood for a moment. She had actually gone along to an NCT coffee morning, but they had all seemed nearer Claire's age than her own, and her comment that children were far easier to deal with when gestating than at any other time in their lives had not gone down particularly well.

Richard was in the kitchen when she got home, tired and thirsty. He had put together the skeleton of a plot for his new, time-travelling detective with the intelligent pet pig. It was only a very rough sketch so far, but he was so pleased with it that he decided he might tell Tessa now, after all. Unfortunately, in setting the scene for this important conversation, he had made her a cup of tea.

As Tessa told Sally later, when you married a writer you expected the occasional mental aberration, but you would think that after ten years he might have remembered she didn't drink ordinary tea.

'Sorry,' said Richard, when she pointed this out, 'I forgot.'

Tessa frowned. 'I'm fed up with you switching off from me.'

Richard, sensing a gathering cloud of pregnant hormones heading his way, decided that this was not an auspicious moment for the planned conversation. You just never knew what would set her off these days. Hormones have a lot to answer for. 'I said I was sorry. I was trying to make an effort.'

It wasn't good enough, Tessa thought. Even a hug wouldn't have been good enough, but it would have been an improvement on the tea. She began to put the shopping away.

'Can I help?' asked Richard, hovering, not wanting to skulk off when he seemed to have upset her, and disappointed because he had quite been looking forward to telling her about his new plot.

'You'd better,' said Tessa ungraciously.

He sighed and pushed his chair back with a sudden scraping sound on the tiles. Charlie jumped and tried to hide behind Tessa, a pointless manoeuvre when he was so much bigger than she was. 'Can't you stop being so bad tempered? I was trying to help.'

'Yes,' said Tessa, feeling the baby kick, 'but you don't try to understand.'

'I do. That's unfair,' he said, wondering, not for the first time, if he was being compared to Tom and found wanting. 'Anyhow, all I did was offer you tea.'

'I hate tea,' she said, 'and I'm tired and hot and pregnant, and I've just fought my way around the supermarket, and now you offer me tea.' She knew she sounded unreasonable, but all she really wanted was a hug, and there clearly wasn't one on offer. Actually, sex would be even better than a hug, but sex was about as far from Richard's mind as the Planet Zog is from Walthamstow. She could tell. Tears prickled behind her eyes.

Richard put the kettle on. 'Do you want coffee?'

Tessa sniffed, not trusting herself to speak.

'Oh, for Heaven's sake!' he shouted. 'I just made the wrong bloody drink and you act as though I'm having an affair. I'll make coffee. Look. Coffee.' He waved the pot.

'I don't want it,' said Tessa, wishing she could turn the argument into a reconciliation, 'I'm not thirsty.'

Richard set the kettle back on its stand with a bang. 'Everyone else drinks tea,' he told it, trying to turn the row into a joke, 'and I managed to marry Coffee Woman.'

'What do you mean, "everyone else"?'

'Just that,' said Richard, 'everyone. All sixty million of us.'

'Everyone you've slept with, you mean,' said Tessa. She couldn't help it. The words just slipped out, or perhaps they were pushed, as all the insecurities of the last few months surged out of the woodwork like erupting death-watch beetles.

'Are you accusing me of mixing you up with my ex-girlfriends?' demanded Richard, outraged.

'Can't think why else you thought I drank tea,' muttered Tessa sulkily.

'I didn't think, that's the point,' said Richard, then, before he could stop himself, 'at least they didn't complain and sulk all the time.' He could have kicked himself, furious to have contributed to such a petty argument's interminability. The argument seemed to have taken on a life of its own, and it was carrying them both, kicking and screaming, whither it would.

'You mean at least they weren't *pregnant*!' shouted Tessa, shocking herself. She put her hands on her stomach as though to block the baby's ears.

Richard sighed, his anger dissolving. 'Is that what all this is about?'

Tessa began to cry. 'Carol was never pregnant. She was always smart and sexy. I bet you never went off her.'

'Carol doesn't matter now,' said Richard, trying to take her hands. 'I didn't *marry* Carol.'

An awful thought occurred to Tessa. She couldn't stop it from jumping out into the maelstrom – the argument was still in charge. 'Did you ever ask her?'

Richard's hesitation gave him away. He did not want to lie, and yet the truth was not going to help matters.

Tessa snatched her hands back. 'You did!' she accused.

'Well, I did once, but it wasn't serious—' he tried to take them again.

Tessa pushed him away. 'Oh, for God's sake, don't make me beat it out of you, just tell me.'

'All right. I asked her. She said "no", we split up. It was twelve years ago.'

'Then why did you lie?'

'I haven't lied,' said Richard exasperated, 'we've never discussed it. I don't know how many proposals *you* had. Anyway it means nothing now – we were young. You actually *got* married to Tom, for Heaven's sake. White dress, red roses, the lot. You don't hear me harping on about that.'

'No,' said Tessa, a tear running down the side of her nose, 'but you've never had to prise it out of me.'

'Look, you're overwrought,' said Richard, 'let's change the subject, shall we?'

Tessa couldn't. 'Not until you've told me about this.'

'There's nothing to tell.'

'But you must have been devastated when you broke up.'

'Not really. The relationship just finished, that's all.'

'You mean,' said Tessa, leaping a few mental light years and coming dangerously close to a conclusion she did not like, 'you cared enough to be in a relationship with her, but you didn't care when it ended. Wouldn't you care if our relationship ended?'

Richard tried to put his arms around her. 'Of course I would. I love you.'

Tessa sniffed. 'You told me I was the only one you'd ever loved. I haven't felt very loved lately, and now it sounds as if you loved Carol.'

Richard dropped his arm. 'You're starting to sound like Hugh. Look, I didn't love her. I was twenty-two years old. I just thought I was in love.'

'How do you know you don't just think you love me?' The baby kicked again, and more tears rolled. Poor baby, you can hear every word.

'Pretty long bloody delusion. Look, Tessa, I don't need this. You're impossible at the moment.'

'That's because you don't love me,' said Tessa, thinking, I know I'm making this worse and worse, but I can't seem to stop digging this hole. I sound pathetic.

'I do love you,' said Richard, 'this isn't about that at all.'

'It's not about tea either,' said Tessa, 'it's about sex.

Loads of affairs start when the wife is pregnant.'

'For crying out loud, I'm not having a bloody affair!' shouted Richard, goaded impossibly. 'Stop being so wet.'

'Now you're shouting,' said Tessa miserably, knowing she had provoked him, and not at all sure why.

'Oh, for Heaven's sake . . .' began Richard again, then gave up and stormed out of the house.

Tessa sat at the table and cried, but it didn't bring him back. Charlie came round and drooled hopefully on her feet, but she didn't notice. Claire strolled through a few moments later. Her mother had her head pillowed in her arms and seemed to be in tears. She hovered, wondering whether to say something, but what? 'Can I have a biscuit?' would sound a bit insensitive, but anything else was far too awkward. In any case, it was probably one of those hormone things. She sneaked away.

A little way away, as Richard drove angrily by, the man from the Council had arrived to check up on Mavis and her hogweed. Cyril Bender picked his way cautiously through Mavis's garden. He had become a cautious man since being given the Health and Safety job at the Council, for he had quickly learned that Suffolk was a perilous place, in Health and Safety terms. He had only recently taken over the job, and wanted to make his mark. On finding Mavis's file, a positive library of hogweed-related letters, he had concluded that this was a client he should visit. If this wasn't a case of wilful hogweed cultivation, then his name wasn't Cyril Bender, which it was. He hoped there would be no unpleasantness – only the previous week the proprietor of a delicatessen had tried to assault him with a Camembert, and who knew what kind of person might deliberately cultivate a Dangerous Weed?

Cyril was entirely red-green colour blind, which gave him an odd view of the world, and the world a somewhat extraordinary view of him. Reds and greens appeared to him as rather neutral shades, but this did not stop him from wearing them. On the contrary, he dressed as though he had undergone total immersion therapy with Rupert the Bear, in a series of clashing red, yellow and orange tartans which sometimes made old ladies gasp and point. Only the dark jacket he favoured over the top protected those he met from retinal burns. His choice of colour seemed inexplicable, since he perceived none of it. He had no idea that, from a distance, he resembled a Belisha beacon.

He was a scrawny man. If he had been a lamb chop, he would have taken only a minute to grill. He wore the kind of spectacles which make everything loom suddenly into your field of vision as if from nowhere. It was hardly surprising, then, that when Mavis Entwhistle appeared from behind a laurel bush, he was visibly shaken, for the combination of Mavis looming and a magnifying lens would have shaken most men.

'Mrs Mavis Entwhistle?' he asked, smiling to cover his nervousness. He had a smile like a muppet with toothache. 'I am Cyril Bender, Health and Safety.'

'Hello,' said Mavis, somewhat struck by his appearance and the crookedness of his smile. 'I'm Mavis Entwhistle.'

It took him a moment to take her in, for he was bemused. She was, he felt . . . indescribable. Cyril Bender stood and admired.

Mavis was not accustomed to admiring looks, except possibly from some zoo animals, and she was rather taken with his sheer gormlessness. 'Would you like to come in for a drink?'

'Oh, I don't drink,' said Cyril, blinking to check that she was real.

So Mavis made herb tea. She had certainly never

intended to drink any of it herself, for the depth of her belief in its powers was immense. Anyone with her preference for celibacy would be highly unwise to drink it in the company of a strange man, even a gormless one who was dressed like a tartan lollipop. Nevertheless, something must have upset her concentration, for drink it she did, and so she was hoist by her own petard, and a pretty hefty petard it must have been. Like Titania opening her eyes after Oberon had decided to have a bit of fun, Mavis looked at Cyril Bender and felt the Hand of Destiny upon her, as awe-inspiring as an advertisement for the National Lottery. Mavis was a victim of her own hogweed.

It was no less startling for Cyril Bender, and here any theory about magic potions only affecting the suggestible rather fell down. In all his years of inspecting drains and other foul wastes, he saw little that was beautiful. (Although once, when spec-less at the zoo, he had thought a hippo rather chraming.) Now he had met his match. 'Mrs Entwhistle,' he said bravely, 'Mavis. I would like very much to take you to tea.'

'I would be delighted,' said Mavis, quite practical now that she knew her fate was sealed. 'Now, about my hogweed . . .'

She still had her wits about her, Cyril could see. Preparing with joyous anticipation to be bribed – such opportunities come rarely in the field of drains and foul wastes – he had already decided to give in without a fight.

Meanwhile Richard, driving to and fro on the Broomhill by-pass, reflected that things seemed to have come to a poor pass. Communication lines were down and mangled in a communication-line mangling place. Whoever would think that such a pathetic row could begin with a cup of tea?

He pulled into a petrol station and filled up, noticing

absently that the maggot machine was chained and padlocked. What was happening to his marriage? His feelings for Tessa hadn't changed. She was still the same beautiful, scatty, insecure, lovable woman she had always been. He was pretty sure her feelings for him hadn't changed. So why are we rowing? But we've always rowed, he thought. It's the reconciliations which are missing. Our rows always used to end in good sex. Reconciliation and sex were one and the same thing.

The trouble was, he just didn't want to go home and have sex. There. He'd admitted it. He didn't want sex. But how could he explain that to Tessa? 'I just don't feel like sex at the moment,' he said aloud, experimentally, to the petrol pump.

'Good job, mate, I only do windscreens,' said the lad on the other side of it, and Richard mumbled an apology. Perhaps he should apologize to Tessa too, but then that would involve explaining about the sex, and he didn't really understand the problem himself. Perhaps it was just best to wait the whole thing out. She wouldn't be pregnant for ever, after all.

In fact, Tessa apologized first when he got home, so he apologized too, for the row, for the tea. He knew it didn't go far enough, of course, but it was the best he could do. Tessa could tell it was half-hearted. Clearly he didn't think he should be apologizing for anything.

'It was such a stupid row,' she told Charlie, when Richard had skulked off, leaving little tangible bits of poor communication hanging in the air, 'it wasn't even a good row. A good row might have cleared the air.' But so would good sex. God, I'm turning into a nymphomaniac.

Charlie put his head on her lap sympathetically. Sympathy was one of his strong points. He had that mournful expression which dogs do so well with their eyebrows, and which psychotherapists have been trying to copy successfully for decades. He sighed loudly and meaningfully.

'You love me, don't you Charlie?' Tessa patted his head.

Charlie raised his eyebrows in a show of quite incredible sympathy. He was sensitive to atmosphere, like most wolfhounds, for his great height meant that he was always up there in the middle when all the emotion was flying about.

'Oh, I know it's my hormones,' said Tessa, 'hormones have a lot to answer for. Look at Olive. Come on, let's take you for a walk.'

Surely only the truly cynical would have commented that a little doggy eyebrow wiggling could achieve quite a lot, when judiciously applied.

'You are a habitual wrongdoer,' said Keith to the teenaged Post Office robber in the dock, 'and I do not honestly believe that fining your unfortunate mother would do a great deal to prevent you from re-offending. Indeed, I have little hope that time will not take you from your present status as the Post Office Pick'n'Mix thief to the giddy heights of Marks and Spencer's menswear. However, because I do have that little hope, and because we are approaching the season of Goodwill to All Men, I am inclined this time to be lenient.'

The sullen miscreant took his finger from his ear, where he had been hoping to find enough wax to collect and roll into a ball to flick at the court clerk, and perked up. His mother glared at him furiously.

Keith waggled an admonishing finger at him, peering over his half-moon glasses. 'I will therefore refrain from sending you directly to a young offenders' institution. They have enough problems to cope with. Instead, you will have a seven-day suspended sentence, suspended on the condition that you attend St

Mary's church in your home town of Broomhill, four times in the next three months, and that you listen to the sermon.' The youth's mouth fell open, and the court reporter awoke from idling mode with a jump. What did the old buffer say? Confident that he now had their attention, Keith continued, 'You must also attend the Bumpstaple Festival of Lessons and Carols on Christmas Eve in St Julian's church at seven thirty, and there you will be required to read one of the lessons. I trust that you will find this to be a formative experience, sufficient to divert you from the path you appear to have chosen.' He banged his gavel firmly on his bench. 'Next case!'

The court reporter could not get out of court quickly enough. Sentencing people to church? Forcing them to read at a carol service? This would get into the nationals! How should she angle it? 'Old duffer magistrate violates defendant's religious freedom'? Or 'Broomhill courts uphold good old-fashioned values'?

Plump for the latter. Why not? It was a good time of year for a cheery story! She was dictating before she had even got into her car.

Chapter Twelve

The national newspaper journalists trailing the local papers for interesting stories were quick to spot the potential in the story of a local magistrate sentencing a young offender to attendance at his village carol service. By the following day, a positive posse of hard and cynical-looking hacks were displaying a forest of long lenses outside the manor, clogging up the mobile phone airwaves for miles around in their attempts to get an interview with Keith, Keith's wife, Keith's dog, anyone who knew Keith, and so on. Chatting amongst themselves, they had come to the conclusion that the 'good old-fashioned values' angle was the one that the editors would go for. It was one of those stories where it would not do to be the single journalist who put forth the opposite view. There had, it was true, been a few civil rights people on Kilroy that morning arguing about the US first amendment, but the mood of the press was going the other way. No-one wanted to be the prat who criticized Keith in print while the rest elevated him to the status of Solomon. He had, after all, they pointed out, offered the offender a choice. He could have chosen incarceration rather than church. He chose church.

Unfortunately for the Press, Keith was not at home. Marjorie was very pleasant to them, though, and invited them all in for tea and cake. They were all quite charmed by her, although the man from the *Sun* thought it was a shame she wasn't showing just a bit of cleavage, an attractive woman like that – it would have guaranteed his story a facing page position. The fruit cake was excellent, and, after pumping Marjorie for all the information they could about Keith, the robbery and the carol concert, they left, replete, to make their deadlines. Each hoped that he was the only one to have thought of doing a follow-up feature on the carol concert itself. Like most journalists, they spent much of their time in search of an exclusive story, but such things rarely exist unless they are not worth reading about. Since they all think the same way, this is hardly surprising. It can be a hard life, for newsworthy people seldom make decent tea and almost never offer home-made fruit cake. In this, at least, Marjorie had proved to be an exception.

They cornered Keith as he came out of the Magis-trate's Court at the end of his session. He was very pleased to see them, but he did not intend them to know it. He gave them a few well thought-out quotes for their columns, mainly along the lines that he hoped a trip to church would enable his robber to absorb some of the Christian virtues which overflowed with such abundance in St Julian's, particularly at Christmas.

They returned to their various editors well-pleased, ready to apply their particular house styles to the facts as they saw them, and Keith smiled to himself all the way home.

'Look at this, Ernest,' said Olive, when she visited him the following day, 'Keith and Marjorie Smythe are in the newspaper.' She felt rather proud that she resided in the same village as a couple who had attracted the admiration of the reporter from *The Times*. 'Listen: "Keith and Marjorie Smythe are the kind of good, church-going couple who form the backbone of rural

England." Goodness, Ernest, listen. "Marjorie Smythe, a most attractive woman, adores her dogs and her life in the sleepy Suffolk village of Bumpstaple." Goodness, we're named. I must cut this out!'

Back in the sleepy village itself, Sally was reading her mother's copy of a slightly less erudite tabloid. Mavis took all the tabloids – she liked to see if her competitors in the world of star-gazing were getting things right or not. You could never take your eyes off the opposition: one of them might pop straight into the National Lottery prediction slot, and Mavis hoped she would be next in line. Well, she would certainly be different from the woman they had now.

'Look at this, Mum,' said Sally, '"blonde, buxom Marjie Smythe" – Marjie! Ugh! – "sits at home cooking, while her JP husband Keith doles out old-fashioned justice to Suffolk's young thugs."'

'What's that?' asked Mavis.

'The Smythes. In the paper,' said Sally. 'It seems that Keith has sentenced some lad to come to the carol concert.'

'Must be quite a criminal to deserve that,' said Mavis cheerfully. She had, Sally thought, been particularly cheerful lately. 'Mind you, he's hardly likely to turn up.'

'He'll have to,' said Sally. 'They'll check up on him. The place will be packed full of probation officers.'

'And reporters, I should think,' said Mavis. She and Sally looked at one another, realization dawning simultaneously. A big audience. 'Clever old Keith!'

Tessa saw it on *News East*, where it briefly attracted her attention away from the back page of *The Times*.

'Look, it's Mr Smythe on TV!' Hugh shouted, and they all temporarily abandoned their breakfasts to rush into the sitting-room and watch.

'I'm not sure I like the sound of that,' said Claire

huffily, 'some yob reading at the carol concert.'

'That'll make two of you, then,' said Hugh, ducking.

'Takes one to know one,' said Claire.

'Oh, do shut up, you two,' said Tessa, 'we want to listen.'

The report showed Marjorie and her dogs in the kitchen.

'She does look so much better without the head scarf,' commented Claire, 'don't you think so, Richard?'

'Can't say I'd noticed,' said Richard. 'Awful shoes.'

True, thought Tessa, they were awful shoes. She wondered if perhaps Marjorie's mirror didn't go down that far. She returned to *The Times*. 'The Outer Hebrides have been put on Duck Alert,' she read. 'The ducks are thought to be approaching the Western Isles.'

'Oh, right.' Richard was reading the sports pages.

'I've decided to elope with the electricity man,' said Tessa.

'Oh, right,' said Richard.

Tessa sighed. 'No-one hears me in this house.'

'I heard you,' said Hugh, 'and so did Spotty Muldoon.'

'Creep,' said Claire, 'just wait until you get spots.' It occurred to her that perhaps Mavis could offer something to help on the spot front. It would be better than taking hormones. Look what hormones had done to her mother. 'Those ducks will be worth a lot of money when they land, won't they?' she said to Tessa.

'I suppose they will,' said Tessa. 'I would have liked one.'

'It's a pity you're not charging an entrance fee to the carol concert,' said Richard, switching back into the conversation as suddenly as he had switched out of it. 'It's bound to be full of reporters now. You might have made enough to spend a few months floating in the sea off the Isle of Lewis, waiting for one to swim your way.'

Tessa sniffed, not liking to be the butt of his humour when she was not the butt of his affection. 'I can think of a few people I'd like to pay to float in the sea off the Isle of Lewis indefinitely,' she said pointedly.

'You could pay me to do it,' offered Hugh hopefully, 'I'm cheap.'

'You'd be useless. You couldn't catch a plastic duck if it was glued to your head,' said Claire scornfully.

Hugh mustered a dignified look. 'Geniuses,' he said, 'are always misunderstood.'

Marjorie was also watching the report. God, she thought, those shoes make me look like a character from *The Magic Roundabout*. One of the dogs sat lovingly on her feet, and she slipped them out of her shoes. 'You can have them,' she told the dog, 'I'm going to wear something else.' Overwhelmed with gratitude, the dog embraced her shoes wholeheartedly. Like most Labradors, he was not mean with his saliva. Well, I couldn't wear it now, Marjorie told herself.

It took her a while to extract the white stilettos from her wardrobe, as the box was right at the back. When finally, after all these years, she put them on, they were too tight. Not only that, they did not look as she remembered them. Balanced precariously on painfully pinched feet, she looked at herself in the mirror, and realized that they looked dated and incredibly tarty. Perhaps she needed a different look.

Robert also saw *News East*, and it gave him an idea. He telephoned Broomhill's local radio station. Put through to one of the programme controllers, he asked them if they would be interested in Bumpstaple's Christmas Eve carol concert. It would make good listening, he told them, he was sure of that.

The controller noted down his offer and promised to pass it on at the next production meeting. After hanging up, she placed it wearily in the stack of other worthy local suggestions, on top of the man who could play 'Jingle Bells' using a banana skin and the woman who believed that some herb biscuits she had bought locally had turned her into a sex maniac and cured her hernia. She didn't even listen any more, as most callers were completely barmy. The ones that sounded plausible were usually TV practical jokes show hosts in disguise. It was better not to get involved.

The following weekend, Claire went to London. She usually looked forward to weekends with her father, as they were times of treats and liberation, of staying up late and being allowed wine, of hearing different, more fashionable swear words than the ones Tessa used – 'Oh Bloody Hell' was so passé – and of sleeping in a room decorated with framed newspaper articles which her father had written. Tessa had once called her bedroom at Tom's The Shrine to Ego, but Claire, not realizing who Ego was, had not understood. Sadly, in the world-wide species race to extinction, Latin teachers were at the front of the queue, so Claire and her peers had been deprived for ever of a source of irony available only to those who have chanted 'bellum, bellum, bellum, belli, bello, bello' and have learned that 'Me transmitte sursum, Caledoni!' means 'Beam me up, Scotty!'

There hadn't been a weekend with Dad for a while, and she ought to have looked forward to this one. She told herself over and over again that she *was* looking forward to it, to the extent that she snapped at Tessa for suggesting that her inability to find the right clothes to take with her stemmed more from her ambivalent mood than from Tessa's failure to buy her enough of them. Tessa suspected that she feared some blonde siren from St Hilda's would strut into Bumpstaple in her absence and pursue Josh for a date. She did not say so, in case she was wrong and thus planted an insecurity in Claire which she would not otherwise have had. Josh was such a nice boy, not the type to be tempted away. Was it because he was a vicar's son? After all, you couldn't imagine Robert being easily tempted, although even vicars must want a sex life sometimes. She herself had only been deprived of hers for a few months, and already she was getting desperate. Pregnant women aren't supposed to get desperate – but then neither are vicars.

Claire did not want her mother to guess at her terrible fear, the fear that the entirety of the hormonally charged fifth form would descend on Bumpstaple wearing skin-tight leggings and see-through tops with visible bras just as soon as she got on the London train. Admitting it aloud seemed to make it more likely, somehow, and in any case she was far too proud to admit to feeling insecure.

Dad and June lived in a trendy three-storey house in Canonbury. It had iron railings, white walls and Habitat Japanese lanterns. They drank cappuccino for breakfast from a big stainless steel monster in their sleek, marble-topped kitchen, and Dad made crêpes suzettes at the table when they had guests. Dad was very good at crêpes suzettes – he always made a point of being very good at everything he did. Those things he did not do, and they included keeping pigs and painting pictures, were not worth doing. That had always been made very clear to Claire.

Dad and June always entertained at the weekend, and Claire had always enjoyed staying up until midnight while people who were incredibly important in London, because they wrote for the newspapers, chatted and laughed and drank. It had always annoyed her that Tessa never seemed to have heard of any of them. Tessa never had interesting dinner parties with wittily sarcastic guests who smoked French cigarettes and drank Campari. Tessa would not allow anyone to smoke in the house, and in any case, her dinner parties were always casual supper parties for friends who were far too familiar to be interesting.

This Saturday night was to be another dinner party. Apparently Felix and Miranda were very big in interior design, and their daughter was Claire's age. June was making something complicated and Italian, and Claire was sent down to the local supermarket for sun-dried tomatoes.

It was a lovely, bright, crisp November day, a glad-to-be-alive sort of day. The pavements of Upper Street reverberated with the roar of passing heavy goods vehicles belching particulate emissions into the Islington atmosphere as they poured from the A1 into Central London, and Claire found herself feeling slightly wistful because she would not see the woods of Bumpstaple today, walk with Josh through the crunchy grass and smell the frost on the leaves of the holly trees as Charlie raced ahead and panted steam. It was not that she missed home, she told herself, for where she was now was far more *happening,* but she did miss Josh. She tried not to imagine him encircled by a crowd of predatory lipsticked girls with jiggling breasts and the kind of fingernails which cello players cannot hope to grow.

Unfortunately, there were workmen engaged in making gratuitous holes in the pavement just down from Canonbury Villas, and Claire came out of her daydream to realize that she would have to pass them. She had got too close, dawdling along thinking of Josh and the breasts of her rivals, to cross to the other side without being obvious.

She suffered from the teenage-girl paranoia that every man everywhere was looking at her with a kind of derogatory lust. Paranoia is usually a delusional state, but in the case of men digging up roads, it can be an appropriate one, as, unfortunately, it was now. These men were being paid weekend rates to do this job, and they wanted to make it last. As Claire approached, they were lolling against their pneumatic drills, bum-spotting. They clearly *had* been working, as they were hot. At least, that was one explanation for their wearing only tight T-shirts and tattoos with their jeans. The cynical might have deduced that they had, in fact, worked just enough to get just hot enough to strip down to their biceps – biceps which had been developed more in the gym than by any genuine exertion with the pneumatic drill. They had the weathered, russet tans of men who do not like to cover any part of their bodies and, by doing so, deprive the female population of a visual treat, and they perked up when they saw Claire approaching.

Claire averted her eyes. She was caught in the awful unresolvable dilemma of whether to smile at them and thus invite sexual innuendo, or look away disdainfully and attract sneers and insults. At fifteen, an indifferent approach is impossible – indeed, by the time most women are old enough to be indifferent they long for the odd wolf whistle to be indifferent to.

The workmen approved of the length of Claire's skirt, they said, and they were quite interested in her cup size. They suggested that she tried a Wonderbra and advised her to replace her Doc Martens with something with a nice high heel. She should, they said, get herself a real man, which would help. They did not pass comment on her face.

Claire stalked past, mortified, even though it was no worse than she had expected. That was the trouble with London. No-one working on the road in Bump-staple would have treated her like that, she was sure. They would all know Tessa or Sally or someone else in

237

the village, and would be ashamed to be offensive lest they were recognized. Suddenly Claire felt rather homesick. It was thanks to June and her bloody sun-dried tomatoes that she had to do this, *and* she was going to have to walk miles around noisy, trendy *sodding* Islington to skirt these *dickheads* and get home. She could hardly ring June and ask her to come and fetch her in the car. Even if June was understanding about it, it would take hours to get the car through the traffic, and June was busy making black pasta and was already in a panic about finishing her cooking in time. *Black pasta?*

Reaching the safe haven of the small supermarket, Claire picked up a basket. There were hardly any trolleys – very few people could afford a whole trolley-load from here. It smelt of supermarkets, but at least they were playing Capital Radio, rather than that awful jingly stuff.

The sun-dried tomatoes were not immediately apparent. After exploring various other sorts of tomatoes which, presumably, were either still wet or had dried in bad weather, Claire looked for someone to ask. 'If it's not on the shelf we haven't got it,' said the girl stacking shelves, without looking up.

'Yes, but where *should* it be?' asked Claire, in her most patient voice – this was not a very patient one, but she tried.

'Sorry, I only stack shelves,' said the girl, uninterested. Her badge said, 'My name is Alison and I'm here to help you.'

Claire sighed. One thing you could say for Olive Osborne, she never left anyone to fend for themselves in her shop. Come to think of it, another thing you could say for her was that she didn't sell sun-dried tomatoes.

'You OK, love?'

Claire turned. It was one of the workmen from

outside. He looked different with a wire basket over his arm and a packet of Thai fragrant rice in his hand.

'I can't find the sun-dried tomatoes,' she said, emboldened by the rice. His buying fragrant rice, rather than the quick-cook variety, put him in a different category from the one to which she had previously assigned him in her mind. A man who ate fragrant rice might know about sun-dried tomatoes.

'Here,' he said, 'have mine, darling. I can always get some more.'

Claire snatched them and muttered a thank you. That look and that 'darling' put him straight back in with the louts.

Walking back, Claire thought that the trouble with London was that she didn't know the rules. Even the road repairers in Islington ate this fancy stuff. It was quite funny really. Mum would laugh; she was always talking about not wasting time stuffing mushrooms, but would Dad and June understand? Somehow she thought not. They'd have to appreciate what pretentious food they were serving in the first place. She wouldn't tell them. For a moment, she found herself wishing she was home. There is nothing more welcoming than a shared sense of humour, and there was nothing to lose at home as she wasn't under pressure to have a good time. She remembered Josh saying, 'I think your mum's great.' Was her mum great? No, hippie pig-lovers couldn't be great, but then Dad could be annoying too, with that habit of wearing black everything, and now June was even making pasta to match him. Claire realized that she would much prefer one of Tessa's big lasagnes, made in the huge dish which didn't quite fit into the Aga, so that she had to keep rotating it to cook it properly.

She sighed, and tried to rediscover her usual enjoyment of her London weekends. It was surely Mum's fault if she wasn't having a good time – she was the one who had brought her up to be a country person. If I'd grown up in London, she thought, then I'd enjoy it here. It's Mum's fault I don't fit in, her fault for splitting up with Dad and living in the sticks.

Still, the little niggling feeling that a weekend at home would have felt much less like hard work persisted into dinner. Felix and Miranda were fashionable in a truly dreadful way, and their daughter was called Portia and thought far too much of herself. She had nothing but scorn to pour on life in the country, and after hearing that Claire not only lived in a village but was also taught by nuns, she affected to treat her as though she was a bit of something someone had dug up at Sutton Hoo.

'Do you really only have one boyfriend?' she asked pityingly.

'One,' said Claire loyally, 'is all I need.'

'Honestly, Darling,' Miranda was saying, 'everyone wants slate now, and sleek is so *in*, you know. Fussy is completely *out*.'

'Oh dear,' said Tom, gently teasing, 'd'you hear that, Claire?'

'What?' she asked.

'Stripped pine kitchens and racks of dried flowers are *out*. Best not to tell your mum, heh?' He grinned conspiratorially.

Claire found that she did not feel conspiratorial. Without stopping to wonder why she suddenly disliked being subtly placed beside Dad and against Mum she said, 'I much prefer our kitchen at home.'

There was a tiny embarrassed silence, then Miranda jumped in. 'Oh dear, I didn't mean to offend,' she said, 'it is only fashion, you know. We're just interior designers. We have to keep up like lemmings. Silly, really. Your mum's got the right idea. I'm sure pine is far more practical in the country.'

240

She meant well, but somehow Claire was left feeling like Worzel Gummidge. She could feel a tightness in her throat. She was supposed to be gracious to Miranda, she knew, but Miranda had been instrumental in her feeling stupid and she did not want to be gracious.

'Come on, Claire,' that was Dad, still teasing, hiding his surprise. He was accustomed to playing on Claire's anti-Tessa stance for a little comradely fun every so often. He had certainly not intended to provoke her into leaping to Tessa's defence. 'I was only joking, you know that.'

Claire shrugged, hating the fact that everyone was looking at her, and June, realizing her discomfort, changed the subject. 'D'you want to sneak out for a smoke?' asked Portia quietly as the adults turned to the state of the property market.

'No thanks,' said Claire, 'I don't smoke.'

'Really? How strange,' said Portia, adopting her archaeologist face again. 'I bet you've never smoked pot, either.'

Claire gave up any attempt at politeness. She was hating the evening. It had been a trendy, smoke-and-eat-nasty-black-pasta-with-squids'-bits sort of evening, and Miranda's perfume was making her eyes water. God knows what squid did to spots. Imagine if they turned black or worse, some other colour. Who knew what was in squid ink? Mind you, she had noticed, smugly, that Portia had spots under her make-up. It would be almost worth a few smudges to see Portia turn into an ink-blot.

'You're a real victim, did you know that?' she said to Portia.

Portia shrugged. She was where it was at, she felt. She had nothing to prove.

The party broke up soon after that. Dad and June were terribly nice, and they didn't say a word about

241

her sulking, but Claire could positively feel their tact. She knew they would tell one another in bed that she was at an awkward age, and that it was nothing to worry about. What a bloody patronizing thing to say. Everyone at school heard their parents saying that about them. They all agreed it made them want to throw up. In a flash of annoyance with Dad and June for something she didn't even know they were saying, although in fact she was right and they were saying just that, Claire thought hopefully that at least it would stop them enjoying sex tonight.

She took the usual train home. She didn't want to upset Dad, or make too much of her wish to be home, so she made herself refuse when he offered to take her to an earlier one. She could tell that he and June thought perhaps she was snappy with PMT – June had left some sanitary towels casually out in the bathroom in case she needed them but was too embarrassed to ask. They were wrong about the PMT, Claire told herself. It was Josh she was missing, he was the reason for her sudden impatience with the atmosphere of repressed tact in London. Mum and Richard certainly weren't part of the attraction of home. As the train swept through Essex, she indulged in her favourite fantasy, the one in which she ran away to some unspecified Utopia and her mother, father, Richard and June appeared on *The Nine o'clock News* weeping and begging her to come home safely. It worked. By the time she reached Audley End, she was quite cheerful.

Tessa, driving over to meet her off the London train, got stuck behind a huge yellow hedgecutter negotiating the road at less than two miles per hour. The man operating it ignored her completely, in an absolute sort of way which he had obviously honed by years of driving tractors along East Anglian roads. She did not dare overtake him on these bends. She sighed and looked at her watch. Claire's train would be in already.

At Audley End station, Claire read a series of complaining letters from frustrated commuters which British Rail had mysteriously elected to mount on the station wall in a glass case. Presumably this was an alternative to doing anything about them. A white-haired man and a smoking youth were waiting with her. The youth was leering, and Claire shut down her peripheral vision and concentrated on the letters.

The first complained about the absence of a breakfast car on the 6.52 to Liverpool Street. Next to it another bemoaned the presence of a breakfast car on the 7.02. On second thoughts, Claire told herself, perhaps British Rail knew very well what they were doing in mounting the letters. She had just begun one from a woman complaining about the quality of passengers on the 9.32 when a voice at her shoulder said, 'What's yer name, then, love?' It was the lout.

Claire summoned up her coldest voice. 'I have a boyfriend,' she said, the resultant blast of dry ice withering her admirer where he stood.

'Blimey. No need to bite my head off,' he said, backing off. A car pulled up and hooted, and he rushed over to get in and be driven away.

Claire glanced over at the older man, and he smiled. 'Hard to fend them off, is it?'

She shrugged, then, deciding he wasn't being sarcastic, said, 'Not my type.'

'Nor mine, actually,' said the man. Claire looked at him, startled. 'Sorry, love,' he said, 'didn't mean to shock you.'

'Oh, I wasn't, I mean, I didn't catch . . . are you . . . ?'

'Woopsy, dear.'

'Oh.' But you're old, thought Claire, I thought only young people were gay – but then old people are just young people a few years on. Does everyone have

243

the same problems, through all the generations? Did Mum have my problems?

Tessa pulled up, flushed, and stalled the Landrover.

'My lift,' said Claire awkwardly, feeling that she had shared an intimacy and should not now leave casually.

The man peered past her. 'Pretty woman. That your mum?'

'Yes. I'm surprised you think so,' said Claire, the anonymity of the encounter allowing her to be direct.

'You don't have to drink sea water to enjoy sailing on it,' he grinned and nodded.

Claire was still trying to work that one out when Tessa started the car again, and with a little nod back, she hurried over to her mother. Her pretty mother, apparently.

Tessa was surprised at the lack of hostility. Normally Claire arrived home from Tom's quite unbearable. It usually began with her arrival in the wrong car, with the wrong-shaped space in the back for Claire's stuff and the wrong sort of door handles. Weekends in London seemed to emphasize the high levels of wrongness with which Tessa surrounded her. Today she had expected her late arrival to make things even worse: for this meant she had kept Claire waiting at what she had once referred to as a 'country-bumpkin station less stimulating than a blank video'. Stations in London, where Tom kept her waiting, sold knickers and cappuccino.

Now, though, Claire slipped cheerfully into the car and said 'hello' with what sounded like genuine warmth. Tessa even got a kiss on the cheek. Claire was glad to be back in Suffolk. She'd take her chances with Hugh rather than po-faced Portia any day, and she might even tell Tessa about the awful black pasta.

'Was that old chap bothering you?' asked Tessa as she drove out of the car park, wondering if Claire's apparent pleasure at being picked up was actually the relief of escape.

The bubble broke, and Claire's usual persona jumped into her seat like a lead balloon. 'Honestly, Mother, not everyone is a pervert!' she said scornfully.

Tessa sighed. At least she hadn't collected the wrong person from the station – she had begun to wonder, for a minute. She concentrated on the gear lever, as her theory that pregnancy somehow interfered with the brain's ability to synchronize gear-hand with clutch-foot was trying to prove itself again.

Claire settled back into her seat and winced obviously and enjoyably every time her mother ground the gears. She was content that the battle lines were properly drawn. Battle lines were familiar, and without them it was difficult to be cross – she had not yet reached the stage of realizing that it is possible not to be cross. She was glad that she would see Josh soon, glad that Tessa's friends did not design steel kitchens and that dinner would not be squid, glad that she could be comfortably cross with Tessa without anyone making a big thing out of it or saying it was her age. She just didn't want her mother getting the wrong idea about it, that was all. She might think she'd done something right and stop trying. Think how awful things could get around here if she, Claire, didn't complain all the time, and in any case, if life ceased to be such a battle, how could she hope to win?

245

Chapter Thirteen

Claire hated rugby. Even the nicest of boys seemed to become complete animals on the rugby pitch. She was not yet at the stage when the sight of those firmly muscled thighs and sweating, masculine bodies grappling in heaps in the frosty air represented the first floor on the escalator to Nirvana. Besides, when Josh was playing he seemed to become completely oblivious to her. She was quite certain that even if she ran naked on to the field he would only come near her if she picked up the ball and went for a try. For this reason, she had elected not to watch him playing for the first fifteen against Ickleford School, even though there was such a supporting crowd of parents and schoolmasters on the sideline that any accusations of bimboism would have been easily countered. She did not go straight home from the bus stop either: she had a dilemma on the go. Hugh waited by the bridge for a while, hoping to goad her into turning red, but eventually the thought of the thousands of uneaten cornflakes in Tessa's kitchen overcame him and he hurried on alone.

Tessa came in from feeding scraps to Lysander, to find Hugh deep in a vast bowl of breakfast cereal. What is it about small boys and cornflakes, she wondered. Claire never did this. 'Where's Claire?' she asked him.

'Dunno,' said Hugh, with the verbal clarity of the honey monster.

'Was she on the bus?' asked Tessa, trying to remember if she had forgotten any important school events. Open day was next week, but her name was already mud at St Hilda's for failing to come and support the inter-house netball competition, even though Claire was only second reserve in the fourth team. (As there were only four teams, it had seemed reasonable to conclude that, as Claire had said, netball wasn't her thing, and Tessa's presence was not essential.)

'Yes,' said Hugh, 'I think she went to see Sally.'

Tessa wondered idly if Claire knew anything about Sally's love life, or the possible presence of Robert being in it. No. Even if there were some sort of secret romance developing, Claire would never notice. She was far too wrapped up in her own romance, and in any case Tessa was sure that, at Claire's age, she would have assumed that a vicar was practically a monk and that Sally, being over thirty, was way past that sort of thing. Claire had seemed to think that Tessa's pregnancy must have been conceived in a test tube, as they could not possibly still be Doing It. Tessa pointed out that of course they still Did It, and so did Claire's father, and why did Claire think he got married again recently if he didn't? Claire professed disgust, then wanted to know exactly *when* they Did It, which rather put an end to the conversation.

She put a cheese pie into the oven, reflecting that recently she seemed not to have made the wrong food or bought the wrong cheese quite as often as in the past. Claire was definitely improving. Was the awkward age coming to an end, or was this a temporary window of opportunity, due to her having Hugh to focus all her angst upon and Josh to alleviate her boredom?

Claire called round to see Mavis, to ask if she could provide a spot remedy. As she asked, she did wonder whether it was a little absurd to think that Mavis might be able to help, when her own appearance was so – well – ghastly. Perhaps Mavis, being well and truly past it, simply had no need of beauty. Like most teenagers, Claire believed that beauty was essential for the entrapment and retention of the Opposite Sex, without whom life would obviously be pointless. The idea that someone might actually be happy looking like a warthog did not occur to her. Only advertising boffins have the same complete inability to understand that there may be another point of view, which is why they are convinced there is no woman anywhere who is not constantly worried about the whiteness of her wash and the shape of her sanitary towels.

Mavis was delighted to see Claire. She offered her a dock leaf and stinging nettle application for the spots, together with a packet of hogweed tonic for Tessa.

'Half the village are drinking it, you know,' said Claire. 'I'm surprised Bumpstaple isn't having a huge orgy.'

'Ssshh,' Mavis eyed the walls suspiciously, 'you haven't told anyone, have you?'

'Of course not,' said Claire indignantly, 'I can keep a secret. Are those biscuits of yours magic too?'

'Dandelion,' said Mavis, 'made from the leaves, dear.'

'What are they for?' asked Claire, fascinated yet horrified to think that she, along with the rest of the choir, had partaken. Perhaps they would all start to look like Mavis. She swallowed.

'They perk people up,' said Mavis, 'make people sing higher.'

'Ah,' said Claire, 'you mean Mrs Osborne.'

Mavis smiled. 'I don't think I specified.'

'You didn't need to,' said Claire. 'Uncle Richard thinks she beats Mr Osborne – and I did see him limping.'

'Ernest Osborne has hidden depths,' said Mavis, mysteriously.

'They must be hidden pretty deep,' said Claire, 'he looked as though someone had done him an injury.'

'Limping or dragging?' asked Mavis, thinking of remedies.

'Kind of a waddle,' said Claire.

'Ah,' said Mavis, 'that'll be the hogweed tonic starting to work. You watch Mrs Osborne – you'll see a difference.'

'Why? What do you mean?'

But Mavis would not elaborate.

When she got home, Claire retreated to her bedroom, pausing only to check that the cheese pie had no spot-provoking butter in it. She blamed her mother's cooking a little less for the spots these days, having discovered that Zoe Ormondroyd, who had never had a spot in her life, lived on fish and chips. Mind you, that meant it must all be in the genes, and where were her genes from?

Upstairs, she sniffed at Mavis's spot potion, then got out the little packet of twenty-one innocuous-looking white tablets which she had obtained from a rather coy lady GP. Should she hedge her bets and take both? A day with spots was a day wasted, and yet if she used both, and the spots got better, she would never know which one had worked and would be forced to continue with both indefinitely.

On the plus side for the potion, it was natural. Mavis's abilities were already proven, and it would not do anything unexpected to her breasts. On the minus side, it smelt like drains and it might stain her face green.

Then there was this Pill. Claire, as a child of the

249

eighties, had a healthy respect for anything which came in a blister pack. On the plus side, it might give her bigger breasts, and it would also confer contraception. On the minus side, look what hormones were doing to her mother, and what if it actually *arrested* her breast growth? She was not sure that she really wanted its contraceptive properties, and she had read somewhere that it was made from the urine of menopausal Italian nuns. She dithered.

Olive, a short distance away, had no such reservations about her HRT. Even if Italian nuns had had direct involvement in the production of her little plasters she would still have used them. She was now in no doubt – her hair was starting to curl. She was a woman in waiting. She was a woman whose husband had an implant. She had already begun to spread the news around the village that Ernest had a groin injury, to explain his odd limp; she had no real concept of what a groin injury was, but since the England cricket team got them they must be OK.

It was that week that things began to get seriously wintry. Every year there comes a morning when that certain numbness of the tip of the nose begins, that willingness to go back indoors for gloves, even though you have already started the car, that feeling that electric lock warmers are not such a naff idea after all, and in Bumpstaple it had arrived. By the weekend, no-one even bothered to mention the frost patterns on the windows any more.

Tessa gazed out of a coffee shop window at Bury St Edmunds market place, a chaotic surge of people and colour which must have had the same feel to it for five hundred years. That sense of an urgency to exchange goods and money whilst shouting unintelligibly in cheerful marketese would not have altered at all.

250

You could tell at once that it was December, for the vegetable stalls were seething with people panic-buying sprouts. They were not content to buy a pound or two, they were buying huge sacks of sprouts. To Tessa, the sacks evoked Dickensian scenes of misery, of worn women endlessly peeling off the outer leaves and cutting neat crosses in the top of each sprout while their families pored over the Christmas and New Year issue of *The Radio Times*, putting stars next to all the TV programmes they wanted to watch. This, she felt, was the unbending tradition of the sprout.

Across the square, in Marks and Spencers, rich people were buying sprouts in which the crosses had already been made by smart shop assistants who did not object to Dickensian tasks, if it meant that they could work for an employer who also provided subsidized hairdressing and on-site cervical smears. (One manager had actually suggested that their customers might like to get their cervical smears there, too. A discreet wave of their account card over by the chicken tikka ready meal, and they could be all fixed up for another three years.) Tessa detested sprouts. She detested their taste, she hated their colour, and she abhorred their smug expectation that neat crosses should be cut in their tops. She believed that sprouts, like radishes and Jerusalem artichokes, were of use only to those who were not embarrassed by flatulence, and otherwise should be fed only to chickens. The thought of what might happen if she fed them to Lysander was too unpleasant to contemplate.

Bury was full of Christmas shoppers and animal rights activists. These latter were always particularly active on the Saturday approaching Christmas, when the cattle markets were going on, and they liked to nobble the mums and dads watching the pretty pink pigs and point out that they were heading in a lorry straight for the land of pork pie. The mums and dads would then be consumed by guilt at the thought that their morning bacon had once run around a cattle pen, rather than evolving spontaneously in slices on a polystyrene tray, and sign the petition.

Tessa normally avoided the cattle market because it made her feel guilty. Today, though, there was nowhere to park other than the cattle market car park, so she wedged the Landrover between Mike's Sunny-farm egg van and an empty cattle lorry, in order to sort out Claire's requirements for Christmas shopping.

They agreed that Claire would shop while Tessa drank endless cups of coffee and spent considerable time queueing for lavatories in Bury's charming selection of tea shops. She was now on her fifth coffee in Le Cafetière. She was not enjoying Le Cafetière, which was ostentatiously and inappropriately French. It boasted a huge crystal chandelier and the kind of wallpaper which little children like to pick off bit by bit. It was testimony to the belligerence of the staff that none had done so, but then children were clearly not welcome in there, and from the sullenness of the waitress, it appeared that this applied even while they were gestating. The waitress matched the wallpaper quite well, in that she was very pink and almost entirely lacking in charm.

Tessa allowed her gaze to drift around the walls, noticing the collection of pencil sketches featuring rather French-looking nudes; closer study revealed that, although their faces differed, their breasts were all the same, which she thought was rather odd. Best not to ask the waitress about that, she thought. She resolved to leave. It was clear that she was not particularly welcome to stay without ordering more food, and she was far too full to do so, indeed, she never wanted to see apple strudel with cream again for the rest of her life.

Outside, the crowds of shoppers seemed to be

surging in one direction. Probably one of those discount traders had set up, she thought, the ones who sell a bale of sixty towels for two pounds to a stooge. As the piped music moved into 'We Three Kings' performed by a pop star, Tessa waved at the waitress for her bill. She heard the song as 'We three kings of Leicester Square, Selling knickers tuppence a pair'. Hugh had better not try anything like that at the concert. Where was Claire?

She paid the bill, leaving a guilt-induced tip for the pink waitress, and put on her coat, then she spotted her daughter, making her way with difficulty through the throng and into the tea room. She was loaded with carrier bags.

'Did you get everything?'

'Most things,' said Claire cheerfully. The endless carols she had heard in shops all about the town had left her mellow and Christmassy. 'I'm just stuck on Josh.'

Tessa nodded, 'I have the same trouble with Richard.' She was conscious of a touch of mother-daughter bonding and tried to take advantage of it. 'I know where you might look.'

'I don't want socks,' said Claire at once.

'Socks? Come on, when have I ever bought Richard socks?' Tessa opened the door and smiled goodbye to the waitress, who ignored her.

'Well. I can't buy him flavoured condoms, can I?' said Claire.

'How did you know about that?' Tessa closed the door behind her and saw that the waitress was giggling. Clearly she must have hidden depths.

'Aha,' said Claire, 'nothing's secret, especially when it's hidden on top of the – what's going on?'

As they headed out into the market place, there was a definite sense of stepping into a current of people, a feeling of being swept in a direction in which you did not plan to go, as if striding into the centre of a herd of stampeding wildebeeste. Why wildebeeste might be stampeding towards Marks and Spencers was not immediately clear, unless it had something to do with the fear of having to prepare their own sprouts.

'Everyone seems to be running away from something,' said Claire, trying to see through the people, but the hundreds of hassled shoppers, weighted with aftershave sets and bargain wrapping paper, were very tangled up in one another, and she could not see between them.

It took them a little while to struggle against the tide across the market place back towards the car but when, eventually, they reached the edge, they encountered a scene of devastation. The contents of three market stalls, which had been selling Christmas trees and mistletoe, were scattered across the ground. A man dressed as Santa rushed past them carrying an inflatable reindeer.

'What's going on?' Claire shouted after him.

'Bullocks,' he called, rushing away.

'Well, really,' said Claire, 'I don't see why . . .' she trailed into silence as several very large bovine creatures lumbered menacingly out of the cattle market gate and into the street immediately ahead. They were, perhaps, fifteen feet away.

'Oh God,' said Claire.

The creatures stopped and eyed them squarely.

'It's OK,' said Tessa, more calmly than she felt, 'they're only bullocks. They're not aggressive.' Such things can be difficult to say with any real conviction when all that stands between you and several hundredweight of rare beef is a heap of mistletoe and Santa's hat.

'They looked pissed off,' said Claire uneasily. The bullocks were milling ominously. 'Do we run?'

'No,' said Tessa, more confidently than she felt,

'walk slowly. Into that shop.' They edged across the pavement. The shop was, appropriately enough, a china shop. It was also closed for lunch. Now Tessa could clearly see the ring through the nose of the big one. Do bullocks usually have rings?

'Damn,' said Claire, 'I'd even have bought a china plate.'

'Oy there you buggers!' shouted a man in a flat cap in broad Norfolk, appearing from nowhere. Tessa opened her mouth to protest, then realized he did not mean her. More men appeared, and began to remove the cattle.

'Thank goodness,' said Tessa, 'I couldn't have run far in my condition.'

'They *were* only bullocks,' said Claire, embarrassed to have been afraid, 'we should just have smacked them and clapped our hands.'

'Good job you didn't,' said the man, coming over, 'them're bulls. Bloody big 'uns.'

'Golly,' said Claire.

'Why on earth are they free, then?' asked Tessa, starting to feel righteously cross.

'Them bluddy animal righters,' said the man in disgust, 'let 'um out, and lost my pigs. They've ruined my best bull.'

'Why?' asked Claire curiously, 'why's he ruined?'

'In with thum cows,' said their companion, 'had 'is early Christmas, 'im. Insatiabull, I call it.'

Tessa thought that was quite witty for a farmer. She sensed a kindred spirit. 'I have a pig,' she said, 'named Lysander.'

The man looked at her pityingly. 'I'm sure you 'ave,' he said, 'but at least your'n isn't shopping in Woolworths.' He sighed and wandered off in search of his errant livestock, who were doubtless having a grand old time in the pick 'n' mix.

'Golly,' said Claire, 'we could have been in real danger.'

'I suppose so,' said Tessa, thinking, I feel so bovine that it's a wonder the bull didn't fancy me. 'I can certainly understand Santa having made a run for it, especially when you consider the colour of his outfit.'

Claire giggled. 'After what that man said, I can understand him taking his reindeer too. It was really a bull's version of a blow-up sex doll, wasn't it? Could have driven him crazy.'

Tessa erupted into laughter. 'Claire! You're not supposed to know about such things!' Thank Heavens our children educate each other, she thought, it's bad enough when you have to explain about erections, without having to cover blow-up sex toys with the facial expressions of surprised tunafish and more orifices than a multi-plug socket.

Claire laughed too. She had read Tom Sharpe. She could make risqué jokes. Laughing with her mother made her feel rather adult and clever, as if she had just reached somewhere important, although she hadn't known she was heading there. 'Let's go for a cappuccino, shall we?' she suggested.

Tessa, delighted to be asked, agreed at once, despite being awash with the stuff. Some moments must be grasped, whatever the possible consequences for your bladder. She would even eat more apple strudel if it would help her daughter turn more quickly into a normal human being.

Marjorie was doing her shopping in Cambridge, where the sprout problem was magnified by the greater size of the Marks and Spencers, although this was more than compensated for by the lack of any rampaging cattle in the street.

Laura Ashley was full of beautiful young girls buying ballgowns for the party season. She almost turned back at the door, the fear of a communal changing room halting her on Trinity Street, but the pull of those crisp cotton blouses and soft coloured skirts called her in, and she took a deep breath and stepped into the sound of King's College Choir on piped CD.

It wasn't so bad in the end. No-one came up and demanded to know whether or not they could help her in the kind of tones which suggested they would rather see her fried. No-one refused to let her into the changing rooms on the grounds of extreme age, and no-one seemed unduly surprised when she couldn't put anything back on its hanger, because the hangers seemed not to be designed to have clothes put back on them.

It didn't take too long to choose, since she wanted everything she tried on. They even sold shoes. Just wait till Keith saw her. Mind you, it was going to be such a surprise that perhaps she had better save it for a really special occasion. She knew of just the one.

Marjorie would have been surprised if she had known that Mavis Entwhistle was also out dress shopping. Indeed, the shop assistants were pretty surprised, for Mavis was not the kind of thing they saw every day, and seeing her simultaneously reflected in five or six mirrors was quite overwhelming. She required a dress so that Cyril Bender could take her to tea at the Angel. She had received a small advance from the specialist publisher to whom she had submitted her small book on hogweed, and she was going to have a dress. As long as it was not orange – her estranged husband Albert's current favourite colour, apparently – then she wasn't too fussy.

Sally knew that her mother was in Cambridge, which was why she and Robert met in Saffron Walden, whence they had driven in separate cars, which Robert felt to be appallingly clandestine for a man of the cloth.

They were both beginning to feel that it would have been safer to come clean to the parish at the very beginning, and print a confession in the magazine, mobile library and all. At least the waiting was nearly over – they had decided to announce their engagement to Bumpstaple after the Festival. They therefore decided to do their Christmas shopping together, because, by Christmas day, presents could be jointly given.

Unfortunately, they had reckoned without the fact that residents of Bumpstaple suddenly seemed to lurk all over Saffron Walden, and were reduced to hiding in a little-known coffee room above a New Age crystal healing and incense shop called Astral Suggestions, planning separate shopping for the joint gifts.

'Have you sorted out the readers for the carol service yet?' asked Sally, who knew that Tessa had given up and handed the problem of sorting them out over to Robert. Since she had done so, poor Robert had spent many sleepless nights worrying about how to arrange it, drinking cups of Mavis's herb tea to send him off to sleep. Although it did help him to sleep, his nights were then filled with rapturous dreams of Sally which, although delightful, left him very tired in the morning.

'I think so,' he said. 'I decided to alter tradition a little. The Bishop will go last, of course, but I have put Marjorie first. The rest slot in between. We're having two poems and seven traditional readings, and I thought I might give Hugh the Betjeman.'

'I wouldn't,' said Sally. 'Hugh's idea of poetry might cause something of a stir. I'm surprised at Marjorie wanting to do it, especially if we do get on to local radio, she's always been so shy. Mind you, she's a changed woman when she conducts the choir.'

Robert smiled. 'Not only then, I think.'

Sally took his hand. 'You did that, you know. You spotted her and brought her out of her shell.'

'Not at all,' said Robert, 'I just opened a door, that's all. It was Marjorie who went through it.'

'Well, I think it was you,' said Sally firmly. 'So many people are different since you came. Even Olive.'

'Ah, Olive is a tough nut to crack,' said Robert. It would have been a breach of confidence to tell her about Ernest and his implant. 'But I think we may see more changes in her before the winter is over.'

'What do you know?' asked Sally curiously, but Robert could not say.

'Oh, just an impression,' he said lightly. 'Perhaps your mother's herb tea has given her a new lease of life.'

'It's probably given her indigestion,' said Sally.

As they left the café via the shop, they did not notice the poster advertising a new book, *The Magical Properties of Hogweed*, by Leila Stargazer, but even if they had, it would have meant nothing to either of them.

In addition to the usual rush of Christmas pop releases in the shops, luxury Christmas puddings with brandy in the supermarkets and Christmas holly leaves on the milk bottle tops, Christmas brought several of the trials of life, namely, black ice, frozen pipes and School Open Day. The only saving grace was that Hugh's open day was not until the spring, when his parents would be back. It is one thing to agree to act *in loco parentis* to Dennis the Menace, but quite another to have to take the blame for him at his school.

Claire's termly trial-by-teacher was something which the years had taught Tessa to dread, as she had always felt disapproved of. At first she felt disapproved of as a single mother, then for introducing a stepfather, and currently it was for being pregnant. That was not all. Long hair, being an artist, wearing sandals, living in a village: all these things seemed to be faults in the eyes of Miss Gromit.

Miss Gromit was head of both Lower and Upper School, so Tessa and Claire had been under her jurisdiction for ten years. During that time, Tessa had come to realize that Miss Gromit blamed parents for everything. Every dropped mark, every forgotten school book, every ink blot on the French homework, every unnamed sock was directly attributable to the life style, dress style and hairstyle of the parents. She shuddered at the memory of the day when Miss Gromit had actually telephoned her upon spotting Claire wearing odd socks.

'Your daughter,' she had said thunderously, 'has told me that a pig ate her sock. This is a Christian school, Mrs Bennett, we do not treat untruths lightly, so you will understand that I had to speak to you.'

'But it's true, I'm afraid,' Tessa had said, 'we have a pig, Lysander, and he is rather partial to socks, especially navy.'

'I do not,' Miss Gromit had replied, 'approve of pigs,' and Tessa was left afraid that her porcine friend might be spirited away after a frank call from Miss Gromit to Social Services.

Now she faced the school gates with Claire and also with trepidation.

It was an excellent school, overflowing with smart, bright girls, with totally browbeaten parents. Despite having put on her cleanest smock and plaiting her hair, she was conscious of the fact that she was essentially different from the other parents. First, crucially, the other parents came in twos. Then, the other parents wore smart jackets and court shoes and were not eight months pregnant. The other parents looked as though they didn't know what a smock was for. The other mothers had bosoms which conformed to the manu-factured range of bra sizes, and the other fathers looked as though they had mobile phones and always got someone in to do their plumbing.

Claire, walking nervously beside her mother, noticed the differences too. It had never struck her before, but didn't the other parents look boring? She'd bet none of those other women could paint even a wall, let alone a portrait of a pig. They were probably all legal secretaries, or ran smart dress exchange agencies. They had fingernails and hairstyles. She realized, with a strange startled jump, that she actually *preferred* her mother to these others. This was odd, because she could clearly recall that last term she had been embarrassed by Tessa's plait, and had wished that Richard had come with her instead, even though her mother was not nearly so obviously pregnant then. This time she could sense some of the other parents looking at Tessa, and it seemed to her that, rather than looking disapproving, the men looked admiring and the women jealous.

She escorted her mother from room to room, showing her displays of art, maths, history, design technology. Tessa was suitably and verbosely impressed. She was actually enjoying herself. Last time, Claire had abandoned her in the clear hope that no-one would then guess they were related. This time, Claire had even put her own hair into a plait, almost as though she intended to emphasize the relationship. It seemed as though Claire was beginning to like her.

Miss Gromit liked to speak to all of the parents at these events. Today, as the allotted time for her five minutes approached, Tessa began to feel jittery. Doubtless Miss Gromit would open with a few choice words on the subject of absent husbands.

She was kept waiting for precisely four minutes. Miss Gromit liked to make people wait a little – it kept them on their toes. Unfortunately, although delayed, the moment arrived, and a green 'enter' light flashed beside Miss Gromit's door. It was intended to make parents feel like recalcitrant pupils who have been sent to explain to the Headmistress why they ran down the corridor, or failed to sew name tapes into their knickers.

'Sit down Mrs Bennett. Is Mr Bennett not here?'

Tessa sat, thinking, I was upset enough with Richard for being too caught up with work. Why should I suffer twice for it? 'No,' she said aloud, 'I'm afraid he couldn't make it.' She couldn't help lapsing into her telephone voice, the one she otherwise reserved for the bank manager and the man who authorized increased credit limits on her Visa, the voice with no dropped aitches and absolutely no dirty laughs.

'Oh,' said Miss Gromit. She wore metal-rimmed spectacles and her hair was iron grey. Tessa suspected that it had always been iron grey, as it matched her so well. Admittedly children rarely had iron grey hair, but then Miss Gromit could surely never have been a child. She probably just evolved out of two rulers and a mortarboard. Tessa smiled.

Miss Gromit did not smile. She proceeded to deliver her assessment of Claire with a precise coldness which seemed to demand explanations. 'Her science subjects and mathematics are a little better. There have been two episodes of late homework, both in chemistry, and one of poor dress – a mismatching sock.'

Tessa opened her mouth and then closed it. Asking whether Miss Gromit intended to mention the sock on Claire's UCAS report would definitely not help this interview.

'Her English and French teachers are pleased with her progress, history has been average, geography better. Frankly Mrs Bennett, there has been considerable improvement in Claire's work this term.'

Miss Gromit's tone was so dour that it took Tessa a moment to take in these encouraging words.

'Oh,' she said, after a second, 'well, I'm very pleased. Claire does try hard.'

The mercury of Miss Gromit's expression dropped. Tessa wondered whether icicles ever formed on her nose. No, they wouldn't dare.

'We must hope that she does not let it all slide away due to an unhealthy interest in boys.'

Tessa frowned. If Miss Gromit hoped to lead by example on the subject of boys, then she must surely realize that any girl who thought that she represented what they could become if they forswore the opposite sex, was likely to get pregnant at once. 'Claire is fifteen, Miss Gromit,' she said. 'Nature decrees that she should have some interest in boys.'

Miss Gromit managed to incorporate Tessa's abdomen in her look. 'I have been a headmistress for twenty-two years, Mrs Bennett, and in my experience there is healthy interest in boys, and there is unhealthy interest in boys.' It was clear which sort she believed Tessa must have had.

Tessa fumed inwardly. If it weren't such a good school, with such nice nuns teaching there, she would have told Miss Gromit to stick her head in a bucket years ago. She resorted to the other parental weapon of unsettling politeness. 'Well, thank you for your time, Miss Gromit. I'm so glad Claire is doing well – Richard and I will look forward to her end-of-term report. Goodbye. Thank you again. Goodbye.' She stood, holding out her hand.

Miss Gromit stared for a moment, unused to lone mothers with the nerve to leave before they were dismissed, then took the proffered hand, still slightly wrong-footed. 'When is the baby due?'

'New Year's Day,' said Tessa, surprised to be asked. Perhaps Miss Gromit was just checking that she wasn't about to give birth on her carpet.

'Oh. Good luck, then,' said Miss Gromit.

Tessa left in astonishment.

Miss Gromit took off her glasses and rubbed her

eyes, sighing as Tessa left. All these bright young women who passed through her care over the years – she recognized them in Tessa. Was Tessa right, that Nature will out and the urge to procreate always comes through in the end, however many 'A' levels you have? Still, she brightened, Margaret Thatcher had children, it did her no harm.

'How was it?' asked Claire, outside. She had been hovering nervously near the doorway, imagining the worst, but pretending not to care when anyone walked by.

'Not bad, really,' said Tessa. 'I don't think she approves of me.'

'Me neither,' said Claire, feeling that they shared a common enemy instead of being two enemies themselves. 'Don't worry – we call her the Gromitosaurus.'

'Oh dear,' said Tessa, 'poor Miss Gromit.'

'Don't feel sorry for her,' said Claire. 'I think she was genetically engineered out of the bits in a piece of amber. What do you do after spending a million years buried in a swamp? Become a headmistress, that's what. Anyhow, you never said "Poor Mrs Thatcher", and she had nothing on Old Dragon Drawers.'

'Claire!' Tessa started to giggle. 'Someone will hear you.' The release of tension upon escaping from Miss Gromit's room was really quite profound.

'Come on,' said Claire, taking hold of Tessa's elbow suddenly, 'come and see the pottery room.'

'Oh, right,' said Tessa, pleased to have been claimed. It did not escape her that Jackie Johnson and her parents were walking the other way, towards Miss Gromit's door. It did not escape Claire either, and she noticed that Mrs Johnson wore even more lipstick than her daughter, and had the same highlights. God, how tarty! I wouldn't want to be seen with her, she thought. It did not occur to her that Jackie might be thinking more or less the same thing about her own mother. She had only just realized that she would much prefer to look like her own mother than any of the others here tonight. She was much too early in the path towards self-knowledge to have any understanding that her feelings, not to mention her problems, were not unique.

Chapter Fourteen

The following evening, Richard offered to take Charlie for his walk. He ran into Robert Peabody as he passed the New Rectory.

'Fancy some company?' asked Robert, who was just getting out of his car.

'Sure.' Richard wasn't sure that he did, but didn't like to say no. He had the non-churchgoer's conviction that vicars talked only in biblical quotes and moral judgements. He had not really spent much time talking to Robert, he had been so busy with his book recently, and in any case there was that funny collar, like a white halo, reminding him of a whole thesaurus of words which he mustn't allow to slip out.

'How's Tessa?' asked Robert as they followed Charlie up through the village. Charlie was more than usually hopeful, for Richard seldom walked him, and therefore he felt that anything could happen. He did not appreciate that there was no real link between the identity of the person on the other end of his lead and the likelihood of finding large, slow, disorientated rabbits in Bumpstaple woods.

'Fine,' said Richard, 'everything's going well.'

They were passing the war memorial and could see Claire and Josh sitting on the plinth, holding hands between smooches. For a moment, for differing reasons, Robert and Richard envied them.

'A wonderful woman,' said Robert, 'many talents.'

'Yes,' said Richard, regret showing in his voice, 'she is. She thinks I don't appreciate her, I'm afraid.'

Robert hid his surprise; he had not expected to hear problems, he had just been making conversation. He waited, instinctively.

'Actually,' said Richard after a moment, 'poor old Tess is rather tired. I'm afraid that pregnancy has been hard work for both of us.'

'Oh dear,' said Robert gently, 'how's that?'

They reached the edge of the woods and Richard let Charlie off. He rushed away in a random manner.

'We just seem to argue a lot at the moment,' Richard found himself saying. 'Nothing major, just little petty arguments which come out of nothing and never really go away. We've lost the ability to finish them and make up. Instead of clearing the air, they just make it more oppressive. Actually, I think we've lost the ability to talk.' He could hardly tell Robert about the sex. Not a vicar.

'May I be blunt?' asked Robert, and Richard thought of Tessa's Third Man joke – 'Yes, as long as I can be Burgess' – and suppressed a smile.

'Please do.'

'Well, in my experience anything niggly is usually down to sex,' said Robert.

Richard smiled wryly. So much for his idea of vicars. 'You could be right.' Then, to his own immense surprise he found himself explaining to Robert that he just lacked the right urges at the moment. He did not realize that Robert had a great gift for extracting problems from embarrassed and shy parishioners. Indeed, it was a gift which he sometimes wished he did not possess in quite such abundance. There were times – in the supermarket queue, for instance – when he would have preferred not to be such a magnet for the unburdening of souls.

'It must seem odd to you, hearing all this,' Richard said awkwardly.

Robert found it rather ironic. Here was Richard, embarrassed not to be having sex when he thought he was expected to, and here was he, Robert, having sex when he was expected not to. 'Not at all,' he said, 'vicars are not celibate, you know. As a matter of fact, it can be very difficult for an unmarried vicar, as our parishioners prefer us not to have sex, and yet we cannot always avoid wishing to do so.'

Richard wondered who he was sleeping with. It had never before occurred to him that an unmarried vicar might not be celibate. It made him feel that this was a man he could talk to. 'I wish we could make things up,' he said wistfully.

'Pregnancy can be a difficult time,' said Robert. 'Expectations are very high, and of course your wife is not just one person at the moment, is she?'

'She thinks I've gone off her,' said Richard, 'and we've always made up our rows in bed before now.'

'And have you? Gone off her, I mean?' asked Robert.

'No,' said Richard, 'it sounds silly, but it's just the loss of privacy, having someone else in bed with us, even though he's on the inside.'

'I see what you mean,' said Robert gravely, 'but have you told Tessa?'

'I've only just really thought it through myself,' said Richard. 'I had put it down to stress of work until now – I've started something completely new, you see. It's quite a responsibility. Anyhow, I'm sure she'd think I was being ridiculous. We both want this baby very much, you know.'

'I have always found,' said Robert firmly, 'that however ridiculous we look when we communicate, we generally end up looking far more ridiculous if we do not.'

'You're right,' said Richard, impressed by the obviousness of it. They should have talked about things long before they reached this point. So silly, what a mixture of embarrassment and awkwardness can do. Well, better late than never. 'Sorry to leave you,' he said to Robert, 'must hurry home.'

'Of course,' said Robert, 'shall I return the dog?'

'Oh yes, please. Thanks!' called back Richard, throwing him the lead. 'Oh, and I hope your love life works out.'

Robert sighed and wished that, just occasionally, he and Sally could smooch behind the war memorial. Unfortunately there are some things even less acceptable from a vicar than love at first sight. Love at first sight was merely extravagant. The war memorial was right out.

Claire and Josh had already parted and gone home, hunger being almost as powerful a feeling as passion at their age. Claire found Tessa in the kitchen, knitting a white cardigan for the baby, having allowed a woman in the wool shop to convince her that he or she might be sexually confused if dressed in an inappropriate colour at such a formative age. 'I just saw Uncle Richard walking Charlie,' she said. 'Are you ill?'

'No,' said Tessa, 'he just feels guilty.'

'What for?'

'Oh, this and that. Me being tired. Have you got any homework?'

'Bit,' muttered Claire, opening a tin. 'Hugh's had all the biscuits again.'

'I've got some of Mavis's dandelion ones,' said Tessa, 'would you like one?'

'Do I look like a masochist?' demanded Claire, to cover her inside-knowledge smirk. 'Anyhow, I saw Hugh giving them to Lysander. He says they make him more obedient.'

'More flatulent, more likely,' said Tessa. 'I must tell him. What about the homework?'

'Biology,' said Claire, who had hoped to get off

the subject of homework. She began to edge out of the kitchen.

'Oh, really?' asked Tessa cheerfully. Biology she knew about. 'Animal, vegetable or what?'

'What,' said Claire, 'that's all.'

'Hang on,' said Tessa, dropping a stitch as her curiosity took hold. 'What's so terrible? Is this sex education again?'

'No. Menstruation,' said Claire reluctantly. 'We have to write about the menstrual cycle.' She made it sound as though she had to do a project on body odour.

'That's not so bad, surely?'

'It's a class project,' said Claire, 'on reproduction. We each had to do a subject. I got periods out of a hat.'

'Oh dear,' Tessa started to laugh. 'D'you suppose that's how it all began? The Angel Gabriel putting everything in a hat, and Eve got the periods and Adam got the willy?'

'Adam must have got second turn, then,' said Claire, 'a woman would never have picked anything which looked that silly.'

'Well,' said Tessa, 'you could have got a worse subject.'

'Oral sex wasn't in the hat,' said Claire, and scarpered with 'Claire!' ringing in her ears.

I never told her about oral sex, thought Tessa. It's like starting diets, there's never a right time. Should I have told her? Should I have been keeping a bottom drawer of condoms for her, and explaining about the strange desires some men have for sheep?

Upstairs, Claire glared at her books in frustration. Where should she start? Should she go for the biological angle, or inject a bit of comment? A witty review of the role of tampons in society, perhaps? She could mention the Bumpstaple Robbery.

She picked up her pen and wrote, 'Why is it that on

TV ads they pour *blue* liquid on to the things with wings?' That ought to upset Sister Angela. Downstairs, Tessa wished that Richard would hurry back with Charlie. They hadn't been very close recently, but she still missed him when he wasn't there. The trouble was, she was beginning to miss him even more when he was. Tonight there was to be a rehearsal of the Nativity play, which they had put within the carol service, and she would have liked to be with him a little first, for a bit of moral support.

Homework tells teachers a lot about their charges. Claire turned her essay on menstruation into a litany of complaint at the advertising industry for using models in tennis kit with false tans who were surely too anorexic to have periods at all, and for making insipidly coy references to sanitary protection for parachutists. Hers was the essay of Miss Angry, who feels that the world is not being run for teenagers, and it owes her an explanation. Hugh, on the other hand, was deliberating on how he could make the set essay title, 'My Favourite Animal', into a futuristic epic involving an invasion of giant caterpillars from Mars who are overcome by a particularly gifted ten-year-old boy who then becomes prime minister. Neither essay was going particularly well, and they were both initially pleased to be called down for an early tea, although such sentiment evaporated rather rapidly when they realized it was cauliflower cheese.

'If this was a film,' said Claire, 'they'd be playing the creepy music right now.'

'Why?' asked Tessa, taking the bait helplessly.

'Because Hugh will start farting at any minute,' said Claire, picking all the cauliflower out of her cauli-flower cheese and leaving it at the side of her plate. This did not leave her with a lot of dinner. 'We may have to evacuate the village.'

'That's enough of that,' said Richard, walking in

from his walk. He had hoped to try to make his peace with Tessa immediately, but was disappointed to find the kitchen full of bickering children and cauliflower, neither of which appealed to him. 'Are we eating early for a reason?'

'Nativity rehearsal,' said Tessa. 'I did tell you. Where's Charlie?'

'Robert's got him,' said Richard, 'he wanted more walk, and I wanted to talk to you. Can't Marjorie take the rehearsal by herself? I thought she was all-capable these days.'

'She is, but I have to be there. I'm sorry,' said Tessa, meaning it, 'they'll need me on the organ.'

Richard supposed that, if it weren't for their recent problems, he could have made something out of that. Tessa thought, he doesn't even make rude jokes to me any more – there was an obvious one there. Richard helped himself to tea. She knows I don't like this vegetarian rubbish, he thought ungraciously. She could have done me a lamb chop.

'I'm sorry this is all there is,' said Tessa, 'I meant to defrost a lamb chop for you, but I got caught up in trying to sort out the script for tonight, and I forgot the time.'

'That's OK,' said Richard, trying to be gracious. Robert was right, he thought, communication is everything. At the moment we're about as awkward as those poor buggers who get dragged on to morning TV just because their next-door neighbour strangles their parrot, or their mother-in-law elopes with an Eskimo.

'What time will you be finished?' he asked, hoping there would be a chance to chat then, but she could not give him a time.

'When I am too fraught to continue,' she said regretfully.

*   *   *

She was soon fraught, for Serena was not co-operative. She wanted to be the Angel Gabriel, and felt that being Mary was just not the same.

'But Mary has the starring role,' said Marjorie desperately, 'you get to cuddle Baby Jesus and sit in the middle of the stable.'

Serena remained sullen. 'I want to be the Angel Gabriel,' she said. Tessa felt that this was not a good time to mention the sex of the Angel Gabriel.

'She's not doing it,' said her arch rival, Abigail. 'I got it out of the hat.'

Indeed she had, as this had seemed the only democratic way of resolving the small war developing over casting. The fact that this method cast Hugh as Joseph was just another manifestation of its shortcomings as a method.

'Why don't you want to be Mary?' asked Tessa, lowering her tone conspiratorially. 'I was once Mary.'

'You're having a baby,' said Serena accurately, 'so it was all right for you.'

'She wasn't always pregnant, stupid,' said Hugh, who thought six-year-old girls were the pits.

'I know that,' said Serena scornfully, 'but the Angel Gabriel had a tinsel thing on her head.'

Tessa, ignoring the many theological and dramatic problems she was creating, said, 'Will you be Mary if you can wear tinsel?'

Serena brightened. 'And wings?'

Marjorie rolled her eyes.

'She'll be wanting to wear her ballet tutu next,' whispered Claire to Josh.

'No wings,' said Marjorie firmly, 'on anyone.'

The Angel Gabriel was most disappointed in this decision, and made accusations about it being all Mary's fault which, when you thought about it, was probably what they said in ancient Palestine too.

However, after a bit of bribery and cajolery, they managed to get everyone into place.

Hugh was all for having a donkey. It was obvious, he said, that they needed a donkey. They couldn't have walked all the way.

'They walked the last bit,' said Tessa, 'now settle down.'

'I think Uncle Richard could look after it,' said Hugh, 'if we had a donkey. He could keep it in the vestry and we could hang carrots on the altar. That way, it would go in the right direction when we let it in.'

'Uncle Richard is terrified of horses,' said Tessa, 'ever since he was a judge at a pony club rally.'

'Did he get kicked?' asked Marjorie, curiously.

'Nearly,' said Tessa, 'but only by the mothers of the girls who didn't win "Best Turned Out".'

'It gets very competitive, doesn't it?' said Marjorie, sympathizing. She had done the pony club circuit for years. It had felt like a reprieve from a chain gang when her youngest daughter finally left home and she didn't have to hitch the trailer to her car any more.

'I suppose it must do,' said Tessa, 'but this was only the five-year-olds.'

'They're the worst,' said Marjorie.

The cast were becoming impatient, so they got started.

In the end it was not too bad. It did have the advantage that everyone knew the story and could guess at the script, and since they were rather short on numbers, there were only two shepherds and two kings. The representatives of the Heavenly Host would be the Angel Gabriel, rendered female by the demand for tinsel, and the Bumpstaple choir. There may have been more unlikely Heavenly Hosts than this, but surely not very often.

The children of Bumpstaple had actually proved surprisingly willing to take part. Perhaps, Tessa reflected, watching them, in this age of computer games and round-the-clock TV quiz shows, children are beginning to hanker after something magical in their lives. Perhaps, as she commented to Marjorie at the end of the rehearsal, they needed to find a meaning in Christmas beyond its function of heralding the start of the Debenhams sale.

'It would be nice to think so, wouldn't it?' said Marjorie, shepherding the children together. She and Tessa were walking them home in a crocodile, as it was too dark to send them home alone, 'but I suspect that it's more because they want to wear tinsel on their heads.'

Tessa hoped that it was more than that. Perhaps the littlest ones just wanted to dress up. Perhaps even Hugh, at ten, was still just accepting the tasks which adults thrust upon him, just as when writing thank you letters to maiden aunts – 'Dear Aunt Lucy, Thank you for the socks. They are a good bed for my hamster Ernie.' But some were there because they chose to be, helping organize the little ones. Perhaps even Claire. On the other hand Claire probably just came along for a snog.

By the time she got home, Richard was deep in a TV detective mystery, and try as she might, she could not pick up the plot. It had all the usual ingredients: an ancient murder, a family secret, an illegitimate child and a gamekeeper.

'I think it's the gamekeeper,' she said finally, 'it always is.'

'Can't be,' said Richard, 'he didn't look shifty when he was questioned.'

'Well he wouldn't, would he,' pointed out Tessa, 'he's an actor.'

'Yes, but he's an actor playing a gamekeeper who didn't do it. If he was an actor playing a gamekeeper who did do it, he'd make *him* a bad actor.'

'I suppose so,' said Tessa, 'but what if the actor's a bad actor?'

Richard got irritated. He got even more irritated when the gamekeeper confessed half an hour later. It was not an auspicious time to begin communicating properly – but then, he reasoned, that was a very good example of exactly why he should.

Tessa, hearing his explanation in the bath that night thought it pretty stupid for an intelligent man. It did help, though, to hear him admit to being off sex. Being off sex was much better than just being off her, she didn't have to take it quite so personally. She wasn't clear why she felt this. After all, it wasn't as though there was anyone else he should be having sex with.

'Don't you see,' he had said, 'it's not because you're not sexy, it's not because you're going to have a baby, it's because *I'm* going to have a baby.'

'Clever bloody you,' Tessa had said dryly. She didn't need it wrapped up. She knew when someone didn't fancy her, and it was quite clear to her that her Mothercare maternity support underwear didn't do a lot for Richard. To be fair, it wouldn't have done a lot for anyone, not even the man in the newspaper kiosk, and that was saying something – he would have fancied a tub of lard if it was wearing suspenders.

'Oh, come on, Tess. I'm trying to explain,' said Richard now. 'It's our baby who's the problem. He's there already, down there, you know, where the action is.'

'Down there.'

'Yes. Listening.'

'Listening?'

'Don't you understand,' said Richard, 'he's here, in bed with us. It's not you putting me off, it's him listening. How can a man make love to his wife when his baby is listening?'

Tessa started to laugh. 'That's really stupid,' she

said. 'Remind me never to go caravanning with you.'

'What?'

'Nothing,' Tessa considered his confession, 'so you don't really regret not marrying Carol the Cowpat?'

'No. Total cowpat.'

'Not even a little bit?'

'Even less than I regret not marrying Lysander.'

Tessa mused. 'Did someone put you up to talking to me?'

'Kind of. Robert Peabody gave me a lecture on communicating. Actually he was a bit odd. I got the distinct impression he's sleeping with someone.'

'Funny,' said Tessa, 'I've had exactly the same feeling about Sally.' They looked at one another. She shook her head. 'No. No, I'd know if it was Robert,' she said.

Later, in bed, Richard gave her a cuddle for the first time in ages, and then he told her about the new book. The cuddle was the more difficult to achieve, but only in that he couldn't hug all of her at once, and when she tried to lie with her head on his shoulder, her feet stuck out of the side of the bed. Any adjustment in her position would have needed a winch, though, and she was determined not to move, not even when the baby kicked sharply somewhere low down, sending a sharp pain down her leg. At least it was a cuddle. It was better than nothing, and if it saved her from trying to flirt with the man in the newspaper kiosk, then it must be a good thing.

'I wondered if you might design the cover for me,' he ventured carefully. 'I know it's not your usual kind of thing, but—'

'Oh, Richard. I'd love to, I really would!' Despite not having a winch, she rolled over, sat up, kissed him.

'My God,' he said, unable to stop himself, 'it's like being embraced by a giant beach ball. No, hang on . . .

kiss me again . . .' It's amazing, he thought afterwards, what a bit of communication does for your sex drive. Odd, really, when he'd thought it worked the other way round. A wise man, that vicar.

'What's he called, your travelling detective?'

'Hugh,' said Richard sleepily, 'he gave me the idea.'

Tessa poked him playfully. 'You're full of other people's ideas. I suppose the nookey wasn't Robert's idea as well, was it?'

'Certainly not,' said Richard, who knew where honesty should end. 'Mind you, he has hidden depths, that man.'

Tessa considered this for a while. Secretive people having secretive relationships. Hidden depths. 'You don't suppose Robert and Sally are having an affair, do you?' she said eventually.

'Humph?' asked Richard, halfway into a dream.

'Do you know,' said Tessa, 'I think they are. It makes a lot of things make sense.' But Richard was already asleep. Tessa smiled to herself. Doubtless they had their reasons for keeping it secret; well, she wouldn't let on that she knew, not even to them. It was rather nice, being the only one who knew.

She dozed off eventually, after a sleepless half hour counting sheep, and dreamed alarmingly of Hugh and Serena, wrapped in tinsel and sporting delightful pink tutus, careering up the aisle of St Julian's at an untidy gallop as their donkey headed towards the altar, intent upon carrots, with shepherds, angels and kings some way behind in hopeless pursuit.

It was in the early hours of the very next morning that the advance flotilla of around two hundred plastic ducks came within sight of land. True, they had already passed near Rockall, but as they were entirely subject to the whims of wind and current, they had been unable to land there.

Now they bobbed along, their whole world encapsulated by the previous wave and the next one. They had no concept of the immensity of their achievement so far, for they were yellow plastic ducks and therefore non-sentient. Even if they had been capable of rational thought, when your whole life has consisted of either floating upon, or freezing into, extremely salty water, and when you have no understanding that most of your kin are more likely to be sucked by a teething toddler than eaten by a hungry sealion, then you accept your lot with equanimity. There is nothing else you can do.

So they had bobbed on, day after day, as the days shortened and the twilight lengthened into the morning . . .

It would not be long now. Duck Alerts had been issued in the Hebrides, Orkneys and across the North Coast of Scotland. There was a bounty on their heads throughout the Western Isles, and there was intense competition between the Scots and the Faroese as to who might land the first duck. The Spanish trawlermen were also quietly confident, but it was largely felt that, as their nets were considered suspect, then any victory on their part would be thoroughly pyrrhic. There were even twitchers on Lewis, that strange breed of men who lie for hours in damp and lonely places just to catch the first glimpse of the greater spotted yellowback or the blue-billed thingummy. Although the ducks were plastic, the twitching community felt that they represented a challenge.

It was impossibly early. Even the morning TV presenters, deep in the gentler landscape of England, were still fast asleep, but somewhere off the Isle of Lewis, Donald MacDonald had gone out to his lobster pots.

Donald MacDonald was a morose man. In a room full of very morose men, he would have stood out as being particularly dour. He had lived all his life on Lewis, and he had spent much of that time being rained upon; but he was not morose because of the rain, for he loved rain. He loved it when it fell in sheets and when it dribbled in spatters, when it appeared out of the mist like a fine dampness and when it thundered in chunks the size of golf balls from a leaden sky. The best days of his life had been rainy days: the day he was born, the day he married Morag, the day of the birth of his son, Donald.

At the root of Donald's moroseness was morning TV, for Donald loved morning TV. He wrote it fan letters all the time. He loved the witty glamorous presenters, the co-ordinated décor, the cushioned sofas. He spent hours trying to get through to the phone-in features. He loved the friendly weather man who leapt around on a floating model of the British Isles like the sugar plum fairy with a testosterone implant, and the swift, bright, make-over team who transformed frumpy flustered housewives into models of style and glamour in the twinkling of an eye. He loved them all so much that he longed with every fibre of his being to be there on TV with them, and he was morose because there seemed little chance of that.

This was because most of Donald's days were essentially the same. They involved a lot of rain, a few lobsters, and endless confusion when the postman arrived as to which items were for him, which for Donald, his son, and which for his father, Donald. They then involved him watching morning TV from the moment it went on air to the moment it went off, when he would watch the other channel which he had recorded. Those who spend all their time watching morning TV rarely have the chance to do anything interesting enough to earn them an appearance on it.

Donald knew this. He could foresee no possible future event which would result in an invitation on to that wonderful padded sofa in front of the eyes of the world. True, there had been one newsworthy event in his part of the world, involving a sighting of four alien spaceships which had been spotted landing in the sea by Jock Mackay of Mars, as their neighbour preferred to be known. The Press had been interested for just as long as it took to find Jock, but then he had rather killed the story by introducing himself as Arcane Zog of the Mercurians, and instead of appearing on morning TV, had been taken to Inverness in a special helicopter. Unfortunately, throughout the excitement, Donald had been at home watching morning TV.

Donald might have given up on fate, but fate had not given up on him. Fate's fickle finger slipped up the west coast of Scotland and gave a little stir to the ocean currents. As a result, as Donald drew in his lobster pots, into his patch of ocean floated a small and weary group of yellow plastic ducks.

He realized their significance at once. They had, after all, been mentioned on morning TV, but in any case there had been a little excitement locally since Stornoway had been put on Duck Alert, for rumour had it that the Sassenachs would pay well for the little plastic ducks. Donald himself had briefly considered joining the Duck Watching Syndicate which had assembled a few miles along the coast, but decided that he probably had just as much chance of finding ducks if he didn't look for them as if he did. Now he had been proved right. Here he was, alone off Lewis, seeing the first wave of invading ducks floating towards him like weary pilgrims catching their first glimpse of Canterbury.

How should he best capture this immortal moment for posterity? Donald MacDonald was quite clear on the answer to that: he fished his camcorder out of the cabin. For nearly a year he had carried it in the hope that he would see something worth recording. Now, thanks to morning TV, for if it were not for morning TV he would not need to leave home so early and would not therefore have been the first out here today, he had.

Delicately, he manoeuvred both boat and camera until the ducks came astern. There were around a hundred of them – clearly a renegade group. Finally, and with considerable dexterity, he managed to video-tape his own scoop net collecting the first of the yellow voyagers from the cold, grey waters of the North Atlantic.

When they were all safely in the hold, he turned for home, well pleased. Never again would Morag complain about the monthly credit plan from the catalogue through which he had bought the camcorder. All it would take was a telephone call. Now, should he phone the BBC in Birmingham first, or ITV in Liverpool.

Later that same morning, Tessa sat in the lounge feeling, as she had told Sally earlier, frumpy, lumpy, dumpy and grumpy. 'Sounds like four of the seven dwarves,' Sally had said. Pregnancy, she felt, was not an easy state. Perhaps if she had bloomed it would have been different; all the books promised her that she would bloom. They had gone so far as to suggest that she would eclipse the Chelsea Flower Show in blooming terms. Her thick glossy hair and glowing wrinkle-free skin would more than compensate for the odd ache, especially as she would have so much *energy*. None of this promised glory had come her way. Her hair was a bush, her face pale, she looked like a pear on stilts, and as for energy, she was about as energetic as Big Ben.

There was such a lot to do, too, for Christmas is actually an exhausting and expensive season which has been tagged on to a religious festival in order to give it a little respectability, like a particularly gaudy tail on a kite. Tessa could not concentrate on any of the things she had to do. She meant to wrap presents, make mince pies, ice the Christmas cake, construct elaborate garlands which would turn the house into a verdant bower of seasonal beauty, and then pull them apart and feed them to Lysander because they looked more like products of an anarchic art class than the tidy elegant creations in *Country Charm* magazine. She meant, above all, to make lists, for lists are the mainstay of every wife and mother at Christmas. Lists, sub-lists, branch-lists, food lists, present lists, Christmas card lists. Lists of which lists she had done. Lists of where last year's lists were kept.

It was all too exhausting, so she gave up and switched on the TV. Morning TV fizzed into life to reveal an incredibly dour-looking kilted man sitting on the pastel sofa between the two presenters. On his knee was a small yellow plastic duck. This, apparently, was Donald MacDonald, hero of the hour, and duck-rescuer extraordinaire. He had not even had the chance to make the papers. Not even the Duck Club had known, for Donald MacDonald had given the exclusive story to morning TV. He had struck a hard bargain. He had been flown to their studio amidst intense security just in time for them to go on air, having telephoned from Lewis at an unearthly hour, and now he was the star of the show.

Tessa watched, transfixed. Even Hugh, who was off school with a tummy bug, did not distract her when he wandered in with a matchbox and offered to open it.

The ducks had arrived! Donald's amateur video of their little yellow beaks bobbing on the grey swell, given a dash of realism by the drops of water on the lens, captured an important moment for Tessa. It was a moment of triumph, a moment which proved, if proof were required, that the odds mean nothing in the end.

It made her morning. If the ducks could do it, then what could she not achieve?

Fired by a fresh sense of enthusiasm, she rooted 'Country Charm, the magazine for country lovers everywhere' – mainly read by suburban interior designers who spent all of their lives wishing that they had thought of small floral prints before Laura Ashley did – out of the wastepaper basket and found again the photograph of the smiling design editor beside her charming wreaths, garlands and trees. The picture had made her own offerings seem so inadequate, but looking at it more closely, Tessa could see that the design editor had fingernails. She could not possibly have made the decorations herself. There had probably been a dozen illegal immigrants slaving in a basement at sweatshop rates to make them. Well, she, Tessa, would make something just as good. She would find her nesting instinct if it killed her.

Hugh was interested in Donald MacDonald, too. He was not actually ill, but he had strong personal reasons for wishing to be off school today: when a boy has lost his entire centipede collection due to an unfortunate tripping accident very close to the staff room door, he may feel it is wise to lie low for a while. Now he sat down next to Tessa, rubbing his stomach sorrowfully to keep up the credibility of his performance, and watched.

'He's very glum, isn't he?' he remarked. 'Do you suppose he's constipated?'

'He's a solemn Scot,' said Tessa, irritated. 'There is a difference between solemnity and bowel trouble, you know.'

'What do you suppose he'll do with the ducks?' asked Hugh, as the programme went into a commercial break.

'I don't know,' said Tessa, 'I missed the first part. He probably won't be on again. Morning TV is like that – just a series of short items.'

She was wrong. Donald's price had been high. Not for him mere baubles or a cheque. Not for him dinner at the Ritz or a weekend for two in Seville. Donald wanted it all. He wanted a whole morning on morning TV. He wanted to be in every item, and he had got what he wanted. A man learns to be stubborn, growing up in a house where kilts are always worn in the traditional way – draughtily.

The producers had earlier torn out their hair over his demands. What could they do about the actress wanting to promote her new play? What about the fashion item? But in the end it proved a runaway success. Viewers phoned in by the dozen to compliment the programme on the inclusion of such a hilarious character. Obviously he could not be real, they said, but keep it up, give him a series. Particularly popular was the item on the weather, when he pushed the ever-cheerful map-hopping weatherman into Liverpool Dock and lectured the camera on the impossibility of simply forecasting 'rain' and expecting Hebridean lobster-catchers to glean any useful information from it. The fashion item on kilts appealed to a lot of viewers, as did Donald's various recipes for salted herring. He was, in fact, such a success that he was offered an indefinite weekly slot as a morning TV 'expert'. He appeared to be that rare creature, an expert on everything. Donald MacDonald's wildest dreams – and, despite his dourness, he had had some pretty wild dreams in his time – had come true.

None of this helped Tessa greatly at the time, for he did not reveal the whereabouts of any of the other ducks.

The Post Office in Bumpstaple closed for a day, rather mysteriously, the following week. It puzzled a lot of people, for a Post Office which has stayed determinedly open after facing an armed robber surely does not close for much, particularly on the last guaranteed posting day for Christmas for postcards to the Maldives. Fortunately, no-one in Bumpstaple was possessed by a last-minute urge to send a postcard to the Maldives that day, so no-one was terribly inconvenienced.

Ernest was delighted that it worked so well. He felt like a new man. He and Olive drank cups of Mavis's herb tea and ate her dandelion biscuits all day, because getting out of bed to make anything else seemed a pointless waste of valuable time.

It was quite wonderful, really, although he was beginning to feel a little tired after the fourth time, and his moustache needed restyling. Still, things down below might no longer have a will of their own, but Olive's will more than made up for it. Eventually they fell asleep, and entered the sleep of the truly replete. It was just lucky it wasn't pension day.

The BBC in London were very interested when Radio Broomhill called them. They had begun to feel, in recent years, that the annually televised Festival from King's College Chapel in Cambridge was, while beautiful, somehow rather exclusive. People queued for days to get in, everyone knew that, so it was always full of the sort of people who think it is fun to sleep on the pavement for a week and live off vegeburgers, whereas those living in the real world finish last-minute Christmas shopping, cook and rush about. As a result, there were never any old people, any families, any children in the congregation. It was not accessible.

When Robert Peabody had suggested to Radio Broomhill that Bumpstaple's Festival of Nine Lessons and Carols might interest listeners, the comment was passed in a pile to a producer. He spoke to a friend of his at Broadcasting House. Surreptitious checks were made that Bumpstaple was an OK sort of place. They checked up on Robert, to make sure he had no embarrassing history of alleged offences, and they sent a man to the local paper to check up on any recent events in the Bumpstaple area. What he unearthed at the *Broomhill Gazette* was enough to convince them. Bumpstaple, the senior executive in charge of programming told them, had everything. It had everything the viewing public like their villages to have on Christmas Eve. It had a pub, a church, a Post Office, and a young offender reading a lesson. Now it would also have the full attention of the BBC's Outside Broadcasting Unit. They wrote it into the evening schedules in place of *Songs of Praise*, which was becoming a bit samey. (One of the producers had suggested perking it up a little with a service from a naturist beach, but Terry Wogan had refused to do it.) They then went on to rearrange the rest of the evening too, as they also had to accommodate the latest star of the screen, a rather odd Scottish presenter who now had his own weekly show.

Chapter Fifteen

The complicated rituals of Christmas shopping, Christmas visiting and Christmas TV programming meant that the last full rehearsal for the Festival had to be a full nine days before the event. It was the last day they could find when everyone could be present.

Mavis Entwhistle hummed tunefully as she made her way down to the church. It had been a good year, she felt. Advance orders for her book were going through the roof. She was wondering when to tell Sally that Cyril Bender was to move into her cottage after Christmas. Sally's reaction did not worry her unduly, for she was certain that Sally had found romance, and that it was only a matter of time before she and Robert declared themselves.

They were having a dress rehearsal, and Tessa's own misgivings about having cast Hugh in the rôle of Joseph evaporated when she saw him in his costume. She had made his gown out of an old blanket tied with dressing gown cord, and the head-dress was a tea towel. Richard expressed fears that he might resemble a young Yasser Arafat, which was not really the intention, but fortunately this proved not to be so, at least, not as far as any of them could tell. His crook was a washing line pole which had had a hasty encounter with a junior hacksaw – 'What is a senior hacksaw, anyway?' Tessa had asked in the tool shop, but they had not appeared to know. Hugh pointed out that

Joseph was actually much more likely to have carried a hacksaw than a crook in any case, but Tessa had visions of Hugh appearing on The Night with a Black and Decker Work Bench strapped to his back in the interests of authenticity, so she insisted he kept to the crook.

The rehearsal did not go well. The choir were about as vibrant and tuneful as a flock of sea-sick crows. Everyone had a sore throat. Even Marjorie, normally laden with energy and enthusiasm, was feeling fed up and dispirited. They had reached that stage in any production called the pre-concert blues, when everyone is bored with what they have to sing, and feels like a change. The rehearsal of the Nativity itself was a little delayed by the disappearance of Baby Jesus – it later transpired that the Angel Gabriel had taken a liking to Him and had taken Him home and renamed Him Penelope. Hugh, ever capable of improvization, replaced the Holy Child with a coconut, which ought to have been fine for rehearsal. Unfortunately, though, just as the Heavenly Host were about to break forth into swelling song, Mary looked into the manger and became hysterical, on the grounds that Jesus was too hairy. Nothing they could do or say, not even Robert's line about Baby Jesus having moved in a mysterious way, would persuade her to carry on.

They tried to run through the readings after that. Robert read first, which seemed silly to Marjorie, as he was the only one of them who didn't need to practise projecting his voice in church. At least he started the ball rolling. Hugh did his piece reasonably well, although he did insist on putting on a Welsh voice for the Angel of the Lord. When Robert said that no-one had ever suggested that the Angel was from the valleys, he became indignant and argued that no-one could prove that he wasn't, either.

'This was ancient Palestine,' said Claire, irritated, 'he wouldn't have sounded Welsh.'

'Well, he could have been to Wales on holiday,' said Hugh, 'but in any case, Dad says the Welsh get everywhere these days.'

By the time he was persuaded not to speak in tongues, everyone was getting rather weary. Marjorie declined to do her reading, saying that she hadn't practised enough yet. Sally read hers beautifully, but then Olive, fiercely competitive, decided that if Marjorie planned to save herself, then so would she. It was Ivy Postlethwaite who finally brought the rehearsal to an ungraceful close. Instead of her Oxford Book of Modern Poetry, she had picked up *The Price of Lust* by Esme Smuts. Since a page was turned down and a paragraph marked, just as in the poetry book, she careered deeply into a Smuts account of seriously expressive lust before anyone was able to shut her up. It was fortunate that the language used in the paragraph was so coy that only those who knew what a manhood was for, and that the centre of a woman's being is not necessarily her stomach, were likely to grasp its meaning, and so no real harm was done.

'At least they say that an awful dress rehearsal bodes well for the show,' said Marjorie to Tessa as they tidied up at the end.

'That doesn't reassure me much,' said Tessa. 'I don't mind if the choir sing flat, but think of the offence we'll cause if we lose Baby Jesus on the night.'

'Don't worry,' said Marjorie, 'I've learned from today. I shall have two spare Jesuses in the vestry.'

Robert cornered Hugh to lecture him. 'Now, Hugh, you must promise me not to pull any stunts with Baby Jesus. This is a very important story you are taking part in, and we may even be on local radio.'

Hugh was indignant. 'I was only trying to help. I

looked everywhere for the real Baby Jesus, but He wasn't here.'

Robert looked at him hard. Hugh had the righteously indignant expression of one who is, usually, in the wrong, but who, on this occasion, is innocent. Robert decided there was no need to extend the lecture to cover what happened to those who used false gods and idols, even if they were only coconuts. 'All right,' he said, 'I believe you.'

Hugh was quite overwhelmed at this. 'Shall I go and get Baby Jesus for you?' he offered. 'I know where Abigail lives, so I can easily find Him.'

Robert suppressed a smile, wishing that finding Jesus was always so simple. 'No, Hugh. I think we should allow Abigail to keep her doll, don't you? I'm sure we can find a suitable stand-in.'

That was when Hugh, encouraged by Robert's faith in him and his motives, decided to plan a really nice surprise for the Nativity. Nothing involving Baby Jesus, of course, for he had promised. He thought hard.

The eventual plan came to him in Tessa's garden, where he had gone to chat to Lysander, who was particularly flatulent today as Tessa's Christmas cake icing had gone wrong, and she had given it all to him. What a plan it was, too! How could he manage it without discovery? Hugh began to plot.

The weather turned seriously cold the following day, and Richard didn't have Tessa's Christmas present yet.

Tessa had all of hers – she had been ordering things for months. Throughout December, gifts had been arriving daily courtesy of the postman. They seemed to have got bigger recently, and Richard was beginning to fear what he might open the door to next. He could imagine it clearly: himself opening the door to the postman, the postman saying, 'Your llama, Mr Bennett, where did you want it?'

It was the last day of school before they all broke up for the holidays, and by the time Hugh and Claire got home, the sky was the colour of pencil lead and there was an ominous silence from the usually howling distant fens. It actually felt rather nice to close all the doors, turn on plenty of lights, and snuggle into the house as though they were preparing to hibernate.

'It's your nesting instinct,' said Richard over dinner, when Tessa mentioned the feeling.

'I haven't really had much of a nesting instinct,' said Tessa. 'If we were herons I'd be the one laying my eggs in someone's chimney on an old bit of straw.'

'Perhaps you're about to give birth,' said Hugh. 'Lots of animals that are hopeless mothers do some nesting just before they give birth.'

'Oh, thanks very much,' said Tessa, 'we'll have less of the hopeless, thank you. Anyway, I'm not due for a fortnight. More apple pie, anyone?'

Richard and Claire were conspiring, she could tell. It was one of those very obvious conspiracies which people enter into just before Christmases and birthdays. Doubtless Richard hadn't got her a present yet, and was going to ask Claire's advice. They sneaked off, the two of them, puddingless. Hopeless, she thought, it was typical of an author, that her present should be an afterthought whilst she had been planning his for ages.

She was correct in deducing that Richard had left her present till the last minute, but not in thinking that he hadn't planned it. What he wanted was coming up at auction in Cambridge the following day, and Claire had found it, by intercepting a missive from the Duck Club the previous week, and even that was down to Hugh, because of something he had seen on TV.

The weather forecast was awful the following morning. The sky was heavy and brooding, with snow clouds which looked as though they planned to bypass the usual picturesque white stage and fall down as dirty grey sludge.

Tessa didn't want Richard to go to Cambridge. 'It's an awful day. It's going to snow. Cambridge will be packed. Look, I have a bad feeling, as if I've eaten a huge, indigestible cowpat. Please don't go today.'

'Cowpats are never indigestible,' said Hugh, 'they've already been digested.'

'Oh, you and your feelings,' said Richard, who did not take Tessa's forebodings of doom seriously. He kissed her thoroughly.

'Yeugh,' said Hugh, 'soppy.'

Richard grinned.

'You should have done your shopping earlier,' said Tessa, uneasy without really knowing why. She wasn't normally an alarmist, what was the matter with her?

'I'm sorry, love, I have to go today,' said Richard, winking annoyingly at Claire, who winked back.

Tessa sniffed. She got the message. Her present was A Great Secret. It had been left till the last minute, and now she was supposed to be grateful that he was going to so much trouble, and she was not supposed to argue. 'Will you take the mobile phone, then?'

'OK.'

'And switch it on?'

'All right,' said Richard, 'I'll switch it on. Look. Here it is, I'm switching it on . . . now.'

Tessa tried not to feel panicky as he closed the door behind him, but after he had gone, she paced the kitchen disconsolately, before deciding to make mince pies. The sky was so dark that she needed the lights on, not just to give a warm reassuring glow, but actually to see. Charlie whinged disconsolately, and pushed against her legs. 'I know, boy,' she told him, 'if I were

293

Dorothy, you'd be Toto.' She grasped the back of the chair, feeling a silly mood coming on. That hadn't happened for a while – things must be looking up. 'Oh no, oh no, here comes the wicked witch of the West!'

'Thanks a bunch,' said Claire, coming in. 'Have we got any wrapping paper?'

'Loads,' said Tessa, 'in the pantry. Do you think it'll snow?'

'I think so,' said Claire, pleased to be asked. 'It looks kind of mean out there.'

It certainly did. There also proved to be no mince-meat in the larder, although, oddly enough, there was even more Sellotape in there than before. It was obviously one of those days. Tessa decided to give in and tune in to morning TV, to spend an hour or so envying the presenters. At least it would feel Christmassy. You can always depend on morning TV to be seasonal when all else is grey and cheerless.

Richard, on the other hand, was having some success in Cambridge, which was relatively deserted. The clouds had loomed threateningly over him all the way in, but so far all they had done was loom, and he hadn't needed to queue to park. The rest of his Christmas shopping was now stashed securely in the car boot, and he made his way to the auction rooms and bought a catalogue. 'Santa Special – Toys and Novelties' proclaimed the cover and, sure enough, when he opened it, Lot number twenty-three was 'One much-travelled yellow plastic duck.'

It seemed that Donald MacDonald, who possessed those traditionally Scottish attributes of canniness and miserliness in great abundance, had put ducks up for sale in ones and twos all around the country in order to maximize their earning potential. Luck had been with him so far, in that no other ducks had yet turned up anywhere else. They would probably be spending another wet Christmas with only the grey seals for company.

Richard sat down on a wooden chair and watched surreptitiously as those who might bid against him for East Anglia's one and only plastic duck to date trickled into the auction room.

Tessa's day was dragging on. Claire was in her room now, wrapping up presents. The ever-smiling TV people had laughed and joked and gone off air while having a very jolly party just after midday. It all conspired to make Tessa feel completely left out of things, especially as the reception had been hopeless, giving Merseyside the distant quality of a transmission via a toy satellite from Vladivostok. A variety of weathermen on every channel she had tried increased her sense of vague disquiet by making dire references to blizzards and gales spreading across East Anglia, making the threat of the next Ice Age as all-pervading as Terry Wogan once was.

Tessa could not settle to anything. Even the sketches she was trying for Richard's book were half-hearted. The baby seemed to be making a trampoline out of her bladder, her back ached, and her sense of unease was as deep as the colour of the sky. She felt a primitive urge to gather her family about her and bolt all the doors, and she went to shut Lysander in his hut. Lysander needed no persuasion. Although he was about as human as it is possible for a pig to be – in fact Tessa felt that, on the scale that linked people to pigs, there were many politicians much nearer the pig end than he – he retained his porcine instinct for bad weather. He curled contentedly in his straw, digesting Christmas cake with an amiable expression.

Tessa shut his door and stared out of the garden across the fields. There was not a bird to be seen, and now she could hear the low howl of wind in the north, where it came to the Fens when it wanted a holiday from Siberia. Around her the air was still. It made her think of the *Ballad of the Ancient Mariner*: something about the eerie quality of the calm, that sense of something brewing just out of sight.

As she went indoors, the first big flakes of snow began to fall, large, thick and intractable, with the kind of cold inevitability which only snowflakes and James Bond's arch enemies ever display.

Claire had come downstairs and was in the kitchen. Tessa was glad that she no longer had to gird herself mentally for confrontation when she saw her daughter. In fact, keeping the peace did not require nearly so much effort these days. It was more than seasonal good-will, for Claire had never displayed any seasonal goodwill in the past. No, Claire was changing. She had passed that awkward stage. She was almost a young woman.

'Why have you shut Lysander in?' she asked now.

'They've forecast dreadful weather,' said Tessa, 'and now it's snowing. Look.'

It was settling already, and the distant banshee wind had crossed Norfolk and Suffolk with deadly speed and was beginning to howl in Bumpstaple.

'No walk for you, Charlie,' said Tessa.

Charlie hid gratefully under the kitchen table. He disliked howling gales and blizzards even more than he disliked incarceration. He didn't understand what Tessa said, but his philosophy of life led him to feel grateful for having what he wanted right up to the point at which it was taken away from him. This was yet another manifestation of his sheer hopeful-ness.

'When's Uncle Richard back?' asked Claire.

'Goodness knows,' said Tessa, 'as long as it takes him to buy Christmas presents.'

'That's dedication,' said Claire, looking for something to spread on a cracker. 'Why is the mincemeat in the fridge?'

'Pass,' said Tessa. 'Where's Hugh?'

'Just come in,' said Claire. 'He was round at the Post Office. Mrs Osborne gives him free sweets.'

Tessa was surprised, as this did not sound like the Olive she knew. 'Surely this isn't still gratitude because of the robbery?' she asked. 'Even for something like that it seems unusual when you think that small boys are normally about as welcome in Olive's shop as Greek Orthodox priests are in a Turkish brothel.'

'She's been funny lately,' said Claire, half wanting to tell Tessa what she knew. 'I think it's that herb tea she's been drinking.'

'Why should that make her funny, particularly?' asked Tessa. 'We've all been drinking it, after all.'

'It's a love tonic,' said Claire, 'it gets people – you know – going.'

Tessa laughed. 'You've been listening to Mavis. She's always fancied herself as a white witch. She thinks none of us know, but if that's a love tonic then I'm a monkey's aunt.' I wish it was, she thought, it might have saved Richard and me a lot of trouble. Mind you, things had been an awful lot better lately. Last night he had even forgotten that he didn't fancy her when she was pregnant. Much as she had enjoyed it, it had been technically quite a feat, as she was shaped more like a spacehopper than a woman. 'Anyhow,' she said aloud, 'if it was a love potion we'd all be very strange by now.'

Claire smiled to herself. She had her own ideas about whether Tessa was a monkey's aunt, for if Hugh wasn't the nearest thing she'd ever met to the missing link, then she didn't know what was.

Hugh wandered into the kitchen sucking a coloured

gobstopper. 'Hi, all,' he said unintelligibly, 'what's for dinner?'

'What have you done to Olive?' asked Tessa, 'Why's she giving you free sweets?'

'She likes me. I saved her from being robbed,' said Hugh smugly.

'I don't believe it's still that,' said Tessa, 'I know Olive. Gratitude isn't part of her nature.'

Hugh took the gobstopper out of his mouth and examined it. To his delight, it was turning from green to pink. 'I can't help it if she likes me,' he said, seriously smug.

'I should imagine,' said Claire, looking with distaste at her cousin, 'that she has a cunning plan to stop your gob, that's all.'

'You're just jealous,' said Hugh, unperturbed.

'I am not.'

'No point in giving you gobstoppers, anyway.'

'Why not?' Claire was drawn into the goading trap by her determination to have the last word.

'They don't make them big enough to stop yours,' said Hugh.

'She did *give* them to you, didn't she, Hugh?' asked Tessa, as Claire seethed and sought withering words.

'Of course she did,' Hugh was indignant. 'I told you, she likes me. I flattered her. Dad says it works every time.'

'How on earth could you flatter Olive?' asked Tessa.

'I told her we all thought she was just like a gazelle.'

'A what?' Claire and Tessa spoke together.

'A gazelle. I said we all thought it, and she said you must come round for tea and cakes.'

Tessa tried, but failed, not to grin. 'I have never,' she said, 'ever,' she tried desperately hard not to laugh, 'accused Olive Osborne of resembling any sort of horned creature, although I may have thought it in my more desperate moments.'

298

'You did too,' said Hugh, becoming irritated at being the centre of a joke he did not appreciate. 'I heard you.'

'When?' Tessa stopped smirking, mystified.

'Last week. You said she was so like one that she must be related.'

A glimmer of light began to dawn on Tessa. 'But I said she was like Vlad—'

'Vlad the Impala,' said Hugh, in an I-told-you-so tone. 'I do know what an impala is, you know.'

Claire started to giggle. 'You really told Olive we thought she was like a gazelle?'

'Yes I did,' said Hugh, 'what's wrong with that?'

Tessa laughed so much that she went into labour.

She didn't realize it at once. Popular soap operas have imbued everyone with the mistaken belief that the time lapse between the onset of labour and birth itself is a mere fifteen minutes of ghastly certainty. In truth, for most people, the knowledge that they are in labour dawns gradually, somewhere in the hours between the odd mild twinge of back ache and the final push. It's rather like the horrible expanding alarm experienced when you see a spider on the wall when you are in the bath, then, as you move to catch him in a glass, see another two out of the corner of your eye . . . and then, glance turning slowly and dreadfully, encounter an entire spider convention crouching in a distinctly kamikaze-like manner on the ceiling directly above your head. The final knowledge that things are taking place on a scale you had not previously imagined, except during nightmares or Stephen King films, is understood by all women who have felt that first apparently innocent twinge.

Tessa, who had become accustomed to backache, only realized that she was in labour when the twinges turned to gripping pains of the kind that soap opera actresses should be forced to experience in the interests of faking them authentically later on when they have to give birth on set (as they always seem to, eventually). She tried not to panic. There was plenty of time. No need to say anything to Claire or Hugh yet, she would wait for Richard.

It was dark by now, partly because it was around four o'clock and the middle of winter, but partly because the sky had closed in like a black jacket. It seemed as though Bumpstaple sat in the eye of a howling blizzard during which screaming giant psychotic snowmen were flinging huge drifting clods of snow at each other. The sky was gloomy to the point of catatonic depression, and empty lager cans discarded in Broomhill High Street that morning were clattering around the village green like the debris of ghostly teenage vandals. It was when the power went off, and the special Christmas screening of *Mary Poppins* went with it that Tessa began seriously to wonder if she was in trouble. Not since *Mary Poppins* first hit London's cinemas, and East Enders heard Bert the chimney sweep's cockney accent has such an obvious problem been spotted so late.

The wind upped its baseline howl by a few decibels, and laid into Suffolk with all its might. A slate fell from the church roof and landed with a thud on the grass, but you would actually have to have been one of the blades it landed on to have heard it. The snow was already knee deep and drifting, and the village outside appeared deserted. Windows flickered cosily with candlelight, and even the streetlights were out.

'Are you coming over?' asked Claire of Josh, on the telephone. 'Uncle Richard isn't back from Cambridge yet.'

'He's probably sitting out the storm,' said Josh. 'Dad went over to see Sally about something and he isn't back either. I'll come over.' He was pleased at the chance to be protector of the women. Well, and Hugh, of course.

Claire hung up, blissfully unaware, for the moment, that as she did so a tree was falling down somewhere on the Broomhill road. Its branches snagged the main phone line, but it held, supporting the tree as it lurched in the wind. 'Josh is coming over,' she called to Tessa.

'Oh. That's good,' said Tessa. She put down her knitting. 'I wonder where Richard is.' She was beginning to feel a little twitched. Perhaps she should ring him. She didn't want him to panic, in this weather, particularly as Claire had taken more than twenty-four hours to arrive . . . on the other hand . . .

'It's late night shopping at M&S,' said Claire, who had been sworn to secrecy about the duck.

'He won't be in M&S,' said Hugh, 'that's for women's knickers.'

'I bet he's stuck on the road,' said Tessa. 'Oh dear. I should have rung earlier. I'm going to phone him.'

'Why?' asked Claire, hoping to reassure. 'You know he'll be fine.'

'He will,' said Tessa, 'but I'm not. I'm afraid I'm in labour.'

'Oh God!' said Claire then, faster, 'Oh God, Oh God. What do I do? Do I need to get hot water and nappies? Oh God!'

'Come on,' said Tessa, 'things could be worse.'

'Only if we were down a collapsed mine being besieged by giant man-eating mine creatures,' said Claire hysterically.

'Oh, rubbish,' said Tessa, more confidently than she felt. 'Labour takes hours and hours. Nothing's going to actually happen. I just wish he was home.' She dialled Richard's mobile phone.

'Hello?' She could hear him, just. It was very crackly.

'Richard, it's me.'

'What? Tessa? Is that you?' His tone told her he was

shouting, but he sounded a long way away.

'Richard, can you get home? I'm in labour.'

'What?' The line was terrible. It hooted dreadfully in Tessa's ear. Was he in the car?

'Where are you?' she tried again. 'I'm having the BABY!'

'I'm—' On the Broomhill road, the telephone cable snapped as the tree crashed heavily and treeishly to the ground.

No tone, no hopeful bleeping, just dead.

Josh arrived in a burst of cold air and a flurry of snowflakes. Several unrelated doors slammed gratuitously. 'Our phone just went dead,' he said, brushing melting snow off his head, 'did yours?'

'I'm cold,' said Hugh, coming down the stairs looking like a mournful Wee Willie Winkie in a scarf and bobble hat, and carrying a candle.

Claire checked the phone. 'It's dead too,' she said.

'Well,' said Tessa, feeling illogically that if she could keep calm and behave normally then perhaps nothing would happen, 'in that case, let's all sit and play Scrabble.'

'Oh, good,' said Hugh, who had overheard his parents playing an after-dinner version in which they scored double points for rude words, and he had consequently formed the impression that it was rather a grown-up game.

'You put the board out,' said Tessa.

Hugh hadn't even had time to close off the board by making three letter words everywhere when Tessa's pains moved up a notch in intensity. This was not conducive to trying to make a word out of four 'e's, two 'r's and a 'j'.

'I'm going for a bath,' she said.

Hugh watched, mystified, as she waddled from the

room. One minute it was Scrabble, the next a bath in a power cut. Peculiar wasn't an adequate word. He looked at his letters. 'Do we get double points for 'snog'?' he asked, hopefully.

'No, you get buried in the snow,' said Claire, and he sniffed.

Upstairs, Tessa wallowed in her bath as only the truly pregnant can. At least the water in the tank was hot, but an entire bottle full of relaxing aromatherapy oil did not make her womb relax in the least. The labour pains were marching on with unmistakable vigour and regularity. It was more bearable in the bath, but she couldn't stay up here for ever. She was in labour, the house was so cut off it might as well be on Pluto, and bloody Richard was bloody out.

Guilt took over as a pain passed. Poor Richard was probably struggling through a snowy Cambridge, staggering under the weight of a huge bag of M&S knickers. I don't suppose there's a silk négligé for me in there, not this time, she thought wistfully.

Richard, four miles out of Broomhill, found himself confronted by blue flashing lights.

'Sorry, Sir,' said the constable, 'this road is blocked. There was a minor knock between two cars, then a horsebox stalled trying to turn round. They're jammed up solid. One or two motorists have taken refuge in that house over there, Sir.'

'Oh, God,' said Richard, beside himself, 'you've got to help me get to Bumpstaple, Constable. My wife's in labour, and the phone lines seem to be down. She's all alone, except for two children, a dog and a pig, and it's all my fault.'

'Oh, my goodness,' the constable appreciated a real crisis. You never knew when it might lead to a starring role on one of those real-life emergency dramas. Better still, it could be worth a nice gold badge on that show about heroes, or even a cuppa on morning TV. He talked into his radio, holding it close to his mouth so that the wind could not whip his words away before they had a chance to be amplified and coded into short wave signals.

Joe at the other end was impressed but unable to help. 'Sorry, Ted, there's no free choppers this side of Northampton. There are women going into labour in cars and buses all over East Anglia,' he said cheerfully, 'it's going to be raining babies from here to Bishops Stortford before the night's out.'

'Sorry, mate,' said Ted to Richard, 'I should take shelter if I were you.'

'No, no, I must walk.' Richard said desperately, 'I've got to get to her. I can't let her do this alone.'

'I wouldn't advise that, Sir,' said Ted dubiously. 'You're three miles from Bumpstaple as the crow flies, and if you'll pardon me, not even a crow could get there in this. The only safe course is to stay put.'

Richard knew he was right, he would never get through. The snow was drifting several feet deep at the sides of the road, and the skies continued to howl and dump vast quantities of snow unrelentingly. Sadly, despairing, he began to make his way past the line of abandoned cars towards the lighted house ahead.

When he came to the jack-knifed horsebox he recognized it – it belonged to the Ormondroyds, Great Barking's answer to the royal family. It was, as Ted had said, completely stuck. As he drew level, the side door opened and a familiar figure stumbled out.

George Ormondroyd seized Richard's arm. 'Excuse me, old chap, have you seen the policeman? These horses can't stay here all night. Howling winds, you know, upsets them terribly.'

'Sir George?'

'Why, Bennett, isn't it? Bloody awful weather, don't you think?'

'Yes, yes,' Richard agreed, surprised that George remembered his name. 'Sir George, tell me, how many horses are in there?' The wind whipped his words towards Southampton.

'What? I must speak to the constable.'

'I said HOW MANY HORSES?' shouted Richard in George's ear.

There is something awfully inevitable about labour.

'I could help,' said Hugh hopefully, 'I've seen spiders give birth.'

'Spiders don't give birth,' said Claire witheringly, 'they lay eggs. They're even further down the evolutionary scale than you.'

'That's rich coming from someone whose main ambition is to become a TV weather girl,' said Hugh nastily.

'Oh do stop arguing!' shouted Tessa. 'I'm not in the mood for arguing.'

'Sorry,' they said, unified and contrite. Josh offered to fetch warm towels, although none of them really knew what to do with them. Even Hugh, that fount of wisdom, seemed lost for suggestions, but only briefly.

'Don't you need ropes?' he asked.

'What for?' wailed Tessa, waiting to do the right breathing, but unable to remember what it was. The throbbing of her TENS machine, strapped to her back for alternative pain relief, was making her bounce rhythmically. It was not making anything hurt any less, it just added a farcical element to the proceedings. She had always wondered why, in James Bond films, the various fitness machines which almost finish off our hero always have a dial setting marked 'red-danger', whose purpose is to be turned to by a sinister gloved hand. What was the point of making a machine so that it could be dangerous? Now she knew that it was not merely to add drama, it was to reflect the fact that it is

305

always possible to have too much of a good thing. Keep calm. Breathe. Think of the sea. Think of the lost ducks, battling on so stoically. Think of endurance, of just weathering the next wave . . .

'They tie ropes to baby calves on James Herriot,' said Hugh.

'Can't you shut him up?' pleaded Tessa to Claire.

'I could send him out for firewood,' said Claire darkly, 'and tell him he's not to come back till he's found Good King Wenceslas.'

'And they use irons,' said Hugh, 'I saw it on Children's TV. Sometimes they use golf clubs.'

'Am I hallucinating?' asked Tessa, feeling another pain beginning.

Outside, the blizzard howled. Snow continued to fall upon snow in a bleak midwinterish manner. Tail backs built up on roads throughout the region as motorists abandoned their cars and descended in droves upon Little Chefs and people who lived in cosy-looking houses on main roads. Shares in Little Chef rocketed the following week, and a lot of houses on main roads were put on the market.

Tessa's contractions were only three minutes apart. She had flung the TENS machine away in disgust. Where was Richard? Bastard!

Claire and Josh were beginning to realize that help might not be at hand. Apart from a few ideas about tying cords in knots, neither of them had the faintest idea of how to deliver a baby. Claire had seen Brooke Shields give birth in *The Blue Lagoon*, but this romantic production was notable for featuring no placenta whatsoever, so it did not solve the puzzle which worried them most, namely, how you tied a knot in the cord when it was fastened to the baby at one end and the afterbirth at the other. They had even examined Hugh's navel, on the basis that, of all of them, his was the most recently knotted, in an attempt to spot how exactly the knot should be fashioned, but it did not provide any clues.

'I am going for help,' said Josh eventually, and this time Tessa did not argue. She, too, realized that her original birth plan – the one with the calm, smiling midwife and the epidural – should probably be abandoned.

Claire watched anxiously from the kitchen window as Josh staggered out against the blizzard and disappeared into the darkness. They had agreed he should try for Sally's, where his father was, but if it seemed impossible out there, he would stop at the nearest house with a light. Claire hoped it would not be Olive Osborne or, Heaven help them, Ivy Postlethwaite.

Half an hour is a long time in childbirth. Tessa, who dared not return to the bath in case she gave birth in it, leaned on chairs gasping and feeling very much like a female Rock of Gibraltar: huge and hard, although, admittedly, not covered in apes.

Claire put Hugh on vigil at the window to prevent him from making any more suggestions. He told Tessa that he thought perhaps she should go outside and squat in the garden, as he had heard his mother say that in Africa women gave birth in the fields, whatever the weather, and it was easy as pie.

'They don't mean weather like this,' shouted Tessa, 'not in Africa!'

Claire, who had run a sink full of hot water, but who had no more idea of what to do with it than she had with the umbilical cord, rubbed Tessa's back during the contractions. She was struck, suddenly, by the worry that Tessa was still fully dressed. Surely you couldn't give birth *dressed*? Shouldn't she take her knickers off? How do you *say* that to your mother? Thank God, she thought, suddenly and fervently, thank God I am no longer a child.

There was a loud banging and crashing in the hall.

'Someone's here!' yelled Hugh, louder than the wind. There was a shriek and a slam as all that was outside tried to get in – with the express intention of blowing everything that was inside, outside – and then there was Hugh with Josh, Robert and Sally.

'Oh no,' moaned Tessa illogically, misunderstanding the presence of her priest in the confusion caused by her pain.

Sally took charge. 'Come on, now, what's happened to your breathing? You look like a chicken who's just realized she's having a turkey.'

'Ha ha, very seasonal,' said Tessa, between breaths, with all the sarcasm her circumstances allowed her to muster, which was not much. 'I'm not laying a bloody egg. Owwwwwwwwooooooo!'

'Tessa, now *breathe*. I have done this before, you know.'

'When?' howled Tessa, not believing it.

'When I was a trainee in Clacton Library,' said Sally. 'Now come on. Think of it like riding a camel.'

'How . . . wwwwch.'

'You know, really wobbly and awkward when you first get on, but once you're up and running then it's really smooth and fast.'

'Till you fall off,' said Hugh, interested.

'Shut up, Hugh,' said Sally.

Tessa began to cry in a gap between contractions. There did not seem to be much in the way of gaps between contractions. 'Thank goodness you're here,' she said, 'Claire's been wonderful, but we were getting scared.'

Claire began to tiptoe out.

'No, you stay here,' said Sally. 'Hugh, dry towels, Robert, hot water in a bowl – and find some scissors and string. Put them in the hot water. Tessa, are you wearing knickers?' It all happened so fast. Sally, trying not to betray the pumping of her heart, had really arrived in the nick of time.

'Oh no!' shouted Tessa. 'Oh no! I want to push!'

'Are you sure?'

'Yes! No! I feel as though I'm giving birth to Wales.'

'How many whales?' shouted Hugh from the door-way.

'Ffffwwwhhhh!' went Tessa, pushing hard in spite of her strong desire to give up and go and lie on a beach. 'Oh no! I can't! Forget it!'

'You have to! Push!' shouted Sally, squeezing her hand.

Claire held the other one, and her breath, although she didn't mean to. She tried not to push along with Tessa, and mopped her mother's face with a flannel. In the hall, Robert was virtually sitting on Hugh to stop him from going to watch.

'But I've seen cows,' Hugh was protesting, 'it's not so different.'

The front door burst open. Richard staggered in in a flurry of blizzard, looking like the Ice Man of the Himalayas. Behind him was a horse.

'Whoa!' George Ormondroyd was shouting. 'Whoa!'

Richard, oblivious to the horse, George, and every-thing else, rushed into the sitting-room, then stopped in the doorway, aghast.

'Push!' Sally was shouting. 'Just one more for the ducks!'

'Yeow! You're hurting my hand!' shouted Claire, who was experiencing more of the pain of childbirth than she had expected.

'Richard!' shouted Tessa, and he rushed forwards and flung himself to her side, where she lay propped up against the sofa.

'I'm here, Darling. You're doing brilliantly.'

'Just little breaths, now, don't push. Just puff,' said Sally, and a little boy was born, just then.

He cried before Sally had time to worry about what to do if he didn't. He was slippery and shiny, and scrunched and red. Wrapping him in a towel and giving him to Tessa was a bit of a fumble – the St John's ambulance course hadn't mentioned that – but the rest went according to plan.

Richard was overwhelmed. His powers of clear speech deserted him entirely and he said 'thank you' and 'oh, darling' and 'hello baby' over and over. For a not terribly new man, he produced a fair few tears, too.

Tessa was exalted. 'Oh, Richard. We'd given up on you. Claire was wonderful. Sally, Sally – you were fantastic. That thing about the camel – it really helped me focus. Did someone teach you that?'

'No,' said Sally, 'I made it up.'

'What about the woman in Clacton?'

'St John's Ambulance dummy,' said Sally. 'Sorry. I wanted to make you confident. It was a first aid course.'

Claire was incredibly impressed. At the baby's birth she had experienced a quite astonishing urge to burst into tears. Sally had, Richard had, Robert had – and Tessa hadn't stopped from crying earlier. It was clearly an adult thing, and OK. She felt grown up, and a part of things: her mother had given birth and she, Claire, had helped. The sense of female solidarity was inspiring. She hugged Sally, hugged her mother, hugged everyone. 'It was fantastic,' she kept saying, 'fantastic.' Just think, she, Claire, must have been worth having if her mother was prepared to go through that again to have another one. Having seen her brother born, she felt that she understood, for the first time ever, what motherhood meant.

'You were wonderful, my darling,' said Robert to Sally, kissing her in the kitchen, where they had gone

310

to find something with which to drink a toast to Baby Rufus.

'Nature took its course,' said Sally, 'I just caught the baby.'

'You're so modest.'

'You're so gorgeous . . .'

Josh, walking in to escape all the crying, ducked back out again. If they didn't want to tell him yet, he wouldn't spoil the surprise, but did they honestly think that he didn't know who crept out of his father's bedroom in the early hours of the morning? Everyone knows that you can't have a teenager and a secret, separate, in the same house.

'Come on,' said Robert eventually, 'someone will come looking for us.'

'Hey, ho, you don't have any oats, do you?' said George Ormondroyd, stumbling in through the kitchen door with a rush of powdered blizzard and a sudden howl of gale.

'Sorry, Sir George,' said Sally, 'we've had ours.' She grinned at Robert.

George Ormondroyd peered at her. 'I beg your pardon?'

'Nothing, really. Have you been outside in this all of this time?'

'No, no. Rubbing the horses down in the Bennetts' old stables.'

'Horses? You mean Richard *rode* home? He's terrified of horses.'

'You would never have guessed,' said George. 'So, you're going to marry the vicar, heh?'

'How did you . . . ?'

'Oh, I hear things around and about,' said George.

'I don't know why we've bothered to keep it secret,' said Sally later, 'everyone seems to know. Perhaps we should just announce it.'

'They're just rumours, they don't know. Let's wait

311

until Christmas,' said Robert, 'today is Rufus's day, after all.'

Outside, unnoticed by everyone except the horses, the raging storm sighed a little, grew bored, and heaved itself further west, leaving a whited-out world and a lot of very tired traffic police. In the Happy Eaters they put on more chips, and, far up above it all, a few stars began to appear.

Chapter Sixteen

The weather cleared the following day, as the storms headed for the home counties, leaving heaps of grey slush stacked around West Suffolk like Dickensian mashed potato. All around the county maternity wards discharged those ladies who had been flown to them by helicopter, panic-stricken that they were about to give birth while cut off by snow, and who had then proved not to be in labour at all, and elsewhere, overworked district midwives rushed around visiting the ones who actually had been in labour, but for whom no helicopter was available. The home delivery rate in East Anglia had zoomed, and not just for pizza.

There was a reasonable congregation in church that morning, despite the slush, and it felt rather comradely. Everyone felt that they had battled against some odds the previous night, and they had a few more to battle through that morning when Ivy Postlethwaite stood in for Tessa on the organ. The music she played bore no discernible relation, either in style, form or content, to the hymns which Robert had selected, or even to any other hymns in existence, but everyone had rather a good time anyway.

'It was like during the Blitz,' said Ivy to Robert, when he thanked her at the end, 'everyone was pulling together.'

'Are you all right?' Sally asked her. 'Is your power back on?'

'Yes, thank you,' said Ivy. 'I did ring the electricity board last night, but I didn't think it would do any good. You do come to realize, dear, that as an OAP your opinions are completely irrelevant. Most people think your powers of observation have left you. That's why I always have such a good time in your library.'

Sally watched her go. 'She's a sharp old thing,' she said to Robert, 'I hope she was only referring to borrowing books.'

'There are hidden depths in Ivy,' he said, smiling at her, 'I never knew she played the organ until she offered.'

'She doesn't,' said Sally, 'couldn't you tell?'

Claire had come to a decision. She was not going to take the Pill. It was a considered decision, she told herself, not at all influenced by the fact that Zoe Ormondroyd had told her that it made you glow in the dark. In truth, she found the little packet rather daunting. She sensed that taking it would mean stepping on to a road which she would never step off again, the road to becoming ancient, going on and on, unremitting, until she was forty. Claire could not imagine ever being forty. She did not want to imagine ever being forty. In any case, deep in her heart, she still rather wanted to be an Enid Blyton girl, and Enid Blyton girls don't have sex. Midnight feasts, ginger beer, kidnapping by smugglers, yes, but sex was right out at Mallory Towers. No. She didn't want sex yet. Sex would change everything.

She explained to Josh that evening that it was a step she was not yet ready to take. Josh, almost as relieved as he was disappointed (for how can you hope to perform successfully when you have not had a chance to rehearse?) made all the right New Man noises about respect and mutual decisions, and wondered privately if there was a use-by date on his condoms. Everything had a use-by date these days, even Marmite and tinned prunes. His father said it was because of the throw-away society we live in, and that the food at the Scott base camp in Antarctica was as edible now as the day when that gallant band left for the Pole. Josh was not so sure. As he pointed out, Dad had been pretty ill when he ate that week-old Scotch egg ('What do you think it's going to do,' he had said, 'hatch into a giant sausage?' shortly before retreating to the bathroom for twenty-four hours on clear fluids only).

'Mum?' said Claire, standing in the doorway in the manner in which teenagers stand when they have something to say about which they feel very awkward.

Tessa wondered if this had anything to do with sanitary towels again. She had bought the winged variety, as requested. Was there now a variety with extra wings, like a sort of sanitary biplane? Or one with propellers, perhaps, and a rear gunner? 'Hmm?' she said aloud, thinking, childbirth has made me strange. She was breastfeeding Rufus, which is, at first, like trying to attach a small and rather angry nozzle attachment on to an over-inflated football which God has equipped with a small and sensitive nozzle quite inadequate for the purpose.

'I've decided not to go on the Pill,' said Claire.

'Oh,' said Tessa, trying frantically to think of some-thing non-inflammatory with which to respond to this rather startling yet welcome, statement. Somehow, 'that's nice, dear,' wasn't quite right. She tried it anyway, as it was all that came to mind.

To her surprise Claire did not erupt into 'Honestly, Mother!'s, but instead said, mildly, 'Aren't you pleased?'

'Of course I'm pleased,' said Tessa, 'although I hope this doesn't mean you've decided to try for a baby.' Oh my God, what have I said? How did that one get out of my mouth? She eyed Claire warily. The old Claire would have been enraged by such an appallingly tolerant response, would have asked rhetorically what she should have expected of a mother who listened to Joan Baez and believed in Flower Power.

It was, though, a teasable Claire who now stood before her, a Claire who was beginning to empathize. This new Claire grinned. 'Well, I thought if I did it quickly you'd still remember what to do and we could manage another home delivery.'

'Ha ha,' said Tessa.

The week crawled by for Hugh, who always found that time got slower and slower as Christmas approached. His parents were due back on Christmas Eve, and with their arrival his freedom would, he knew, be somewhat curtailed. Before then, he hoped to embark on a money-making scheme with the help of Freddie Cartwright and *The Cambridge Book of Christmas Carols.*

Whereas some people feel that Christmas is not the same without carol singers, there are others who find them a little wearing when they turn up absolutely every night, managing no more than 'We Three Kings of Orien-Tar' before banging on the door and demanding money. It was for this reason Tessa ruled that Hugh should only be allowed out carol singing once, and that would be with the official village carol singing group, and not with Freddie.

'Can't I ask Freddie too?' pleaded Hugh.

'Certainly not,' said Tessa, who had decided that this would effectively put Robert and the other singers in the invidious position of demanding money with menaces, for if Hugh and Freddie weren't menaces then what was?

'But we'd be ever so good,' said Hugh, thinking that you could tell she was his mother's sister.

'You can,' Tessa told him, 'have too much of a good thing.'

Hugh was annoyed. He had reckoned on having the monopoly on Bumpstaple's carol singing this year; last year, he and Freddie had gone dressed as choirboys and had raked in a vast profit. Now, not only was he limited to the Friday before Christmas, but Josh, Claire, Sally and Robert were coming too and, worse still, the profits were going to charity.

Still, on the evening he took it with good grace, and it was a glorious night. The blizzards of Rufus's birthday had been replaced with the kind of bracing, brittle weather in which the stars and the sky seem to have expanded impossibly, and in which the ground has that footprintable coating of crunchiness familiar to those who never defrost their chest freezers.

Tessa was half sorry not to be going with them, but it would make a welcome change to hear their singing from a nice warm room, especially as Richard was making cocoa. She watched Robert and Sally closely when they came with Josh to call for Hugh and Claire. No surreptitious looks of suppressed passion were obvious. They were very good, you had to grant them that.

They set out in jolly mood, calling from house to house, and singing a whole carol at each. This was particularly embarrassing at those homes whose occupants insisted on opening their doors halfway through the first verse. This was worst at the Osbornes, where the door was flung open just as soon as the words 'On the first day of Christmas' had been uttered. Olive Osborne always liked to get her money's worth, and by the time the twelve drummers had been drummed into oblivion, Olive's sitting-room would have made an efficient refrigerator. She and Ernest, in their dressing gowns despite it being barely eight o'clock, ought to have been frozen. Strangely, though, they looked quite warm. Ernest had done something astonishing to his moustaches: the ends stuck up, like

317

Kitchener's. It rather suited him. Olive was so flushed that Robert asked her if she was all right.

'Wonderful, thank you Vicar,' she replied, thereby attaining a level of weirdness which made them all a little uncomfortable. Claire remembered Vlad the Impala and started to giggle, and Robert bade the Osbornes a hearty 'goodnight' lest they all should do the same. Olive, whose determination to get her money's worth out of things, was responsible for the flushes she and Ernest wore, for they wore little else, did not even notice. She had shut the door.

'Don't know why we sang for so long,' said Hugh, 'she only ever gives us five pence.'

'Well, she gave us two pounds this year,' said Josh, who was holding the collection pot.

'She's flipped,' said Hugh.

'It's probably mad maggot disease,' said Claire, giggling.

Robert looked at Sally. 'Are we missing out on some great cosmic joke, here?'

'Only Hugh,' said Claire.

'That's rich,' said Hugh, 'coming from someone who treats an innocent little pet like it's the creature from the deep.'

'If it had been in *your* knickers,' said Claire, 'you'd have screamed too.'

Sally began to laugh and, perhaps it was the spirit of Christmas, but something made all the others join in.

Later, after counting up, it struck Hugh that having a vicar on the team had really improved the takings. 'You should have seen it,' he told Freddie Cartwright on the phone as soon as they got back, 'when they opened the door and saw the vicar, they went back and got *paper* money.'

'Wow,' said Freddie, 'what's your cut?'

'Not a sausage,' said Hugh reluctantly. 'Charity job.

Still, I thought we might ask if we could rent him for an evening. I'm sure it would be worth it.'

Sally, overhearing from the kitchen where she was serving up mulled wine, grinned to herself and was forced to agree. He was definitely worth renting for an evening.

'But it's going to be televised live on BBC,' said Tessa, absently stroking Rufus's ginger head as he fed voraciously. 'What if I need to breastfeed?'

'Oh, come on, Tess,' pleaded Sally, 'you must play. We can't do it without you.'

'I'm hardly *Songs of Praise* standard,' said Tessa. 'You could get in someone much better than me.'

'No we couldn't,' said Claire, 'we need *you*, Mum. If the TV people want to show Christmas Eve in a little village church, then they expect a little village organist, not Rachmaninov.'

'Well, he'd be dead,' piped up Hugh, who was under the kitchen table trying to catch a silverfish. 'People would write in and complain.'

'Shut up, Hugh,' said Claire, without malevolence.

'Look,' said Richard, 'it seems to me that if you want to do it then you should. Blow the BBC, Claire's right. We didn't do this for them in the first place, and in any case, the choir is hardly King's College, Cambridge.'

'You'll see,' said Sally, with bravado.

'Well . . .' began Tessa, flattered by the persuasion, particularly Claire's.

'If you feel up to it then, we beg you,' said Robert.

'Do you? Feel up to it, I mean?' Richard squatted in front of her and looked her in the eye.

'Of course I do,' said Tessa crossly, 'I've had a baby, not a hernia repair. It's a natural thing to do.'

'In Africa they have them in the fields,' said Hugh from under the table.

'He's like a record with the needle stuck,' said Claire. 'What is it with you and fields?'

'I just meant it's easy to give birth. It has to be, or we'd die out.'

'Starting with you,' said Claire, 'if you talk that rot too much. It's a good job you'll never have to give birth.' She felt that she spoke with the authority of one who now had some insight into the process.

'You never know,' said Hugh.

'Stop bickering, you two,' said Richard. 'Tessa, are you sure you want to do this?'

'She started it,' muttered Hugh. Claire pulled a face.

'Yes,' said Tessa firmly, 'I do. Robert, will you get the TV crew to promise not to film me if I have to feed Rufus between carols?'

'You could even do it while you were playing the hymns if Uncle Richard held Rufus in place,' said Hugh.

Tessa felt that expecting the assembled media to ignore such a spectacle was perhaps expecting too much of good faith, even at Christmas. 'Frankly, Hugh,' she told him, 'the opinion of a boy who started a sword fight with his Palm Sunday cross last year is the last I'd go by when deciding how to act in church.'

Hugh fell silent while he tried to work that one out. It seemed most unjust to him to bring up past misunderstandings for which he had already been told off. Anyway, it had all been the fault of the Archbishop of Canterbury – fancy giving toy swords to a load of boys in church, then expecting them to sit quietly. He had said this at the time, but it only seemed to make things worse.

'So, will you do it, Mum?' asked Claire hopefully. 'After all the rehearsals, it wouldn't be the same with someone else at the organ. All the choir will think so.'

'Oh, I'll do it,' said Tessa, 'after all, I should have realized there was a chance of this happening when I took it on in the first place. They do say that second babies are often earlier than the first.'

'You are a star,' said Sally, kissing Tessa's cheek. 'D'you hear that, Rufus? Your mummy's a star.' And so it was decided.

Marjorie awoke feeling nervous on the morning of Christmas Eve. It was only six o'clock. Keith was listening to the farming news downstairs, which he did every morning. The dogs, banished from the bedroom at last, were conspicuous by their absence. It was peaceful.

She had butterflies in her stomach, and they were using crampons to scale the sides. Would they have trampled quite so hard if St Julian's were not being invaded by the TV crew? She thought they probably would, actually. It is not the millions you can't see which inspire the fear, but the few that you can. Had she done the right thing, hiding the new clothes from Keith until this evening? It was hard to say why she hadn't shown him already – perhaps, she thought, it's because I like myself in them so very much. She was terribly afraid that he would hate them, hate the altered her, that he might betray his dismay at the transformation by some twitch of the eyebrow or setting of the jaw. Until that happened, until he told her that he preferred her old clothes, she could still enjoy looking forward to putting on the clothes, like Cinderella, and seeing admiration shining in her husband's eyes.

She padded downstairs in her slippers to make some herb tea. The dogs greeted her enthusiastically. Keith, wisely, had bypassed them and gone to his study, so she was the first non-dog they had seen in hours. They betrayed their pleasure wetly. She made two mugs, put food down for the dogs and opened the back door. Their new employee would be over to walk them at eight. Then she took Keith his drink.

He switched off the radio as she came in. 'Herb tea, is it? I wondered what it was. Thought perhaps you'd been making up some sort of a tonic for men of a certain age.'

'Not me,' said Marjorie, 'it's Mavis Entwhistle's recipe.'

Keith choked. 'Good Lord!'

'I'm sure it's harmless,' said Marjorie, 'everyone's been drinking it.'

Keith pulled her onto his knee. 'Do you know, my dear, I don't think I tell you nearly often enough quite what a wonderful woman you are.'

Marjorie blushed, too overcome to think of saying that he never actually told her at all. 'I say. What brought this on?'

'Oh, this and that,' said Keith, embarrassed, 'you know me. Still waters run deep. Perhaps this herb tea went to my head. Let's go back to bed.'

Marjorie took his hand. 'Must be powerful stuff to turn off the farming news.'

'Nonsense,' said Keith, 'seeing you in your night attire just reminded me that there are much better ways to start the day, that's all.'

Marjorie, removing that very night attire a few moments later, reflected that something must have changed when a nightie she had worn for five years suddenly became an erotic garment. After all, it could hardly be anything to do with Mavis's herb tea.

Sarah and Miles, Hugh's parents, arrived back from America that morning, loaded with shopping. Tessa's sister always reminded her of the classic Jewish housewife as portrayed in bad American sit-coms, the kind in which even the canned laughter sounds forced. Strangely, Sarah was neither Jewish nor a housewife, but when she breezed into the kitchen, sweeping Charlie ahead of her so that he fell over his own feet in his rush to hide under the table, you never would have guessed.

'Tessa! How are you? You look bushed. Has Hugh been any help? I told him to help, but does he listen to his mother?'

Tessa smiled faintly, knowing that any question marks within the monologue were entirely accidental, and did not indicate that a response was required. Sarah seemed to switch off her ears when she turned on her voice – perhaps, thought Tessa, that was why Hugh so rarely paused for breath. If he stopped speaking for a moment, there was a very real chance that he might not get a chance to start again for days.

Tessa often wondered how Sarah and she could possibly have come out of the same gene pool. They were so different, right down to the fact that Sarah had just required enlargement to reach the dizzy heights of a 'B' cup, whereas she, Tessa, seemed now to be developing the kind of bosom you have to carry around in a shopping trolley.

Hugh and Freddie Cartwright wandered in, equipped with gobstoppers from Olive. Revoltingly, they were comparing them. 'Well,' Hugh was saying, 'mine was that colour as long after I started it as yours has had, and I bet that by the time yours has had as long after you started it as mine has had now, yours will be . . . Mum! You're back!'

He peered at his mother in fascination. He had told all of his friends that she had gone to America to get some more breasts, and none of them had ever seen a woman with four breasts before. He hoped she would let him have a proper look – he wanted to see where she had had them put. It did not occur to him to think it odd that a woman should feel the need for an extra pair – the adult women of his acquaintance were, he felt, all so peculiar that anything went, really.

'Where are they, then?' he asked eventually from behind her.

'What?' Sarah looked at him, at Tessa, at Freddie.

'Your new breasts,' he said crossly, hating the feeling that they all knew, and he didn't.

'What you have failed to appreciate, Hugh,' said his mother dryly, 'in the ten years for which you have had your eyes so far, is that you actually have to point them at things in order to see them.'

'Well, they're not on the front,' said Hugh, 'I looked, and you've only got two there. Freddie reckoned they'd be on the back.'

'And where did you think they'd be?' asked his mother, while Tessa shook with silent laughter.

'Above the others,' said Hugh in all innocence, 'what's the matter? What's so funny?'

Tessa had her face in her hands.

Claire poked him scornfully. 'You don't get extra ones, stupid. You alter the ones you've got.'

'What's the point of that?'

Claire could not think of a reply that would not be embarrassing.

'Vanity, son,' said his father, rescuing her. 'Most women want to look like the dummies in shop windows.'

Hugh grinned at Claire. 'They've got the brains for it.' He wasn't going to let her get away with calling him stupid in front of Freddie.

Claire glared. 'It's a shame they don't do brains too,' she said, 'we could get Hugh done.'

Hugh was back on the subject of the breasts. 'How do you choose what to have?' He imagined all the breasts stacked in rows in a kind of breasts superstore.

'You don't,' said Miles, 'although I think you pay by the ounce.' He grinned at his wife. 'Mind you, Hugh's idea isn't bad.'

Sarah sniffed. 'Well, they certainly wouldn't have

324

needed to remove the old ones just to put a new pair where I wanted them to be. It's called Mothers' Droop, and I blame Hugh. You'll be next, Tessa, off to the clinic.'

'Not me,' said Tessa, smiling at Claire, 'I've got my man, so now I can go to seed.'

'You mean you haven't already?' Richard winced as she kicked him.

It struck Claire that they seemed a lot happier. There had been a sense of underlying strain, unnoticed at the time, but now it was noticeable by its absence. She must tell Mavis. 'Anyone for a cup of herb tea?' she asked.

Mavis faked her surprise excellently when Sally told her about Robert. Since George Ormondroyd had dropped his comment on the night of Rufus's birth, she had been worried that Mavis might hear it somewhere else first. It made no difference that, as Robert said, the rumours were the result of idle gossip, for they happened to be true.

'Doesn't it worry you,' she asked Robert, 'that we have behaved as village gossip predicted?'

'Why should it?'

'Well, village gossip is well-known for wild speculation and unlikely scenarios.'

'Are you suggesting that we're wild, or that we're unlikely?'

'Wild, I think,' said Sally, some time later.

Mavis, however, had news of her own which not even village gossip would have dared to predict, even in its most insane moments – although when you considered that most village gossip originated from, or passed through, Mavis herself, perhaps that wasn't so surprising. 'Of course, I shall be taking in a lodger after Christmas,' she said, 'a Mr Bender, so there's no need to worry about me.'

Sally gaped. 'From the Council?'

'That's right,' said Mavis defensively.

'Mother! You're not going to be cohabiting!' said Sally, pretending shock. 'When were you going to tell me?'

'When you told me about Robert. You should talk, Sally Entwhistle,' said Mavis comfortably, 'don't think I don't know when you creep out of my house at night.'

'You mean you really did know all along?'

'I am a mother,' said Mavis. There seemed no point in saying anything about the hogweed.

Tension built. As the day crept on, the popularity of the Broomhill Festival of Nine Lessons and Carols became gradually apparent. Parked cars began to build up late in the afternoon, and the BBC live transmission vans set up on the car park of the Cricketers Arms. Even Olive, a woman not easily impressed, was amazed by the numbers. The pub landlord, overcome by the spirit of Christian season-ality, produced mince pies and mulled wine in vast quantities and, avoiding an opportunity for profiteer-ing, sold them at a modest price to the gathering TV technicians and gentlemen of the press. Half a dozen hot dog vans and an ice cream man turned up in the hope of muscling in on the action, although only the ice cream man did a truly roaring trade. There must be something about the jingle of an ice cream van which sends people of otherwise unquestionable sanity rushing for frozen vegetable fat despite the fact that their extremities are already turning blue and threaten-ing to drop off. The Associated Press reporter set up his in-car sound system to play a medley of Christmas favourites by Bing Crosby.

Over in the New Rectory, Damien Hobbs, the young offender whose sentence had stimulated the press interest in the first place, was rather bemused by it. He and his mother, Irene, had come over to see Robert, to go over the reading he had to make. They all sat rather awkwardly at the kitchen table while Robert made them tea, until the ice was broken rather unexpectedly by the resurfacing of the penis mug from its apparently self-imposed exile. This made them realize that, despite being a vicar, Robert was probably good for a laugh.

'I think it's a grand idea,' Irene told him, 'the number of fines we've had. The poor lad has to steal to pay them. It's a scandal.'

'I think it's dead scary,' said Damien, looking nervously out towards the church.

'You ought to be pleased, getting on the telly,' said his mother, 'even Terry Wogan isn't live on Christmas Eve.'

'It's not the telly that bothers me,' said Damien, 'it's the old women. They can't half give you grief.' He had found attending church in Broomhill quite terrifying, as every octogenarian in the congregation had had a go at him for trying to rob Bumpstaple Post Office.

'I know just how you feel,' said Robert sympathetically, 'after all, the millions watching TV are invisible, aren't they? It's the ones you can see that count.'

'That's very clever, that is,' said Irene, 'you ought to be on telly too.'

Robert thought, a little sadly, that it was rather a pity that so many people these days thought that this was the greatest thing there was to aspire to. Mind you, perhaps they were right: look at that Donald MacDonald, you couldn't say he wasn't happy. 'That's very kind,' he said, 'but, you know, there's more to most vicars than meets the eye.' He tried hard not to think of Sally as he said it, as she had said a similar thing to him in quite a different situation, but failed. Not thinking of Sally had become totally impossible. No, it had been impossible from the first instant he saw her. Well, once the concert was over they would tell the world. Their waiting was nearly over.

Chapter Seventeen

By half past seven, the church was packed more tightly than Harrods on sale day, and were it not for the fact that Robert had reserved at least a dozen front pews for villagers, none of them would have squeezed in at all.

'Wow,' said Aunt Sarah, uncharacteristically impressed, as she and Miles stepped over cables and dozing journalists to get to their seats, for the decorations were splendid. Olive had done most of it the previous day, correctly leaving it greenery-free for Advent. Her decorative style was normally of the neatly symmetrical, rather repressed variety, using the kind of arrangements which are to a florist what a blue rinse is to a hairdresser. This year, though, she must surely be possessed of some strange wildness, for the whole church was lushly bedecked with greenery. Holly and ivy tumbled down the walls, and all over the carved oak half screen which edged the choir stalls. A great bunch of lilies, surely the epitome of extravagance, stood beside the altar; they had spent the last four days in Ernest's greenhouse, with the heater and the humidifier on to persuade them to open. Bunches of cinnamon and clove-studded oranges hung over the ends of the pews, and the font was buried beneath so much greenery that the overall effect was evocative of the temples of Angkor Wat after the Cambodian jungle had grown all over them. Even the tree was not the usual six-foot green tinsel one which Olive had always insisted upon in the past, because, she claimed, real ones made her sneeze, but a magnificent Norwegian spruce, glowing with Christmas lights and laden with oranges, grapefruit, apples and pears, an oddly culinary touch which Olive had spotted in *Country Homes* magazine.

The choir were hiding in the vestry, in a state of collective panic. Only Olive was exhilarated, for after the exercise tests she and Ernest had run on his implant over the last few days, the BBC live transmission unit seemed but a minor thing to her.

Hugh was missing. Since it fell upon him to open the proceedings, this ought to have caused some concern, but everyone else was too caught up in trying to adjust their hair in a three-inch mirror, which only showed a fraction of a face at any one time, to worry.

Richard, cradling his baby son and kissing his soft, scented, kiss-provoking cheek with a pleasure which astounded him, sat at the back so that Rufus could be passed to Tessa if, as she put it, he needed a boob job. Sarah and Miles, however, were firmly directed to the front row by Robert, and now sat wondering over and over again how the Hugh they had given birth to could possibly be the same Hugh who was to be the lynchpin of the carol concert. Sarah was so nervous that it had actually taken a few sherries just to get her into church. Miles was pleased – she was always far more malleable after a few sherries.

'I thought I knew Hugh,' she whispered now. 'I never knew there was a new Hugh, did you?' She giggled and hiccuped.

'Sssh,' said Miles, 'just because you've got new boobs doesn't mean you can't be shut in the vault if you're naughty.'

Sarah sniffed. 'If my son is anything like I expect him to be, we might be queuing to be shut in the vault by the time this is over.'

Next to her, the Bishop's wife overheard and wondered what sort of an evening this would prove to be.

Oliver Bush was there, beside the Bishop, with his wife, Rose. Rose wore the kind of suit normally worn by women who do not mean to be eclipsed. She had spent much of the day trying to set her VCR to record the programme in which she was about to star – sadly she had not succeeded, she only thought she had. The channels on her TV were wrongly set, and she had in fact programmed it to record James Bond.

She did not look nearly as tired as Ernest Osborne, who sat in the pew behind. He had had a hard few days, in an appallingly literal sense. He was sure that Olive would not sing flat today, his only worry was that she might sing sharp. He was proud of himself, indeed, as he had said to Olive, after his recent performances, he was a man who could hold himself erect in any company, and there was no arguing with that.

There was a mild commotion at the last minute as Cyril Bender arrived, looking a little like an escaped extra from Children's TV. He had put on the red checked waistcoat and orange checked trousers: to him, they were a nicely contrasting pair of beiges. He squeezed on to the end of the front pew ostentatiously, for he was proud to be Mavis's man.

Hugh turned up just as they were beginning to panic. He would not say why he was late, and Tessa, who knew him and who might therefore have been suspicious, was already playing soft seasonal music and was not available to notice. Outside, in a large transmission van laden with antennae, stressed people in headphones listened to the end of the previous programme and prepared to roll into the introduction.

All over the country, those people trying to recapture the spirit of Christmases they had once known, or thought they ought to have known, turned off James Bond (which had been shown before) and switched to BBC2. The national grid exprienced one of the greatest surges of the year as millions put on their kettles for a nice cup of tea, to better enjoy the idea that they were religious after all, and Christmas was not just an excuse for too many nuts, too much drink and an awful lot of wrapping paper.

At the BBC in London, the controller who had put his career on the line over a live village carol service chain-smoked as the bank of screens moved into the previews. Technicians flicked switches, and in the studio the voice-over began.

'Good luck, everyone,' said Robert to the nervous choir. Since some of them were also in the Nativity, they were not quite a uniform crowd, as amongst them were Joseph, Mary, and a heavily-tinselled Angel Gabriel. To Tessa's relief, Mary had finally been bribed to forgo tinsel on the condition that she got to keep Baby Jesus afterwards. 'Remember,' he added, 'this is our Christmas service, for our village's worship. That matters much more than the TV cameras and the Press.'

They lined up tensely at the door. Robert took his place at the front, with Josh in front of him carrying a candle. They opened the vestry door and Tessa, watching in one of her mirrors, saw her cue to finish on middle D. The BBC sound man prayed that the volume was set correctly, and that no-one near to him would blow their nose.

'Once in Royal David's city
Stood a lowly cattle shed . . .'

Hugh's dulcet tones echoed around St Julian's with a purity only ever found in choirboys who keep beetles in their pockets. Indeed, if the congregation had seen the contents of Hugh's pockets, those of a nervous disposition might well have run screaming from the church, but they did not see, and his being dressed as Joseph of Nazareth rather added to the poignancy of his performance as the choir progressed slowly up the aisle.

The old carol brought tears to the eyes of many of those in church, and in London, the BBC controller drew a little less heavily on his cigarette and sank a little further back in his seat. Sarah, listening to her son, was momentarily overcome by the feeling that she had produced an angel. Only momentarily, though, for then she remembered what he had put in the muesli that time. It is not nice to find mice in your cereal bowl, however undernourished someone claims they were previously.

The collection of hardened hacks from the world of the Press did not cry, but they did stop looking quite so patronizingly tolerant, and began to wonder whether their wives and children were watching. The *Sun* photographer did have a tear in his eye, but that was because the man from the *Express* had blocked his shot by standing on his toe.

The gentlemen of the Press may be rather hopeless in many respects, but when it comes to a good carol, they can certainly do their editors credit. The combination of villagers, reporters and locals who wanted to be on the TV raised the roof with the second verse, and viewers all across England, Scotland, Wales and Northern Ireland forgot their tea and wondered about perhaps going to midnight Mass this year.

Marjorie, conducting the choir with proud delight, could not believe that they were singing so well. There was no obvious warbling. Olive and Mavis were singing what everyone else was singing. Both of them were in tune. She sent a little prayer Heavenwards. This felt like a magical evening. It felt as though all sorts of things were coming right in their little church.

As the carol finished, the congregation settled back

to try and recapture something of the two thousand Christmases that had gone into this one – in particular those Christmases which everyone imagines Dickens knew, peopled with nice, charitable Victorians, in which every star seemed to be the star of Bethlehem, back to make a special guest appearance, just for the one night.

Marjorie had the first reading, which was the Betjeman. Keith watched her in great admiration. She had a natural gift for reading and she looked, to his eyes, truly beautiful. Indeed, when she had come downstairs earlier this evening in that lovely new outfit with that hairband and those lovely court shoes, he had felt quite overcome. He had discovered himself feeling quite, well, *desperate* about her, so much so that he had been completely unable to conceal it. Even so, it had only been when he told her how much he adored her that he realized quite how long it was since he had said the words with quite so much passion. The resulting kiss had made him determined to repeat them more often. Much, much more often.

He hoped that she would like her Christmas present. It had occurred to him that perhaps the Range Rover was a bit too much for her, if she wanted to shop more. He had initially intended to buy her a nice Volvo estate, but had spotted the little bright blue runabout in an advert in which a very charming French girl featured very prominently. Marjorie had liked her hairstyle, so Keith bought her the car. Not a truly informed choice, perhaps, but advertising is a powerful thing.

Marjorie read the magical words of the poem as Hugh, along with the rest of the cast of the Nativity, crept out through the side chapel in order to come back in via the vestry, by the end of the first lesson. He was

333

therefore unchaperoned for several crucial minutes. Unchaperoned and unstoppable. He hurried round to the Old Vicarage to collect that which he had prepared earlier, whilst the rest of the group assembled excitedly and unknowingly in the vestry.

As Marjorie sat down, Keith leaned forward from his seat on the end of the choir stalls, and reached for her hand to squeeze it. The BBC cameraman, instructed to catch one or two examples of villagey-ness for a bit of heart warming, caught the movement, as did Damien, sitting in the readers' row opposite the Bishop. Nice couple, he thought, nice of them to give me the job looking after their dogs.

Robert stood and welcomed them all to St Julian's: the congregation, the Press, the invisible, watching multitude. He said a few words, for he did not want to interrupt the flow of things, but he reminded them of what they had gathered to remember. Then he introduced the Nativity.

The narrator came out first, and as she did so, Hugh arrived with his surprise, to find Mary frantic with nerves.

'What have you brought him for?' she hissed.

'Authenticity,' said Hugh, who had looked it up. 'Anyway, he felt left out.'

'Joseph didn't have a pig, stupid,' said Mary.

'No, but there was probably one in the stable,' said Hugh, who had thought long and hard about this, 'and he wants to be in it.'

There was no arguing with that. Mary knew that if Hugh claimed direct communication with a pig, then he must have it. She was impressed.

'Mary and Joseph had to travel to Bethlehem, the City of David, to pay their taxes to Caesar,' said the narrator, and they were on.

The camera swivelled as Mary, great with child, Joseph, and the pig, Lysander, wearing a rope lead wound with holly berries and secured behind his front legs to prevent escape – no-one could say that Hugh failed to learn from his mistakes – walked up the aisle to where the manger lay.

'Focus in on the pig!' shouted the technicians in the van into the headphones of the cameraman. 'Kids and pigs, close-up. Now!'

Tessa watched in frozen horror. This was Lysander the flatulent, the very same pig who had eaten Ivy Postlethwaite's straw hat and Mavis Entwhistle's sage patch. She, Tessa, had no illusions about this pig. This pig could not be trusted. What should she do?

The presence of the TV cameras kept her silent and rigid. After all, she reasoned, what would be worse, the sight of a wild lactating organist pursuing Mary and Joseph and their pig to Bethlehem like a Government Health advert about mad cow disease, or the sight of the pig, alone, running amok in church, stealing the decorative oranges and little bunches of kumquats while no-one, absolutely no-one, admitted he was theirs?

She avoided Richard's eye and prayed fervently that Lysander would not eat Baby Jesus's straw – or, worse still, Baby Jesus Himself.

Those who knew Lysander watched in fear and dread, but the strangers in the congregation were charmed, as they assumed that this must be a particularly tame and pliable Gloucester Old Spot, for they were unaware that there is no such thing.

Lysander played his novel rôle with aplomb. The kings and shepherd arrived at the manger, bearing an assortment of tea caddies and a lovely woolly lamb who, sweet though he was, lacked a certain authenticity when set beside Lysander. They ended with the second carol, 'Away in a Manger', and all around the country, viewers remembered halcyon days at infant school when they were too young even to have smoked behind the bike sheds.

Lysander even allowed Hugh to lead him back to the vestry, to the huge relief of all those in the know. Even when he was found snoring in there much later on, no-one guessed that Hugh had given him a large bowl of Mavis's herb tonic and a handful of dandelion biscuits. These had put him in a happy, dreamy, helpful mood which would last for hours. Hugh had found this out by chance when he was trying to retrieve Lysander from under the altar during a practice run.

After fast-moving characters from the stable in Bethlehem had replenished the ranks of the choir, Robert read the second lesson. As he read, Lysander slipped into dreamy sleep in the vestry, and Hugh encountered a new problem. Larry the Lizard had woken up and absconded from under his robes! Where might Larry be?

The choir sang 'In the Bleak Midwinter' in perfect harmony. Tessa probed the two parts with her musician's ear, and could find no fault. It was incredible! What could have happened to Olive and Mavis, to turn them from crows to nightingales in just a few weeks?

Olive thought she knew. Those little patches had made her a new woman. Mavis, on the other hand, was quite sure that herb tea and biscuits had rung the changes. Cyril Bender of course had his own ideas as to what had put the sparkle in Mavis's eye.

Mavis stopped singing suddenly halfway through the second verse, as she came to terms with the certain knowledge that something was walking down her back. She might be endowed with The Sight, but it did not equip her with eyes in the back of her head. She had never met Larry, Hugh's lizard, and so her mind turned to mice, and large, man-eating spiders. Of the two, she would have preferred the spiders. She froze.

As Mavis was of a size to exert her own gravitational field, Larry had a long way to go before he got out, and on the way he encountered all sorts of things which lizards do not normally encounter, and so he explored them. Mavis, feeling little cool feet on her inner thigh, fought desperately hard not to make a grab for the area – not only would it look terrible on screen, but she was terrified of squashing something unspeakable. Fortunately, just then they all sat for the third reading.

It was a pity Larry did not understand Josh's reading of 'The people that walked in darkness', as he might have found it rather appropriate. He wandered down Mavis's leg and headed along the pew, beneath the choir robes.

'O Little Town of Bethlehem' was gloriously rendered. By this stage, the BBC were really in the swing of things, and the man in London was on his mobile phone trying to persuade the technicians to try and find the pig and bring him back. The duty office was being swamped by calls from pig-lovers who feared that he might be on line for stuffing chipolatas in the morning.

When Ivy Postlethwaite read the fourth lesson, Claire winked at her mother. 'The lion shall lie down with the lamb' was a major improvement on the works of Esme Smuts. Tessa winked back, enjoying having a daughter.

The BBC camera man focussed in close on Ivy, wanting to show the large print text from which she read. It was one of those little personal touches, he felt, which marked Bumpstaple's service as genuine, unrehearsed TV. He focussed in so closely that you could read the name engraved on Ivy's best piece of gold jewellery, the big gold locket she wore, unusually, outside her jumper in honour of the occasion. The name engraved upon it was quite clear for all the watching millions to see. It was Esme Smuts!

337

Of course, it would not be until the following day that most of the villagers would hear of the unmasking of the mysterious Esme Smuts in their midst – and Rose Bush had to wait longer than most, since she had only managed to record James Bond. There was no doubt, though, in the mind of the BBC controller. There had always been rumours that Esme was a batty old woman who was obsessed by sex and who plagiarized the rude bits from other books. Certainly the truth explained a great deal of the sameness of Esme's novels: Ivy's memory was not what it used to be, and she was plagiarizing her own work. It was entirely possible that Ivy Postlethwaite did not realize herself that she was Esme Smuts, but then perhaps that didn't really matter.

After they had sung 'Silent Night', a carol with particularly magical qualities, Claire read the story of the annunciation. It gave Tessa an odd quiver, hearing her daughter read, 'Behold the handmaid of the Lord', and realizing that Mary, so long ago, might have been only the same age as Claire. It gave Josh a quiver of a different sort, reminding him of what they had discussed so recently. Claire was right, they should wait. When she was sixteen she would feel differently, and that was in five months, three days and three and a half hours. If one of them wasn't sure, he thought, then it wasn't right, although if he were truly honest with himself, he was just a little relieved to put it off for a while.

Tessa saw him watching Claire. How quickly they grow up, she thought, her gaze moving to Richard cradling the sleeping Rufus. For a moment the urge to go and pick her baby up was almost overwhelming, and she had to press her arms across her chest to stop herself from springing a leak and flooding the nave. Imagine the headlines, she thought: 'BBC mobile unit cut off from dry land,' 'Vast bosom of organist defeats

338

live transmission.' The feeling that they were not her breasts, but two over-inflated footballs persisted.

The cameraman saw her hug her chest, but did not zoom in. This was not, he told himself, because Hugh, protecting Tessa, had threatened to drop a tarantula down his trousers if he showed her in close-up. Nevertheless, he did not like spiders, and he wasn't taking any chances; he had known a boy just like Hugh when he was at school. There's one at every school — only one, generally, as there isn't room for two.

Hugh did not actually possess a tarantula, although he would very much have liked to. He had asked Santa for one on several occasions but, unaccountably, Santa had so far failed to oblige. The last Santa he had met had, when Hugh had explained what a good keeper he was to all the bugs he kept about his person already, ejected him forcibly from the fairy grotto.

Hugh was to read next. He had still not located Larry, lost beneath the choir robes. As far as the BBC were concerned, he had already stolen the show with his solo and his obvious affection for the pig.

His reading should have been simple. It was from the first chapter of the Book of Matthew. Unfortunately, though, he had been studying it in some detail and had decided that he rather liked all the bits at the very beginning when all the begatting was going on. Why limit it? It made things much clearer when you got the whole story.

'Abraham,' he began in dulcet tones, 'begat Isaac, and Isaac begat Jacob and Jacob begat Judas and his brothers.' He looked sternly over the lectern like a miniature headmaster, to make sure they were all listening properly. 'Judas begat Phares and Phares begat Esrom and Esrom begat Aram and Aram begat Aminadab and Aminadab . . .'

Tessa sighed. Did he plan to read the whole of the New Testament, she wondered, or would he limit himself to the gospels? The TV controller in London frowned. He didn't remember this bit from King's College.

Hugh was warming to his subject. 'And Jesse – that's a man, you see – begat David the king. He was the one who beat Goliath, you know, with a catapult, which just goes to show what good weapons they are. And David begat Solomon, of her that had been the wife of Urias. Urias got a raw deal, really. His wife was called Bathsheba because she had a lot of baths. Anyhow, she had Solomon, the one who wouldn't cut up the baby . . .'

The Bishop raised his eyes skyward.

'Come on, Hugh,' whispered Robert under his breath. Had he been wrong to entrust Joseph's visit by the angel to a boy who had, after all, already tried to exchange Baby Jesus for a coconut? Still, it was not the result but the intention that mattered. If Hugh felt that it was important the congregation should understand about Joseph's ancestry, who was to argue? He smiled and sat back.

Hugh was there. He had stumbled slightly over Zorobabel who begat Abiud, but he was there, through all the forty-two generations to the birth of Christ. '. . . and they shall call His name Emmanuel . . .'

The Bishop held his breath. Would he stop at the end of the chapter? He did. The BBC were impressed. Hugh's reading had, they felt, completely compensated for the technician's inability to reawaken Lysander. (He did find a coconut in the vestry though, and decided to take it home for his wife.) Hugh had still failed to catch Larry, who scarpered around the corner of the choir stalls during the next hymn and then froze, chameleonishly, on a pale green tile.

After the hymn, there was an expectant hush. Then it was Damien's turn to read the story of the birth of Christ. A couple of flash guns did go off, despite

Robert's prior request that they should not, and his mother applauded very loudly at the end. The applause spread a little, and under its cover Hugh was able to crawl along between the choir stalls in pursuit of his lizard. Mavis saw him and sent him a furious look, but since it differed very little from her usual expression, he did not notice.

After the seventh lesson, Robert led them in prayer. Across the country the small but motley band of families whose TV sets are equipped with the little black boxes which calculate viewing figures all decided not to turn over for the Nine o'clock News. There was only one household not at home watching, and that was because Mavis Entwhistle was in church. No-one can say how it came to pass that Mavis was selected as being representative of some section of the population, but it did give her a thrill to know that what she did with her box actually affected the viewing figures. Tonight she had left her set tuned in to BBC2. In this way she had personally added five thousand to the viewing figure for the carol concert, resulting in it having the highest viewing figure of the season, with five thousand more than *Inspector Morse.*

Olive's reading of 'Journey of the Magi' came after the prayers. Robert had decided that the best way to prevent her from complaining that modern poetry, in which people cursed and grumbled, was inappropriate, was to get her to read it. Now she was truly proud. This was real poetry. It was culture, so it could curse and grumble all it wished.

She read very well, for she was a woman fulfilled and therefore capable of considerable vocal passion. Even the sight of the green thing which Hugh had pursued past her a few moments ago did not shake her new-found self-assurance.

As she looked up from the lectern, for she knew her piece by heart, she noticed a pair of BBC technicians in the vestry trying to lift that pig onto a wheelbarrow. It did not concern her, she had other things on her mind. She had spent much of the concert daydreaming, and it struck her that the Magi in Eliot's poem had clearly seen something rather appealing in girls bringing sherbet. The Post Office sold sherbet. All right, it had a liquorice stick in it, but that could be remedied. She would surprise Ernest tomorrow morning.

Ernest was exhausted. Had he known that he would wake up the following morning surrounded by dozens of sherbet fountains and Olive in a négligé he might well have bedded down with Lysander, for an exhausted man with an inexhaustible implant, and an inexhaustible wife, is in a difficult position. Indeed, Olive had a lot of difficult positions in mind. Perhaps he should drink some more of the herb stuff, he thought, it seemed to have done her a lot of good.

'O Come, All Ye Faithful' showed off the choir's abilities with descant. Hugh had stopped looking for Larry, and was pulling stretched-mouth faces at Serena, who sat opposite him. Serena was still holding Baby Jesus, who, she felt, should not be left alone. This pleased the cameras, as Serena was six, blonde, charming and dressed as Mary. Hugh, though, became convinced by her smug look and her furkling with something he could not see, that she was holding Larry hostage. He ducked down behind his pew again and began to work his way round to Serena, scurrying across the central aisle just as the Bishop stood to deliver the last reading.

Larry, who had been having a fantastic time just being green on his green tile, was swept up by the Bishop's robe and began to hoist himself upwards. 'In the beginning was the Word . . .'

Rufus stirred a little, and Richard lifted him up to his shoulder, stroking his downy head and being nuzzled in return. The whole miracle of new life seemed to him, not normally a particularly religious man, to be intensified this evening. It was almost as though between them, with their pigs and their lizards and their gremlin children, they had opened up a little snicketway to Heaven, just for the one night. He was no longer sorry that he had not been allowed to record James Bond. It really didn't matter.

Rose Bush, wife of the rector of Great Barking, squeezed Oliver's hand. Her pink suit actually looked rather good on her, and she was feeling relaxed and happy, despite her initial annoyance that Bumpstaple had eclipsed Great Barking this year both in the concert stakes, and by the presence of the Bishop. The Bishop's wife had such awful hats, she told herself, Great Barking didn't really want a woman with the Titanic on her head in the front pew.

Oliver was glad that Robert had pulled it off. The pig, he felt, had added a particularly brave but charming touch, and although the lizard on the Bishop's shoulder was hardly traditional, it did seem to be listening.

The camera had closed in on the Bishop and the lizard, a still shot destined to appear on the front pages of the Christmas editions of the broadsheets. The tabloids carried Damien, for when it comes to the crunch the headline, 'Young thug gives lesson to Bishop' is rather more enticing to some editors than 'Wizard with a lizard', which *The Times* man came up with – and he had had half a bottle of ginger wine.

They finished with 'Hark, the Herald Angels Sing!' Hugh was still wrestling with Serena on the floor between the stalls, convinced that she had Larry. It was only during the last verse, when the Bishop quietly asked Robert if he could borrow Hugh, that he realized his mistake. He got up, now watching the Bishop's shoulder carefully.

The Bishop handed Hugh the closing prayer to read, feeling that as he had begun the service it would be nice for him to end it. Hugh took his chance and seized Larry. He then decided to seize his chance to get out of the kind of trouble he was sure he would be in.

'Thank you all for coming,' he ad-libbed, and the Bishop gazed at him in alarm. This was not what was written on the card.

'We do hope you have enjoyed it, and I hope no-one will be cross with Lysander, my Aunt Tessa's pig. He wanted to come because Baby Jesus's stable might have had a pig in it. I know it probably didn't have a lizard, but it might have. I tried to get a donkey, but my Uncle Richard said I must be nuts because it runs in the family.'

Grannies across Great Britain dissolved into their TV sets at his butter-wouldn't-melt face, an expression long-rehearsed for just such an occasion as this. It cut no ice with Tessa or his mother any more, but it got the grannies every time.

Robert whispered something in Hugh's ear. Hugh grinned. 'And before I finish . . .' Tessa held her breath. What now? A request for a centipede from Santa?

In London they had over-run, but the controller did not care. This was wonderful TV. He was far too excited to smoke. The alternative magic show could wait. It is well known that children and animals attract a far greater audience than halved women with feathers on their heads. They stayed with Bumpstaple.

'Our vicar wants to tell you that he wants to marry Sally Entwhistle.'

'Ooooh,' murmured those in the congregation who knew them but who had not already guessed. This made it a very quiet 'ooooh.'

'Say "yes",' hissed Mavis frantically.

'I told you so,' whispered Olive to Ivy Postlethwaite.

'I've based my last book on them,' whispered back

Ivy, surprising herself by remembering, 'it's called *Desire in the Library*.'

'I'll look forward to that,' said Olive, who had seen the locket, 'I've read all your others this week.'

Sally had joined Robert and Hugh to say 'yes'. This was the sort of spontaneous TV that spontaneous-TV programme producers spend the best years of their life trying to capture. The Bishop, taking advantage of the general level of grinning soppiness, seized back the initiative and got in the closing prayer before Hugh could interest the congregation in any more of his unusual pets. The Bishop had once worked in South America, and due to an incident in a Peruvian village involving a skinful of apricot brandy, had a terrible fear of llamas. He now suffered from camelidophobia, as it is better known. It had returned him to England, as he had even developed tremor in the face of vicuña, and you can't go far in rural Peru without meeting a vicuña. Whilst there was no reason to expect an imminent invasion of vicuña here in Bumpstaple, Hugh had already introduced one foreign species, and the Bishop's view was that you never knew what might be lurking outside to jump on you and pull all your hair out.

Tessa began to play, and the choir paraded out. The credits began to roll at the BBC in London, and the Duty Office reverberated with paeans of telephoned praise. Several producers of comedy drama also rang, asking for Hugh's name, and the live unit at Bumpstaple took off their headphones and cracked open the champagne. Up in Stornoway, Donald MacDonald watched proudly. This was TV. He was a part of it, and he loved it.

Hugh, Claire and Josh wheeled Lysander home before Tessa could see the state he was in. They did not want to upset her: Uncle Richard had issued dire warnings as to what might happen if they disturbed her hormones so soon after Rufus's birth. Claire and Josh had both

345

felt a new surge of relief that they hadn't done anything peculiar to Claire's hormones, yet.

Everyone else was involved in a positive orgy of feel-good-ness, the sort of thing which governments would do anything to package up for distribution at election time. Everyone wished everyone else Merry Christmas as the church bells rang out, Tennysonishly, to a wild sky.

By midnight, they had all gone. The church was empty even of snoring pigs, and it waited, calm and patient, for the morning service. In the Old Vicarage, Richard and Tessa had finished putting presents under the tree. Now they were cuddling under the mistletoe, while Rufus slept on a sheepskin on the sofa.

'I've got something for you,' said Richard.

'What, again? Already?' Tessa put her arms around his neck, enjoying the fact that all of her body could now be pressed against him at the same time.

Richard brought the gift out from behind his back. 'Happy Christmas,' he said.

'Oh,' said Tessa, when she saw the plastic duck. 'Oh. Where did you find him?'

'Aha,' said Richard, 'that's between me and Claire.'

'Does he have a name?' she asked, examining the duck minutely for traces of icebergs and walruses. He was, it's true, rather pale for a yellow duck, but he seemed otherwise relatively unscathed.

'He was named after the man who found him,' said Richard. 'Donald.' They dissolved into laughter.

'Do you know,' said Sally to Robert that night, 'I got the feeling that half of them suspected us all along.'

'Actually,' said Robert, 'I think they all did. Even the Bishop.'

Sally wondered whether to tell him about the latest offering from Esme Smuts. No, perhaps not.

*   *   *

He had travelled eighteen thousand miles, a long way
for anyone who is not a sperm whale or a tuna. He had
braved pack ice and winds like knives, ridden currents
so cold and cruelly remote that the only men to go
anywhere near them had been in submarines from the
world's more secretive establishments. He had swum
with penguins and Arctic terns, floated with jellyfish
and porpoises, had almost been eaten by a sealion
. . . and now he sat on a mantel shelf in Bumpstaple,
between a pink teddy bear and a vase of chrysan-
themums. Seven years after being lost to a freak wave,
the plastic duck was home. He had made it.

Epilogue

'I thought that these were good for half a million times,' said the registrar at the private clinic.

'So they are,' said the consultant, 'usually.'

'It seems incredible that he managed to break it in under a month.'

'Oh, he didn't. It was his wife.'

'How come?'

'She kept using it when he was asleep. Hazard of the job, I'm afraid.'

'Poor bugger. I bet he was miserable.'

'No, not really. He wants another one done straight away. You know, he swears by some herb tonic he's been drinking. Says it's given him the energy of a man of thirty, to match the willy. Offered to get me some, actually.'

'Did you accept?'

'Of course I did. I may be a surgeon but I'm not a complete fool.'

THE END

A Wing And A Prayer
Mary Selby

In the quiet village of Great Barking, strange doings are afoot. Up at the Hall the squire, Sir George, seems to have exhausted his wife Angela – leaving her quite unable to contemplate the rigours of hosting the annual village fête in the Hall grounds. Caroline, the doctor's wife, has her time taken up with her three tiny children, but feels that as a newcomer to the village she should offer her own rather more modest garden as the venue for this important local affair. But who is to open it? Will Sir George's elderly mother, now somewhat unpredictable, be asked, as tradition dictates? Or should Sarah Struther, the voluptuous lady potter who prefers to work unencumbered by clothing and who has just been featured in a smart Sunday newspaper, be invited?

The village fête committee decides that a commission to Sarah to fashion a special pot for the fête, to be entitled The Organ (suggesting the need for funds to combat dry rot in the organ loft) may be a better idea, little suspecting that the title may be open to misconstruction. And in the churchyard the tall privet bush has been lovingly fashioned by old Jacob Bean into a shape so curious that coachloads of sightseers start arriving to view it . . .

0 552 99672 6

BLACK SWAN

Just For The Summer
Judy Astley

'OH, WHAT A FIND! A LOVELY, FUNNY BOOK'
Sarah Harrison

Every July, the lucky owners of Cornish holiday homes set off for
their annual break. Loading their estate cars with dogs, cats, casefuls
of wine, difficult adolescents and rebellious toddlers, they close up
their desirable semis in smartish London suburbs – having turned off
the Aga and turned on the burglar alarm – and look forward to a
carefree, restful, somehow more *fulfilling* summer.

Clare is, this year, more than usually ready for her holiday. Her
teenage daughter, Miranda, has been behaving strangely; her
husband, Jack, is harbouring unsettling thoughts of a change in
lifestyle; her small children are being particularly tiresome; and she
herself is contemplating a bit of extra-marital adventure, possibly
with Eliot, the successful – although undeniably heavy-drinking and
overweight – author in the adjoining holiday property. Meanwhile
Andrew, the only son of elderly parents, is determined that this will
be the summer when he will seduce Jessica, Eliot's nubile daughter.
But Jessica spends her time in girl-talk with Miranda, while Milo, her
handsome brother with whom Andrew longs to be friends, seems
more interested in going sailing with the young blonde son of the
club commodore.

Unexpected disasters occur, revelations are made and, as the
summer ends, real life will never be quite the same again.

'A SHARP SOCIAL COMEDY . . . SAILS ALONG VERY NICELY
AND FULFILS ITS EARLY PROMISE'
John Mortimer, *Mail on Sunday*

'WICKEDLY FUNNY . . . A THOROUGHLY ENTERTAINING
ROMP'
Val Hennessy, *Daily Mail*

0 552 99564 9

BLACK SWAN

A SELECTED LIST OF FINE WRITING AVAILABLE FROM BLACK SWAN

99564	9	JUST FOR THE SUMMER	Judy Astley	£6.99
99629	7	SEVEN FOR A SECRET	Judy Astley	£5.99
99618	1	BEHIND THE SCENES AT THE MUSEUM	Kate Atkinson	£6.99
99648	3	TOUCH AND GO	Elizabeth Berridge	£5.99
99537	1	GUPPIES FOR TEA	Marika Cobbold	£6.99
99593	2	A RIVAL CREATION	Marika Cobbold	£5.99
99622	X	THE GOLDEN YEAR	Elizabeth Falconer	£5.99
99488	X	SUGAR CAGE	Connie May Fowler	£5.99
99610	6	THE SINGING HOUSE	Janette Griffiths	£5.99
99685	8	THE BOOK OF RUTH	Jane Hamilton	£6.99
99392	1	THE GREAT DIVORCE	Valerie Martin	£6.99
99480	4	MAMA	Terry McMillan	£6.99
99503	7	WAITING TO EXHALE	Terry McMillan	£5.99
99606	8	OUTSIDE, LOOKING IN	Kathleen Rowntree	£5.99
99672	6	A WING AND A PRAYER	Mary Selby	£6.99
99607	6	THE DARKENING LEAF	Caroline Stickland	£5.99
99620	3	RUNNING AWAY	Titia Sutherland	£6.99
99650	5	A FRIEND OF THE FAMILY	Titia Sutherland	£5.99
99130	9	NOAH'S ARK	Barbara Trapido	£6.99
99643	2	THE BEST OF FRIENDS	Joanna Trollope	£6.99
99636	X	KNOWLEDGE OF ANGELS	Jill Paton Walsh	£5.99
99673	4	DINA'S BOOK	Herbjørg Wassmo	£6.99
99592	4	AN IMAGINATIVE EXPERIENCE	Mary Wesley	£5.99
99639	4	THE TENNIS PARTY	Madeleine Wickham	£5.99
99591	6	A MISLAID MAGIC	Joyce Windsor	£4.99